FEARLESS

By Jessie Keane

JESSIE KEANE

FEARLESS

MACMILLAN

First published 2018 by Macmillan
an imprint of Pan Macmillan
20 New Wharf Road, London N1 9RR
Associated companies throughout the world
www.panmacmillan.com

ISBN 978-1-4472-5435-5

1 3 5 7 9 8 6 4 2

A CIP catalogue record for this book is available from the British Library.

Typeset by Ellipsis, Glasgow
Printed and bound by CPI Group (UK) Ltd, Croydon, CR0 4YY

Visit **www.panmacmillan.com** to read more about all our books
and to buy them. You will also find features, author interviews and
news of any author events, and you can sign up for e-newsletters
so that you're always first to hear about our new releases.

This book is dedicated to Cliff –
who still has a lot to put up with . . .

ACKNOWLEDGEMENTS

To all my Romany and bare-knuckle sources, thank you. You truly are Fearless, and you've been so generous with your time. To my *other* sources, way to go, guys. To my editor Wayne Brookes and the rest of the team who have helped my books achieve bestseller status – and to my ever-patient agent Jane Gregory – thank you.

I have to mention here the people who keep me sane throughout the long process of writing a book – Tess Gerritsen's right when she says it's like climbing a mountain. Cliff, of course, who gets the food in order when I forget to eat, and Steve and Lynne Ottaway for the belly laughs and the lunches. So many contacts, helpers, friends, comrades and fellow panellists – Laura Wilson, Susan Wilkins, Fanny Blake, Jake Kerridge, Louise Marley, Elly Griffiths, Peter James and all the rest, thank you so much for all your invaluable input along the way. Also the Crime Writers' Association, who have been so fabulous when I've been under pressure, and the International Thriller Writers . . . thanks to one and all.

And last but never least, my Facebook and Twitter pals and everyone else who joins me online from time to time and has helped propel my books into the *Sunday Times* Top 10 bestseller charts.

Happy reading, folks. Keep going. There's plenty still to come.

Rikker it adrée tute's kokero see an' kek'll jin
Keep it secret in your own heart,
and nobody will know it.

PROLOGUE

2001

The torch was weaving back and forth in Aysha Flynn's hand, which was shaking hard. Its cone of light, feeble in the country blackness of the night, was wavering all over the place.

'Hold it *steady*, damn it,' snapped Connor.

Aysha put both hands on the torch. Teeth chattering with nerves, she tried to do as her brother said. Connor was steady as a rock, usually, wise beyond his twenty-five years. But this time? Doing a thing like this? She really thought he was demented. He'd been acting strange and out of character ever since those two Milo bitches had arrived in England.

'This is wrong,' she told him.

They were inside a tiny church, way out on the far edge of nowhere in the south of England. No one came here any more. The place was near-derelict; no alarms, nothing. The church hadn't been in use since Gilbert White trotted past it on his famous white horse in the eighteenth century. It had never been big enough to seat more than twenty people, tops. It had no electricity, no heating or light. It was a place of deep peace and tranquillity.

Tonight, it was being desecrated.

We're going to be cursed for doing this, thought Aysha with a shudder.

Even at night, the place wasn't locked up. No point. There was nothing here to steal; no altar cloths or silver candlesticks, no crucifix – even the pews were gone. Connor Flynn, with a pickaxe in one hand and a sledgehammer in the other, had led the way up to the big gravestone at the top of the aisle, in front of the disused altar; last resting place of Polly James, 1745–1762, fiancée of William Cody. The inscriptions had almost been worn away by footsteps over the years, but Aysha could still read them, just about.

MAY SHE REST ETERNAL

Jesus! Spooky, or what?

Polly James had died the night before her wedding, it said. And then there was the old wedding rhyme:

Something Old
Something New
Something Borrowed
Something Blue

Connor tried to get the pickaxe under the edge to lift the stone. But it was huge and too bloody heavy for one man to budge. So now Connor flung the pickaxe aside and took up the sledgehammer again. He was taking aim . . .

Oh shit, thought Aysha.

. . . and the hammer swung fast, up and then down. It hit the ancient stone and bounced off.

'Fuck,' said Connor, peeling off his shirt and tossing it aside.

Despite the bitter chill, there was a sheen of sweat on his brow and an alarming intensity to his face when the torch-

2

light caught it. Aysha watched him, thinking that this was crazy, that they couldn't be doing this, that he must be wrong.

Connor shot his sister a look. 'Steady,' he said, and swung again. He was here to prove a point, and he wasn't about to stop until it was done.

'Connor, we shouldn't—' said Aysha.

'We have to,' he cut her off, and swung again, and again, and . . .

Suddenly it happened: the stone cracked. Connor hit it once more, and the crack widened into a fork and split. Connor downed the sledgehammer, grabbed the pickaxe again and levered one of the smaller sections away. It tipped up and then crashed to the side, echoing mournfully in the tomb-like silence of the church. Dust plumed up, and Aysha recoiled, coughing. Connor levered the pick under the remaining section, and heaved. That too gave up and fell aside.

'What the hell is *that*?' asked Aysha, her voice shaking as she focused the torch's beam on what was revealed.

Connor leaned forward. He'd hoped to find nothing but an ancient skeleton. It was Aysha who stretched down a hand. With a shiver of revulsion she brushed away dirt from the stuff Connor's blows had revealed.

'It's fur,' she said.

'Fuck it,' said Connor.

He hadn't wanted to believe it, but here was the proof: the tales the Milo women had spun him weren't lies at all; they'd been telling the truth.

There was a heavy crash behind them as the door was flung open. They both spun around as footsteps came thundering up the aisle. Aysha let out a panicky cry as she saw the men running toward them out of the gloom. Then one of them lashed out and caught Connor a vicious blow on the head. He fell.

The last thing Connor heard before blackness took him was his sister Aysha's terrified screams.

BOOK ONE

1

April 1975

On a sunny spring day, twenty-one-year-old Josh Flynn and seventeen-year-old Claire Milo walked away from the gypsy camp that had been their home since childhood. They trod a path they had been using for as long as either of them could remember. Others of their *jeal* – their kin – had used it too. Not long after the war, a distant Flynn cousin who farmed outside Winchester in the south of England had quietly opened up a *puv* – a fallow field – so that the Romany Flynn, Milo, Grey and Everett clans – plus a few others – could set up a permanent camp there and stop their travelling.

'Where you two off to then?' asked Shauna Everett, passing by, her eyes alighting on Josh. She smiled flirtatiously at him. At *him*, not at Claire.

Claire felt her hackles rise. Bloody Shauna Everett, she was always giving Josh the glad eye. And ignoring *her*, like she was nothing.

Keen-eyed and opportunistic, that was Shauna. Claire had known her all her life, and hated her just as long. At eighteen, Shauna was tall, dark-haired and olive-skinned, pure gypsy with flashing conker-brown eyes and a seductive smile that she never wasted on women. Only men ever got the benefit. She was also tough, brassy, sharp-tongued and quick-witted; everything that quiet, pretty and patient blue-eyed blonde Claire – who didn't look Romany at all – was not.

Claire hated the way Shauna always put herself forward, wearing revealing tight jeans and clinging, plunging tops; everything was out there in the shop window. Shauna would always jostle her way to the front of the queue and grab whatever she wanted out of life. And she wanted Josh. Claire knew it.

'We're not going anywhere special,' Claire told Shauna coldly, and walked on.

Claire saw the hatred in Shauna's eyes. *Well, it's mutual*, she thought. Shauna Everett might be good-looking but she was a right old whorebag. It wound Claire up, the way she was always smirking at Josh. Claire had often seen Shauna hanging around with the Cleaver boys. The Cleavers weren't Romany; they were *gorgi* pig farmers from up the lane. Shauna had been spotted necking with them at parties and dances, and they were nothing but backwoods scum that no decent woman would touch with a bargepole. She could see two of the Cleavers lurking over there by the vans right now – big bastards with dirty old macs and mud-spattered boots on, their faces covered in scruffy beards – fat Rowan, and Ciaran with his one blind eye. They were watching what was going on.

Claire thought that Shauna's flirting with those dead-leg Cleaver boys was just window-dressing, anyway. She had seen the looks Shauna shot Josh at the same time as she was pretending to be all over the Cleavers like a rash. *She's trying to make Josh jealous*, thought Claire. Well, she was wasting her time. Josh belonged to *her*, not Shauna.

As they walked on down the dell and away from the camp, Claire squeezed Josh's hard-muscled arm and smiled up at him. No doubt about it, Josh was a prize to be coveted and she was proud of him. He was tall with a fine fighter's build and a head of thick pale-brown hair that always bleached to blond in the summer. His profile was strong and his heart-stoppingly pale grey eyes gave him an almost luminous aura. All the girls looked at him, not just Shauna, but he belonged to Claire. He had been hers since they were small. While 'grabbing' was the norm among gypsy folk – where a boy fancied a girl and wrestled her for a kiss or even more – that had never happened with Josh. He treated Claire with absolute respect. Although she was seventeen, she was still as pure as the day she was born.

'It's beyond me why you bother,' said Rowan Cleaver as Shauna moodily flounced over to where him and his brother stood.

Shauna's eyes had followed Josh and Claire out of sight. Her face was grim as she watched the happy pair walk away, hand in hand. She turned to Rowan.

'Why don't you shut the fuck up?' she said.

Rowan laughed. Rowan was always the one loitering in the background, giggling like a hyena. He was his older brother Ciaran's lap dog and his younger brother Jeb's whipping boy, everyone knew that. If Ciaran or Jeb said jump, Rowan asked how high.

'He got a point, ain't he,' said Ciaran. 'Josh Flynn ain't never going to look twice at you, gal. He's been mooning over that Claire Milo ever since he could crawl.'

'That's the truth,' said Rowan, grinning.

'So just be grateful for what you *have* got,' said Ciaran, snaking an arm around Shauna's waist and pulling her in close.

Shauna quickly pushed herself free of him. The youngest Cleaver boy, Jeb, she could just about stomach. He was good-looking, if you went for the brutish heavy-muscled sort. Ciaran wasn't all that, though. That ugly milky-white eye gave him an evil look. A pony had kicked him in it when he was eight years old, blinding that eye in an instant. As for Rowan, he made her want to throw up. But all three Cleaver boys were useful in their way. A lot of people were scared of them, but they were always willing to do favours for Shauna. It was all a matter of knowing how to handle them – and Shauna had it down to a fine art.

'Ah, she's pissed off because the Flynn boy's always off with that Claire,' said Rowan.

'Give it up, gal,' said Ciaran. 'Serious. You're wasting your time.'

That put Shauna's back up. The worst thing was, she feared it was true. But she *wanted* it to be different. And, over the years, Shauna had got used to having what she wanted. Her parents had never done fuck-all for her, so she'd grown up tough, fending for herself, grabbing everything she could get out of this Romany life but always finding it wanting. She wanted *more*. She wanted *better*. And she was bloody well going to get it.

'I could have him if I wanted,' she said.

'Yeah, and there goes one of our pigs, flying over that hedge,' laughed Rowan.

'I could,' insisted Shauna.

'Bollocks,' said Ciaran, and the two Cleaver brothers turned away.

2

The beauty of the day helped Claire brush Shauna and the Cleavers from her mind. She and Josh trod the path they always followed, crossing the dell and on down past the row of poplars shimmering in the breeze, then between the fields with their fast-greening crops of wheat and barley, and on down to the little church.

The mouldering building was surrounded by an old graveyard, lichen-covered stones standing around like drunks among the overgrown grass which was now studded with pale yellow and sugar-pink primroses.

It was *their* special place – Josh's and Claire's. As children, they had played here. As young teenagers, they had shared their first kiss; and now, as adults, here they were again, talking and laughing together in low whispers, their arms wrapped around each other, Josh so tall and handsome and tough, Claire with her tumbling blonde hair, as lovely as the spring day.

'Let's go in,' said Claire, dragging Josh after her.

Inside, the church was still and peaceful. Claire led the way up to the altar, stepping on ancient stones inscribed with details of the departed. Before the altar she stopped, looking down at the very last one. Polly James, fiancée of William Cody, lay here. The inscription said that she had died of a fever the night before her wedding.

1745–1762
MAY SHE REST ETERNAL

'Look. That's the old wedding rhyme,' said Claire, tracing the words with her toe. 'Something old, something new . . .'

'Yeah, I know,' said Josh, smiling indulgently. She was his angel, sweet and soft-hearted and full of warmth, always championing the underdog. Claire was never loud or pushy, but she had a core of iron and would take shit from no one – not even him. She was strong in her quiet, determined way, and he admired that. He was lucky to have her, and he knew it. 'I've read the damned thing a thousand times.'

'Don't swear in church! It's unlucky.' Claire stared down at the stone and crossed herself. 'Poor girl.'

'Let's go outside,' said Josh. 'It's fucking cold in here. Catch a chill and I'll be in no state to fight.'

'Ah, you're soft as a gorgi,' she joked. A gorgi was a house-dweller. But his mention of the fight soured her mood. She wished he *wouldn't* be fit enough to step into the ring, not ever. She hated the bare-knuckle fight game and feared for him every minute she knew he was in the ring. She was the soft one, not him. But Josh had grown up fighting, like his father and his grandfather before him; and she was – for better or worse – in love with Josh.

For a while she'd hoped he'd settle for the sort of labour the other Romany lads did. He'd given it a try, done his stint on the driveways, laying razor-thin tarmac bought off council surplus for the roads, and some tree felling. He'd dealt scrap metal and done a bit of horse trading at the fairs. He'd creosoted turkey sheds and picked fruit. But when he'd stepped into the ring for the first serious bout of his life, he'd been lost. He was a fighter; it was in his blood. He couldn't help it.

Claire noticed that Josh seemed distracted. His face when she smiled up at him was deadly serious. In silence he led the way back out into the sunshine.

'Josh?' Claire caught up with him, touched his arm. 'What's up?'

'Got something to ask you. Something important.'

'Go on then.'

Josh got down on one knee in the long grass.

'Claire – will you marry me?' he asked.

Claire let out a scream and put both hands over her face.

Josh squinted up at her. 'What's that mean? Yes? No? Fuck off?'

Claire started to cry. Then she started to laugh. 'Oh Christ! Josh!'

Josh grabbed her around the waist and pulled her close to him. 'What?' he asked.

'It means yes! Of course it means yes!' howled Claire, wrenching herself free of him and haring away up the dell.

'Where you going?' he called after her, still kneeling in the grass. He groped in his pocket – Christ, he'd forgotten to give her the bloody ring, he'd been that nervous!

'Got to tell Mum,' she threw back over her shoulder, and ran on.

Josh laughed then and stood up. Claire's mum, Eva, would be tickled pink; her dad, Pally, probably would be too.

As for Josh, hearing her say yes had made him the happiest he had ever been.

3

There would be a big engagement party in one of the barns soon, and then there would be the wedding. The Pole funfair family were going to be setting all the rides up especially for the event, and everyone was thrilled, anticipating the mighty calliopes roaring out 'Hi Ho Silver Lining' as the painted horses on the roundabouts dipped and spun and the waltzers whizzed around.

An autumn wedding would give them just about time enough to prepare, and they would need every moment. It was so *exciting*!

Every Romany girl starts planning for her wedding the minute she is past her first Communion, and Claire was no exception to that rule. Communion was a big event in itself, but a wedding was huge. The groom would buy a new van and get it on site at the ready, and after that he would bring home the money any way he could – by fighting, in Josh Flynn's case – while the woman he married would keep house and raise their kids.

Claire Milo had already been collecting Coalport and Royal Doulton china to adorn the van that she and Josh would share as newlyweds. She couldn't wait to marry him; if anything she loved him more than ever now. For her, the only fly in the ointment was his love of the boxing ring. That worried her. She couldn't understand why it meant so much to him when he never seemed to win. Undaunted by his dismal record, he trained endlessly in one of the spare sheds; he had weights set up in there and a punchbag to keep himself fit. He even had a 'manager', that rascal Cloudy Grey. Claire avoided seeing Josh fighting. She knew he'd like her to attend the fights, but she couldn't. The thought made her feel sick. Seeing someone punching him, hurting him? Maybe it would be different if he won a match once in a while, but strong and fit though he was, he never seemed to.

So the plans for the wedding went ahead, and so long as Claire didn't think about the fighting thing, all seemed fine. Then one day she was round behind the vans. Her grey lurcher, Blue, a cross between a Saluki and a greyhound, was sitting at her feet. Blue was a brave dog, the best; he coursed for hares with Claire's dad. The catgut on his chest and belly glistened in the sunlight from where he had charged through barbed wire after his quarry and had to be stitched up afterwards. Blue was the best dog in the whole of the southern counties, all the way up to London. Claire cried over each new injury Blue suffered; she'd had him since he was a tiny pup. But her dad wasn't so soft-hearted. If the dog got cut, Pally stitched it up himself; soon as Blue was mended, out they went again.

Claire was grooming one of Pally's piebald horses, pulling the colt's ears and talking low to him as she worked, when someone grabbed her arm. She whirled around, startled. The horse shied and she steadied him. Blue stood up and growled.

It was Shauna Everett.

'Oh, it's you,' said Claire. What the fuck did *she* want?

Blue had his teeth bared, staring at Shauna.

'You don't shut that fleabag up, I'll kick its teeth down its fucking throat,' said Shauna.

Claire touched Blue's big head, and he subsided.

'This right, what they're all saying?' asked Shauna, staring intensely at Claire.

Yeah, she might be a slapper, but she was a looker, Claire thought. You had to give her that. Shauna was strong-featured and strong of body. She wasn't dainty like Claire, and there was no compassion in her eyes. She didn't like dogs, or horses. But the men always seemed to like her well enough. All except Josh, of course.

'I dunno. What you been hearing then?' asked Claire, carrying on with the piebald's grooming, wishing she'd go away.

'About you and Josh Flynn. Saying you're going to be married this autumn.'

'Well, that's right,' said Claire, carrying on brushing, little puffs of dust coming off the piebald's coat in a cloud. 'We are.'

'Christ! You're joking,' said Shauna.

Claire stopped brushing. She turned and looked at Shauna's grimly set face. 'Why would I be joking?' she asked.

Shauna's gaze grew spiteful. 'Because, *stupid*, he could do about a thousand times better than you, any day of the week.'

Claire half-smiled at that. 'Oh, you mean *you*? Sorry – don't think he's interested.'

'You think that, do you?' Shauna stepped forward. Blue started that low-level growl at the back of his throat again. 'I *mean* it,' said Shauna.

'Shut up, Blue,' said Claire, watching Shauna warily.

She'd had run-ins with Shauna her whole life, all the kids in the camp had. Shauna was the leader, the strong one, and she bullied the rest of them mercilessly. Claire had endured a lifetime of Shauna's insults and snide remarks.

She'd been on the receiving end of a punch or two, and the odd smack upside the head. And she knew Shauna was royally pissed off about her and Josh finally making it legal.

'Yeah, shut up or I'll shut *you* up, you stinking mutt,' said Shauna to Blue.

Then her dark eyes fixed on Claire. 'Christ, who'd believe it? Josh Flynn, throwing himself away on the likes of *you*.'

Claire's heart was thumping, but she refused to be intimidated, even if Shauna *did* put the shits up her. Yes, Shauna was jealous. But Claire was the winner here, she had to remind herself of that. Shauna was too forceful, too bold, for Josh's taste. Claire was the one he wanted.

'Josh loves me,' she said. She showed Shauna her left hand, the cheap imitation diamond glittering. Soon, Josh would buy her a better one. He'd promised. And Josh always kept his word.

'Yeah? Christ knows why,' Shauna sneered, eyeing the ring. She felt sick, seeing it. So it was *true*. All right, she might muck around with the Cleavers and a few others, but that meant nothing. What she felt for Josh was real. He should be *hers*.

Claire glared at Shauna. 'Look. It's a fact. So why don't you go and find your own man, you low-life bitch? Like one of those deadbeat pig-farmer Cleavers you're always hanging around with. I think that's more your level. I heard they *fuck* those pigs – and knowing them, I believe it. How about one of *them*?'

'Why you—' Shauna looked shocked for a second. The little mouse was actually answering back instead of running snivelling to Mama like she always used to do.

Shauna shot out a hand and grabbed a handful of that silky blonde hair, yanking it hard toward her so that Claire stumbled forward with a shriek of pain, half-tripping over Blue.

'Get *off*!' yelled Claire, struggling to break free. The piebald was jumping around in alarm, struggling against its halter, which was tethered to the back of the van.

In a blind rage, Claire swung the currycomb in her hand and it struck Shauna's jaw. Shauna fell back. Blue started barking. He lunged at Shauna and sank his teeth into her leg, then when she kicked at him he yelped and leapt away.

'Fucking mongrel *hound*!' said Shauna, staggering back with a hand to her scraped jaw.

She stared down at her leg. Blood was starting to seep from the bite, colouring the torn denim to purple. Her eyes when they met Claire's were vicious.

'You're going to be sorry,' she spat out, panting with temper.

Shauna turned away from Claire. Then she turned back.

'That crack about finding my own man?' she rapped out. 'For your information, I fucking well have, bitch. His name's Josh Flynn and he's *mine*. He just don't know it yet.'

4

Shauna got back to the family trailer and stared at her reflection in the mirror. Her chin was scratched from where Claire had struck her. She bathed it. Then she stripped off her jeans and poured some of Dad's neat gut-rot whisky over the bite that mutt had inflicted on her. It stung like a bitch, but she was so mad, so fucking *incensed*, that she barely felt it. At least the bleeding had stopped.

Then she put on clean jeans and stalked around the trailer, irritably picking up this and that, fuming, unable to believe that dopey cow had summoned the nerve to turn on her like that. She kicked the couch, but really she wanted to kick *her*, Claire Milo. She wanted to wipe her out, never again to see that pretty-pretty face with those sickeningly soft blue eyes.

Finally, unable to settle, she snatched up the keys to Dad's pickup and left the trailer. She got in the pickup and drove.

As Shauna pulled up outside the Cleaver place, she thought not for the first time that the untidy bastards ought to do *something* to make the place look a bit better. Granted, they were only pig farmers, but the betting and other things meant they always had cash on the hip, so why didn't they tart the place up a bit? It was damned near derelict, the gates hanging from their hinges, the porch leaning at a sharp angle. The farmhouse itself was dark, its roof mossy and missing some tiles, and the wooden cladding on the eaves was crumbling from years of neglect. The house was set close to the northern edge of a pine forest, and even on a day like today, which was bright and sunny, very little light penetrated the gloom around it.

There were several scruffy dirt-caked old trucks parked at the front, and she could hear a big dog barking monotonously inside the house. Looking out over the fields to the front of the place, she could see the pigs churning the ground to mud and hear them grunting – about a hundred in all. This was how the Cleavers made their living: breeding hogs and growing them on before sending them to market. She could smell them, too. Yeah, maybe that bitch Claire was right. The Cleavers *were* low lifes. But they were useful ones.

Jumping down from the pickup, she paused, looking at the statue of two grinning, rutting pigs perched above the sloping porch of the house. She felt a shudder of distaste go through her. Fucking *oiks*, these Cleavers. But she was going to do this, whatever it cost. She knew what she wanted, and here was where she'd get it.

'Hiya, gal,' said a voice behind her.

Shauna turned. It was Jeb, the youngest Cleaver boy, bull-necked and slope-shouldered. An axe hung casually from his right hand, and he was clutching a bundle of firewood against his chest with his left. He was better-looking than his two elder brothers Ciaran and Rowan, his hair blacker, his eyes nearly black too, with an intensity of expression in them that said *Don't ever mess with me*. But she did, all the time.

'Hi,' she said, and smiled.

'Come for some fun?' he asked, and she nodded.

Fun first, she thought. Then she'd get down to business.

'So where are they all today?' asked Shauna as she and Jeb lay naked in bed an hour later. The radio on the dusty bedside table was playing 'Sugar, Sugar' by the Archies.

'Dad's at market with Rowan. Ciaran's out the top field,' said Jeb, rolling over and clasping her tit in a crushing grip. 'Damn, you're hotter than hell, girl. You really are.'

Shauna suppressed a wince of pain. She was meant to be *enjoying* this, but she didn't. She never had. She'd been 'doing it' with Jeb and with Ciaran – less often with Rowan, and a couple of times with their dad, Bill – since she was twelve years old.

She'd worked out early that a romp between the sheets made men blind and biddable. Even at a young age – an *illegal* age, but who gave a shit about that – she had insisted on a condom. It was also understood that when she put out, favours would be required in return. All she had to say was 'I need some cash, how about it?' and she'd be showered in fivers. And when she told the Cleavers, 'I need to get even with so-and-so, will you see to that for me?' whoever had crossed her would end up being sorted out down some dark alley.

So the Cleavers were useful. *Very* useful. They weren't in the same league as Josh Flynn, of course. Shauna was *obsessed* with Josh Flynn, dreamed about him day and night. She fantasized that whichever grunting, gasping man was pumping away on top of her – whether it be Jeb, or half-blind Ciaran, or sly grinning Rowan or even their old man Bill, who was easy to tap up for a few fivers – was Josh. That way, she got through it and out the other side. Fun first. Usually *their* fun, not hers. Then business. And today she had something very specific in mind.

'I want to talk to you,' she said.

'What about?' He was kneading her tit like he was squeezing dough or something. It hurt. Shauna pulled away, stroked his belly, kissed his chest, which was thickly matted with black hair. All the while, she was thinking, *Josh, Josh, you can't do it, you can't throw yourself away on her. I won't let you.*

'That bitch Claire Milo . . .'

'You never did like her.' Jeb grinned. 'Ciaran says it's pure green-eyed jealousy. That you fancy Josh Flynn for yourself.'

Ciaran's not as stupid as he looks, she thought.

'Truth is, she set her fucking dog on me. You believe that? Look.' Shauna held up one long shapely leg so that he could see the bite mark Blue had left her with.

'Jeez. That's nasty.' Jeb ran his hand up her leg to her thigh. Quickly losing interest in her injury, he went up further and began probing the damp hollow between her legs, his eyes intent on that.

'You ever thought of shaving your bush?' he asked, fluffing up the black hair there with his fingers. 'I could do it for you. Be a right turn-on.'

Shauna felt a stab of arousal at his words. Sometimes, Jeb could *really* light her fire, and she sort of hated herself for it when he did. Yes, he was an animal, but he was a sexy one.

'No,' she said. 'I've never thought of that. And this? You seen this?'

She redirected his attention to her face and the graze on her chin.

'That her too?'

'Hit me with a currycomb.'

'What, Claire Milo? Girl's a mouse. Saint Claire, the

22

lads call her. Good as gold and scared of her own fucking shadow.'

'I'm telling you, she did it.'

'You're after Josh Flynn.'

'What if I am?' Shauna propped herself up on one elbow and stared into his eyes. 'That won't alter nothing, Jeb. There'll still be you and me. You know it. Ain't we always been there for each other?'

'Yeah.' Jeb's eyes narrowed. 'You been there for Ciaran too. Rowan told me. And you done Rowan. You even done Dad – Rowan told me he saw the pair of you at it out in the yard, Dad with his pants round his ankles. Poor old cunt musta thought it was his fucking birthday.'

Shauna lay back down. Sneaky bloody Rowan. He ought to keep his fat mouth shut.

'Actually, I think it *was* your dad's birthday,' she said.

Jeb's head turned and he looked at her. Suddenly, he started laughing. Shauna joined in. Then Jeb grew serious. He clutched at her chin, hurting the scratches there. He stared into her eyes.

'But I got first dibs on you, right? I got first call. That's not going to change, OK? Not ever.' She pulled her chin free of his grip and nodded. 'All right, you can *have* Josh fucking Flynn all week and twice on Sundays, but you and me, that's for keeps, you got that?'

'That's not going to change,' said Shauna. First thing she could, she was going to kick every one of these fucking hillbilly Cleavers to the kerb. She had a plan. A *big* one. But for now, she needed them. She needed them to do something special, something *important*.

'Jeb . . .' she started, her voice wheedling. 'Will you do something for me?'

'Yeah, but first . . .' he said, pointing down his body to indicate that he was ready for action again.

Shauna sighed and reached for a fresh condom, ripping it open with her teeth. She snapped it on, pushing it down over his erection. Then she climbed aboard, slipping his cock inside her oily wetness and riding him like a bucking bronco, making plenty of noise because he liked that. And she dreamed, dreamed, *dreamed* . . . of Josh Flynn.

Then, when Jeb was finished, she told him what she wanted done.

5

'Oh my God! Oh my baby!' cried Eva, clutching a hankie to her streaming eyes as she stared at the vision standing before her.

They were in the home of the woman who made nearly all the gypsy wedding outfits in the country; she was known throughout the land as the go-to person for a knockout dress. Claire had been in the changing room with her sister Trace assisting her, struggling into the vast wedding gown that had been a work in progress for months. Now she came out, and her mother was instantly in floods of tears as she stared at her eldest daughter in a dress that was like something out of a fairy tale.

Claire looked like an angel. The dress was a huge beautiful powder puff of a gown, sparkling with five thousand crystals and studded with artificial pearls. It looked wonderful and Claire felt like a queen wearing it. No matter that she could barely stand in it, let alone walk. The finished gown that they'd all slaved over for so long was a triumph. It weighed around five stone and Claire thought she'd have to take it off soon because the corset on the bodice was killing her, and her hips felt bruised and would soon start to bleed. But fuck it, who cared? The dress was *fabulous*.

'Mum? What do you think?' she asked, beaming with pride.

'You look lovely,' said Eva. 'Breathtaking.'

Even Tracey looked pleased, and Trace was a real misery, unlike sunny Claire. The glass was always half-empty to dark-haired and painfully plain Trace, never half-full. It was as if the fates had bestowed all the good looks and warm nature they had to spare on Claire, and forgotten sixteen-year-old Trace's share.

'So everything's nearly ready then,' said Claire, squeezing her sister's hand.

Trace was to be Claire's bridesmaid, one of seven, and Claire had chosen stunning turquoise gowns for her attendants to wear on the big day, and dainty feathered bouquets for them to carry. The wedding was going to be the Romany 'do' of the year. The church was booked, the wedding breakfast sorted, the flowers selected, the photographer set straight about which family groups to do on the day; they wanted a *huge* wedding album, the very best. There would be one of the relatives' carriages all spruced up and pulled by two dazzling white ponies to get Claire and her dad Pally to the church, and there would be a monster truck kitted out like a disco to get Josh and his best man there on time.

She knew Josh hated the fuss and would have been happier with a simple register office do, but all the graft was done now.

'I can't believe it,' said Claire, eyeing herself in the full-length mirror. Soon, she and Josh would be man and wife. She couldn't wait.

Her big day was coming at last.

Then her smile faded. Since that scrap with Shauna, she'd been troubled by dark dreams – almost like premonitions. Maybe she *did* have the Sight, just a bit. She hoped not. Because the dreams all seemed to involve horror and pain, and finding her dear old dog Blue dead.

'You OK, lovey?' asked Eva, watching Claire's face.

'Fine!' It was nothing. They were just silly dreams. Nothing more.

Josh had the new van on order and everyone had cleared some space on the site ready for its arrival, so that was sorted too. Claire was so happy she felt she was going to burst.

Later on, she met up with Josh on the steps of her folks' trailer. Night was drawing in, and Pally had set a cheery fire going in the middle of the clearing. By the light of that and the tilley lamps, Josh thought that Claire looked lovelier than ever. Blue was tucked in under the trailer steps, on guard, and the stars were bright in the heavens.

'Not long to go now 'til the wedding,' said Josh, kissing her.

'I love you, Josh.'

'I know. I love you too.'

The kiss deepened, grew passionate. Claire pulled away, smiling. 'Not until the wedding, though. We agreed.'

'Christ, you're a hard taskmaster,' said Josh, but he was smiling too. He could wait. He'd found the perfect girl; he wasn't going to spoil things by rushing at her. He hated all this bloody wedding claptrap, but it was her day, so he was going along with it. His smile faded. He had to say this now. 'You know the fight, on Saturday?'

Claire's eyes grew serious as they gazed into his. 'Yeah. I know.'

'Matty O'Connor. That man's a legend,' said Josh.

And not long after that, they'd be married. Ever since she'd got wind of the upcoming fight, she'd had nightmare visions of Josh being carried up the aisle to her on a blood-soaked stretcher. Josh never won. She couldn't figure it out, but it was a fact. He *always* lost. So how the hell could he stand against a beast like Matty?

'He's the champion,' said Claire. 'I know that. The king of the fighters.'

'Well then?'

'Well . . . what?' She felt her stomach clench with dread. *Knew* what was coming.

'I'd like you to be there, ringside. I know you've never been before, but this is going to be different. And it's time you were there, supporting me, or what will everyone think?'

Claire looked troubled. 'I don't care what anyone thinks, Josh. I just don't want to see you getting hit, that's all. And how the hell can it be different?'

'Claire . . .' Josh stood up, paced around a bit.

'*No*, Josh. It can't be, can it? You're fooling yourself. And against Matty? It's time someone spoke some sense around here. He'll knock you to hell and you know it.'

'No, he won't.'

Matty was a huge raging bull of a man, a cousin of the Cleaver family, and there were rumours that he'd actually *killed* a man in the bare-knuckle ring with his ferocious right hook. The community had hushed it up, seen the widow right, made sure the *muskras* – the police – were none the wiser. But to Claire it was terrifying to think of it.

Christ, she hated the very idea of Josh coming up against that brute. She was so scared for him. After a fight like that, maybe he wouldn't make it up the aisle at all. Maybe he'd be *dead*.

'How is this time going to be different? How can it be?' she asked, her eyes filling with tears.

Josh put his arm around her shoulders.

'You don't know the fight game, do you,' he sighed.

28

'Listen. Here's what's been happening. I've been throwing fights because Cloudy's told me to.'

'Throwing . . . ?'

'Losing them. Deliberately. People have been betting on me to lose.'

Claire stared at Josh.

'I get paid well. So long as I lose.'

'So . . .'

'I'm sick of it. This time I'm not losing. I'm going in there to win.'

'But these people who are betting – do they still expect you to lose?'

'Who gives a shit? I've had it with the whole thing. I'm kicking Cloudy into touch and I'm winning, and then we'll see who's king of the gypsy fighters.'

'Won't there be trouble?'

'There might be. Who bloody cares? But this once, I *need* you there.'

'Oh Christ,' moaned Claire.

'Please.'

'All right. I'll be there.'

But as soon as she'd said it, she wished she could snatch the words back. The thought of the fight dimmed the pleasure of the upcoming wedding festivities and wearing that fantastic dress, being queen for the day.

I'll just have to get through it, she thought. *Grit my teeth and do it.*

There was nothing else she could do. She kissed Josh goodnight and went back into the trailer. Neither she nor Josh saw Shauna loitering near the end of the van. Blue did. He crouched ready to pounce, hackles rising, lips pulled back in a snarl. But Shauna vanished into the shadows and was gone.

6

It was the night of the big fight. Matty O'Connor, the long-standing legend, against Josh Flynn, an upstart youngster who lost far more often than he won. Everyone had come to see it, because Matty always drew a crowd. No one thought it would be a decent contest, but what the hell, this was *Matty O'Connor*. Everyone knew he would see Josh off in the first round.

The crowd inside the barn was going crazy, cheering 'MATTY, MATTY, MATTY!' over and over again until Shauna Everett felt that her head was going to burst wide open with the noise of it.

Thirty-five-year-old Matty O'Connor, who had been the all-round reigning bare-knuckle boxing champ for five years, the undisputed king of all he surveyed, was – as predicted – hammering the crap out of young Josh Flynn, Claire Milo's fiancé, in the makeshift ring.

It wasn't anything fancy, this ring; the corners were marked out with gas bottles and they'd strung lengths of rope between them so that it looked right, even if they were fighting on a dirt floor. Spectators were standing on hay bales, and lights had been slung up on extension leads that trailed out from the farmer's house to this big oak barn.

The heat inside the barn tonight was nearly unbearable.

This summer the sun – 'Phoebe', Claire's mum called it – had burned down on the country without end, wilting plants and trees, drying streams to nothing, yellowing the grass. There seemed to be no relief anywhere from the heat.

'MATTY!' everyone around Shauna was bellowing.

Fuck Matty, she thought.

Shauna Everett's eyes were glued to Josh. She still couldn't believe a man who looked like him could be intending to chuck his life away on Claire Milo. *She*, Shauna, was the woman he deserved, not that gutless little blonde cow. Shauna could see Claire standing across the ring with her sister, Trace. Claire was white-faced and cowering as Matty and Josh fought. Shauna could see how sick Claire was feeling. Whereas Shauna herself felt quite turned on by it all, quite excited. Who wouldn't be, watching Josh? He was gorgeous – a real hunk of a man.

Win, Josh! Come on then, win! she thought, willing him to do it.

She'd passed word along to the Cleavers of Josh and Claire's little chat. The boys were pissed off, but forewarned was forearmed so they wouldn't make a loss on it. They thought it was unlikely that *anyone* could stand against Matty, anyway.

But Shauna wondered. If Josh *did* win – by some miracle – then things would change for him. Wild men and suicide fighters would seek him out, because he would be king of the gypsies, the strongest, the toughest man going. Pro boxers would fight him, too, and that was where the money was; if he was clever, he could be made for life.

Shauna didn't think Josh was *that* clever. His impending marriage to Claire, for instance – what the fuck was that all about? She knew Josh and Claire had been together as kids, but for God's sake! Claire was not a woman whose stature would complement Josh. And that fucker Cloudy, that so-called 'manager' of his. She knew that Cloudy had been – mostly at the Cleavers' instigation – setting Josh up for the past few years to always be the fall guy.

But big handsome Josh himself had impressed her when she'd listened in the other night. He was determined to win this time and make a name for himself. She didn't see why he couldn't, if he set his mind to it. He was as fit as a butcher's dog and he was a southpaw, a leftie, and that made him difficult to fight. Yes, Josh had possibilities.

Possibilities interested Shauna. Her own family were travellers from way back, just like Josh's and Claire's. Now they were settled, but it was in the blood, what they were. You couldn't escape it, everyone said that and it annoyed the hell out of her. Shauna wanted to try and make the break from this life. She wanted to aim big, to reach the top or die trying. No measly two-up-two-down in Where-the-Fuck would ever do for her. That wasn't enough. She wanted it all: a massive house, a fancy car, holidays in Mustique like Princess Margaret took. And a boat moored up somewhere, a proper gin palace with two fucking great outboards, not one of those stick-and-hankie sailboats. She wanted power, she wanted speed. And she was going to get it. Tonight, things were going to change. She'd already made sure of that.

The crowd were shouting louder and louder as punch upon punch landed on Josh. The heat and the bloodlust and the stench of sweat was almost choking in here.

'MATTY! MATTY! MATTY!' they roared.

'Come on, Josh! Hit him *back*!' yelled Shauna. He was supposed to *win*, wasn't he?

Josh was faltering on his feet, shaking his head. There

was blood coming from a cut on his brow, and his knuckles were red. Matty closed in.

Fuck, thought Shauna. He was fading.

'COME ON, JOSH!' she screamed.

7

Blood spattered Claire Milo's face and she winced with revulsion and looked away. Fuck this for a game. She was never, ever going to come ringside again. She vowed that on her mother Eva's life. She heard punch after sickening punch landing on flesh, like someone pounding a piece of meat. She couldn't watch; she had to keep her eyes down. All around her, the crowd roared its encouragement, even her dad was shouting like a lunatic, but she seemed to be on an island, removed from it all.

'Look, Claire, look!' screamed her sister, nudging her hard in the ribs.

Claire raised her eyes and forced herself to look.

Inside the ring, Matty and Josh were still knocking lumps off each other. They were both stripped to the waist, drenched in sweat and soaked with blood, their own and each other's. Josh was tall and muscular but he looked like a no-hoper beside the champ; Matty was squat, solid as an oak door, his red hair plastered to his head as he moved quickly around the ring with Josh dodging blow after punishing blow. Josh was kidding himself, she could see that now. Matty would win. Matty was a legend, he *always* won.

'Oh shit,' moaned Claire, thinking that she was making an awful, awful mistake.

Nanny Irene said she was. Nanny Irene had the Sight;

she'd predicted all sorts, deaths and births and all manner of shit. She had it, in spades. Mum had it too, she'd seen Grandad's death in a dream. Claire was so fucking glad she *didn't* have it: the Sight was a curse.

When Claire had said she was going to marry Josh, Nanny Irene had straightaway insisted on a full reading. Nanny was almost the last of the gypsy wise women, regularly prescribing a Traveller's Joy infusion for rheumatics, henbane for gallstones, belladonna and warty caps for other ailments. She still bound open wounds with cobwebs, and never left a single scar.

The old woman had got out the tarot cards, dimmed the lights. She told Claire to shuffle the pack, then she had stared with her bootblack eyes at her granddaughter. They'd been sitting at the table inside Nanny's bow-top wagon, which was parked up behind Mum and Dad's big trailer.

'Pain, that's what I see,' Nanny Irene had said, turning over cards, shaking her grey head. 'Pain and suffering, girl, you mark my words. Don't do it.'

Now, almost drowned out by the baying crowds though they were, Nanny Irene's words clanged around in Claire's head like death bells. Her mum and dad had laughed it off, of course. But standing ringside, watching the man she was about to marry getting himself beaten in the ring despite all his assurances to the contrary, she could see that Nanny Irene was right. She was marrying a bare-knuckle fighter from a long line of them. *This* would be her life now, if she went through with the wedding. A life of pain and suffering.

Ah God, the wedding.

It should all be so perfect.

But it wasn't. It couldn't be. She could see that now. *This* was what she had to look forward to. A lifetime of living with crippling anxiety every time he stepped into the ring, and then bathing his wounds after fights, or shipping him off to hospital if it was really bad.

'Come on, our Josh!' shouted Sam, Josh's mate who was in his corner, acting as his second. 'Finish him!'

Claire's attention returned to the fight and she cringed with revulsion. This was the way Josh earned a crust, the way his dad had, and his grandfather too. Since way back, the Flynns had been doing this, setting up illicit matches in farmers' barns and at horse fairs and funfairs. This was the way Romanies settled their differences, too; they fought. They didn't call the muskras or whine to the courts. They went head to head, bare-knuckle, and the winner won the argument.

Pikeys, the gorgis or house-dwellers called them.

But really they were the fearless ones, the people who lived life on their own terms and fuck what the rest of society said about them. Claire wished *she* was fearless, like Josh. Like that bitch Shauna was too. But she knew she wasn't.

'Come the fuck on, *break!*' shouted the man in the white blood-spattered shirt and red braces who was trying to referee this whole damned thing and mostly failing.

Claire looked around the crowds. She saw Cloudy there; he styled himself Josh's 'manager', and was shouting louder than anyone. He was going to be furious if Josh *did* win. But he wouldn't. He couldn't. Then her eyes slipped onward and she saw dark-haired, flashing-eyed Shauna Everett standing in among the jostling throng of people, grinning straight at her. *Smirking* at her. Mocking her.

Fucking Shauna.

Claire forced herself to drag her eyes away from Shauna's. She looked on, around the heaving, screaming crowds. The Cleavers were in, mob-handed. There was Bill, the father, who was shorter than his three sons but still huge, broad as an ox. Then Ciaran, the eldest boy, with that distinctive milk-white blind eye. Rowan the middle son, solidly fat and grinning as if at some private joke; and Jeb the youngest, who with his black hair and beard almost verged on handsome. Catching her eye, he winked at her. Claire looked away with a shudder.

Whenever she passed the Cleaver place – and mostly she tried not to – Claire thought that it looked sinister, like an indication of the type of people living there. No one ever saw the boys' mother. Rumour was she'd left, run off years ago, and good luck to her.

Then Claire's eyes drifted back to the ring and she got a shock.

Matty was sagging against Josh, clinging up close so that Josh couldn't punch. Josh shoved him back, away, and the crowd roared as Josh's left fist smacked hard into Matty's jaw. Matty reeled and then lurched back and swung a haymaker at Josh.

The crowd went crazy. Josh's mate Sam looked like his head was going to come off his shoulders; his face was beetroot-red as he yelled himself hoarse, urging Josh to finish him.

Josh ducked. Matty charged in. Claire looked away again.

This was the first time she'd been ringside, and it would be the last. She was revolted, horrified, and filled with a fear so gripping that it churned her stomach and made her bowels clench. She was either going to mess herself or throw up, she didn't know which.

'He's down, he's down!' screamed Trace, elbowing Claire in the ribs.

Oh Christ, oh no, not Josh . . .

Claire steeled herself to look. She couldn't bear it, but

she had to. She looked . . . and there he was, on the ground.

Matty.

Matty was down, not Josh. Josh stood over him, sweating, bloody, weaving on his feet, panting hard.

'He's won, he's won it!' yelled Trace.

The man in the red braces counted down from ten and then he lifted Josh's arm into the air. A thunderous roar went up. Sam ran in and lifted Josh clean off his feet in triumph, a grin as wide as a mile on his face.

'You bastard, you done it, you done it!' he was shouting over and over again.

Someone dashed in and threw a bucket of water on to Matty, who stirred groggily but didn't get up.

'The winner!' shouted the man with the braces, yanking Josh's arm skywards again.

All around Claire, people were now shouting *fix*, booing.

'I lost a fucking monkey on this thing,' growled a man by her ear.

Josh stood there, exhausted. His 'manager' Cloudy was forcing a smile on to his face but not meaning it. Claire saw Shauna Everett break away from her place near the Cleaver lot. Jeb Cleaver was watching her boot-faced as she went shoving her way through the crowds. Shauna ran over to messy, sweaty, bloodstained Josh. She shoved Sam aside and planted a congratulatory kiss on Josh's cheek.

That *cow*.

Shrugging off Trace's clinging hands, Claire went in the other direction, fought her way out, through the crowds and out of the barn door and into the superheated air of the night. This summer had shaped up hotter than the devil's handshake. The tarmac had bubbled up on the roads and people were having to queue at standpipes for water. Claire breathed in hard, feeling the air almost scorching her lungs. Above her, a million stars studded the heavens and she stared up at them, tears running down her face. She felt but did not see people surging past her and away.

She stood there, half-fainting, disgusted, appalled.

A whimper made her look down. There was Blue, her faithful old lurcher, tied up to the barn door with a length of string. She untied him and knelt to give him a hug. Then with Blue leading the way, she started for home.

8

The inside of Cloudy's big Morecambe trailer was like a palace, crammed full of rugs and sofas, large hand-painted plates lined up all along the walls. There was a black fat-bellied stove in there, cold now, but it chugged out massive heat in the winter. After the fight in which he had taken down the reigning champion, Josh was standing before the cold stove like a schoolboy getting a carpeting.

'You effing little *cunt*,' said Cloudy, pacing the rug so hard he was nearly wearing a trench in it.

'Cloudy—' started Josh.

'Shut it.' Cloudy stopped his pacing in front of Josh and held up a pudgy gold-ringed hand. 'You were meant to lose that bloody fight. You knew that. You agreed to it. What the fuck you playing at, boy?'

'I agreed to it because you *pushed* me into agreeing with it, as per usual. I didn't want to,' said Josh.

'Oh, you *didn't want to*?' Cloudy came up close, right in Josh's face. Josh could see beads of sweat standing out on his flushed red skin. 'That's a fucking comfort, that is. I'll think of that when the Cleavers are breaking my legs. *And* yours.'

The day had started out good, Josh thought. Big protein-packed breakfast, a short run, a bit of cardio. And then he'd won the fight. But now, this. For too long it had been playing on his mind that nothing about the fight game was honest or straightforward. That you won or lost according to whoever had the most clout and the biggest wedge riding on the outcome. And he'd had enough.

Usually, it was the Cleaver mob who dictated who won and who lost, and they wouldn't think twice about coming down heavy on anyone who crossed them.

And Cloudy, who Josh had once – long ago – respected, looked up to, Cloudy was deep in their pocket. Fact was, with Cloudy's nose so far up the Cleavers' arses, Josh would *never* win matches like he wanted to.

He'd known he could take men before, hard men that he'd met on the way up, he knew it and yet he'd caved in to Cloudy's demands. He'd been doing that for a good five years now, accepting hefty payments to throw fights, even when he *knew* he could take down anyone he came across. Even Matty O'Connor, who was the hardest of them all. A legend. Josh knew he could do it.

And, tonight, despite all the pre-match chat from Cloudy, despite the bungs and the whisperings and the pats on the back – *Good boy, that's my Josh, you're a star* – he knew that this time he was playing the game *his* way. Fuck the money, he wanted to *win*.

And tonight, at last, he had.

Now here was Cloudy, bawling him out like he was a schoolkid.

Well, fuck *that*.

Cloudy was leaning in close, and suddenly Josh's head was humming and all he could see was that red angry face, the big check suit, the dirty grey sweat marks on the collar of Cloudy's shirt. A good boxer never lost his temper, always kept his cool. But not tonight. Not any more.

He reached out a hand and, almost gently, placed it on Cloudy's throat. He watched as Cloudy's eyes widened in shock. Josh felt the soft sponginess of Cloudy's neck, but Cloudy's mouth was still moving, the shouting was still going on, so Josh squeezed.

Cloudy stopped shouting. His eyes bulged as Josh lifted him off his feet. A groaning rasp came from Cloudy's mouth, and his hands scrabbled at the front of Josh's shirt. Josh held him there, easily. Josh was six foot six inches tall, and packed with well-honed muscle. Cloudy was soft as butter. Josh kept Cloudy dangling there, looking at him. And then he dropped him.

Cloudy staggered, seemed about to fall. Then he righted himself, grabbing at his throat, staring in disbelief at his protégé.

'What the . . .' he whispered.

'You ever shout in my fucking face again, you fat bastard, and I'll finish the job,' said Josh, stabbing a finger at Cloudy's shirt front to emphasize his point.

'What the fuck's happened to you?' gasped Cloudy. 'Ain't I been good to you, boy? Ain't I seen you right?'

'Oh, you been a prince,' said Josh sourly. 'You've made a pro loser out of me, you've made me a fucking *joke*.'

'I got you good money. I did *everything* for you.'

'You got me the dregs,' snapped Josh. 'And that's all you'll ever get me.'

'You should have talked to me if you're unhappy,' whined Cloudy. 'We could have worked something out.'

'You mean you'd've talked your way out of it.'

'Serious, boy—'

'Don't call me boy. I ain't your boy.'

'All right! But you never told me you weren't happy with any of this.'

'You fixing me up to be the fall guy every time? Why would I be happy with that? I'm the best bare-knuckle fighter there is.' Josh shook his head. 'I'm sick of you, Cloudy. I'm tired of this shit.'

Josh had worked everything out. He had a bag packed. He'd get straight over to Claire's now, grab her and they'd elope. Yes, he was sick of all *this*, but truth to tell he was even more sick of all *that*, too – the wedding. The vast, never-ending fuckfest of a wedding with Claire's mother Eva clucking around him, saying he had to do this, go there, be so-and-so, like he was a shop-window dummy or something.

At least his own mother, widowed years ago when Dad had an accident on a building site, was too old and gin-soaked to care about weddings one way or the other. Josh had been a late baby, unwanted and unloved. Mum had always preferred the bottle to her son, and Dad had used Josh as a punchbag on a regular basis. When the news came that a dumper truck had crushed the life out of the old bastard, Josh could remember feeling nothing but relief. But still – the roughness of his upbringing had made him tough. There was that to be said for it. And tonight he was going to make his move.

They'd duck out of all of it, him and Claire. They'd run away together, tonight. She loved him. She'd be pissed off at him for a bit, but that would pass. Later, they'd come back, get the new van and, if need be, piss off somewhere else, start afresh, away from this place.

Everything would be OK.

He knew it would.

9

Josh left Cloudy's and picked up his travelling bag from where he'd tucked it under another van nearby. Across the clearing, he saw his friend Sam illuminated by the light spilling out from the open door behind him. Sam was sitting on the steps of his family's big trailer and raising a beer can to his lips.

'Josh!' Sam called, catching sight of him.

'All right, mate?' said Josh.

'Beer?' asked Sam, rising to his feet.

'Nah, no time for that. Going to see Claire.'

Sam's grin lit his face up. 'What a fucking night, eh?'

'Yeah. Great fight.' Josh wouldn't say more than that. Sam didn't know that Josh should have thrown the fight. Sam didn't know *shit*, and Josh wasn't about to set him straight.

'Punched his bloody lights right out, you did.'

'Yeah.'

'King of the fucking gypsies,' said Sam, coming over and bear-hugging Josh. Then he drew back, still beaming, and slapped Josh's back. 'Get on over to your girl then, Josh. We'll have a pint later.'

Josh walked on to Claire's folks' place, parked up just over the clearing. As he approached, Blue hopped to his

44

feet and snarled. Tied though he was, Blue was ready to have a go.

'All right then, Blue?' said Josh, and Blue's tail swished slowly from side to side.

Blue knew Josh; Josh was his friend.

Josh stepped past the dog as it resettled on the ground beneath the van. He went up the steel steps and knocked at the door. There was no answer, but he could see light coming through the curtains. He knocked again. Finally, Claire opened the door and stood there, unsmiling.

'Can I come in then?' asked Josh, trying to gauge her mood. She wouldn't like what he had planned; he knew it. Every girl wanted a big wedding, the works, didn't they? And she and her mother had been planning it all for so long. But then, he'd always been able to sweet-talk soft-hearted Claire into anything.

Claire stepped back from the open doorway, saying: 'Christ, look at the state of you.'

Josh hadn't even thought about the state he was in. His left eye was swelling half-shut from one of Matty's pounding right-handers. His chin was bruised and cut, and one of his teeth was wobbling in its socket. His knuckles were scraped raw. Luckily, his shirt covered his midriff, which was a fucking mess by anyone's standards. At least she couldn't see *that*. Or know that he'd spat blood after the ferocity of the fight. He was used to the knocks he took in the ring, though: it was his job. And now he had proved he could take down the best, he was buoyed up, fizzing with determination.

'I didn't see you at the fight,' he said by way of an opener.

'I was there,' said Claire, walking over to an armchair and sitting down.

She was pissed off about something, he could see that.

Probably the fight. She was so soft, Claire. He liked that about her, but she was going to have to get used to it. There was a smear of blood on her cheek.

'What's this?' he asked, coming over to where she sat and touching her face. She flinched. 'You cut yourself?'

'It splashed on me,' said Claire, her voice wooden, her eyes hostile. 'While I was ringside. I think it's yours.'

'Ah. Right. Well, I won it, Claire. That's what matters. I got the prize money and I won. Where's your parents then?'

'Gone down the pub for a lock-in with Trace. I wasn't in the mood.'

'Just as well.' Josh sat down in the other chair and dropped his bag on to the floor. All the aches from the fight were coming out; he'd be stiff as a board tomorrow morning. But he couldn't worry about that now.

Claire's eyes went to the bag. 'What's that for?' she asked.

'It's what I got to talk to you about.' Josh took a breath. 'All this fucking wedding stuff, Claire. I've had enough. It ain't me.'

'What?' She was staring at him blankly.

'Claire.' Josh sat forward, clasped his hands between his knees. It hurt his middle, but he didn't wince. He was used to pain. He looked her straight in the eye. 'I was meant to throw the fight tonight. And I didn't.'

Claire pushed her long blonde hair back from her face. Her blue eyes stared right back at him for a long moment. Then she said: 'Yeah, you told me. So?'

'Claire, listen. Let's just go, shall we?'

'*What?*'

'Fuck the wedding, I hate all that shit anyway, you know that. We'll elope. Go somewhere and do it quiet in a register office.'

She was still gazing at his face. Staring at him, he thought uneasily, like she didn't even know him.

'Claire? Say something, even if it's only "fuck off".'

He half-grinned nervously. Josh thought how much he loved this girl, his gentle dreamy Claire, always off around the horses, smoothing them and nuzzling into their shoulders, or wandering the fields, picking cowslips. Time and again he'd gone with her to that tiny church in the dell and she'd said, "Couldn't we get married here? It's so lovely." They'd lie in the long rustling grass and watch the skylarks flying above in the blue sky, singing their sweet thrilling song. Those moments were heaven to him, snatches in time he would always remember.

She took a deep breath. Then she said: 'Josh. There's not going to be a wedding.'

Now it was Josh's turn to stare. 'You what?'

'You heard. Standing there tonight, seeing what you did, I knew right then and there that it was all a mistake.' Tears started to roll down her face. 'Oh, Josh! I've always loved you. You know that. Even when we were little and playing half-naked in the dirt – my mum used to tie a rope around my middle sometimes and tether me to the van to stop me wandering off, you remember? And you'd always untie the damned thing and then off we'd go. I loved you then and I love you now.'

'Well then . . .' What the fuck was happening here? Josh had assumed he'd come storming in and she'd roll over, do as he said. But this was all wrong.

'Well then *nothing*. I can't live day to day watching you get punched to fuck, Josh. I can't do it. And I won't. So it's off. The fighting game's horrible. Cruel. And it's full of bent bastards making money on the backs of idiots who are too busy punching each other's lights out to even notice. I saw a bit of it tonight, and I don't want it, Josh. And so I don't want *you*.'

'But – Christ, Claire! The wedding . . . ?' He couldn't believe what she was saying.

Claire stood up abruptly. Her eyes wouldn't meet his.

'I told you. There ain't going to *be* a wedding. Not a bloody great one and not a hole-in-the-corner one either. It's *off*.'

She walked over to the door and opened it, tugging off her engagement ring. She handed it back to him. 'Here. Take it.'

'Jesus.'

How could this be happening? They'd always been together, a pair. Big rough Josh and gentle Claire. And now, he'd lost her. Wanting to show himself off, be the big man, he'd lost it all. She wasn't going to run away with him, she wasn't going to be his Claire any more.

'Claire . . .' he started. 'Wait. All right. Say I agree to the big wedding, just as you want it. What if—'

'*No!* Fuck off, Josh,' she said, her voice harsh with barely stifled emotion. 'Just go, will you? Do the decent thing and piss off.'

10

Crying her eyes out, Claire paced around the trailer's hot interior for several minutes after Josh was gone. She'd lost the man she loved, but she couldn't have gone through with it. She knew it. She was too soft. She couldn't bear to see him hurt. And yet . . .

If she went after him right now, she could still make things right. But . . . shit, the wedding. She hadn't realized the depth of his hatred for all things marriage-related, she hadn't known that he detested the whole huge-wedding business. Why hadn't he just *told* her that, for God's sake?

Because he was thinking of me. Me and my girly big-wedding dreams.

If she *did* go after him now, he would think it was OK to just elope. And it wasn't, not in her eyes. Mum would be devastated if it was all called off. And truthfully? So would she. If she was going to marry at all, then she wanted her big day. And Josh didn't, so it was all impossible, and it was best that it ended now.

But her heart was breaking.

Unable to settle, wondering how the hell she was going to tell her parents and Trace, she went to the door of the trailer and out, down the steps into the semi-darkness of the campsite. Blue whined and she undid the string tying him. He jumped to his feet, eager for a walk.

She set off up the track toward the lane, knowing her way even in the pitch-blackness of the night that folded around her out here in the country. Soon her eyes gained their night vision and she trod more confidently, Blue tugging at her arm. She was relieved to at least be moving, to be out in the open while her mind wrestled with all her troubles.

God, she had so many.

She'd lost Josh.

That was the worst of all.

Out in the lane, owls hooted and foxes wailed, but she wasn't afraid, she knew the sounds, she was used to them. Claire barely noticed them now. She had too much sorrow to contend with, too much pain. And humiliation too. She was going to look such a fool in front of everyone, having to call off all the arrangements. Shauna Everett would laugh at her. God, that bitch would love it.

Still crying helplessly, she halted as Blue gave a growl and stopped dead in front of her.

'Oh Christ, Blue, don't mess around. Not now. It's only a ruddy badger or a deer, that's all,' she choked out.

But now Claire could see it wasn't. By the dim moonlight she could see figures moving ahead of her in the lane. Coming closer.

She stiffened. 'Who's that?' she called out.

They didn't answer.

She felt the chill of fear.

Blue was growling steadily, his hackles raised, his head lowered, ready to spring. Then one of the figures came in close and she heard Blue snarling in earnest.

'You better shut him up,' said a female voice Claire recognized.

'Shauna? That you?'

No answer. Claire was pulled off-balance as rough sacking was dragged over her head, stifling her. Someone hit her, hard, and the dark world went darker still.

11

When Claire came to she felt sick and dizzy. Her head was pounding, her whole body was in motion and there was an awful pressure on her stomach . . . someone was carrying her over their shoulder, she realized. The sacking smelled dusty against her nose and she thought of Blue. Where was he?

The answer came straight away. She could hear him growling and whimpering, somewhere close by.

She could also hear the wind, sighing over the fields, and now a door was creaking open and the sound was familiar. They were inside now, inside a cool and silent building that echoed with the footsteps of whoever had grabbed her.

It was . . .

It was the church in the dell.

Blue's growling went up a notch. He should be *biting* someone by now, she thought. Why wasn't he?

Suddenly she was set down on her feet. She staggered. The sacking was pulled off and a torch shone into her eyes. Shaking, unsteady, she winced, put a hand up to shield them. She felt a sticky patch of blood on her brow, where she'd been struck. Wondered if she was going to vomit. But then they were yanking her forward, dragging her up the aisle and . . .

'Jesus,' moaned Claire as rough hands pulled her to a standstill.

Ahead of her were more torchbeams, highlighting a horror. The grave of Polly James, the one at the top of the aisle in front of the altar, the one she knew so well, had been opened. Inside was Polly herself, the white wedding gown she'd been buried in turned yellow and crumbling with age. Polly's skull was grinning up at them all as if in welcome.

Standing beside the grave was Jeb Cleaver, his fist wrapped around Blue's string in a tight, choking grip. Blue's muzzle was bound with gaffer tape. His eyes were frantic, pleading. Jeb pulled the string tighter and Blue whimpered in pain.

'Don't . . .' said Claire, swallowing bile.

Then she saw the knife in Jeb's free hand.

'Don't!' Claire surged forward but strong hands held her fast. She looked back. It was the oldest Cleaver, Ciaran, his blind eye blank, the other one full of mockery at her weakness. She couldn't move, couldn't help. She looked back to Jeb. Her voice faltered. 'Please don't hurt—'

Jeb swiped the knife in one swift movement across Blue's throat. The whimper turned into a choked cry of agony. Blood spurted. And Blue went limp. Jeb unwrapped the string from his fist, letting Blue collapse, dead, to the floor.

'No!' Claire shouted, her face twisted with anguish. 'Oh God, what have you *done*?'

'The same as we'll do to you, if you don't fucking well clear off,' said Shauna Everett's voice behind her.

Gasping in shock, Claire turned her head toward that voice. In the huddle of torchlit bodies, she could see Shauna standing there. Open-mouthed with disbelief, Claire stared at her.

Shauna's dark gaze held Claire's steadily. 'I *told* you you'd be sorry.'

'You bitch, you horrible cruel *cow!*' cried Claire.

Jeb moved, grabbing Blue's lifeless body by the front legs and tossing him in on top of Polly James. Ribs snapped and dust rose in the torchlight, mouldy and stinking of the grave, as Blue's body thumped down on the skeletal remains.

'You see that?' said Shauna, pointing.

'I'll get you for this,' said Claire, panting against Ciaran's restraining bulk. 'You *bitch*, you'll pay for this.'

'I said, do you *see?*' said Shauna more harshly, grabbing Claire's chin and directing her gaze to the grave.

Claire said nothing. Horrified tears poured down her face. They'd killed Blue.

'Because *that* is what is going to happen to you if you don't fuck off, Claire Milo,' said Shauna. 'This ain't a joke. I'm not playing with you. I'm serious. You go – anywhere, I don't give a shit – tonight, and you don't come back. Not *ever*. You stay away from the camp and you don't contact your folks ever again. I hear you've been in touch with your mum or dad, or that twat of a sister of yours or that mad old bat your Nanny Irene, and *this* is what's going to happen to them. You got me? They're going to get their throats cut, just like that damned dog of yours. You *stay away* from them all, and from Josh Flynn.' A satisfied smirk twisted her face. 'Good fight, wasn't it? And he won, just like he said he would.'

'How . . . ?' Claire stared at Shauna and then, despite her panic and revulsion, she realized. 'He wouldn't tell you that! You been listening to us talking.'

'Damn sure she has,' said Ciaran. 'And fucking good job, or we'd have lost a packet.'

'The wedding's off,' said Claire, feeling nausea rising up

to choke her, feeling literally sick with fear. But if they were talking about her going, then perhaps she was going to get out of this unharmed. And Shauna would be pleased with the news that the wedding was cancelled. That at least might make her see reason.

'You what?' It stopped Shauna in her tracks.

'It's off,' gasped out Claire. 'I hate the fight game and I wanted a big wedding. Josh loves to fight and he don't want all the fuss, he . . . well, we couldn't agree. It's off. It's over.'

Shauna was shaking her head. 'I don't believe you.'

'It's true.'

'Nah, you're lying. You're *lying*. Listen – I want you gone. That's all I want. You, out of the way, for good. Or you and your whole bloody family go the same way as that vicious mutt of yours. That's a promise.' Shauna reached into her jeans pocket and pulled out a wad of notes. 'Take this.' She stuffed the notes into Claire's skirt pocket. 'You take this money – I got it out of your bottom drawer; your wedding savings, eh? – and you fuck off.'

Shauna went over to the wall of the church and snatched up a suitcase Claire recognized. It was *hers*. And of course it would have been easy for her to get into the Milo trailer. No one on the site ever locked their doors; there was no need.

'I packed some of your stuff for you,' said Shauna, dumping the case at Claire's feet. She came in close to Claire, stared at her, nose to nose. 'So you go tonight, you got that? And you *never* come back. I hear so much as a whisper that you've been in touch with anyone on the campsite, I'll get them. And then I swear I'll come and get *you*.'

Claire was trembling with terror. She nodded. Right now, with Blue dead in front of her, Ciaran Cleaver restraining her and Shauna looking at her like that, she would have agreed to anything. 'All right. I'll go.'

'Good,' said Shauna, and moved away down the aisle. Then she glanced back at Ciaran, at Jeb. 'All yours,' she said.

Claire watched her go for a moment, then suddenly she knew what was to happen next. Ciaran shoved her from behind. She sprawled forward and fell on to the hard flagstones, bruising her knees and her arm. Pain seared through her left wrist. Jeb came closer too. Panicking, Claire started to scrabble to her feet. Jeb shoved her back down.

'No!' she cried out, but Ciaran was on her in an instant, pinning her with his weight.

'Hold her,' he said to Jeb, and Jeb grabbed her flailing arms while Ciaran started pulling at her clothes.

Oh Christ, help me! thought Claire.

But no one came. No one helped.

Outside in the hot still air, Shauna heard Claire's screams. No one else would, of course; the church was well out of the way. She heard Claire's frantic cries, and she relished them.

Now, with that troublesome little cunt out of the way, the field would be clear. Josh Flynn would – at last – be hers. She would make sure of it.

12

When Shauna got back to the camp, she felt a guilty start as she saw a big figure moving across the clearing. He had a bag in his hand and was lit by bright moonlight, the dying fire and the fainter glow of the tilley lamps.

'Josh?' she called out, feeling her cheeks go red. She was thankful for the semi-darkness. Her hands were shaking and her guts churned up. She had committed herself to a great goal now, and standing right here in front of her was the prize at the end of it: Josh Flynn. She'd wanted him for so long, and now . . . She thought of Claire Milo down there in the dell, getting God knew what done to her by the Cleavers. She had caused that. And the killing of the dog. But this was all part of the plan and it was no good having doubts now. She had to press on with this.

'Josh?' she said again when he didn't answer. 'What the fuck's going on?'

She was glad nobody else was about. And that her folks were out. They were *always* out, they'd been out nearly every night of her life. Even when she was tiny, they'd be off boozing or down the bookies, and they'd never given it a second thought, they'd just left her in her cot, alone. They were a cold pair. Maybe they'd made her that way, too.

Shauna couldn't see Josh's eyes, but his movements

were slow and almost bewildered as she approached him. Shauna reached out, took one of his big hands in hers. 'Josh? What's going on?'

'Nothing,' he said, sounding strange, his words almost slurring. He shook her hand off, went over to the Milo trailer and banged on the closed door. 'Claire!' he shouted. 'Come on, Claire, open up. Let's talk!'

'Don't she usually take the dog out walking late?' suggested Shauna. 'I don't think she's in there, Josh. What's up? You two had a row?'

His eyes turned toward her. He seemed almost to *see* her there for the first time. 'The wedding's off,' he said.

Christ! So it *was* true, what Claire had said. Images flipped through her mind. Dark blood spurting from Blue's throat as Ciaran cut it. Claire, her face white as snow as she pleaded with her. Those terrified screams, echoing around the dell.

'That's it. I'm through with all this shit. I'm clearing out,' he said.

'You're doing *what*?' Shauna choked out a laugh. Josh had been here all his life, just like she had.

'I'm going, Shauna.'

'Don't be daft. Going where?'

'Anywhere. Anywhere that ain't *here*.'

'Wait a minute.' Now she grabbed his hand and held on to it. Despite the heat of the night, his flesh felt cold. 'Come in for a mo, OK?'

She tugged and for a moment he resisted; then his shoulders slumped and he followed, meek as a lamb. She went up the steps to her family's trailer and he went too. Then she closed the door behind him and went to where Dad kept his whisky. She slopped some into a glass and handed it to Josh as he stood there in the centre of the room, dwarfing everything around him.

Josh took the drink, raised it to his lips, drank the liquid down in one long swallow. He still held his bag in his hand. His face was bruised, his knuckles red.

Feeling nervous, Shauna flicked on the radio. Now it had come to the crunch, she felt unsure and she was wondering if she really could turn this thing to her advantage. Abba were singing 'Waterloo'. Well, Claire Milo had for damned sure met *her* Waterloo tonight.

'What you talking about going for, then?' she asked, her smile covering her anxiety. 'You're a big man now, Josh. You beat Matty O'Connor.'

'I wasn't *supposed* to,' said Josh, putting the empty glass aside. 'I was supposed to throw the fight. Cloudy had it all sorted. But I didn't do it.'

'Right,' said Shauna.

'It's all over – me and Claire. That's all off,' said Josh.

'Why's it off, Josh?' she asked. Christ, this was a miracle. It was a bloody *gift*. Tonight her and Jeb and Ciaran had done things – *bad* things, she supposed – and maybe they hadn't needed to even bother. But no. It was better – neater – this way.

'Claire don't like the fight game. She can't take it. And after tonight, not throwing the match, I suppose I could be in the shit. So I'll clear out and things will cool down.'

'I saw her there tonight. At the fight.' *And later.*

'Yeah. She don't like it, Shauna. She *hates* it.'

Shauna saw raw pain in his eyes. He'd been with Claire all his life, he *loved* the silly bitch. Shauna couldn't see why. Josh was a king in the making; Claire? She'd never measure up to him, not in a million years. *Shauna* was the one he should be with. And now – if she played her cards right – he would be. Everything was falling just right.

'So where will you go then?' she asked.

'Far away from here as I can. No point staying.'

'If you keep fighting, drawing a crowd, all those that lost money on the fight will come after you.' The Cleavers hadn't lost a penny. She knew that. But Josh didn't.

Josh shrugged. 'Once they cool down, they'll forget it.'

'Josh, you can't just go.'

'Watch me.'

'Then . . . I'll come with you.'

Josh blinked, seemed to focus on her properly. 'You what?'

'I'll come too. Keep you company.' There was no way Shauna was letting Josh just vanish out of her life now. Tonight was a turning point for both of them. Claire was history. They – she and Josh – would be a great match. All she had to do was make Josh see that.

'Don't be fucking daft,' he said.

'I'm serious, Josh. I got nothing to stay here for. Only Mum and Dad, and they're off out every night getting pissed, they're never here. They don't give a shit about me. And I don't give a shit about them.'

Josh stood there, staring at her. Then he shrugged, indifferent.

'All right,' he said. 'If you want. Pack a bag. And hurry the fuck up.'

13

It was gone twelve by the time Josh parked up outside a tatty-looking little B & B with a *vacancies* sign up, on the outskirts of Andover.

'You'd better stay here, let me go in first,' said Shauna, picking up her handbag and carryall. 'They take one look at that beat-up mug of yours, they're going to slam the door in both our faces.'

Not waiting for a reply, she went up the path to the house. She banged on the brass knocker. It was some time before lights were switched on inside the house and a sixty-ish man in a dressing gown came to the door, opening it halfway.

'What the fuck time d'you call this?' he asked.

Shauna turned on her megawatt smile, hitting him with the charm offensive, tucking her left hand into her coat pocket.

'I'm sorry it's so late. We broke down on the road, got the car started again, and we just need a place to bed down for the night. When we saw your sign, my husband and me, we thought you might still be able to put us up. I know it's late. I'm sorry.'

She could see the man thawing. He stepped back, running a hand over his dishevelled hair.

'You come far then?' he asked.

'All the way down from Yorkshire,' lied Shauna. 'We're visiting my husband's parents in Bournemouth – his dad's sick.'

'Well . . . I'm sorry to hear it.'

'You've got a room free then?'

'Yeah.'

'I'll go help my husband fetch the rest of the stuff,' said Shauna, and nipped back down the path before he could change his mind.

She threw open the car door. 'We're in,' she said to Josh. 'We're a married couple and we've come from Yorkshire and we're visiting my folks in Bournemouth. My dad's ill. OK?'

Josh nodded, picked up his bag, and together they went into the B & B. The hallway was shabby, with a dusty grandfather clock gloomily ticking away the hours. There was a half-moon table against the wall with the day's papers on it. One of them showed that London had had its hottest day in thirty-five years, and in Malaysia ten Japanese terrorists who took over the US Embassy had left for Libya. Shauna saw the B & B owner's eyes open wide in alarm when he saw Josh.

'What the fuck happened to you then?' he demanded.

'He had a fight with his brother. Boxed his ears proper for him. The brother didn't want to come with us, his poor old dad on his deathbed too, I think that's disgusting, don't you?' said Shauna. She was so convincing, she half-believed it herself.

'Families got to stick together,' said the man, stepping back as Josh and Shauna crowded into the hall.

'That's right,' said Shauna. 'That's what we told him, but he wasn't having none of it.'

'I'll show you up,' said the man, and led the way up the dingy carpeted stairs.

He paused on a landing lit with a forty-watt bulb that cast a depressingly low light. 'In here,' he said, and opened a white-painted door, stepping inside and flicking on a stark circular fluorescent.

The bedroom was tiny, dominated by a double bed covered by an orange candlewick bedspread. There was a window with purple curtains pulled closed. It was hot as hell in here, stifling.

'Bathroom's at the end of the hall, my missus has the plug. You want a bath in the morning, ask her for it.'

Shauna stared at the man. Fuck's sake! She'd heard of tight, but that was *water* tight, like a duck's arse.

'Breakfast is sharp at eight downstairs. And it's twenty quid, all in. Money up front.'

It wasn't exactly cheap, but at least it was a bed. Josh got out a twenty and it vanished into the man's dressing-gown pocket faster than you could say knife.

'Sleep well then,' he said, and went out the door, closing it behind him.

Josh put his bag on the bed and Shauna followed suit. There was nowhere else to put their things, except on the floor. No lamps by the bed, there wasn't even room for a chair. She went straight to the window and flung it open, but there was no cooling breeze; the night air was humid as a damp flannel.

'Well, here we are,' said Josh.

'Yeah,' said Shauna, and suddenly she was nervous.

She'd wanted this for a long time – but now it was actually happening, she felt awkward. If she had ever daydreamed about her and Josh – and she had – the scene would go like this: Josh would fall on his knees and propose to her, say he didn't know what the hell he'd ever seen in Claire Milo, that he'd kicked the dozy bitch aside. That he wanted Shauna, he always had. And then there would be wedding bells, blissful marriage, the works.

But . . . this wasn't that. Josh was still in love with Claire. Shauna was here because she had insisted on keeping him company. She felt a stab of despair at the situation. But she was tough; she'd make the best of it. Now that drippy tart Claire was off the scene, he would come to see that Shauna was the right woman for him. He *had* to.

'Better get some shut-eye then,' said Josh, and took both bags off the bed and tossed them on to the floor. He threw back the covers.

Shauna looked dubiously at the purple nylon sheet. She sniffed, guessing that it hadn't been washed after the last occupants of the bed had departed.

'Jesus,' she grimaced.

'It's a bed,' he shrugged.

'I'm not taking my clothes off to lie in *that*,' she said.

'Keep 'em on then,' he said, his tone weary, and he kicked off his shoes and lay down.

Shauna's mouth dropped open to rage at him for the insult. The clear message was that he didn't give a toss whether she was buck-naked or fully dressed, but then she shut up. What was the point? This was a start, that was all. The rest? She could work on it.

'Turn the light off,' he said, yawning.

Shauna turned it off, stumbled over the bags in the darkness, cursed. She groped her way to the bed, took off her shoes, lay down, and tried to sleep.

14

Sometime during the night, Shauna awoke to feel Josh's arm around her and his hand cupping her breast through her clothes. She lay perfectly still, not wanting to break the spell. So much for his pretended indifference. She *knew* there had always been a spark between them, and this proved it.

But then, she thought again. Men weren't fussy. Hand it to them and they'd lap it up, her mum had always told her that and she was right, drunken old cow that she was. Then she felt Josh's big hand fiddling with the buttons on her blouse, pushing aside the thin material; he'd reached her bra.

He's half-asleep. He don't even know it's me, she thought. *Maybe I should stop him.*

But then . . . she'd dreamed of this, fantasized about it so much. She *wanted* it.

Yes, she'd mucked about with the Cleaver brothers, tried her best to make Josh jealous, but she had never been even faintly interested in them, not really. Compared to Josh, they were nothing; he was the prize. And now . . . here he was. She had him.

Slowly she reached around, popped the bra open, then felt a shiver of lust as his hand quickly fastened over one naked tit, hardening her nipple in an instant. Helplessly she ground her hips back against his, felt the hardness there, wished he'd do it to her, right now. *Do it*, she thought. *Please* do it.

She heard him give a moan, felt his breathing quicken against her neck, then his hand left her breast and he was working the button on her jeans loose, tugging down the zip, pulling them off her.

His hand was sliding inside her pants now, touching her where she was most sensitive, feeling her readiness. She gasped as his hand moved away, wanted to say something, to protest, to say, *Don't stop, please don't stop*, but he was pulling her pants down, over her thighs, her knees, her ankles, and she was naked down there, and she was panting too now, her blood aflame with desire.

Josh pushed her on to her back, got between her legs. She couldn't see him, she couldn't see anything, all she could do was *feel*. She heard him fumbling with his clothes, heard the zip of his jeans go down, heard him pushing them out of the way. Her hands reached out and she felt him then, his cock naked and hard as iron, throbbing and somehow threatening but silky too, and she pulled him in almost frantically, wanting this, wanting him.

When he was there, right at the spot, she pushed up with her hips, taking him inside her, impaling herself on that big hard column of flesh. She felt such pleasure, such unbelievable thrills of desire, that she moved as he moved, pounding into her, taking her, filling her just as she had always longed for him to fill her. All those others had been rubbish, nothing but a rehearsal. *This* was the real thing.

Then he said it, *moaned* it.

'Oh Jesus, Claire . . .'

Shauna stiffened. He really *was* half asleep – and he was dreaming he was fucking that dopey little cow Claire.

He could get me up the duff, thought Shauna.

But he'd said Claire's name, not hers. Still, that wonderful thing between his legs was still thrusting inside her and her feelings were all over the place. She wanted to stop him, to push him away from her, because for God's sake he didn't even know it was her. But she wanted him to go on too. His movements quickened then, and he groaned.

He thinks it's her, thought Shauna in fury, feeling spikes of passion rock her, making her stomach clench, making her clasp him even harder inside her.

She didn't care *who* he thought she was, not right now. He was in despair over that Milo bitch, and he was taking blind, mindless comfort the way men always had, always would. For her, the pleasure was too intense, almost unbearable. He moaned again, and seemed to get bigger, harder, so that she cried out, not hurt but amazed.

Now he was almost pulling out from her, pushing back in, deeper, harder, fuller.

Shauna cried out again.

Josh pushed in hard, madly, and was still for a while, pinning her there.

Then he pulled out of her, flopped back on the bed. Shauna felt wetness on her thighs. Maybe he *had* given her a baby. That would be a hell of a result. A quiet, nice, *decent* man like Josh? He'd have to marry her then; he'd feel obliged to. Gasping and with their limbs tangled together, Shauna cuddled in against him.

'It's me, Josh,' she said quietly. 'It's me. It's Shauna.'

But he didn't answer.

'Josh?' she whispered.

His breathing had deepened. He was asleep.

Shauna tried to sleep too, but she was too excited. Everything was starting to happen for her. Her life was beginning at last – her *real* life, with Josh Flynn.

15

Claire supposed she must have slept at some point. Or just passed out with the terror of what was being done to her. When she came back to herself she was lying, shivering, on hard stone and as she lifted her head a shaft of pain lanced straight down her neck. She let out a groan, pushed herself up so that she was sitting. Her wrist hurt. Her knees were scraped. She was . . . oh Christ in heaven, she was naked.

And then it came back.

It *all* came back.

Claire let out a choked cry as she looked around her, at the cool echoing interior of the church, at the relentless morning sun creeping through the stained-glass windows, throwing puddles of colour on to the stone slabs of the aisle. She caught her breath on a panicky sob. Oh God!

There was the grave, right in front of the altar, filled in now – but last night it had been open. Her hand touched a piece of cloth on the floor. It was her skirt. Discarded like a rag. The horror of the memories poured into her brain then, like iced water. The two of them clawing at her, bruising her, invading her. The pain. The humiliation.

Oh God oh God oh God . . .

Panic-stricken, shuddering, Claire stumbled to her feet, her mind whirling with remembered images so vile that she felt her guts start to clench and bile rising into her throat. Jesus, and they'd . . .

They killed Blue.

She started to cry, great wracking sobs, and her bleary eyes looked toward the grave in front of the altar.

Blue was in there.

She remembered Shauna Everett shoving a bundle of notes at her, and then . . . ah shit, then . . .

She couldn't even think of it. She hurt everywhere and the shaking was bone-deep now as her brain skipped away from all that had happened here last night. Shuddering, she snatched up her clothes and started to pull them on, her fingers frozen, her movements jerky with shock and pain.

She'd always known Shauna was a cruel cow. She *knew* that. But she had never for one minute imagined the lengths she would go to just to get rid of her. She had underestimated Shauna. And oh God, it had cost her. It had cost her so dear.

Somehow her feeble hands managed to fasten her skirt. She felt filthy, ashamed. Soiled to her soul. She didn't want anyone to see her, her life was over. Josh was gone from her and she had to clear out, she had to do this now. She couldn't ever go home again. A stark image surged into her mind again, of those two animals laughing as they attacked her last night, thrusting into her like she was a piece of meat.

Oh Christ!

She had to get out of here. She had to get *away*. Because if she didn't, Shauna would be mad. And then God knew what she would do. Now Claire knew what Shauna was capable of. For the moment she was alive and if she wanted to stay that way then there was nothing for it but to do as Shauna said and *go*.

Claire picked up her blouse and pulled it on with shaking hands. Her wrist throbbed, hot with pain. Her neck ached. She was black and blue with bruises and between her legs – *oh God* – she was hideously sore, and wet. She felt in the pocket of her skirt for the money that Shauna had put there last night. It was still there. She was surprised at that; she wouldn't have put it past those godless bastards the Cleavers to have taken even that from her, along with her dignity and her virginity. They had taken everything else.

She managed a few tottering steps to the grave in front of the altar.

Blue. Oh my poor sweet Blue.

Her eyes lingered on the inscription there.

*Something Old
Something New
Something Borrowed
Something Blue*

Shauna's idea of a joke, putting Blue in there? Claire didn't know. She turned away, crying, beaten, bloody and sore, and staggered out of the church and away.

16

Josh knew where all the travelling folk were at any given time; all the Romanies did. There were the horse fairs, run as regular as clockwork, and then there were the funfairs, set up all over the country on bank holidays, with legal boxing booths being a big feature of the entertainment.

Unable to sleep, tormented by the thought of all that he had lost, he dragged his aching body from the bed and left Shauna Everett in the land of nod. He crept down the stairs and unbolted the door and let himself out into the warm night. Crossing to the car, he took off the handbrake and rolled her down and out to the gate, then started the engine and switched on the lights and turned the car south.

He drove until he saw the signs. *Pole and Co Fun Fairs*, they shouted, showing great grinning clown faces painted in brilliant reds and yellows. *Fun's the game and Pole's the name!* He turned the car down a long gravel driveway. Up ahead against a charcoal-grey sky he could see the outline of a big wheel, the massive cone of the helter-skelter. The big top was up, flags luffing in a sultry breeze.

Josh drove on, past the fairground, and found himself in a huddle of cars and caravans. The dogs started barking the minute he switched off the engine. He didn't get out of the car, he wasn't a fool. Some of them would be roaming loose, patrolling the site. As he sat there, a black-faced Alsatian came and stood its big forepaws against his window and let loose a thunderous barking.

Josh leaned on the car horn. It didn't deter the dog, who was quickly joined by another, and then another, all surrounding the car and baying for Josh's blood. Josh sat there and fought the urge to open the door and let them in to tear at his flesh. Maybe he deserved that. Maybe he would even welcome it. If Claire was gone from him, then the best part of his life was over.

Then he thought of last night, and Shauna. He'd felt so down, so lost. He knew he'd had her, knew damned well he'd taken comfort in a female body. It could have been anybody's. Turned out, it was Shauna's. As soon as it was done, he regretted it. Somehow, he had to go on with his life. Right now, he didn't know how.

Finally, after minutes of Josh leaning on the horn, the dogs going demented, a light came on in one of the bigger vans, illuminating the windows. A curtain was shoved aside and someone peered out. Then the door was flung open and a bulky man came down the steps, zipping his trousers and pulling his braces up over his vast, grey-vested beer gut.

'What the fuck's happening here?' he asked, swiping angrily at the dogs as he came.

They stopped barking, turning away and loping off into the semi-darkness.

Josh wound down his window. 'Mr Pole? Mr Linus Pole?' he asked, looking at the man who peered in at him. Pole was red in the face as Father Christmas. He was plump, with thin greying hair, an aggressive hazel-eyed stare and a big waxed handlebar moustache.

'Who wants him? It's the middle of the effing night.'

'Josh Flynn,' said Josh.

'Who? Flynn, you say?'

'I beat Matty O'Connor in a fair fight yesterday evening.'

'I know Matty. Course I do. Everyone does. Man's a legend.'

'Well, he's beat.'

'You're fucking kidding me.'

'No, I ain't.'

Now Pole was looking at him differently. 'Well – what can I do for you, Mr Flynn?'

Josh shrugged. 'Where there's fairs there's fights. I can beat any man you got on this site, Mr Pole. Set it up and I'll prove it.'

Pole relaxed a notch. He'd set up more fights than he'd had hot dinners; they were always good earners, and he liked to earn.

'You ain't *seen* the boys we got on this site,' said Pole.

'Don't have to. I can beat 'em.'

'Cock-sure, ain't you,' said Pole, but he was smiling.

'I know my own abilities.'

'Come on over to the van, let's talk.'

17

Shauna managed to sleep at last, and she woke when daylight crept through the curtains. The events of yesterday evening rushed back to her – getting rid of the Milo bitch and that damned hound of hers, leaving the campsite, arriving here and then falling into bed with Josh, who'd had her during the night. Had her, thinking . . . what? That she was really Claire? No. She reckoned that Claire was still a virgin – well, she *had* been until Ciaran and Jeb got hold of her. She thought that Josh had used her, like she was just anybody. That enraged her, *killed* her, but she would work on him, she would alter his feelings. She was hell-bent on that.

She flopped on to her back and stretched out a hand, a smile starting on her lips – and then she realized he was gone. Shauna shot up in the bed, her eyes casting around in the gloom. She could make out her bag, there on the floor. His wasn't with it.

'Shit! No, no, no . . .' She flung herself from the bed and yanked back the curtains, feeling her heart thudding in her chest as she stared down at the driveway and saw that Josh's beat-up old Ford Zephyr was gone too. Her mouth was dry as dust. She turned, groped for the clothes he'd pulled off her sometime during the night. That *bastard*. He'd screwed her and left her.

She yanked on her pants, her jeans, her bra and shirt. Glanced at her watch. Seven a.m. Hopefully Scrooge and his lady wife wouldn't be up, getting the breakfast started. It wouldn't be anything fancy anyway, she thought. Dry toast and a scrape of marge, maybe.

Shauna grabbed her bag, opened the door as quietly as she could. She didn't want to bump into that ugly bugger and have to start explaining where her 'husband' had got to. Wounded and furious, she crept down the stairs and heard a loo chain pull somewhere in the house. Hurrying, she slipped outside into the dewy morning. She trotted down to the road, looked left and right, then headed south, back toward the campsite. She reckoned for sure that he'd gone back there, looking for the Milo bitch, hoping to change her mind over the marriage. On the way, she was going to find a phone box and call up a taxi. She had cash enough for that.

Fucking Josh Flynn.

18

By the time Josh had concluded his business with Linus Pole, it was daylight. Josh turned the car around and set off again, while the sun rose on another blisteringly hot day. Last night had turned into a waking nightmare, but today was a new day and he was going to see Claire and talk her round. He was going to roll over about the big wedding. Use that as a sweetener. He couldn't just give up on her. She'd been upset after the fight, but today she would see reason. He knew it.

But when he got to the campsite clearing, all hell was breaking loose. As soon as he saw the flashing blue lights of a police car, his guts clenched in alarm. Muskras, here? It was unheard of. He drove straight on, and stopped two hundred yards along the lane. Then he got out, walked back to the clearing. Sure enough, there was the police car, parked up beside the vans. He *hadn't* dreamed it. Its radio was burbling away, unheeded.

Josh looked around, feeling his heart pounding hard. There was his mum's van, the curtains pulled shut. Cloudy's big Morecambe was over there, the curtains closed, a light burning behind them. Claire's folks' van was lit up like Crystal Palace, the door wide open, yesterday's washing still out on the line. He could hear raised voices coming from inside. Eva, Claire's mum, was wailing. Young Trace's voice was deeper. And Pally's, deeper still, and Nanny Irene's aged croaking. Now a muskra was coming down the steps. Josh saw that Blue was not at his usual post under the van.

Josh walked along the edge of the camp and came up close to another van. The dog tethered under it snarled, but he shushed it and it subsided; it knew him. Then Josh walked around the front and over to the policeman.

'What's going on, mate?' he asked.

'Who are you, sir?' He looked about ten.

'Bertie Mackey. I live over there.' Josh pointed to a trailer across the clearing that was still closed up for the night. 'What's happening?'

'Girl called Claire Milo's been reported missing,' said the copper. 'Run off with her boyfriend, I reckon, 'cos he's gone as well. Took her dog too, by the sounds of it.'

Josh felt his heart contract with shock. Claire was missing? Shit, what was going on?

'Stay here, will you, sir? I'll just be a moment . . .' The policeman went back inside the van.

Josh stood there, sickened and reeling. Claire, gone? Gone *where*?

Claire was a stay-at-home type of girl. She wasn't flighty and flirty like Shauna, who regularly stayed out overnight doing God knew what. Everyone in the camp knew that. This wasn't like Claire. Not at all.

He stumbled back along the lane to his car and got inside. For a while he sat there, dazed.

Where the hell could she be?

Then someone started thumping on the window.

He looked up.

It was Shauna.

19

'You *arsehole*,' she said when he wound the window down.

'What the fuck you doing here?' asked Josh, his mind spinning. He'd left her at the B & B and he'd been about to go *back* there, but now here she was, wandering the streets.

'What am *I* doing here? What are *you* doing here, more to the point.' Shauna's face drew into thunderous lines. 'Been back to try and see Claire, have you? Changed your mind, I suppose.'

'I haven't seen Claire.'

'You bloody bastard! You low-life *cunt*!' said Shauna, and hit him.

'Hey!' Josh raised a hand to fend her off. Unable to strike, Shauna got madder still and kept pummelling at him until he grabbed her wrist. She was so crazy with rage she barely felt the pain of his grip. 'Stop that!' said Josh.

Shauna was breathing hard. 'What the *hell* have you come back here for, if not to see that little twat?'

'All right! I came back to talk to her.' Josh turned haunted eyes toward her. 'I thought she'd be calmed down by now, that she'd reconsider. But Claire's missing. I just talked to the muskra and he told me.'

'*What?*' Shauna, eyes averted, started pacing up and down beside the car. 'What do you mean, missing?'

'As in, *gone*. Vanished. That ain't like Claire. You know it.'

Shauna stopped walking and shook her head. She was furious and offended. He'd fucked her overnight and then come back for the one he truly loved. If she'd felt any shred of guilt at what she and the Cleaver boys had done to Claire, this crushed it once and for all. She was *glad* they'd marked that bitch's card now. 'Look, what probably happened is she was upset when the two of you parted company, and she's just taken herself off somewhere. She's sulking.'

Josh thumped a scraped and bloodied fist against his forehead. 'Oh Christ. I've fucked it all up, haven't I. This is *my fault.*'

Shauna was staring at him. 'We got to get out of here,' she said. 'We got to put all this shit behind us.'

Josh stared at her like she'd sprouted horns. 'What? My girl—'

'*Don't* call her that, you fool. She *ain't* your girl any more, can't you see that? She's cleared out, ain't you got the message? She's *dumped* you, and run off. Come on. Let's go.'

Shauna stomped around the front of the car and got in the passenger seat, slamming the door after her.

'You're a cold-hearted bitch,' said Josh.

'Oh shut up. One of us has got to think straight.'

'This is my fault.'

'Yeah. Maybe it is. So what? Is this the life you see for yourself, Josh? Is it really? Living on a campsite 'til you die?' Shauna looked at his face. 'You're king of the gypsy fighters now, Josh. You've made the break. All you got to do is accept it.'

Josh was staring at her. 'Cold as fucking Christmas, ain't you. I notice no one's panicking over *you* going. Mostly because you're always out on the tiles, ain't you? Sometimes you're gone for days, like a fucking alley cat. Your folks wouldn't miss *you*.'

His words stung. But they were true. Everyone knew Shauna's parents were shot away. Her mum had famously once knocked her husband out cold while he sat in his armchair by cracking a bottle full of whisky over his head. They both drank like fishes and fought like tigers, and it was pretty much known all around that Shauna had dragged herself up. So she had gone off, made her own amusements from an early age. Trotted off along the lane to the Cleaver place, where at least she was welcome. OK, she was welcome because she gave them uncomplicated sex, and they liked that. And what right did Josh Flynn have to criticize her? He'd liked her well enough too, in bed last night.

Shauna bit her tongue to stifle the angry words. One way or another she would make him forget Claire had ever existed.

Together, they could *move on*. She wanted more out of life than grubbing around for money, people spitting on the ground and calling her an effing pikey when they passed by. With Josh's talents and her looks, they could go far. Provided he'd stop looking back and look toward the future instead.

'So what are you doing here?' asked Josh. His brain felt scrambled. Suddenly, his whole world was in chaos.

'Looking for you, numbskull,' said Shauna.

'You thought I'd run out on you.'

'And you fucking well did, didn't you? And if she'd been here this morning and changed her mind about blowing you out, you'd have left me there to stew.'

'I went to do a bit of business too,' said Josh, his face troubled. *Claire. Where the fuck was Claire?* 'I got a fight lined up for tonight.'

Shauna glanced at her watch. It was seven thirty in the morning and already it was hot.

'Start the fucking car up then,' she said irritably. 'We got time to make it back to Crap Towers and get what passes for breakfast down our necks.'

Josh's stomach rebelled at the thought of food. He had to find Claire. And Shauna was buzzing around his head like a mosquito, annoying the hell out of him.

'Don't look like that,' said Shauna. 'We've paid for it. We're bloody well going to eat it.'

20

They left the B & B right after breakfast, which wasn't much; no full English. Josh only poked at his food with a fork anyway. He didn't eat.

'We're out of bacon,' said the podgy wife of the irritable man serving as mine host, as she slapped their plates – *cold* plates – down in front of them. On each plate was a couple of spoonfuls of baked beans, a thin sliver of black pudding and that was it.

'You out of bleeding eggs too?' asked Shauna, thinking that they should have swerved the breakfast and driven on to a transport café instead.

The woman only shrugged. 'And you're *not* married, are you, the pair of you?' she accused, glaring at Shauna's naked ring finger. 'Bloody disgusting, I call that.'

'Oh shut your fat yap,' said Shauna.

'Get out of my house!' ordered the woman.

They piled back into the Zephyr and sat there on the driveway.

'Where you reckon Claire's gone?' asked Josh.

Who gives a shit?

'She'll be fine,' said Shauna. 'She's off feeling bad about blowing you out and cheating everyone of the big wedding party, that's all. Christ knows what Eva and Pally had to go and start calling the police out for. That's mad.'

'They were worried about her,' said Josh.

'What, enough to call the muskras?' Shauna laughed. 'That's not the way we do things. You know that. They've taken leave of what little sense they've got.'

Shauna was looking at Josh. He was big and tough and handsome as hell. He was born to be a champion and that was going to keep them both in style. But at the centre he was soft as shit. She was going to have to get him out of that little habit of being too caring, too considerate.

'Let's go,' she said, and Josh started the car.

'First I'm going back to see if Claire's shown up,' said Josh.

Shauna let out a sigh, but thought better of arguing. 'All right,' she said. 'But you're wasting your time.'

Let him get that cow out of his system, once and for all. Then they could move on.

21

Josh parked the car out on the lane and turned to Shauna, who'd been quiet on the drive back to the campsite.

'Coming then?' he asked.

Shauna looked at him. 'No, I'm not bloody coming. I *told* you. I'm done with this place.'

'You don't even want to tell your folks what's going on?'

'I'll send them a fucking postcard,' said Shauna.

Josh got out of the car. 'I won't be long,' he told her, and slammed the door closed.

Shauna irritably watched him walk off down the track. In search of Claire Milo, who was long gone. She had *better* be, anyway. Already, Shauna felt this part of her life was over and done with, and it galled her that Josh wasn't letting go so easily. But he would. Eventually, he'd have no choice but to let the damned thing drop.

She heaved a sharp sigh and settled down in her seat. Then a dirty pickup truck came around the bend in the lane and juddered to a stop in front of the car.

Shit, she thought as Jeb Cleaver got out of the passenger side and came strolling over with that distinctive rolling gait of his. He walked like he had so much between his legs he could barely contain it, she thought, not for the first time. And she ought to know. She clambered out and met him halfway.

'We shouldn't be seen together,' she told him. 'You should go.'

What if Josh came back and found Jeb here with her? Ciaran was behind the wheel, staring at her – looking like a real creep with that milk-white blind eye. They were *all* creeps, the Cleavers. With luck, they'd have outlived their usefulness to her once she had Josh where she wanted him.

Instead of answering, Jeb pulled her in for a kiss, his meaty arms enfolding her. He stuck his tongue in her mouth and Shauna forced a response, feeling so tense that for a moment she was revolted.

'We did you a big favour last night,' he whispered against her lips.

Shauna tried to pull away. If Josh came back . . .

But Jeb held her tight.

'You did yourself a favour too, didn't you, with Claire Milo,' she said.

'Fresh meat is always the best,' said Jeb with a grin.

'And she's gone,' said Shauna, wanting it confirmed.

'We looked down the church not half an hour since. Refilled the grave, too. Nobody there.'

Shauna nodded, satisfied. Then a thought hit her. What if that little cow had snuck back to the campsite. Hid out in that brand-new trailer Josh had bought for them to live in when they were married? She wouldn't, would she? No. She wouldn't *dare*.

'You have to go,' said Shauna urgently.

'Just one more kiss . . .' said Jeb, and started slobbering over her again.

Shauna endured it. For the time being, she needed to keep the Cleavers sweet. So she smiled at Jeb while wondering how Josh's search of the camp was going.

★

In sombre mood, Josh unlocked the brand-new trailer he'd bought in such high spirits to house his new bride. Claire also had a key, and he hoped she was in here, *prayed* she was – and then he stepped inside.

It was empty.

He looked around it, pained by all the hopes and dreams that had been invested in the place, which were now going to come to nothing. Then he left the trailer and went and banged at the Milo family door.

No police here now, thank God. Pally Milo opened the door to him, and silently ushered him inside. Eva, Claire's mother, was sitting on one of the couches cradling a huge white crystal-covered dress in her arms. Her face was wet with tears. Her daughter Trace sat there beside her, silent.

'Claire's wedding dress,' said Pally as he and Josh stood over the two women.

'The muskras didn't find her then?' asked Josh. He didn't want to look at the dress. It hurt too much.

'Nah, we . . .' Pally looked uncomfortable.

'He phoned them, told them she'd come back home and not to worry,' burst out Eva, giving her husband an evil look.

'We can't have the fucking muskras swarming over the place,' said Pally. 'Be reasonable.'

'Claire's *missing*,' said Trace.

'I thought she might be with you,' said Eva, looking at Josh with such hope that he felt pity for her.

'I wish she was,' he said. 'She isn't.'

'Is that the truth?' demanded Pally.

'The Everetts are saying their girl Shauna's gone off on one of her benders again,' said Trace, looking at Josh. 'But that's nothing new.'

Josh kept quiet. If he let on Shauna was with him, there'd be blood on the carpet. Accusations would fly. Everyone would think that was the reason Claire had vanished, because he'd been playing around with Shauna. And that wasn't true. So it was best to say nothing.

'You've been out looking for her? Checking round the area?' he asked instead.

'Every able-bodied man on this site's been looking for her – in the woods, all up and down the lanes, down the dell, everywhere. She ain't here. She's *gone*,' said Pally, eyeing Josh with hostility. 'And where the fuck have you been? If I find you had anything to do with this . . .'

I had everything to do with it, thought Josh, disgusted with himself. Making her attend the fight. Asking her to ditch her big wedding plans and go for a hole-in-the-corner affair instead. He'd upset her too much, and now she'd fled.

'She must have intended to go,' said Trace. 'Her suitcase has gone. And some of her clothes. It's not like she . . .' Her voice trailed away.

Not like she's been abducted, taken by force, raped or murdered.

No. If she'd taken some possessions, Josh thought, that must be a good sign. She'd packed up and gone of her own free will. But where?

'Where would she go?' Josh asked. He couldn't look at Eva. This should have been building up to the happiest time in a mother's life, seeing a daughter marry, and now it was all destroyed. Eva's heartbreak was too raw. It made him feel ashamed.

'Maybe to the cousins in Ireland?' said Pally.

'Give me the address,' said Josh.

'I'll phone them from the village,' said Pally.

'Give me their damned address.'

'Let him have it, Pally,' said Eva, so Pally did.

22

The ring was set up behind Pole's funfair at midnight. At this point Shauna was thinking, *It's too soon, this is ridiculous*. Josh had only last night taken a hell of a pasting off Matty and now he was going toe-to-toe with another monster of a man. Added to which, he seemed numbed by the sudden turn of events with Claire. At the moment she didn't know whether he was going to just lay down and die, or kill some bastard with his bare hands. It could go either way.

This match wasn't going to be a 'straightener', a stand-up fist-fight like the one he'd had with Matty. This one was going to be 'all-in', and that was worse, much rougher, an 'anything-goes' type of bout where eyes could get gouged out, kicking was all right, biting too, and if ribs were broken or if anybody happened to die of a busted spleen, that was a shame, but it was OK.

Paul Lean was Linus Pole's nephew and he *was* a monster. He was nearly seven feet tall, and solid as a bulldog, his nose flattened and knocked sideways so often that he *breathed* like a bulldog, too, with a rasping wheeze. You heard him before he ever came into view, and when he came into view that was enough to make quite a few men shit themselves and run the other way.

But not Josh. Tonight, a desperate madness swamped

him. The betting was under way and the ref was in the ring. The two of them – Josh looking almost lightweight, his head and middle black with bruises, and Paul like a brick wall – were squaring up when the bell went and they were off. Screams and cheers and shouts went up all around the ring and Shauna, standing in Josh's corner, was jostled and shoved as everyone yelled suggestions as to how *they* would despatch him. Paul was their boy, their favourite. Josh, big as he was, looked like a child in contrast.

But Josh had a long southpaw reach and he was in a crazy mood over losing Claire; dancing around the ring, he suddenly charged at the big man and took him by surprise, landing a killer left on Paul's jaw. A sudden hush fell as Paul staggered back, then Josh surged forward with a flurry of left and right hooks that left Paul sagging against the ropes, but even then Josh showed no sign of letting up. Despite the glazed look in the man's eyes, he kept pounding Paul's huge head and torso.

Inside three minutes, it was over.

Paul hit the dirt and lay there, spark out.

The ref came forward and yanked Josh's hand into the air.

Silence from the crowd.

Shauna thought you could have heard a pin drop. Everyone was stunned. Christ, *she* was stunned too. Josh turned in the ring, not a blow having landed on him, and slowly the clapping started. It wasn't much, people had lost their shirts tonight and they felt cheated of more rounds, but it had been done fairly, so they clapped, and Josh returned to his corner and Linus Pole was there with his winnings.

'Fuck me,' said Pole, slapping Josh on the shoulder and handing him his envelope with the winner's prize – a thousand quid – inside. 'You're a handy man, Mr Flynn. Fearless

Flynn, that's what we should call you. You went through our boy like a dose of bloody salts.'

'Thanks,' said Josh, who had barely broken sweat.

Linus Pole looked around and lowered his voice. 'I done OK out of a few side bets.'

'Side bets?' echoed Josh, his eyes blank of emotion.

Linus winked. 'Thought you looked handy,' he said. Then he looked across at the crowd and added in a low voice, 'No offence, but if I were you I'd make myself scarce now. People put a lot of money on Paul to win. I'll see you tomorrow, yeah? Like we said?'

Josh nodded. Shauna handed him his shirt, and he shrugged it on. He still ached all over from Matty's punches, but he'd mend. He always did. Shauna glanced back at the big man on the floor. He was still down, his eyes closed. An older man was fussing over him, slapping his cheek, calling out his name. Probably his dad. Now she looked at Josh with new respect. Josh had a big talent, that was for certain. A talent that they could easily exploit. And they would.

'We'll get you some more fights lined up,' she said, smiling up at him.

'Not yet,' said Josh.

'Why not?'

'I'm off to Ireland on the ferry, day after tomorrow.'

Shit, thought Shauna.

23

Claire was exhausted. Everything around her seemed unreal. She was used to the quiet campsite, talking to the horses, walking Blue around the meadows and down the lanes. But now there was only the noise of engines and of people, *so many people* all around her, chattering and moving and laughing, while she floated in a dreamlike bubble of isolation.

She'd walked, then caught a bus from the nearest village into Winchester, and from there she'd got the train up to Liverpool. There she boarded the ferry for Dublin. She had a passport, she'd had one for a year or so, since Josh had said he might take her away to Spain or somewhere like that on a trip when they were wed, so she'd better be prepared. It hurt her to even think about that now.

When she arrived in Ireland she checked into a B & B near the docks because it was late, and then she tried to sleep. But she couldn't. Nightmare images of the happenings in the church kept swirling around her brain. Blue, thrown dead into Polly James's grave. And the Cleavers, grunting as they took it in turns to use her, hurting her, bruising her, laughing all the while about popping her cherry and saying she was good, she was fresh meat. She had to put a chair against the locked door to even lie down on the bed and rest. Sleep was out of the question, she was

91

too afraid for that. They might come after her again, and Shauna would be with them, cruel Shauna who had left her there for them to have their fun with, like she was nothing.

Claire felt like she would never sleep again.

On the strength of that thousand-quid win in the ring, Shauna encouraged Josh to splash out on a three-star hotel instead of a B & B. She looked around the place with interested eyes. It was OK, she thought. Passable. But the windows were painted shut and it was stifling hot overnight.

Still, Shauna was determined to make the best of this. It was a blow, Josh's determination to shove off to Ireland in search of Claire Milo – fat chance he had of finding her! – but he was a man, and she was used to manipulating men. Already they were distancing themselves from the campsite, and all she had to do was keep going, keep him occupied, and one of these days he was going to forget he had ever known the Milo bitch. She was coming to realize that getting rid of Claire was only half the battle; the other half was getting her out of Josh's head.

He was a great man, she thought, perfect for her: quiet, intelligent, strong as a bull ox and a stayer – a natural introvert who would bounce off her extrovert nature and not clash with it. All she had to do was convince him of what a winning team they would make. There was a deep well of sensuality, as yet untapped, in Josh, and she was going to exploit that to the full.

After they'd checked in and eaten, Shauna took a bath and came out into the bedroom swathed in a small towel. Aware of Josh's eyes on her as he lounged on the bed, she went over to the dressing table and let down her dark hair, brushing it out with long languorous movements. Then she stood up.

'God, it's hot in here,' she said, turning to the bed, letting the towel fall to the floor. She smiled at Josh. 'You like me like this, don't you, Josh? Naked?'

Josh said nothing. His eyes were fixed to her body.

'Let's get these clothes off you,' she said, coming over to the bed, starting to unbutton his shirt. Then her hands went to his belt, to his fly, to his underpants, and she stopped. 'Oh, what have we here then?' she asked, smiling into his eyes, fondling his erect cock, her full dark-nippled breasts swinging inches from his face.

Josh felt ashamed of his arousal, like he was betraying Claire. Shit, he *was* betraying her. But . . . God, Shauna was so *hot*. She was a real eyeful. And he felt so low over this business with Claire, so fucking ashamed. Despite all his bumps and bruises, despite his pain over all that had happened back at the camp, he responded to Shauna. Soon they were sweating like pigs and Shauna was bouncing up and down on his prick, moaning with pleasure.

When she at last climbed off him and phoned down to ask for a fan, they told her they didn't have any.

'Then move your arse and get a maintenance man up here first thing in the morning,' she snarled at the girl on the end of the line. 'Get these windows opened.'

'Don't fucking bother them, Shaun,' said Josh. All he wanted was peace, what was she shouting the odds for? 'I'll stick a key in there and do it myself in the morning, but I'm knackered now. Let me sleep, for God's sake.'

Shauna had never in her life before stayed in anything so good as a three-star hotel, but she quickly concluded that it wasn't anything to write home about. All decent gypsy women kept their homes immaculate – her drunken old bint of a mother being the exception to the rule – and this place was far from that. She would tell Josh to book them into a four-star establishment next time. That would have to be better than this. She settled down, pulling a sheet up over to cover them both, and Josh started to snore.

Things weren't so bad, she thought. She smiled, feeling quite happy. She had Josh by her side, even if he was – for now – still stewing over what could have happened to Claire Milo. But Josh would accept the situation in time. And they could earn handsomely. What more could anyone ask for?

Then he whispered something that sounded like 'Claire'.

Damn it!

Who was she kidding? This Milo business was far from over. Yes, he was screwing her heartily, and indulging her with this hotel instead of a B & B. But he was *still* going to leave her without a backward glance and set off for Ireland in search of that bitch among the Milo relations over there in Moyross.

Somehow she had to get that fucking woman out of his brain once and for all.

24

Josh felt wound up, sick at heart and full of shame. But he met Linus Pole the next day down at the gym in the local town as agreed, even though he found it hard to focus on anything but Claire. He *had* to find her. Had to make everything right again between them. Being with Shauna only made him more aware of how much he missed Claire's quiet, calming presence.

There were kids sparring in the rings and Josh – despite his turmoil – thought it looked a nice set-up, better than anything he had ever experienced. Very civilized, with head guards and boxing gloves. A man was sitting in the corner watching the fighters and their coaches with Linus. The man had swept-back grey hair and narrowed eyes. He looked about fifty and his skin had the grey-brown tinge of a smoker who fired up one cigarette off the back of another.

'This is my mate, John Finlay,' said Linus when Josh joined them. They shook hands, and again Josh focused on the nicotine-stained skin and bitten fingernails. John was a man under stress. Josh knew *that* feeling. 'John, this is Josh.'

'Quite the fighter, I hear,' said John, his eyes moving over Josh's lithe bulk.

'I do a bit,' said Josh, thinking only that tomorrow he would be on that ferry to Ireland, and with any luck, Claire would be there and they would be reunited. She was the love of his life. He adored her, and longed to have her back. *This* time, he wouldn't be such a fool. Whatever she wanted of him, she would have.

He felt deeply guilty over his involvement with Shauna. But Christ, he was a man and she fucked like a rabid stoat, that girl. Paraded around naked in front of him until he felt so hard for her he wanted to throw her on the floor and do it to her right then and there. She drained him dry. She leapt on him like a she-bear every opportunity. *Devoured* him. And he couldn't resist her. He *ought* to, he knew that. But he was so miserable, so wretched, that he couldn't.

'John's had a spot of trouble,' said Linus.

'Bought a pub,' said John. 'A free house too, not tied to a particular brewery. Thought it would be a damned good investment. But it's a fucking nut house and I can see now why the last lot sold up and scooted.'

'What, getting trouble then?' asked Josh, not really interested.

John and Linus exchanged a look. Linus nodded.

'I dunno if it's something you'd want to do,' said John. 'But Mr Pole here thinks it might be of interest to you. Truth is, the place is bedlam, night after night. Stabbings. Even a couple of shootings. I can't go on like this. Way I see it, I either do something drastic or get out. I'll make a loss, but what the fuck.'

'How much?' asked Josh. All right, he was broken over Claire, but in the meantime life went on. He had to *earn*. Hotels were expensive.

'To straighten things out in a month?'

'Should be long enough,' said Josh.

John named a sum. Josh kept his face blank to hide his surprise at the size of it. He thought briefly of Cloudy, lining his own back pocket while keeping Josh on basic. As his own manager, he was already doing better than he could ever have hoped for. Providing he didn't get himself killed in the process, of course. Then again, if he couldn't find Claire, who cared if he did.

'I'll be in Ireland for a bit,' he said.

'When you get back then. As soon as you can,' said John.

'All right. It's a deal.'

25

When Claire arrived in Moyross council estate and found her way to the part where piebald ponies and donkeys were tethered on the grass out front, she knew she was in the right place. She remembered the exact house number from visits with her parents when she was small. Her Milo cousins lived here. They were going to be startled to see her, she knew that, but she was going to tell them nothing of what had happened to her. She couldn't speak of it, anyway. Couldn't bear to. All she was going to say was that she had come travelling.

They would welcome her, she knew it. They saw little of each other, the Irish branch of the Milos and the English, but they were family, the door was always open. She didn't want to put Mum, Dad or Trace at risk, so she would tell them she'd had a ruck with her folks and so please not to tell them she was here. They would respect that.

Before she turned up cold on their doorstep though, she supposed she ought to buy them a gift or two. She walked over to a row of shops and found an off-licence where she bought a bottle of brandy. In a sweet shop she bought sherbet lemons and flying saucers for any little ones, and for the lady of the house she bought a large box of milk chocolates.

Then she braced herself, somehow fixed a smile on her

face, and started to walk back to the house, one of an identical row of pebble-dashed houses all squashed in together, side by side. She was about to cross the road when a taxi pulled up outside the house of her Milo cousins. She paused. In her mind flashed an image of Ciaran and Jeb Cleaver. They'd followed her. It was *them*.

Terror gripped her and she stopped dead in her tracks, her legs starting to shake. Then she turned and, trembling, struggling to breathe, she walked unsteadily to where she could take shelter among the other houses. She stopped there, her small suitcase and her shop purchases still in her hands, and peered around the corner.

It wasn't the Cleavers.

It was *Josh*.

Claire stood there, quivering, feeling sickness rising in her again. Tears starting to dribble down her face as she stared at him, so beloved, so familiar. Her Josh. His hair disordered by the gusting wind, his face solemn. But . . . she couldn't approach him. She couldn't let him know she was here. She was filthy, soiled now. Used and discarded by those monsters. And Shauna had said to stay away. If she didn't, if she so much as spoke to him, what else might happen to her? They might come at her again. Hurt her. Abuse her. Her whole body shuddered with terror at the thought. They'd already killed Blue. They could kill her, too. And Mum. Dad. Trace. They were all three still there at the campsite, unaware. Sitting ducks. She *couldn't* put them in danger. They might even hurt Josh – against the three of them, and their old man, he wouldn't stand a chance.

No.

As Josh got out and the taxi drove away, as he walked up to the front door, she thought that Mum and Dad must have given him this address in the hope that she would be here. And – so nearly – she would have been. But by going to the shops first she'd missed him by inches.

Thank God.

Ireland wasn't far enough. He'd tracked her down in days. She couldn't let that happen again, she had to go further. She started walking, faster and faster, away from Josh, away from Delmege Park. She had to get out of here. Before long, she was running and she only slowed down when she got to a small shopping centre.

Trying to calm herself, tormented by the sight of Josh there, looking so anxious and unhappy, she gazed in shop windows, hardly seeing a thing until she came across a travel agent. There was a picture of a vast city in the window, buildings forming canyons between the streets. She stared at the picture for a long time. Then she pushed the door open and went inside.

26

Josh had built his hopes up and now they were dashed again. Claire wasn't with the cousins in Moyross. Devastated, he realized he didn't know where else to look. He just didn't have a single clue. He went back to England, to Shauna at the hotel.

'Well?' she asked him the minute he got to their room.

Josh shook his head, put down his overnight bag. 'I'm going to get a bath,' he said, and went into the bathroom and shut the door and turned on the taps.

Minutes later, he lowered himself into the warm water and closed his eyes, thinking, *That's it, then. She's gone. I can't find her.* He'd blown it. It was finished now. Over and done. He'd lost the only woman he would ever love, the only one who understood him, who knew him better than anyone else ever had.

Then Shauna came into the bathroom wearing her silky purple dressing gown. He looked up at her and felt a jolt of irritation. Christ, was there no rest from her? She followed him everywhere. What was he even *doing* here, with her?

'No luck then?' she asked.

'No luck,' he said.

'Ah, never mind,' she said, and slipped the robe off. Nothing underneath it. Of course not. She knew exactly how to turn him on, and it disgusted him how easily she did it. Sometimes he felt he hated her for it. Other times – like now – he hated *himself*.

'Scootch up then,' she said, and stepped into the bath with him, lowering herself into the water so that her nude breasts bobbed invitingly on the surface. 'This is nice,' she said, leaning back in the water, her toes finding his penis and kneading it gently. 'Don't you think?'

'Yeah,' he said, feeling himself harden.

'We've got a good thing going, you and me,' said Shauna, her dark eyes intent on his face.

'Have we?'

'Yeah, we have. I'm just the sort of woman you need, Josh. Serious. I'll take you far. That's a promise.'

'Huh,' said Josh, half-smiling at that. He looked down at his cock, which was now rearing out of the water, hard as iron, demanding attention.

'Oh, look,' said Shauna. 'He likes it.'

Shauna knelt up in the bath and leaned forward, catching his penis between her tits and moving silkily back and forth. Josh moaned.

'You think Claire would ever have done this for you?' asked Shauna, her voice purringly seductive now as her cool flesh massaged him.

Josh didn't answer. No, he didn't think so. Claire was shy, reserved. Shauna had an openly sexual attitude and big fabulous tits. He thought Claire's were much smaller. He'd touched them, of course, but he'd never seen her naked, much as he'd wanted to. That was special, something they had been saving for after the marriage ceremony. Something that now would never happen. Tomorrow he was going to have to go and see Pally and Eva, tell them the bad news that he hadn't found her in Ireland. He let out a long, deep sigh and submitted to Shauna's expertise.

What could he do?

He couldn't find her, his true love.

But by Christ, he thought as Shauna slipped his cock into her warm, wet mouth, Shauna Everett was a fucking fantastic lay.

27

Claire stayed on at a quiet B & B near Moyross and applied for her visa. Then, when it came through, she used up some of the money to book herself a flight. Within days she was on a plane, packed with families, all of them happy and chatting and off on holidays. She sat alone, cut off from the rest of humanity, feeling herself to be so filthy, so disgusting, so *used*.

The flight was long and tedious, cramped and awful. But as it went on, a sense of calm came over her. She was going where they wouldn't reach her. Not the Cleavers, not Shauna Everett. She was saying goodbye to all that, starting afresh. She thought then of the country lanes, wide skies and open fields of her home and shuddered with pain and longing.

But this was for the best. She would be safe, and so would her family. Somehow she had to try to forget all that she'd been through, which was easier said than done when every time she closed her eyes she relived Blue's horrible death and the events that followed. She turned her face to the window and shed quiet heartbroken tears as she thought of the anguish she must surely be bringing on her folks. And Josh. Most of all, she cried over Josh and their lost future together.

When the pilot announced over the tannoy that they

were preparing to land at John F. Kennedy Airport in New York, she fastened her seat belt and braced herself.

Her new life would begin here, now.

She had to be strong, and start again.

For her, there was no other way.

28

When Josh eventually turned up at John Finlay's pub, he got a surprise. He'd expected a rat-hole of a place, but it was actually not a bad-looking gaff. Nicely done out, hanging baskets all over the front of it and the paintwork neat and clean; clearly, this place had cost John a pretty penny. Outside, on the far edge of the car park, there was a line of lavishly customized Harley-Davidson motorbikes. Josh went over and admired the machines. Then he headed inside and the atmosphere was thick with trouble. Josh could smell it the moment he stepped through the door.

The bar staff looked jumpy, and there was a long-haired group of bikers in denim cut-offs and leathers decorated with either skulls and crossbones or patches on the back identifying where they were from and which club or 'chapter' they belonged to. One of them had two Nazi-like SS lightning bolts below the words 'Filthy Few'. Having come across bikers in the past, Josh knew that this meant the man wearing it had committed murder on behalf of his 'chapter'.

The bikers were making a lot of noise. Black Sabbath were screaming 'Sabbra Cadabra' on the juke. Get a few skinheads in here, Josh thought, and things would *really* kick off.

'Pint, please,' said Josh to the scared-looking blonde girl

at the bar. She had a look, just a faint look, of Claire when she dipped her head and pulled the pint. It clenched at his heart to see it.

Jesus, Claire, where are you? What happened?

He'd been back to the site again several times after telling Pally and Eva that he hadn't found Claire in Moyross. Every time he found himself hoping against hope that there would be good news; but the Milos told him that Claire had not come home. The grief and pain of it all ate at him, chewed his innards.

Claire was gone from his life. And gone or not, she'd made her feelings plain to him. Now he had Shauna, who was sticking to him like glue. And what a live wire *she* was turning out to be, fucking him senseless night and day.

The barmaid placed his pint on the mat and took his money.

'John the owner asked me to call in, said you had trouble.'

'I don't know nothing about that,' she said quickly.

'Worked here long?'

She shook her head. 'Just a week.'

Looking at her expression, Josh was certain she wouldn't be hanging around for much longer. No job was worth aggravation. Except *his* job, of course. In or out of a boxing ring, he was used to having to fight his corner. That was the Romany way. As soon as she'd rung up the sale on the cash register, she scuttled out the back, passing John who was just coming to the front of the bar.

'Hello, Mr Flynn,' he said. 'Thought you were going to be in Ireland a while?'

'I was. Now I'm back,' said Josh. 'That them, is it?' He nodded to indicate the gang.

'That's them.'

'*All* of them?'

'Yeah, bastards. Frightening all the decent punters away. Picking on people having a quiet drink.'

'You had words with them?'

He shrugged. 'You bloody serious? Look at the fuckers. Old Bill's been in once or twice. Done fuck-all, of course. Don't look now, but they're giving you the once-over.'

Josh turned slightly, leaning an elbow on the bar. Sure enough, a solid eighteen-stoner with grey hair pulled back in a ponytail was rising from his seat, leathers creaking, and coming over. It was the one with the intimidating SS flashes on the back of his jacket. His mates were grinning and nudging each other as they looked on. The biker made a show of running his eyes over Josh from head to toe, then said: 'You don't want to come in here, mate.'

'Why's that?' asked Josh, swallowing down the last of his pint.

'Because we *own* this place, arsehole.'

To Josh, everything seemed to slow down then. His breathing steadied and he was aware of his heart, beating. Of the music, pounding in rhythm.

'Do you?' asked Josh.

'Yeah, we do. So do yourself a favour and fuck off out of it.'

In a lightning-fast movement, Josh smashed the glass on the brass edge of the bar and then shoved it straight into the biker's crotch. The jagged edge ripped through the leather as if it was cotton and went straight into the flesh beneath. A yodelling howl of agony shot out of the biker's mouth. Then Josh's left fist pistoned out. It connected with the biker's nose and blood sprayed as the bone broke with a *crunch* and his nose split in two. The biker staggered and collapsed to the floor.

'Hey! Hey!'

The others were coming at a run, but Josh had thought

this out. Four of Linus Pole's men now shot in through the front door and joined Josh in the fight. It didn't take long. It certainly wasn't Queensberry rules. Biker gangs were tough, but gypsy men were *born* fighting – from the time they were little kids, theirs was a world of challenges issued and accepted.

When the gang was all laid out groaning, Josh grabbed the leader's leather jacket and, ignoring his screams of pain, hauled him over to the window. Josh showed him the line of motorbikes which were now burning merrily outside. As they watched, the petrol tanks started to blow, one after the other.

Whumph! Whumph! Whumph!

'Almost pretty, ain't it? Like firework night. Looks like you'll be walking home, arsewipe,' said Josh.

He shook the gang leader's jacket and the man whimpered and clutched at his cut and bleeding crotch. Josh put his head very close to the biker's shattered face and stared into his eyes. 'You listening? Good. You don't come anywhere near this place, ever again. You got that? Or next time I'll chop your fucking legs off and then you won't even be *able* to walk home, you understand? Answer me.'

'Ugh,' said the man past the blood and snot pouring out of his pulverized nose.

'That's a yes?'

The man nodded his head.

'Good. Now. Fuck. Off,' said Josh, and together he and Linus Pole's men threw the bikers out the pub door and on to the pavement.

29

'I'm pregnant,' said Shauna as they ate in the restaurant of the four-star hotel they were now staying at, since Shauna had complained that three-star wasn't good enough. Christmas was coming soon. The blast-furnace heat of the summer was long past, nothing but a memory.

Josh choked on his steak-and-kidney pudding. 'You're *what*?'

Shauna stared at him. They'd been smashing the life out of each other for months now, using no protection at all, and yet he looked almost comically surprised at this turn of events. Men! It was what she'd longed for, of course. *Planned* for.

'I'm going to have a baby. *Your* baby.'

Josh downed a gulp of best bitter and she could see him trying to take it in.

'So this kind of alters things,' she said with a triumphant smile.

As Shauna spoke, Josh felt a devastation so deep it was almost grief. This was something he should have shared with Claire, not Shauna. A kid on the scene would change everything. A baby would tie him ever more firmly to her, when he knew damned well he was still in love with Claire. No one had ever touched him as she had, no one ever would. But he'd accepted that she was gone from his life now. What else could he do?

It was still Claire he craved, but Shauna offered it on a plate night after night. Shauna had cast her spell over him and now . . . now he supposed he was fond of her. Well – if not fond, then he was certainly *used* to her. She was dynamite in bed. With Shauna, there were no holds barred. You could do whatever you liked. Anything. And that made him so hot for her. He knew he should have shown more sense, used condoms, but he'd been depressed and that had made him careless. He'd been thinking of splitting from her after Christmas, going back to his *real* life at the camp. Now what the fuck was he going to do?

Somehow his life with Shauna felt like a fitting punishment for his stupidity at mishandling things with Claire. Making her come to that bloody fight, bottling the big wedding, behaving like such a fucking idiot. With Claire gone, his life was nothing. He had fucked up, royally. And now? Being tied to Shauna was the price he had to pay for it.

Yes, her pregnancy would alter things. It would alter *everything*.

He put down his pint glass. Looked her in the eye.

'We'd better get married then,' he said.

His life had taken a wrong turn and now there would be no going back. Marrying Shauna was the decent thing to do. If you got a girl up the duff, you owned up to it and walked her down the aisle. He remembered his mate Chalky, telling the boys down the snooker hall when he'd knocked up his girlfriend and was in the glooms about it.

Well, that's you finished then, they'd said, laughing.

Now, here he was, in the same situation – and it didn't feel very funny.

Shauna stared at him, her cheeks reddening with emotion.

'We've had a wild time together,' she said.

'We have,' agreed Josh.

Wild, and certainly different. After the fight at Linus Pole's fairground and that sorting-out he'd done with the biker gang at John's place, Josh had found himself much in demand with all sorts of people: boxing promoters, club owners, they all wanted him, and the pay was out of this world. But after he'd failed to find Claire there was a sadness that he couldn't shake off. The pain and the guilt because it was *all his fault* refused to leave him be. He'd sold the new trailer, given up on the dream of him and her together. *This* was going to be his life now, and he wished he felt happier about it.

Shauna was picking over her fish with a critical eye. She flicked a glance up at Josh's face. He seemed miles away, and that irritated her. Was he still thinking about *her*? That thought soured her delight at her pregnancy. But Josh was going to marry her. He'd just said it! So he *must* love her a bit. Maybe. Ah, she was seeing shadows where there were none, imagining he was thinking of Claire when he was just a bit distracted.

'Not too keen on this place,' she said. 'Look at the state of this!' She prodded at the fish with her fork disdainfully.

This was a four-star establishment, but still she wasn't impressed. Josh, keen to keep in shape, had told her all the gym equipment in the hotel basement was on its last legs and the steam room was out of order. In their room, ants crawled and the maid didn't have a clue how to clean. Where Shauna came from, that was a cardinal sin. Gypsy women were great home-makers.

And they said there was a chef in the hotel kitchen? That ponce couldn't fry a piece of fish without leaving it raw in the middle; the idiot couldn't even boil an egg without letting it boil dry and scalding the shell. Gypsy women never gave people food poisoning, either, and she'd heard rumours about this place from the other guests. Next place they stayed in would be five-star. They could afford it. Or . . .

'I've been thinking. We can't keep flitting from hotel to hotel, not with a baby on the way,' she said, watching his face. Christ, he was so handsome. What a fantastic man, and he was all hers! 'It's time we settled somewhere, don't you think? You're doing so well with the fights and stuff. We could buy a house.'

Josh was taken aback. He was going to be married, he was going to become a father and he was going to buy a house. He looked at Shauna and felt apathy overtake him. But maybe the deal wasn't all bad. She was beautiful. Iron-willed and mouthy as fuck, yes – but a real strong gypsy woman with smooth olive skin, long dark curling hair and conker-brown eyes. She'd make beautiful babies, he could see that.

Christ though – a house, a proper house, like a gorgi would live in?

'We can afford it,' said Shauna, a frown forming like a small thundercloud on her brow.

Maybe they could. Money was pouring in. He stared at her set, determined face.

'We'll go and look at some soon,' he said. 'And we'll pop in the register office, set a date.'

30

There was a new estate going up, diggers and dumper trucks zooming about the place, concrete lorries backing up, bricks arriving by the ton, and at the edge of all the building activity was a show home, set up as a sales suite. Girls in fitted suits were in there, passing out brochures to prospective buyers, making pots of tea and doling out fancy biscuits.

Shauna and Josh looked around the show home, and Shauna felt like she was going to explode with happiness.

'I want it,' she said, dazzled by fitted Formica kitchen units, the posh avocado suite in the bathroom and décor that a professional had worked hard on, all burnt oranges and soft mossy greens. There were huge pot plants in corners, big rugs and mirrors everywhere. Outside, you had your own actual back garden, all fenced in so that no one else could intrude, with a freshly laid lawn in its centre and shrubs planted all around.

It was so beautiful and so different from what she knew – the muddy country clearing with its trailers, its grazing piebald and skewbald horses, the haphazardly strung washing lines, the scent of rabbit stew and the flickering camp fires at twilight – that she could have cried.

The sales girl beamed.

'I want this one. The show house,' said Shauna.

'That could take some time . . .' said the sales girl.

'How long?' asked Shauna.

'Up to three months.'

'That's fine,' said Shauna, who knew she wouldn't be ready to drop the baby until well after that. Meanwhile, they could ditch the hotels – she was sick of them – and rent a place until everything came good.

'Shall we go over to the office, put some figures together . . . ?' asked the girl.

'Yeah,' said Shauna, grabbing Josh's hand and pulling him along like a tug guiding an ocean liner into port.

'Might have some more work going, if you're interested, Josh,' said John.

It was New Year, they were sitting in the bar of John Finlay's pub, and everything was coming along nicely. No more trouble, since the biker gang had been sorted. There were punters in, decent people, spending plenty. The whole atmosphere of the place had changed. It was busy, everyone bustling around. There was laughter, music, and the cash registers were ringing like mad.

'Friend of mine's got clubs in London, he needs someone reliable to sort out the doors for him.'

'Sounds OK,' said Josh, thumbing through the newspaper. Agatha Christie the writer had died, and the SAS had gone to Northern Ireland. He folded the paper, put it back on the table.

'This is where you reach him.' John handed Josh a small rectangular purple card. 'I said you might be in touch, but it's up to you. Maybe you're up to your arse in work, I dunno.'

Josh took the card. He had a lot of fights lined up, cash on the hip; this was all working out OK. Maybe he'd bother with this new contact, maybe not. He was going to need all the money he could lay hands on, because Shauna was never, ever going to be a cheap date; he did realize that. Her tastes were expensive. Show her a picture of ten sofas and she'd go for the dearest, every time. And now there were houses and even a baby to be considered, too. She was like a runaway train, unstoppable.

'Thanks,' he said.

'It's a pleasure. I owe you a lot.'

They chatted on into the evening and then at around eleven Josh drove back to the hotel.

He went into reception, trying not to think about how much all this lot was costing him. He and Shauna had already sorted out a place to rent, so they'd be fucking off from here soon, and just as well. Halfway across the floor on his way to the lifts, a bulky bald-headed man blundered up from a chair and grabbed the front of his coat.

'*There* you are, you bastard,' the man said, alcohol pouring in waves from his breath.

It was Pally, Claire Milo's dad.

31

'You fucker! You got her here with you then, my little girl? What did you do to her, you sod? What *really* happened?'

Pally Milo was pushing against Josh like a bull against the side of a pen, but Josh was thinking that there was no way he was going to flatten Claire's father. The best he could do was pull him in close to restrain him as boxers often did, and shout in his face: 'What you on about, Pally? Claire's not with me.'

'You liar, you filthy good-for-nothing . . .' panted Pally.

'It's the truth.'

'Liar!'

'God's honour, Pally. On the Sacred Heart, I swear. I've *told* you. I ain't seen Claire since the night I had my fight with Matty. Get your hands off me, you silly old bugger.'

All the receptionists were squawking in alarm, and Josh could see the doorman turning, hearing the commotion and about to come in and sort it. If he started a brawl in here, Shauna would do her nut.

'My poor Eva's still in bits! Why'd you have to do it eh? Why'd you just have to run off the two of you, and cheat everyone like that?' demanded Pally, twisting uselessly, his hot whisky-soaked breath puffing in Josh's face as Josh restrained him.

'I *told* you, Pally.' Josh put steel into his voice now.

'Listen to me, will you? We didn't run off. That's rubbish. Claire ain't with me. We parted company on the night I fought Matty O'Connor. I haven't seen her since. That's the truth. I looked for her in Moyross, you know I did. And I came back to the site. But she never showed up.'

'You're a miserable coward and a *liar*,' shouted Pally, but his movements were getting weaker. He was very drunk, and against Josh's youth and superior strength he was wearing himself out.

Josh watched the man weaken with pity in his eyes. So Claire *still* hadn't come back. Pally was getting himself drunk and no doubt Eva was still clutching Claire's bridal gown and wailing for him to do something. But there was nothing he or anyone else could do; Claire had obviously made her decision and left them all behind – him included. It hurt, but what could he do about it?

'I don't lie, Pally,' said Josh as Pally's movements slowed to nothing and they just stood there, two big men locked together. 'If Claire's still missing, it's because she's gone off on her own steam somewhere. It's nothing to do with me. I've told you all this before. She told me she hated the fight game and she blew me out, that's the truth. I accepted that, and went my own way.'

Still, Josh knew in his heart that if he ever saw her again he would want to plead with her to give him a second chance. He loved her. He'd love her until they boxed him up and dumped him in his grave. But now Shauna was carrying his baby. He had new responsibilities. All that love he'd shared with Claire must be forgotten.

Pally's myopic eyes were blinking at Josh's face from inches away. Slowly, sensing the man's changing mood, Josh pushed Pally away so that he stood straight. The doorman came in. Josh turned his head, shook it. The doorman didn't withdraw. Josh was just glad Shauna hadn't been down here to see Pally lowering the tone, showing them up among the gorgis.

But then, as if some vengeful god had read his mind, there she was, coming out of the ground-floor lounge, walking a couple of steps and then freezing in surprise as she saw the two men there.

'I can't help you, Pally. Now go home. Go on,' said Josh, but it was too late.

Pally had seen Shauna standing there.

He pulled back from Josh and stared at her like she'd arrived in a puff of smoke. For a moment his face was blank; then Josh could see that he was adding things up, working things out. Pally's eyes swept over Shauna, took in the slight bulge of her pregnancy; then they returned to Josh's face and his lips trembled with contempt.

'So that's the way of it,' said Pally. '*This* is why Claire cleared out then. You and *her*. We all wondered where she'd got to, and now we know.'

'No. That's not what happened, Pally. Not at all.'

'You fucking *cheat*!' yelled Pally in Josh's face. 'God rot you. I hope your bollocks fester, you arsehole. And as for *you* . . .'

Pally lurched toward Shauna and Josh quickly put himself in between the two of them.

'You're nothing but a *whore*,' shouted Pally.

'Fuck off, Pally, before I do something I'll be sorry for,' snapped Josh, wrestling the older man to keep him clear of Shauna, who was frozen to the spot.

'Ah, don't worry. I'm going,' said Pally, and Josh released him. 'My girl was always too good for the likes of you, anyway.'

As he passed her, Pally spat at Shauna's feet. '*Slut*,' he muttered, and moved on, out of the swing doors and back into the night.

32

Josh and Shauna moved into a rented flat over a chippy in the East End of London the week after they'd looked at the show house on the new building site. The week after that, Josh drove his old Zephyr back from the bank, where he'd kept an appointment with the manager. Shauna was still bending his ear over how much she wanted to get that show house, to not be at the mercy of landlords, so against his better judgement he'd gone to the bank to see how the land lay. He wished he hadn't bothered. He was wondering how he was going to break the news to Shauna, but she was waiting at their new rented place that was never going to be big enough or good enough for her – she'd already made that perfectly plain – and the instant he was through the door she was on him.

'Well? What did they say?'

'Turned me down,' he said.

In fact, the bank manager had said a lot more than that, none of which Josh felt inclined to share with Shauna. With a look on his face that said there was a bad smell in his office, he'd listened as Josh listed the things he was doing to earn a decent crust, including some legal boxing bouts – although most were not legal at all – some door work, some landscaping and even lately a bit of tarmacking with some of his old Romany contacts. Then he'd asked whether

Josh could produce three years' worth of books, certified by an accountant.

Josh couldn't. He didn't *keep* books. Who the hell did in their right mind? Next thing you knew, the taxman was on you and you were in double-deep shite. Cash in hand was always king. But that didn't cut no ice with banks and accountants. So, a mortgage? No chance. He could go and whistle for *that*.

'Turned you *down*?' Shauna's face was thunderous. 'They *what*, those bastards? How could they? You're a good earner.'

'Without a steady income, Shaun,' he said, taking her in his arms. 'Jesus, thinking about it I must have been crazy to even go near a bank. As far as the taxman's concerned, I don't even exist. There's no chance we can get a bloody mortgage, it's too damned risky.'

'Then what the hell are we going to do?'

'Look, we're renting and that's good enough for now. This place is all right, ain't it?'

Shauna looked outraged. 'All *right*? It's a poxy little flat over a chip shop. We both *stink* of chip fat.'

'Don't go getting yourself upset, it's bad for the baby.' Josh thought that was uncalled for. This place wasn't exactly *Ideal Home* material, but it was good enough. It was several steps up from a trailer, that was for sure.

'Fuck the baby and fuck *you*,' snarled Shauna, brushing his arms away from her. 'I want *my* place, Josh. My own home. To mix with decent people, not to have everyone looking down their noses at me, calling me a gyppo.'

'Who'd dare call you a gyppo?' Josh almost had to laugh at that, but her scowl wiped the smile off his face. 'Look, Shaun. It ain't a long-term thing, the renting,' said Josh soothingly, making calm-down gestures. 'It's only to tide us over, make us comfortable until the baby comes. Then we'll have more cash behind us and we'll see what can be done.'

'More cash? With a baby? They cost a fucking fortune, any fool knows that.'

'What, a *baby*? A tiny little thing two foot long? How can *that* be?'

'Well, there's schooling to think about. A good primary. Then a grammar school, and further education, maybe university . . .'

'*University*?' Josh echoed in disbelief. 'What you talking about, girl? You and me, we can read and write and add up, and that's where it ends. Some of our kind can't even do that and you know it. What makes you think our kid's going to go for all that?'

'We'll make sure he does. That's the way people get on in the *real* world, Josh,' said Shauna. 'They get a proper education, a *good* one, and they make contacts that help them along in later life.'

Josh stared at her face. Their whole lives had been spent in the camp and visiting others like it, plus the horse fairs and funfairs, *that* was real life to him. He didn't under-stand what she was talking about. They'd had their support network among their own folk and their kid would too. He said as much.

'You're mad,' sneered Shauna. 'All that's finished for us. We've left it behind. And a good job too. It's time we stepped up in the world, Josh, and getting our own house is just the beginning. That's why I'm so fucking cut up about you being turned down. But there are other banks, we'll try them.'

'No,' said Josh. 'We won't. Today taught me that it's a no-go.'

'Then we'll *never* have a place to call our own,' said Shauna, and burst into tears.

'Oh, don't start,' said Josh, pulling her back into his arms. Female tears alarmed him. He didn't know what to do when a woman cried. 'I told you,' he said gently against her head, kissing her hair. 'We do this first. Then, later, we buy. We buy a fucking palace, cash on the nail, the way things are going.'

Shauna drew her head back and stared into his eyes. Her cheeks were wet with tears and he thought she had never looked more beautiful. Yes, she was loud, demanding and a pain in the arse. She wasn't gentle dreamy Claire, that was for sure. But she wasn't an ugly mare, either, and she was carrying his child.

'You promise?' she sniffed.

'I do.'

He'd messed up so much, but this time he was going to get it right. He wasn't going to let Shauna down. Like it or not, he was committed to her now, and to their life together. It was their wedding on Saturday, he was going to be a married man with responsibilities; it was time he got his act together and did as she said: put the old life, the simple wild and free life he'd loved so much, behind them.

33

Claire had enough money to rent a studio apartment in Brooklyn. It was old, mould-ridden, up three floors and no lift. Still, it was a place to stay, a roof over her head. At night she lay awake listening to the foreign sounds of the city – the sirens, the gunshots. People moving in the hall outside, calling up the stairs, laughter, faint music.

When she went to bed, it was with a kitchen knife hidden under her pillow and a heavy tallboy positioned in front of the door. But sleep – once so easy in the deep dark country night, snuggled in the warm cocoon of her parents' trailer – now eluded her. She lay wide awake, nervously listening to the sounds, wondering if one of those people out in the hall would come and try the door, try to *get in*.

Hours, she lay like that, tense, anticipating attack.

Sometimes she was so exhausted that she did sleep. And then she dreamed. Of running as if through treacle, unable to get away, and people jumping on her, pulling her down to the ground, hurting her, while Shauna Everett stood over her, laughing, cheering on her attackers. Then she would wake, screaming, run to the toilet and vomit.

And there were worse dreams. *Nightmares*. That Shauna was chasing her, intent on killing her, and Claire thought she'd escaped, that she was safe. But then she stumbled across the dead bodies of her loved ones: her mum, her dad. Trace. Even once – horrifically – Josh. Maybe she *was* cursed with the Sight like Nanny Irene, and this was a psychic warning to her, saying *Stay away, keep clear, keep yourself safe and those you love protected,* or this *will happen.*

She found a job dishwashing in a dirty roach-infested diner, and worked there, keeping her head down, not making friends, trusting no one. Her hands grew red-raw from hot water and detergent, and her guts churned constantly. She was beginning to think that coming here had been a horrible mistake. She was miserable in this vast, sprawling, noisy, dirty city, when all she had ever known was country stillness and fresh air, the free Romany way of life she'd loved so much.

Before too long she decided that she'd get a better job in a nicer place. Make more money. The cash was starting to run low.

On her last day at the diner she left without a single soul saying goodbye to her. She came home to her little apartment, pulled the tallboy over the door, and sat down on the thin mattress of her bed and thought of Josh, so far away, gone from her forever. Her life, like her dreams, had become a nightmare; she was tired, lost and utterly alone.

Josh, she thought, and lay down and let the tears come. *Oh, Josh.*

34

On one of her rare days off from her new glistening career washing pots in a not-much-better establishment, Claire left Brooklyn for Manhattan. She window-shopped wistfully in Bloomingdale's then peered in upscale restaurant windows, looking for staff vacancy signs. She found a couple of possibles.

She went into Central Park with the paper and her lunch, sat down on a bench and flicked through the news as she ate, seeing that Cuban-backed forces were winning in Angola. Halfway through the sandwich, she felt sick. This was normal for her, lately. And even though she wasn't keeping food down, she was gaining weight; her clothes felt uncomfortably tight around her middle. She was ill and she knew it; those horrible bastards had infected her during the rape, they'd given her some terrible disease. But she had no one else to depend on except herself; she had to struggle on, find a better-paying job, and fast.

Flicking to the jobs section, she trawled through endless ads, but nothing caught her eye until she came across one for 'hostesses' at a club called Sylvester's. Claire squinted at the ad suspiciously. There was a checklist. You had to be over eighteen but under twenty-five. Whether you were married or single, childless or with kids, it didn't matter.

You had to have charm, be cheerful, attractive, intelligent, with common sense and a good speaking voice.

Claire thought about it and found that she just about fitted the bill. The ad went further, detailing an eight-hour day and a five-day week, but what really stunned her was the wages. The figure quoted sounded *way* too good to be true. Still . . . her money was nearly gone, and if she saw another pile of dirty dishes she felt like she might run off screaming.

Her mind made up, she sat there in the weak New York sunshine and filled in the application form. Then she bought stamps and an envelope and posted it. Nothing would come of it anyway, she knew that, because nothing good had happened to her in a very long time.

35

Shauna splashed out on a white chiffon dress for the wedding; Empire-line, so that it flowed out from under the bust and hid the worst of the bump. She bought some white slingbacks with Cuban heels and a bouquet of red carnations and then gazed in the mirror and thought she looked OK. Plump, but still a looker, no doubt about that. Josh was lucky as fuck to have her.

They dragged in some witnesses off the street outside the register office, and quick as that, the deed was done. Josh looked a bit dazed. Suddenly, he was a married man with a kid on the way.

'Happy, darlin'?' Shauna asked him as they came down the steps to his ratty old car. *That* was going to have to go, Shauna thought. Damned rust-bucket. They were going places, but not in a crappy thing like that.

''Course,' said Josh, and kissed her.

They honeymooned in the Lakes, then Josh drove them back to London.

'Got a surprise for you,' he said on the way.

'What?'

'A surprise.' He tapped his nose. 'You'll see.'

It was a new rental, a small terraced house in Bow. Josh carried her over the threshold and dropped her to her feet. Shauna looked around. It was neat, clean and newly decorated. While they were away, Josh had arranged for all their stuff from the flat over the chippy to be brought here.

'Like it?' asked Josh.

Shauna was still staring. It was bigger than the flat, where the stink of stale chip fat had made her want to heave. Yes, it was OK. But like it? No. She wanted better than this. Still, he'd made the effort, tried to please her.

She flung herself into Josh's arms. 'It's bloody great,' she lied. 'Is there a bed upstairs?'

'Am I the business or what?' preened Josh, hugging her. 'Yeah, there's a bed. You think I'd forget *that*?'

'Let's go christen it then,' she said, and tugging him by the hand she led the way up the stairs, laughing.

'But the baby . . .' fretted Josh.

'Fucking's good for babies in the womb,' Shauna shot back. 'Especially to bring on labour when the time's near – did you know that?'

'No. I didn't,' said Josh.

'Well, you do now.'

36

'You know the Playboy clubs?' asked Sylvester Drummond as Claire Milo sat in his office being interviewed.

Claire nodded her head, smiled sweetly. *Everyone* knew about the Playboy clubs. Sylvester was the owner of this place and she already had him pegged as an oddball. He was fiftyish, skinny and clumsy – he'd just greeted her, then knocked the stapler clean off the desk. He was a plain man, narrow-shouldered, all bones and sharp angles. Nothing she would have expected in a club owner. His hair was a thin fluff of pale brown, and his face was long and solemn, enlivened by nice brown eyes.

Sylvester straightened and replaced the stapler on the desk. 'See, they got these fabulous girls in there. Bunny Girls. All kitted out in coloured corsets with bunny tails and ears. These are *classy* women. Not waitresses. Well, they *are* waitresses I guess, but a step up from that, you see? There's all sorts of rules and regulations the girls have to follow: they have to do the Bunny greeting, the Bunny stance, the High Carry, the Bunny crouch and the Bunny perch, and most important there's the Bunny *dip*. You know what that is?'

Claire shook her head, still smiling sweetly, wondering where the hell all this was heading. All she knew was she needed this job. Badly. She felt constantly sick. Really sick, like maybe she was dying, but she tried to look interested in what he was saying.

'No matter. It's a way of presenting clients with their drinks, it's *elegant*. You hold a tray of drinks in one hand, and you dip backwards to place a coaster on the table. You dip back again to place the drink on there. Got it?'

Claire nodded. She didn't care what she did. Why should she? The only thing that mattered was the pay, and that was good. She only hoped her health was going to hold out for a while. Her sudden lack of vigour alarmed her. With such strong gypsy genes, very little real illness had ever troubled her. But now, for the first time, she knew what it was like to feel sick, and weak. And she hated it.

Gypsy genes.

She still missed the campsite, and her family, and Josh. Longed for the still nights of the English countryside, the simple pleasures of cooking fresh-caught rabbit over an open fire, of chatting to her sister. She thought of her wedding dress, how proud she had felt to wear it, how much she had been looking forward to becoming Josh's wife.

All gone now.

All in the past.

'Otherwise you do it from the front and your hooters fall out in the client's face, and that would not be good, you got it?'

Claire gazed at him. She'd drifted off. 'Sorry. What?'

'Hooters,' said Sylvester.

'Got it,' said Claire. *Hooters?*

'Good!' He pressed a buzzer on his phone and presently the door behind Claire opened. 'This is Gina,' said Sylvester to Claire. 'She *was* a Bunny once, way back. She's a real lady, and she manages this place. Gina here's going to teach you how to do everything. All right, Gina?'

Gina came up to the desk. She was a grim-faced matron

of solid build and to Claire it seemed impossible that this matriarchal figure had ever cut a dash as one of those famous jet-setting Bunnies. Gina cast a look at Sylvester, then glanced down at Claire. 'Come on then,' she said.

Claire followed Gina out of the door, and Gina closed it behind them.

'How can your "hooters" fall out in the client's face if you're wearing a costume?' asked Claire. She didn't like the thought of anything revealing. Suppose one of the punters tried to grope her? She felt sweaty with fear at the thought. Even being alone in the office with Sylvester, who looked harmless enough, had made her shake.

Gina gave her a look. 'They can, believe me.'

'Why's he so obsessed with the Bunny girls? I mean, couldn't Hugh Hefner sue him for infringement or something?'

'What we have here is just a pale imitation of Hugh's set-up,' said Gina. 'He ain't going to bother with us. What's that accent?'

'English.'

'It's cute. Follow me and I'll show you.'

Half an hour later and the whole thing was clear.

'I can't wear this,' said Claire, turning back and forth in front of a full-length mirror in a tiny dressing room at the back of the club.

Her 'costume' was tiny too. It was a corseted velvet swimming costume – hers was pale baby-blue, but the others hanging up on rails around the room were all colours of the rainbow, to suit different skin tones. There was no tail, no ears. There was a pair of dangerously high heels, fishnet tights, and right now Gina was stuffing balls of cotton wool down the bra part of the costume to help Claire's breasts fill out the D cups. Trouble was, by the time

Gina finished stuffing, her hooters really *were* in danger of popping out the top of the thing, and she could see why the Bunny dip was a necessity.

Gina paused as Claire spoke, and looked at her with her gimlet eye. 'You want this job?'

'Yeah, I need it, but . . .'

'Then you wear the costume.' Gina stuffed some more cotton wool down Claire's frontage. 'There. What do you think?' she asked, standing back.

Claire looked in the mirror. Her figure had somehow morphed from normal to wildly voluptuous in the space of a few minutes. It made her feel horribly self-conscious and uncomfortable. Christ, was she really going to do this? *Could* she do this? Men would look at her in this get-up and think she was easy, wouldn't they? And then they might try to touch her. She shuddered, hard.

'You all right?' asked Gina, staring at her face. 'It's not too tight?'

'It's fine,' said Claire. 'Um. Sylvester, the owner. He don't seem the type for this.'

'Well, he ain't. Not really. His dad started the club, not him. I was there when the old man ran it and I was sure when Sylvester – the club was named after him by his dad – well I was *sure* that when he took over the whole thing would hit the skids. But it didn't.' Gina was looking at Claire's waist. 'You know, you could stand to lose a few pounds.'

'Yeah. OK,' said Claire, thinking it was impossible. The weight was going on, no matter how little she ate.

The money, she thought. *Just keep thinking of the money.*

This place paid so much better than any of the other waitressing jobs she'd had. 'So . . . you're going to teach me this Bunny dip?'

'You'll get it in no time,' said Gina, and cracked a smile.

37

Claire found her new job to be a piece of piss. *Dead* easy. All her anxieties about wearing a skimpy costume had gone within about a week of starting work at Sylvester's because the place was run on very strict lines. No touching from the punters, that wasn't allowed. The girls were treated with respect. If they *weren't*, there were bouncers on the door who would throw any chancers out on to the sidewalk and never let them back in again.

Gina, the den mother and manageress, gruff though she was, became a friend. And the other girls were friendly too. Good workers were welcomed in the club, and Claire was a very good worker indeed, shipping trays of drinks around the place, smiling, always giving her best even when she felt like shit, which she did, often. She thought she was doing fine, all things considered, until one day Sylvester called her into his office up on the first floor.

'Claire? Yeah, come in, sit down,' he said, standing up, eyes darting to her face and then away, hands nervously jangling the keys in his pockets, knocking over a pot of pens and then scrambling around picking them up.

Claire sat. He slapped the pot of pens back on the desk and then closed the door behind her. She felt a panicky twinge. But this was Sylvester. It was OK. 'Tiger Feet' by Mud was thrumming up through the floor.

'Is something wrong?' she asked anxiously.

Yes, the job was good, but her relentless weight gain was not. Claire was sure this summons was about that. Sylvester would – in his very nice way – tell her that she had to lay off the doughnuts. But Gina had already been on her case about that – and she wasn't eating much. The seamstress who altered all the girls' costumes had been in a couple of times, letting her outfit out at the seams. But it seemed like a battle she couldn't win. She wasn't comforteating and in fact sometimes she felt too sick to eat at all. But in her heart of hearts she was still shattered by all that had happened to her back in England. Her dream of a perfect world had been an illusion, cruelly ripped apart in one horrible night, and it haunted her. The loss of her old life tormented her, too; that perfect Romany life, free of constraint, free of care. She missed it every day, missed Eva and Pally and Trace, but knew she mustn't get in touch, *couldn't* let them know anything about where she was or what she was doing. She had to keep them safe.

And Josh! Would she *ever* get over the loss of him?

'No, nothing wrong. Not at all.' He shuffled a few papers and then sat back, smiling at her. 'Gina's been telling me great things about you,' he said.

'Oh?'

'Says you're a fantastic asset,' he said.

'Well . . . that's kind of her.' Claire could hear a *but* coming.

'Kind, shmind.' Sylvester made a dismissive movement with one long-fingered hand. 'She knows a good worker when she sees one. Says you're real efficient. Got a good head for figures and the clients like you.'

'So . . . ?' Claire hadn't a clue where this was going.

'So how about taking on a new role? Assistant to Gina.

More backroom stuff than out front with the clients, how about that?'

Claire felt her innards shrivel with shame. He'd noticed how fat she was getting. Gina certainly had, she'd called in the seamstress and stood boot-faced and disapproving while the woman fussed over Claire with the tape measure. God, she'd tried so hard not to stuff her face, tried to eat sensibly. She really had. But her body seemed to be ballooning out of control. And now she saw it in Sylvester's face. The awkward sideways glances, the nervous paper-shuffling. He knew, all right. And this was his kind way of handling it. Pushing her to one side, out of sight of the paying customers.

Sylvester cleared his throat. 'Gina will be retiring next year, so this is a real good step up for you. What do you think?'

Claire's cheeks were burning with embarrassment. But . . . this would work better for her. She couldn't entirely shake her self-consciousness in the skimpy costume, and her nervousness around the male customers. She would be happier in a backroom position. There, she could hide from the world.

'I'd like that,' she said.

Sylvester let out a breath that seemed very like relief. 'Good, good!'

Yeah, of course he's relieved – now he won't have to watch me expand ever outward until one day I pop right out of the bloody costume and he has to fire my arse.

'Thank you,' she said humbly, grateful. She was damaged goods, after all. And now she was an embarrassment to her boss.

'No thanks necessary,' said Sylvester, and quickly ushered her out of the office.

38

Claire loved working behind the scenes at the club and gradually she was taking over more and more of the everyday running of the place. Being in the background suited her very well, because she knew damned well she was ill. Actually, she was dying. Her periods had stopped, which for certain meant that she was terribly sick, and she was still getting fatter all the time. Living on Waldorf salads didn't count for shit. There was something in her stomach, a disease, tumour, and it was killing her inch by inch.

Free of that damned costume at last, she swathed herself in big pinafore dresses and voluminous poncho tops, and beavered away in the smaller back office beside Sylvester's own. And, bumbling though he was, laughably clumsy and inept as a man, she grew fond of him. Sylvester *was* odd, but he was also a gentleman, considerate and kind. And it hurt her when she discovered that his health too was poor. Being in closer proximity to him, she was aware that he often slipped tiny pills under his tongue.

'It's angina,' Gina told her when she asked.

'Oh the poor thing,' said Claire. Always one to fuss over sick animals and lame ducks, this news touched Claire's tender heart. She liked Sylvester and was sad he was unwell.

'It's under control.' Gina gave Claire a sharp look. 'You know he's sweet on you, I suppose?'

Claire stared at Gina in surprise. 'No, I didn't know that.'

'Well – don't take advantage.'

'No. Really, I would never—'

'Plenty would.'

'Gina.' Claire was getting annoyed. 'I'm not interested, OK? Not in Sylvester and not in anyone else.'

Claire was always hunched over her desk – *Gina's* desk, really, which they now shared – sorting invoices, phoning wholesalers, chatting to accountants on the phone, keeping the whole thing rolling along.

Working helped her stop thinking about the thing that was slowly killing her. Bad things had happened to her and this was the culmination of all that badness. She was on her way out. She was dying, thousands of miles from all that she had known, all that she had ever cared about. She would never see Josh again.

Then one day Sylvester called her into his office again.

Oh Jesus, thought Claire, sitting down, expecting to be fired, expecting disaster.

'You OK?' asked Sylvester, his eyes on her face.

'Fine, fine,' said Claire. 'Problem?'

'No, not at all.' Again he was shuffling papers, looking awkward. This time he managed not to drop anything, though. 'Listen. There's a room upstairs, you know that, right? We keep a stack of the old files up there.'

'Yes. Sure I know.' Where was this going?

'We could clear it out. It'd be better for you to be here, on the spot, rather than schlepping in from Brooklyn day in day out. You could move in. Would you like that?'

Claire stared at him. She thought of her apartment in that shitty rundown old building across town, where she had to pull the furniture across the door to feel safe at night. And even then, she didn't.

'Yeah,' she said, wondering why he would do that for her. 'I would like that. But . . . Gina doesn't live in.'

'She has family. You don't though – right?'

Claire shook her head. Not only that, her visa had lapsed and now she was an illegal.

'Better for me to have you on the spot,' he said. 'If I have a query, I can get hold of you straight away. You know I'm thinking of expansion. Another club like this one, just across town. So I'm busy, and I need someone here, someone reliable.'

'OK,' said Claire. The journey to and from work was exhausting for her. So to live over the club would be wonderful, so much easier.

Sylvester beamed with pleasure. 'That's good. I'll get the boys up there tomorrow, we'll make it nice for you.'

Claire looked at him in wonderment. 'You've been so kind,' she said.

'Hey, we got to all help each other, ain't we?' His eyes lowered to her swollen belly. 'You poor kid. Father's long gone, I guess?'

'What?' Claire stared at him, yanking her cardigan over the tell-tale bulge of her illness.

'The father.'

'The *what*?' Claire was clutching at her stomach. At the tumour. At this mound of death.

Sylvester held up his hands in a soothing gesture. 'Hey, I'm not judging anybody, don't think that. Well, I would judge the *father* for sure, the rotten bastard clearing off and leaving you like this. So come on, honey, tell me – when is the baby due?'

39

Gina and Sylvester had been unbelievably kind. True to his word, Sylvester set the doormen to work, emptying out the room on the second floor. Until now it had acted as a junk room for old files and assorted bits of crap, broken chairs and old light fittings from the club down below. Now it was cleared out, repainted, and Gina made the arrangements for Claire's few thrift-shop possessions to be moved over from her Brooklyn place and installed. Within a month, the room was homely and habitable.

When Sylvester had spoken the word 'baby' to Claire, she had felt her whole being twist in anguish. Now at night she lay in bed over the club and looked down at the mound of her belly and thought, *You bastard thing, I hate you!*

She was carrying a *child*.

Those awful *scum* had done this to her, put this dreadful thing inside her. A tumour would have been better. An end to it all. But this wasn't an end, this was a whole new beginning, and the thought of that destroyed her.

'It'll all work out,' Gina told her. 'You're not the first unmarried mother in the world. And you're among friends here.'

Claire nodded in agreement, but secretly she seethed. How the fuck could Gina know what she'd been through, all that she'd suffered? Gina had a marriage to a good man, and two daughters. *She* hadn't been raped. She would retire and live a happy life with her family. But what did Claire have?

Nothing.

Nothing except this *thing* that was invading her body, sapping her strength.

And now it kicked.

Claire lay in the darkness and felt the thing kick inside her. She caught her breath. Remembered *them*. The child, the *thing*, would look like them. Dark. Repulsive. She turned on to her side, buried her face in the pillow and sobbed.

A tumour would have been better.

Better by far.

She was sitting at her desk one day, checking invoices, when she was aware – quite suddenly – of warm wetness underneath her. Surprised, she half-rose from her seat and looked at it. Then she reached out an unsteady hand and touched it: yes, wet. Suddenly she felt a deep, gnawing pain in her back and then something worse, like a giant hand clutching at her middle and squeezing hard.

'Jesus!' She gripped the desk as it went on and on.

Finally, it subsided. Trembling, Claire made her way around her desk and over to the door. Without calling for Sylvester, who was in the next office, she went up the stairs alone and into her room on the second floor. The next contraction hit her hard and she stumbled over to the bed, face creased in pain, and lay down there, clawing at the mattress, flooded with horror at what was happening to her.

She should have been married and happy with Josh, living in their brand-new trailer as contented as a pair of lovebirds, and having Josh's baby. Instead, she was going to give birth to a Cleaver monster that had been foisted on her by rape.

'Noooo,' she screamed, crying, doubled over in agony.

'Claire? Claire!' It was Sylvester. He was standing in the open doorway. She recoiled in shame. He looked at her lying there and his eyes went out on stalks. He said: 'Don't worry, honey. It's OK. I'll fetch Gina, right? Hang on!'

It seemed to go on forever. All the rest of that day and into the night, the contractions kept coming and Claire felt that she was going to die, that this thing was going to kill her.

'I'm gonna call an ambulance, get you over to the hospital,' said Sylvester two or three times, but each time Claire shook her head: no.

This was bad enough, having this happen to her here, among friends. In a cold impersonal hospital, with strangers poking and pushing at her? She couldn't bear the thought of it.

'She don't want that, Sylvester, so let it go,' said Gina sharply, as Claire clutched at her hand and screamed the place down. 'Go on now, I'll see to her. I had my own two at home and Cyrus cut the cord himself, I know what's to be done.'

Sylvester retreated, left the two women alone in the room. Sweating, straining, Claire gasped out 'Thanks' to Gina, and then the contraction eased. She looked up at that hatchet face and said: 'I'm scared.'

Gina's expression softened. She squeezed Claire's hand. 'Don't be scared. This is a natural thing, animals do it all the time. You just breathe between the contractions, and pretty soon this baby'll get itself born.'

'Oh – *Christ,*' gasped Claire as another one hit.

'Go with it, babe,' said Gina, dabbing at her brow with

a cool cloth. 'You gonna tell the daddy about this?' she asked when the pain had subsided once again.

Claire shook her head.

'He don't want to know, uh?'

Claire screwed her eyes up and tears spilled out. The pain was awful, far worse than she had supposed it could be, and it was building again, slowly, creeping up on her without remorse, like a tiger in the night. She felt suddenly that she had to push.

'Jesus! Look, I can see the baby's head now,' said Gina. She turned eyes alight with excitement on Claire.

Claire pushed, groaning with effort, needing to get this *thing* out of her right now.

'Again! Come on, Claire!' Gina shouted. 'Come the fuck *on*!'

Claire felt as if she was turning inside out as she pushed and pushed and . . .

There was a feeling of release and then a blood-soaked thing spiralled out from between her legs. It started crying immediately, and Gina scooped it up, wrapped it in a blanket.

'It's a girl,' she said, beaming from ear to ear. She placed the blanketed infant on Claire's stomach. 'Look, babe, isn't this wonderful? You got a little girl.'

Claire looked. The thing didn't have the dark hair and glaring eyes she had expected. Instead there was just light blonde fluff above a red, puckered face. But even so, she recoiled.

'Get it away from me,' she said at once. 'I don't want it.'

'Oh come on . . .' Gina looked startled.

'*I said get it away from me!*' yelled Claire.

40

'I don't know what to do,' said Gina to Sylvester as they sat in his office days later. 'I know some women go through a hard time and they find it hard to tolerate the child. But *this* . . .'

Sylvester looked glumly over at the baby, which was for now slumbering peacefully in the cot they'd made for her out of the bottom drawer of his filing cabinet. She was a pretty little thing, and snug in there, and safe. Gina had nipped out and got the kid some formula, because Claire refused to feed the baby herself. She wouldn't even *look* at the poor little thing.

'Well, I don't know much about babies,' he said. *Or* women, come to that. He was useless with women, didn't really know how to approach them or speak to them. But he liked sweet-natured Claire more than any woman he'd ever met, and it pained him to see her suffering like this.

'I've tried to take the baby up there, time and again, but she won't have it. She gets hysterical. In fact . . .' Gina chewed her lip, her expression troubled.

'What?' prompted Sylvester.

'I think I'd be scared to leave the kid with her. I don't know.' Gina wiped her hand tiredly across her face and fastened her eyes on the baby. 'I think . . . she might try to harm it. Or herself.'

'Who, *Claire*?' Sylvester was shaking his head. Claire was the gentlest woman he knew. The nicest. Everyone loved her. She would never harm a child.

Gina looked bleakly at Sylvester. 'We have to do something. And . . . Christ, I don't want to, but I think it'll be best for the poor kid.'

'You've thought of something?'

'I have,' said Gina sadly.

Gina gave it one last try with Claire, but Claire just cried and turned her face to the wall. It was no good. So when Cyrus collected Gina from work a few days later, she took the baby with her. He drove over to Clinton Hill and parked up outside the place.

'She sure about this? The mother?' Cyrus asked his wife.

Gina looked down at the baby, sleeping so peacefully. Such a pretty child, and no trouble.

'You know what I think happened?' said Gina.

'No, what?'

'Some bastard forced her. And now every time she looks at this child, she sees that man. *That's* what I think.'

Cyrus straightened his glasses and heaved a sigh. 'It's a wicked world,' he said.

Gina looked at him, her husband. Flabby and plain, but he was a good man. Not a man who would ever consider doing such a thing to a woman.

'Well then, I'd better just do this,' said Gina.

41

Gina gathered up the baby and stepped out of the car. She walked on to the sidewalk, looking left and right. It was quiet. She'd deliberately picked a quiet time. Standing there, she looked up at the big iron gates, standing open in front of her: *273 – CONVENT OF SRS OF MERCY* soared high above her head on the arches over the gates. A gust of wind caught her coat and she shivered. But she was doing a good thing for this child, the *best* thing; she had to remember that.

She went through the open gate and ascended the steps to the big wooden door at the top. The door was slightly ajar, and she heard voices in the hall. Male and female. There was the sharp scent of new-cut wood in the air. Sudden alarm made her stop there, listening. Now it came to it, how the hell was she to explain this? The baby was unwanted by its mother. Gina had already tucked a note in with the baby, naming its mother and giving her address – *stupid!* Would the Sisters come back at Claire, try to coax her when it was clear that she wanted nothing to do with her daughter?

Gina tucked the blanket firmly around the child. The sliver of paper brushed her fingers and she thought, *I'll take the note out.* But then she hesitated. What if one day Claire *wanted* to know her child? And wasn't it cruel, to deny the little girl the chance to know her mother? From the other side of the door there was the sound of footsteps approaching, and she bent and placed the baby in its blanket on the step in front of the door. Then she turned and hurried down the steps, across the sidewalk and back to the car.

'Let's go, Cyrus,' she said, getting in. She wasn't an emotional type of woman, but right now, it was all she could do not to weep.

Dave Vance was a carpenter by trade and he loved wood. His trade didn't pay much, not nearly enough to give his wife Josephine the lifestyle he knew she ought to be enjoying. And she was brighter than him – a teacher. He had always felt in his heart that she deserved better than he could provide. They'd been married five years and it was a great sadness to her – mainly to her but of course to both of them – that she had so far been unable to conceive. It broke her heart. She cried when her period came every month. A child would have made their happiness complete, rounded them off just nice.

But *that* was all by the by. For now, he was working with his hands, making a living. Barely. He adored wood in all its textures, the hardwoods, the soft ones you could carve like butter. But he hated fucking wooden doors. They jammed or rattled, depending on the time of year and the humidity. This one, which the good Sisters of Mercy had hired him to attend to, was currently jamming, so he had been planing the convent's front door for an hour now, skimming off a tiny bit here, a little bit there, until he thought he had it just right.

'It'll be loose in the summer if I do this,' he'd warned the Sisters as they'd fluttered around, plying him with coffee and cake.

'No matter,' one smiley-faced Sister had told him. 'It's the jamming of the door that's the nuisance. We like the door to open freely, to let everyone in. People come to us, they don't want their way obstructed.'

From inside the hall, he opened the door, closed it. Perfect, right? He smiled in satisfaction. He opened it again . . . then stopped dead.

There was a baby wrapped in a pink blanket out there on the doorstep. He stood stunned for a moment. Couldn't believe what he was seeing. The baby was gazing up at him with sleepy blue eyes. He looked left and right. Jesus, someone had left the kid here for the Sisters to find. A *baby*. A real little treasure, and someone had just left the . . . it must be a girl, the blanket was pink . . . they'd just left the little girl here, abandoned.

Josephine would so love a little girl.

The thought jumped into his mind. Could he do it, just pick her up and take her?

Even before he was sure he could, even before he had time to reason it out, talk himself out of it, he was doing it. He gathered the child up and went down the steps, his heart thudding away in his chest like he was committing a crime, which maybe he was. He crossed to his old battered workhorse of a Ford van and tucked the baby inside on the passenger seat, closing the door gently.

She'll cry now, he thought. *Create a hullabaloo. Then the Sisters'll come down the steps and call me a wicked man for snatching an infant away. What the fuck am I doing?*

But the child was silent.

Dave ran back up the steps and pushed open the door. 'All done for today,' he shouted down the hall. 'See you tomorrow, Sisters!'

'Sure thing, Dave!' drifted back down the hall.

Dave gathered his tools together with shaking hands

and returned to his truck. He got in, glanced at the baby, who was watching him calmly. Still feeling like a criminal, he gunned the engine and roared off home.

42

'My God! What have you done?' was the first thing Jo said to him when he came in with the baby in his arms.

Josephine stood in the kitchen of their shabby downtown rented apartment, stirring tomato sauce for pasta with a wooden spoon. Or she had been. Now she grew still and stared at this apparition. Her husband, big craggy Dave Vance in his dusty wood-smelling work shirt and jeans, was standing in the kitchen doorway holding a baby in a pink blanket.

A *baby*.

She dried her hands on her apron and hurried forward. It was a tiny girl, blonde fluffy hair on her head, sweet pink cheeks, heart-meltingly calm blue eyes that looked up at her.

'Whose is she?' asked Jo, thinking that Dave had gone mad and that this was *her* fault, giving him so much grief about wanting a child. Now he'd stolen one and got himself in all kinds of trouble, just to please her.

'Nobody's,' said Dave. 'She'd been left on the doorstep at the convent. I was fixing the door and I just walked outside and there she was. So I picked her up and brought her home.'

Jo gave him that *don't fuck with me* look he knew so well. 'You're kidding, right?'

'No. I'm telling you the truth, Jo. God's honour.'

Jo was leaning forward, craning in to look closer at the child. She raised a hand, touched the baby's chin, and it caught hold of her finger and held on. 'Oh, she's so beautiful.'

'What's that?' Dave was frowning.

'What?' Jo was smiling at the baby.

'That scrap of paper in there. Here, you take her.'

Gently he handed the baby over to his wife. Then he took out the note that was tucked just inside the blanket, and while Jo stood there in raptures, staring at the baby, he read it aloud.

'Sorry, Sisters, but Claire Milo don't want this child. Please find a home for her. We (the mother's friends) can be contacted if needs be at the Sylvester club in NY, but please don't ever take that as licence to come around here and try to persuade Miss Milo against her decision. It was hard made but she stands by it and won't be moved.' He stopped reading, looked at his wife cradling the baby.

Jo looked up at Dave. 'We can't keep her though. Can we?'

Dave gave it some thought. 'You think they'd try to take the baby off us? The Sisters? Or that this Milo woman might change her mind, want the baby back?'

'Both those things,' said Jo, cuddling the infant.

'The Sisters don't know we got her. No one saw me pick her up, I swear. They don't even know she *exists*. And this note seems pretty definite about how the woman feels. And *she* don't know where we are, either.'

'People change, though.' Jo was looking fretful. This was marvellous, unbelievable. But it could all be snatched away in an instant. 'The mother could change her mind tomorrow, call the police, anything could happen. You were working at the convent. It wouldn't take them long to put things together, would it?'

'All right.' Dave was biting his lip. He'd found the child on the steps of the convent, it was almost like God had left her there for him to stumble over. This was a gift, a miracle, and they couldn't just pass it by, could they?

Jo was shaking her head. 'We have to take her back,' she said, but her eyes were locked on to the baby, and she was smiling. 'We have to.'

'There's another way. A *safer* way,' said Dave.

'What?' Jo was looking up at him now, and there was wild hope in her eyes.

'Look. We move, yeah?' Dave was nodding, thinking fast. 'Your sister down in Baton Rouge.'

'Virginia? You mean Ginny?' Jo was glancing between his face and the baby's like a metronome. She was holding a baby in her arms, a real live baby, and hardly registering what he was saying. She'd longed for this, and now it had been dropped into her life.

'How many sisters you got? Just the one, yeah. Honey.' He touched her hair in a warm caress. 'This is what we've always wanted and *we can have it*. If you're nervous of the cops, worried about her changing her mind, then let's just go. Right now. Let's pack up and skedaddle. Nothing holding us here, that's for sure. We can stay with Ginny until we sort ourselves out. What do you say?'

Jo looked down at the baby. Gently, she stroked the little girl's cheek. Then she looked up at Dave and her face was so full of joy that he felt choked up.

'I always dreamed when I had a little girl I'd call her Suki,' she said.

'Then let's do that,' said Dave, swallowing hard. 'We'll get her christened as our own. Nobody will know any different, not even Ginny. You can tell her you wanted to surprise her with the baby, she knows the troubles we've had and she won't question it. She'll be fucking delighted. Let's pack this thing up, all right? Let's take Suki down south and start again.'

43

The worst thing about it, Claire thought, was the leaking breasts. Within a fortnight of giving birth to the thing, she was back at her desk, filling in forms, interviewing staff, chasing suppliers, as if nothing had ever happened. Gradually, her stomach regained its shape but her breasts seemed to have a mind of their own. They seeped milk constantly, so that she had to wear pads inside her bra to soak the stuff up.

'That'll go,' said Gina when she confided in her. 'It'll pass.'

'Yeah, but *when*?' Claire's whole face screwed up in revulsion.

'You still sure about all that? Me taking her to the Sisters of Mercy and everything?'

Claire looked at Gina. 'I don't want to talk about it, or hear about it,' she said flatly. 'It's done and gone. All right?'

Gina held up her hands. 'OK. Anything you say.'

Sylvester didn't seem to know how to approach Claire after she'd given birth and brushed her baby aside. Stammering, blushing like a schoolboy, he asked after her health.

'I'm fine,' she snapped at him.

And then he called her into his office one morning and

said: 'Well, the day's come. Gina goes at the end of next week.'

'Is it that time already?' Claire was sad.

She'd miss Gina; Gina had taught her everything about this job, and been a firm friend to her in a time of great need. Almost like a mother. But not quite. Claire longed for her own dear mother Eva, and Pally, her dad. And even Trace, her misery-guts of a sister, and that old doom-monger Nanny Irene. But all that was so long ago now and so far away, another place, another life. *This* was her life now. She had to make what she could of it and be strong, because to even think of reuniting with her family was madness. They would suffer for it if she weakened. Suffer like poor Blue. The image of his dying was burned on her brain forever. So she couldn't afford to do that.

'Yep, it is.' Sylvester looked at her. 'So you want me to advertise the position? Or you want to step in when she goes? Means more pay.'

Claire opened and closed her mouth several times. Then she smiled. 'I'd love the job.' But suddenly a thought hit her and the smile faltered. 'Sylvester – you know I'm an illegal, don't you? My visa ran out ages ago.'

'Guessed as much.'

'That don't worry you?'

'No. It don't. Half the pot washers downstairs and all across this city are the same. We've never been troubled over it.'

Claire gazed at him. Sylvester might be a little strange in his ways, but he wasn't a fool; she reckoned he must be paying the precinct's beat cops to turn a blind eye. 'Then I guess I'll take the job.'

'That's good news. First part of it's organizing Gina's farewell party, OK?'

★

The party went with a hell of a bang. There was music, balloons, a chocolate devil's food cake with GINA splashed across it, and all the girls and bar staff and door boys gave her a fabulous send-off. Sylvester made a stumbling speech, and everyone applauded warmly. It was a happy occasion, tinged with sadness. The end of one era, the beginning of another.

When Gina had gone home to Cyrus and the girls were clearing up the mess, Sylvester called Claire to one side.

'So!' he said. 'Manageress now, yeah?'

'Feels strange,' she said, nodding.

'You'll walk it. Tomorrow we'll have lunch and discuss it all, OK?'

'Fine,' said Claire, and felt for one moment something like real happiness. It was the first time she'd felt such a thing since she'd lost Josh.

44

Much to her surprise, Claire found that she easily managed the job of stepping into Gina's shoes. The whole baby thing was long forgotten now, she had closed her mind to it; it had been a nightmare, but it was over. After that first lunch with Sylvester – nothing fancy, just a bite to eat in one of the local diners – they went out for lunch many more times, talked business, had a chat and a laugh.

Claire liked Sylvester. Yes, he might be awkward and a little *odd*, but he was gentle and he was harmless. She liked that about him and felt sorry for him because of his poor health. He seemed to be slipping more and more of those tiny pills under his tongue as time went on.

Sylvester's physical weakness made her feel safer still. Bullish men made her nervous. Even now she suffered the odd flashback, the feeling of someone creeping up on her in the night. The old dreams of someone hurting her, of people attacking Mum and Dad, or her sister, or even Josh, were fewer now, but she still had them whenever she was under stress. Then she would wake up sweating and fearful. All she could do was hope that one day she could leave the past behind her and move on with her life.

So it was lunch in the diner on Valentine's Day. No big deal. Nothing to either of them. They were friends, not lovers. The very idea was ridiculous. Sylvester was *much* older than her, they looked more like father and daughter out for lunch together. So what he had to say when they'd finished lunch on that Valentine's Day shocked her to the core.

'Claire? Will you marry me?'

The diner was packed and noisy. She thought she'd misheard him. 'What?'

'I said, will you marry me.' Sylvester was blushing like a boy. He held up a hand. 'Hear me out, will you?'

'Sylvester—'

'No, just listen. I like you, Claire. I've always liked you. And I know you've had troubles in your life, and I hate the idea of that. What I would like . . .' His voice trembled. 'What I would like is to keep you safe. To treasure you. Because I think a great deal of you, Claire. I really do.'

She sat there, stunned. The waitress came over and refilled their coffees, and went away again. Sylvester kept his eyes fixed on Claire's face.

'Listen . . .' she started, unsure of what she was going to say.

'Think it over, will you?' His voice was pleading.

'Oh God. Sylvester. I can't.' She really couldn't, and for reasons that she couldn't possibly explain to him.

For one thing, she could never bear to have sex with anyone. That was gone for her. The very idea terrified her. For another, he was old. And she was still young. And another thing, a very important one. She could only ever love Josh. No one else would do for her. Not even a kind man like Sylvester. She was strictly a one-man woman.

'I'm sorry,' she said, touching his hand across the table. 'The answer's no.'

Sylvester nodded and held up a hand. The waitress brought the bill and he settled up while Claire pulled on her coat, struggling for normality. She couldn't believe he'd said that. But he had. Then as they left the table he caught her hand, and to her shock brought it to his lips and quickly kissed it.

'I really like you, Claire,' he said. 'And don't worry. This doesn't change *anything*. I promise you that.'

It was a sweet thing to say, and she nodded and smiled at him. 'I like you too, Sylvester,' she said. 'And thank you for asking.'

She was glad afterwards that their last words together had been kind and friendly, because next morning when she got into her office she got a call from the hospital saying that Sylvester Drummond had been rushed in late last night with heart failure. They'd tried to save him, but there was nothing they could do.

Sylvester was dead.

45

Claire felt awful on the day of Sylvester's funeral; numb with grief. He'd been her true friend, a quiet supporter ever since she'd started work at his club, and she was going to miss him badly. All the girls showed up for the service, and Gina and Cyrus too, plus the bar and kitchen staff, and the door boys – even the club's suppliers. The church was packed with his friends.

No relatives, though. Sylvester had never married, and he'd been an only child of elderly parents who were already gone.

'Sad, ain't it,' sniffed Gina as they paused outside the church after the service. 'No kin of his here to mourn him.'

Cyrus patted his wife's arm. Claire nodded. She felt bad over Sylvester, and guilty. She didn't tell Gina – she couldn't tell anyone – that Sylvester had proposed to her on the day he died. She thought that maybe he had died of a broken heart and she hated herself for disappointing him, but what else could she have done? It was possible that her rejection had wounded him far more deeply than he'd shown. But . . . how could she have said yes?

'You ever think . . .' Gina started as Cyrus moved away, leaving the two women there together.

'What?' asked Claire.

'About the baby.' Gina's eyes were sharp on Claire's

face. 'Do you ever think of her? Are you sorry you let her go?'

But Claire shook her head. 'No. I'm not sorry. Don't talk of it again, will you, Gina? I don't like it.'

She didn't want to be reminded of that, now or ever. She'd come a long, long way from the gypsy camp of her youth. Now she was the manager of a thriving club in a bustling city; a success in business, if not in life. She'd lost Josh. Her family. Her innocence. And she'd just lost a dear friend. But she was stronger now. Adversity had made her tougher, more resilient.

After Sylvester was laid to rest, Claire caught up with Gina again.

'Come back to the club,' she said to Gina. 'We've laid on a spread for Sylvester. All the girls would love to see you, you know they would.'

'OK,' said Gina, and they all went back together and celebrated Sylvester's slightly eccentric life. Afterwards, when it was over and the girls had cleared everything away so that the club would be ready for business in a couple of days – for two days it would be closed in respect of Sylvester's death – Claire went upstairs to her room and cried over the loss.

She wondered what would happen to the club now, to all of Sylvester's dreams for it. He'd never expanded the business as he'd wanted to – she suspected his ill health had let him down on that – but he'd lived for the club, it had become his family home. Without him, it was going to feel very strange, working here.

Dear Sylvester.

Such a kind man. The sort of man any woman should be happy to love. He deserved a lot better than her.

★

Nearly a month after the funeral, it became clear that Sylvester had thought very highly of Claire, whether she accepted him as a husband or not. She took a call from his lawyer, telling her that Sylvester had left the club – and everything in it – to her.

46

By the time Connor Flynn came screaming into the world, Shauna had the nursery fully kitted out and was making inroads into the furnishings for the rest of the house, too, costing Josh a fortune in the process. He was making some wedge, doing lots of door work and bare-knuckle bouts. Linus Pole was keeping in touch and pushing plenty of booth sessions and 'out the back' straighteners his way. He went down the gym on the corner of the street often, worked out there with the weights, beat the fuck out of the other boxers. Kept himself fit.

'You could be world class, with a bit of polish,' said the old geezer who trained the kids down there.

All Josh knew was that he needed a lot more dosh. He wasn't pulling in anywhere near enough. Shauna was high-maintenance. Just today he'd come home from the gym, taken a bath and sat down to eat his dinner – Shauna was a great cook – in front of the TV.

Then Shauna told him there was a new three-piece suite coming on Monday, she'd bought it on the never-never. That old thing they'd bought second-hand from an ad in the corner-shop window was tatty, she was tired of it.

'You what?' he said, dropping his knife and fork, feeling the steak lodge in his throat. That 'old thing' was less than a year old, and in pristine condition.

'You heard. And that fucking Zephyr, Josh. You know, what we ought to have is a Rover, something classy like that . . .'

Her eyes were alight with excitement. When it came to spending money, Shauna got really turned on.

'You take the bloody cake, you do,' he said, slapping the table so hard the cutlery jumped. 'What the *fuck*? You didn't think to talk to me first? Shaun, we're getting up to our neck in debt here.'

'That's rubbish, you earn plenty,' she said, starting to scowl.

'Yeah, and I've got to carry on earning plenty to keep up with you,' said Josh.

'Meaning?' she fumed, her face falling into stubborn lines.

'Meaning, take it bloody easy! *Ask* me before you go spending a fucking fortune on stuff we don't even need.' Josh stood up, his dinner only half eaten, thinking – and oh *shit* he shouldn't think like this, *this* was his life now, the kid and Shauna – that Claire would never have done such a thing. Claire would have been happy with anything, however humble, so long as she was with him. He stormed from the room, slamming the door into the hall shut behind him.

'Who says we don't need it? Only *you*, you mean bastard!' came Shauna's shout from behind the door.

Upstairs, the baby started bawling its head off. Josh put his jacket on to go down to the pub and was rifling through his pockets for his car keys when he came upon the purple card John had given him. He thought about Shauna, the Money Monster. Christ, he was spitting mad at her, the silly cow. He had red bills piling up, demands for payment coming out of his ears. The rent was a week overdue. He paused in the hall and picked up the phone and dialled the number on the card. It was answered almost instantly.

'Carlton?' said a female voice.

'Is Mr Houghton there, please?' said Josh. Upstairs, the kid went right on crying. No sign of Shauna.

'Who wants him?'

'Josh Flynn. A business acquaintance of his, John Finlay, said Mr Houghton might have some work for me.'

'Hold on.'

The phone hit a solid object and the woman yelled: 'Mr Houghton! Phone! Says he's Josh Flynn.'

Josh waited. More crying from up the stairs. The sound set his teeth on edge. Then a male voice came on the line. 'Well, you took your fucking time,' it said.

'Mr Houghton?' asked Josh.

'I've been waiting on this call.'

'Sorry.' Fuck *you*.

'Never mind. So when can you come over?'

'Soon as you like.'

'Tonight. Seven. Ask for me on the door,' said Houghton, and put the phone down.

The baby was still screaming.

'You going to sort that bloody kid out?' Josh shouted. Something hit the kitchen doorway and shattered and fell to the floor. Probably what was left of his fucking dinner. Even their *food* was ridiculous. Steaks, salmon, trout – nothing but the best for Shauna Flynn. She'd be necking *foie gras* and bloody caviar next, off a silver spoon. Well, fuck *her*.

Josh left the house without another word to his wife.

47

The Carlton Club was up West, just around the corner from Annabel's where all the celebs and royals hung out. Josh scrubbed around his previous plan to spend the night down the boozer and went straight to the Carlton. Outside, it didn't look anything special, with two skinny pimple-faced youths trying to puff themselves up and look big on the door. He told them he was here to see Mr Houghton and one of them went off indoors ahead of Josh, beckoning him to follow.

Inside wasn't much better. There was a jazz trio up on the half-circle stage trying to liven the atmosphere, bored hostesses were propping up the bar with empty trays, and a handful of punters sat at the dimly lit circular tables. The place would have seated ninety, but there couldn't have been more than twenty in tonight and, from the look of them, they probably wouldn't be coming back again.

Josh grabbed the youngster's arm. 'It always like this?'

The youth nodded, said nothing. He led the way through the club and paused beside a red door at the back, knocking. Then he opened the door and Josh stepped into Mr Houghton's inner sanctum. It was a bare room with filing cabinets, a cheap desk and chair, nothing stylish about it. Behind the desk sat a man who slapped the phone back on to the cradle then looked up with weary eyes as Josh came in.

'What *now*?' he asked irritably.

Josh looked at Houghton. He was a half-bald little monkey of a man in his fifties with a thin wrinkled face, but there was an air of authority about him.

'I'm Josh Flynn,' said Josh. 'John Finlay at the Crown asked me to give you a bell.'

'Oh, right. Yeah. The boxer,' he said with more interest.

'That's right,' said Josh as Spotty left the room, closing the door quietly behind him.

'Take a seat then. I'm Dave.'

Josh did. 'So what's the problem, Dave?' he asked.

'Druggies,' said Dave, running a hand through his thinning hair. 'Druggies in here day and night, shooting up in the bogs. That useless pair of tossers I got on the door, I think they're taking a slice of that action and turning a blind eye when the dealers come in. It gives the place a bad name. Makes the punters stay away. I need someone solid out there, someone who'll kick arse.'

'I could probably take the job on,' said Josh. He thought of Shauna, running through the money like it grew on ruddy trees. His mate Linus Pole had a few handy lads who'd be pleased with this work and enjoy the rucks that would inevitably occur. He didn't fancy doing more door work himself, but he could certainly subcontract it out to them and carry on with the fighting. 'Provided the deal was right, of course.'

'Sure, sure. We can discuss all that.' Dave's eyes were bright with interest. 'Bare-knuckle then?'

'Whatever's going,' said Josh.

'John said you were a champion. Among your own kind.'

'He's right.'

'But no ambitions to go further with it? Go pro?'

Josh shrugged. 'Whatever brings the wedge in, I'm happy to take on.'

'Then I reckon we can do business,' said Dave. 'We'll discuss the door stuff further, yeah?' He pulled open a drawer and yanked out a sheet of headed notepaper. 'Maybe some other stuff too. That's my home address,' he said, scribbling it down and shoving the paper across to Josh. 'There. John said you're married, right?'

'Married with a kid. Little boy. Connor.'

'Come out to dinner on Sunday and let's see how we go. Bring your old lady, she can meet my Phil. Don't bring the ankle-biter though, Phil can't stand 'em until they're teenagers.'

Josh took the paper, folded it, put it in his pocket. 'That's kind of you. Thanks.'

'Come at four, we eat around six. OK?'

'Fine,' said Josh.

'Where the fuck have you been?' asked Shauna from the bed when he got home later. He'd tried fumbling around in the dark, but his boots had hit the floor with a clatter and she'd woken up. 'Shh! You'll wake the sodding baby, I've only just got him back down.'

Connor was peacefully asleep in his cot under the window. Josh went over and stood for a moment, looking at his sleeping son, lit by moonlight, cosy as a bug in a rug. He reached down, touched a finger to one chubby little cheek. The baby didn't stir. Josh smiled, and then he thought that – *ah, shit!* – this should have been his and Claire's baby. He stopped smiling and sighed.

'He's fine,' said Josh, turning away from Connor. 'I been up West, doing some business at the Carlton.'

Shauna sat up. 'Ain't that one of the clubs all the nobs go to?'

Josh peeled off the rest of his clothes and climbed in. 'It is.'

'What they after then?'

'They got trouble with druggies. Want someone on the door to stamp it out.'

'You could do that with one hand tied behind your back,' said Shauna.

'That's true,' said Josh, relieved that the temper tantrum of earlier in the evening was over. She was like a penny firework, Shauna. She blew up, then ten minutes later she was smiling again. 'Also, the owner's invited us over to his place for dinner. Not tea, *dinner*, he said. On Sunday.'

Shauna looked at him, outlined dimly by the light of the moon. 'Dinner,' she echoed.

Josh's head turned and his teeth flashed in a grin. 'That's what the nobs call it. And if they eat at noon, that's called lunch.'

'Luncheon,' said Shauna, who took a keen interest in all matters upwardly mobile. 'Like luncheon meat. And you ought to say napkin, not serviette. Bet you didn't know that.'

'It's a whole new world,' said Josh, yawning and settling down. He didn't give a fuck about napkins or serviettes. Crystal chandeliers and mansions didn't do it for him. He felt a bit treacherous thinking it, but he knew Claire wouldn't have given two hoots for any of this social-climbing bollocks that Shauna seemed so caught up in.

Shauna snuggled up.

'Where's their place?' she asked.

'Dunno. Henley, think I saw on the paper he gave me. I'll show you in the morning.'

'What the fuck am I going to wear?' wondered Shauna.

'You got lots of clothes.' Shauna had a wardrobe bursting with stuff. All of it bloody expensive, too.

'I'll have to buy new,' she said, and grabbed his cock.
'Shauna . . .'
'Shut up,' she said, and got to work.

48

Shauna got the shock of her life when she opened the front door the following morning and found Jeb Cleaver lounging on the step.

'What the fuck are you *doing* here?' she barked out, shocked, looking left and right. Josh had only just left, heading off to the gym. Five minutes earlier, and he'd have come face to face with Jeb, and she didn't like the idea of that at all.

'Cool down,' said Jeb. 'What sort of welcome is that? I saw your old man go out and thought I'd come say hello.'

'Fuck it, you'd better come inside,' she said, and Jeb strolled in. Shauna shut the door quickly. 'He'll be back soon. What do you want?'

Jeb was leaning against the hall wall now, looking around. 'Nice place you got here. How'd he get the dosh for *this*, then?'

'Never you mind. How did you find me?' snapped Shauna.

'Yeah. About that.' Jeb's eyes sharpened on her face. 'That was bad, Shauna. You moved on from your last place, and the one before that over the chippy, and both times you didn't tell me your new address. Luckily the new people had it or I guess we'd just have lost touch. And I'd hate that to happen, wouldn't you?'

Oh sure, thought Shauna. She'd hoped that would be the result. But here Jeb was, turning up like a bad penny. She looked at him with his scruffy beard and mac and boots and thought that the very last thing she needed in her life at this moment was Jeb Cleaver and his no-mark brothers and their horny old goat of a dad. Sunday, they were going to dinner with the nobs in Henley. *That* was where she was headed.

'You're not answering,' said Jeb with a pout. His eyes were hard as they stared into hers. 'You know what Rowan reckons? He reckons you've had your use of us and now you've just turned your back.'

'That ain't true,' said Shauna, although it was.

A wail went up from the kitchen.

'Look, I've got to . . .' said Shauna and turned away from him.

She went into the kitchen where Connor was sitting in his blue romper suit in his high chair at the table, eating chunks of banana. He looked up as Shauna came in, and grinned.

'Cute little fella,' said Jeb, following behind her. He moved closer to Connor, reached out a grubby hand and touched the baby's cheek with it. 'Hey, boy, how are you?'

Shauna felt an electrifying jolt of protectiveness surge through her as Jeb stood beside Connor. She moved, placing herself between them. Jeb saw the alarm on her face, and smiled.

'He Josh Flynn's then is he?' asked Jeb.

'Well he sure as hell ain't *yours*,' she said.

Jeb's smile broadened. Then he reached out and touched Shauna's cheek. She flinched away. Suddenly his smile vanished. He grabbed her face and held her there, squeezing the flesh until she groaned with the pain.

'I can understand that you like to better yourself, gal,' he said softly, leaning so close that his breath brushed her face. 'I got that. That's fine. But you know the one thing you should never do?'

Shauna couldn't speak. She half-shook her head.

'You should *never* forget where you came from. You should *never* forget your roots,' said Jeb.

But that was exactly what Shauna wanted to forget.

Jeb released her and she sagged against the kitchen table, her cheek throbbing. Connor was looking up at the two adults looming over him, curious, not frightened.

Now Jeb was smiling again. 'We're going to stay in touch, you and me,' he said to Shauna. 'We're buddies, ain't we. Lovers too. You carry on, gal, you climb just as high as you like, but don't forget one thing – I'll be right alongside you. 'Cos I got first dibs on you, no matter about Josh Flynn or fancy clothes or cars or whatever else takes your eye. Remember?'

Shauna nodded. All she wanted was for him to get out. All she wanted was him away from her baby, and from her.

'Josh will be back any minute,' she said, hating the tremble in her voice.

'Yeah.' Jeb's eyes were on her face. 'See you then.'

And he turned and walked off down the hall and out the door.

49

'Oh my God. I mean, *wow*!' said Shauna as they pulled into Dave Houghton's drive in Josh's old car.

Actually, they couldn't pull in. They had to stop ten feet into the drive as they were met with a big set of closed iron gates with two concrete lions atop plinths on either side. There was an intercom. Josh got out of the car, pressed the button.

'Yes?' said a faint female voice.

'It's Josh Flynn,' he said.

'Come up,' said the voice, and there was a whirring buzz and then inch by slow inch the gates opened.

Josh got back in the car. Shauna flashed him a big grin as he put the car in gear and tore on up the drive.

'Jesus!' She laughed out loud when they pulled up in front of the house after nearly a quarter mile of driveway had flashed by. 'Thank God I got some new clothes for this.'

Josh stopped the car and turned off the engine. There was a Rover parked nearby, and a sporty little Triumph. He looked up at the house itself. What a fucking drum! It was white, huge and modern. It was a bloody *mansion*.

'Blimey,' said Josh, smiling at his over-excited wife.

Shauna was lit up like a Christmas tree. To be fair, Josh thought she looked fucking fantastic. Her almost black hair

174

was piled up on top of her head, her body had long since regained its pre-birth shape, her make-up was faultless. She was wearing white hooped earrings and big dark shades. A teensy little bag sat on her lap – it had cost a small fortune – and she was wearing a dress that was orange and white stripes, with a long-zippered front and a big cut-away in the back to show off her lovely tanned skin. It was the sexiest thing Josh had ever seen, that dress. It looked good enough – almost – to take away the pain of the cost of the damned thing.

'Let's get in there then,' he said, and for the first time Josh looked at his old Zephyr – he didn't actually care much about cars, he wasn't impressed by them in the least – and thought, Christ, what a heap of junk. She's right, I *do* need a new one.

Shaun looked like a film star today, and she'd been in a mad pelt of excitement over this dinner, double-checking that the babysitter was lined up – she was – and then pulling Josh's wardrobe open and looking at his clothes with a critical eye.

'I thought I'd wear that jacket,' Josh had said, coming into the bedroom to get dressed for the evening out, picking up his usual tan-coloured effort.

'You will not,' said Shauna, standing in front of the dressing table and tugging heated rollers out of her hair. 'It's the dark jeans, the white shirt, the grey jacket to match your eyes. I've laid it all out, ready.'

Now they were actually *here*, Shauna was dubious. She took in the house, the grounds, the expensive cars parked out front. Thought of that visit from Jeb, him saying *never forget your roots*. But fuck that. *This* was what she craved. All of this.

'You didn't tell me it was Blenheim bloody Palace,' she said.

'I didn't know,' said Josh. 'Come on, Shaun. They're just people. They don't bite.'

'If you say so.'

'There's no way those tits are real,' said Shauna to Josh an hour later, as they stood for a moment alone in a conservatory that wouldn't have disgraced Kew Gardens.

'Shaun!' Josh said, laughing and glancing around in case the lady of the house had returned and heard. She hadn't.

'These are real though,' said Shauna, and with a cheeky grin she yanked down the zip on the front of her dress and gave him an arousing flash of nude dark-brown nipples. She wasn't wearing a bra.

'Shaun! Behave!' But Josh was grinning. One of the best things about Shauna's figure was her big perky tits, and she knew it. Not even breastfeeding Connor had altered the beauty of them, and Josh had only to see them to get a hard-on like a concrete pole.

Shauna picked up her champagne flute. 'I'm telling you. No *way* are they real,' she said.

Josh sighed. Shauna had taken against Dave's wife on sight. And vice versa. From the very first greeting, it had been clear that the two women were not going to be buddies. Philippa, Dave's missus, was a tall patrician blonde with an elitist manner. She had an ex-model's slim hips and long legs and – yes, Shaun was probably right – impossibly full, pert breasts that looked weird perched upon her skinny ribcage.

Dave seemed a lot older than Philippa. In fact, he looked like a weathered little gnome standing by the side of his glamorous wife, the poor cunt. There was no doubt that he was loaded and had probably *paid* for those plastic tits on his credit card.

'There you are, the pair of you,' said Dave, joining them, bottle of Bollinger in hand. 'Top-up, anyone?'

He refilled both their glasses. Josh thought that Dave was already half-cut and that was only on a couple of glasses of bubbly. You wouldn't take *this* cunt out on a Friday night with the lads; one whiff of the barmaid's apron and he'd be flat on the floor.

'Phil's dynamite in the kitchen,' he said with a smile. 'Dynamite at hiring catering staff, anyway,' he added, and although he was half-laughing there was something bitter in the way he said it. 'Come on through to the lounge. You haven't seen it yet, have you?'

The lounge was massive, full of large gold-damask-covered sofas, some modern but obviously priceless occasional tables and three matching chandeliers, all lit up down the centre of the room in a dazzling line. The entire length of one wall was glass, and when you stood in front of it you could look out over a vast sweep of sloping lawn to willows dipping their branches into the dark, fast-flowing River Thames. Ducks and swans glided past. The setting sun glinted on the water.

'It's a hell of a view,' said Josh.

'It's what sold the place to us. We've only been in two years. Can be a bit of a pain in the arse with the river so close, because apparently it does flood here sometimes. But we're on a slope, as you can see, and just as well because the council do fuck-all to clear it. The rates we pay, you'd think they'd cut back the weed, do a bit of dredging of the silt and shit that builds up – *something*. But so far we've been lucky and the river hasn't burst its banks. Philippa's been costing me a fucking fortune, doing this place up. It's great, don't you think?'

'It's fantastic,' said Shauna, green with envy, taking off her shades and drinking in the full splendour of it.

My God, to own a place like this. To wake every morning to that view and think, *This is mine*. This was what she wanted. Something *exactly* like this. She thought of Jeb Cleaver, showing up and trying to intimidate her. Trying to drag her back to what she used to be. Well, she wouldn't let him. *This* was the way forward. This was what she deserved – and she was fucking well going to have it, or go bust trying.

'Right!' said Philippa, coming in from the kitchen and clapping her hands as if they were children to be assembled into straight lines and marched off down the road. 'Dinner's ready, let's sit down.'

The dining area was a candlelit nook beside the big bank of windows. There was a circular table that looked like marble, and thickly padded high-backed chairs. Neither Josh nor Shauna had ever seen such luxury. The soup was already on the table, waiting for them. There were warm fresh-baked rolls in a wicker basket, and curled pats of butter. And there was a young woman in a black dress and white waist apron, standing discreetly outside the kitchen door, ready to serve them.

When Shauna took a mouthful of the soup, it was stone cold. She glanced at Josh. He was eating it, saying nothing.

'What?' he asked her.

'The soup's cold,' said Shauna.

Philippa gave her a look across the table that could have curdled milk. 'It's meant to be cold,' she said. 'It's gazpacho.' Philippa's eyes dropped to the spoon in Shauna's hand. 'And that's a dessert spoon. *That* one's the soup spoon.'

'I get 'em mixed up myself,' said Dave kindly. 'All the time! Phil bends my ear about it too, but does it matter what you eat the damned food with? I don't think so.' He sent his wife a warning look.

But the warning didn't seem to get through. Despite Dave trying gamely to hold up the conversation and keep it civil, Philippa pulled Shauna up on her use of the wrong knife and fork: 'You work your way inwards, it's quite simple,' she said.

When Shauna tried to refill her own glass of water and the waitress hurried forward and took it out of her hand, Philippa said in a patronizing voice: 'That's what she's there for, Shauna. You don't have to do that yourself, really.'

Towards the end of the meal, when Shauna had fallen silent and was simmering away like a bloody volcano – Josh knew the signs so well – Philippa dropped her final bombshell.

'So you're *gypsies*, David tells me. How intriguing.' She turned her baby-blues on Josh. 'Bare-knuckle fighting, how *macho*. And what about Shauna?' She gave Shauna a wide-eyed look. 'What is it? Mud-wrestling? Selling pegs or lucky heather? Something like that?'

And that was how Philippa Houghton ended up *wearing* the pudding course.

50

'How bloody dare she! That fucking *cow*!' spat Shauna in a loud whisper when they got back home and she was yanking off her earrings in their bedroom. They'd paid off the babysitter and she'd gone. The baby was sleeping peacefully in his cot. Now Shauna was kicking off, big time.

Josh said nothing as he pulled off his clothes. Shauna had ranted all the way home in the car but he had sat silent at the wheel, thinking, *Well, that's fucked then*. Dave Houghton wouldn't want his services now that his wife had been on the receiving end of a bowl of strawberry pavlova. Philippa's shriek of outrage still echoed in Josh's brain, cream dripping off her face and strawberries lodged in her hair – and in fact it could almost have been *funny*, if it wasn't such a pain to lose a contact like Dave when they so badly needed the extra income.

'Well *say* something,' Shauna demanded.

'What do you want me to say?' Josh tossed his shirt on to the chair. 'You just fucked up a good earner, is *that* what you want me to say?'

'Keep your bloody voice down, will you? She shouldn't have talked to me like that,' hissed Shauna, ripping the grips out of her hair. 'Like I was a fucking nobody, telling me about which cutlery to use and that the soup was meant to be cold.'

'It *was* meant to be cold.'

'You know what I mean! It was the way she said it, looking down her bloody nose at me.'

Josh could see that Philippa's words and attitude had cut Shauna to the quick, wounded her deeply, but it was because Shauna was so desperate to be better than she was – the product of a travellers' campsite. Shauna wanted more than that, *much* more, he knew it. She wanted to mix with society types and rich bastards, to be accepted. And tonight had been a painful reality check. He felt offended and angry on her behalf. She was, after all, his wife. And – it was true – she *had* been made to look a fool by that over-made-up tart Philippa.

But . . . even now, he couldn't help but compare Shauna's volcanic outburst with Claire's easy-going good nature. Claire would have *laughed* at Philippa's hoity-toity ways, not thrown her toys out of the pram like Shauna had. And he would have shared in the joke with her, too; their eyes would have met across the dinner table, and they would have both suppressed a grin.

But Shauna wasn't Claire.

'Never mind, Shaun,' he said. 'Gawd, you know what? I'm still hungry.'

'We just had dinner,' sniffed Shauna, unzipping her dress.

'Call that dinner? Oh, it *looked* damned good, didn't it, all laid out poncey with twirls of this and slivers of that. Two mouthfuls and it was gone, even though it was damned pretty. I didn't know whether to eat it or fuck it.'

A hint of a smile played around Shauna's mouth when he said that. She grabbed her dressing gown and yanked it on. 'You want some sandwiches? I'll bring them up, we'll eat in bed. And a beer?'

'Yeah, that'd be great.'

★

Dave phoned a week later. Josh was sitting in their – admittedly poky – little lounge, dandling Connor on his knee while Shauna got dressed upstairs. *Here we go*, thought Josh. Now for the piss-off-and-die speech.

'So, when you coming in to the club?' Dave asked.

Josh was astonished. 'Blimey. I don't know. When d'you want me?' If Dave wasn't mentioning the car crash that was last weekend, then neither was he, that was for sure.

'Come on Friday. Have a look around, see what's happening, see what you think. OK?'

'Yeah, all right then.' He didn't know whether or not to bother. Shaun wouldn't like him working for the Houghtons after her set-to with Philippa. And he didn't know whether he wanted all the grief that would entail. But . . . they needed the money. *Shit*, did they need it. He had bills coming out of his ears.

When Dave put the phone down, Josh looked at Connor, who was watching him wide-eyed, his finger stuffed in his rosebud mouth. 'What d'you make of that?' he asked, and Connor grinned, bounced his chubby legs up and down in his pale blue rompers, and let out a shout.

Shauna came downstairs and into the lounge, pulling on her cardigan. 'Who was that?' she asked, bending, taking the baby off him. Connor grizzled, but she rocked him and he stopped.

'Dave Houghton.'

Shauna's face took on a pinched look. 'Well, I hope he's not expecting a fucking apology,' she fumed.

'He asked me to come in on Friday, start work.'

'What, after that flipping fiasco?' Shauna looked gobsmacked.

'What the hell. It was nothing,' said Josh, hoping to make light of it.

'It might have been nothing to *you*, but to me it was bloody humiliating.'

'Maybe Philippa will apologize.'

'She can *stuff* her apology up her arse,' said Shauna, taking the baby out to the kitchen to fetch his milk. She'd stopped breastfeeding and had switched Connor on to the bottle now. 'She'll be sorry she ever tried to make a berk out of me.'

51

'They call cannabis "green petrol",' said Dave as Josh sat in his office with him on Friday evening. Out in the club, a girl singer was crooning 'Downtown', the big Petula Clark hit. 'They grow it up in the Rif mountains of Morocco, place called Ketama. They call it *kif*. It keeps about a million families off the breadline up there. Well, what else can they do? Can't grow olives or wheat on that soil. But cannabis? Grows like a bastard, that stuff.'

'OK,' said Josh. He'd never done drugs, but he'd known a few who had, silly sods. All his life he'd been conscious of being blessed with phenomenal health and exceptional strength, so what would he want to go and abuse his body for, just to get high?

'But there's no money in cannabis on the streets any more. Now what we get mostly is Charlie.'

'Cocaine,' said Josh.

'Comes in through Ireland. Standing joke is, the Irish Navy is a pedalo and a couple of inflatable bananas. They can't patrol all that coastline, it's wide open.' Dave shrugged. 'What the hell, people got to make a living, I understand that. But when it hits home, right here in my club, then I got to draw the line.' Dave paused and looked at Josh. 'John said you're a sound man. Trustworthy.'

'I am,' said Josh.

'You reckon you can sort it out?'

Josh outlined his plans. He'd talked it over with Linus Pole and Linus was happy to let two of his best boys do one fortnight on the door, then another two would do the next. Josh would handle the cash, pass them on their bit. Linus would, of course, get a cut too. It would be fine.

Thoughts of Linus made Josh think of the other thing they'd discussed when they'd met up. Linus hadn't been keen to break it to him, but he had given Josh the bad news anyway: Josh's mother had finally died in her sleep after years of heavy drinking. At first, Josh didn't know how he felt about it. After a while, he realized he was relieved. His mother had stood aside and watched his dad batter him as a kid for years. And Josh had never forgiven her for it.

Dave was nodding, his expression thoughtful. 'Look . . . do you think you would be able to handle something else? It's a bit . . . delicate.'

Josh refocused, wrenched his mind away from his mother's sad ending. 'In what way delicate?'

'In the way that things are a bit *personal*, you understand?'

'No,' said Josh. 'I don't.'

Dave paused, looked down at the desk, pushed the newspaper around with one gnarled yellow index finger. Josh glanced at the headlines. Sadat was talking to the Knesset, and in Rhodesia they were still wrestling with black majority rule. Jimmy Carter's home church in Plains, Georgia, had ended its colour bar, and trouble was looming in England over public sector cuts. Then Dave heaved a sigh. 'Thing is,' he said, 'I have a friend.'

'A friend.'

'Yeah. A *close* friend.'

Josh watched Dave's face. He didn't know this man well yet, but he didn't dislike him. Their wives had brawled like mongrel bitches, but that was hardly Dave's fault. Still, Josh felt he was treading on unsteady ground here. 'Go on,' he said.

'A *boy*friend,' said Dave, and Josh could almost have sworn the ugly little cunt was blushing.

Josh said nothing. Dave was a married man, and he'd believed him to be straight. But now he was saying he wasn't. Well, it was his business if he wanted to bat for both sides. Josh didn't care one way or the other.

'This *boy*friend's name is Andrew Meredith. I met him when he came in as a punter and we . . . well, sort of hit it off.'

'Right.'

'This was about a year back. Phil don't know nothing about this, of course.'

'No. Of course.'

'And I want it kept that way.'

'So what's the problem? Does this friend fit in with the drugs scene here?'

'Andrew . . .' Dave paused. He *was* blushing. 'Andrew's a toff. Went to Eton. Good family. Had it all, all his life. Not like me. Grew up rough, I did. Council estate. Started making money selling stuff down the market, took it from there. Now I got restaurants, this club, snooker halls, box- ing clubs, and a very expensive wife and kids.'

'I know *that* problem,' said Josh with a wry smile.

'Jeez, didn't those two go at it last Sunday?' Dave almost smiled too. 'I have to apologize about Phil. She can be a bitch.'

'It's forgotten,' said Josh, although he knew it wasn't; Shauna never let an insult rest.

'I got two kids, you know. Love 'em to bits. A girl and boy. Both at private school, going on to great things I hope. So, anyway. Andrew likes a bit of rough, fancies himself a gangster, although he ain't, not really. It's a game to him and I keep telling him it's dangerous, but will he listen? No, he won't. He keeps a luxury yacht down at Poole and goes over to Spain and Amsterdam, sometimes to Ireland too – as I said, that's a real soft target – taking the money out to pay for the coke he gets there, loads of it, *tons* of it. And for some time he's been dealing in the club and enticing the wrong sort of people in. Makes the decent punters nervous, and they stay away.'

'So . . . get rid of him. If it's a personal relationship, end it. Call it a day,' said Josh.

'I can't,' said Dave.

'Why not?'

'Because I had that conversation with him. I said, stop it or it's over. Go and have your fun elsewhere, I don't want this kind of trouble.'

'What did he say?'

'He said, "I'm not stopping a fucking thing. And if you *ask* me to again, I'll tell your wife. I'll tell Phil how her ever-loving husband likes to take it up the arse from a posh boy."'

'Christ!' said Josh.

'Yeah. Which would mean I'd lose a lot. I mean, a *lot*. Phil would cane me for as much as she could get. I know that woman and, believe me, she can be vindictive. She'd take my kids away from me. Turn them against me, tell them things about me that would make them sick to their stomachs. She would blacken my name around town. Tell everyone I'm an arse-bandit. Ruin me in business.'

'So you're in a bind,' said Josh. He could understand where Dave was coming from; he was a father himself and the thought of anyone trying to take his little boy away from him made him want to tear someone's head off.

'You can say *that* again.' Dave sank his head into his

hands, ruffled his thin hair so that it stuck out like a rumpled baby's. In that moment, Josh thought Dave was the most pathetic spectacle he'd ever seen. Scared of his wife. Scared of his boyfriend. Scared of what might happen if he just let things slide. Scared of what *would* happen if he didn't. Poor bastard.

'You're a tough nut,' said Dave, staring at Josh. 'I can see that. Grew up rough and had it hard, yeah?'

'That's about right,' said Josh, thinking of life in the camp, Dad always at him when he was small, hammering him with his fists.

'So what would *you* do? In this situation?' asked Dave.

'I think Andrew's got to go.'

'Go?'

'He can't be allowed to blow the whistle, tell all to Phil. She'll fuck with your finances, lose you your kids and make you look bad with your mates. He can't be allowed to go on dealing in your club. So yes – I'd say he has to go.'

'That sounds sort of permanent,' said Dave with a nervous laugh.

'Sounds like what you want.'

Dave's nervy grin faltered and fell from his face. 'Yeah.' He swallowed. 'But . . . you wouldn't do it anywhere near the club, would you? Keep me well out of it. He goes down to Marbella in April, you could do it there.'

Josh's eyes widened. 'Wait on. I didn't say *I* would do anything.'

'I'd pay well,' said Dave.

'No – what?' Josh was shaking his head. Facing a man head-on in a fair fight was one thing. This was something else. 'What are you saying here? You want me to warn him off?'

Dave hesitated. Then he said: 'No. I want this thing *settled.*' His eyes met Josh's. 'I want this permanent.'

'You want . . .'

'Yeah, I want him gone.'

'Christ. Well . . .'

'Two hundred and fifty thou to make it go away,' said Dave, his eyes suddenly pleading.

'You *what*? Just wait a fucking minute . . .'

'All right! *Five* hundred thou,' said Dave in desperation.

Josh's jaw dropped. He didn't know what to say.

Dave was nodding. 'That's right. Half a million quid to get rid of my problem. How does *that* sound?'

Josh thought of Shauna, always pecking his head over the next purchase. This was bad, what Dave was asking of him. The idea of it sickened him. But it would pay better than anything else. Better than anything he'd ever done. It would buy them a house. A future. *Everything*.

'He's already set it up for us,' Dave was saying quickly. 'It would look like a drug deal that's gone wrong.'

Josh was shaking his head. No. He couldn't do this. He *couldn't*.

Could he?

52

Shauna was surprised when Josh said he had to go away for a couple of days, but he gave her fuck-all in the way of detail.

'Where to?' she asked.

'Not far. Got a fight lined up. That's all I'm saying, Shaun.' That's all she got off him these days, the silent treatment. Maybe he was cut up over the news of his mother dying, but she didn't think so. She knew they had been far from close.

'What about the funeral?' she asked.

'I ain't going.'

Josh had given Linus Pole money, more than Shauna thought they could afford, to sort out his mother's burial and headstone. Josh went about the place scowling, and he was making some mysterious purchases. Shauna kept quiet, but she was curious by nature and when he was in the bath she went to the wardrobe where he'd put the latest stash of secrets, and had a look.

The thing – whatever it was – was in a cream gabardine-type bag and when Shauna tried to lift it, it was heavy. There was a drawstring at one end. She pulled it loose, and put her hand in. Felt cold metal. Frowning, she rummaged inside and drew out a big Magnum pistol. She looked at it in astonishment. Then she drew out the other item inside the bag. It was a shotgun, both barrels sawn off. Carefully, she tucked both guns back into the bag, retied the string and closed the wardrobe door.

Later, when Josh came out of the bathroom, she said: 'Josh, it was sad about your mum. Really sad.'

'Yeah.'

'But what we got to do now is, we've got to go on, put our old life behind us. Forget about all that.'

'I know.' Josh thought of Claire and felt his heart wrench in his chest. Yeah, his old life was gone. *She* was gone. So what did anything matter any more, really? He had a job to do, and he was going to do it. Look after his family, even if he *did* still sometimes yearn for what he'd lost.

Next day, Josh kissed his wife and son goodbye, loaded his holdall into the car and then drove away.

His mood was grim. All right, he didn't care about his mother. He never had. But her passing had been a milestone for him. She was his last link with the camp and the life he had lived there. It was all a memory now, gone and forgotten. No . . . not forgotten.

Josh knew he would never, ever forget Claire – and he hoped she was somewhere fine and well and happy. As to his own life, now Shauna was right – he had to go on with it. So he'd phoned Dave Houghton and said he'd do the job. But he insisted he'd pick the time, and the place. Marbella was out. He wanted to do it here, in this country. He wrestled with his conscience over taking the job, but they needed the money, badly. The bills were piling up fast, red bills, and people had started coming to the door demanding payment. And Shauna never let up about the lifestyle she wanted. So it was up to him to provide for his family, to embrace this new life even if it wasn't the one he would have chosen, even if he would have been so much happier back at the campsite, with Claire.

Dave had given him a picture of Andrew Meredith and told him that Andrew had a place down in the New Forest, miles off the beaten track, where he often spent weekends. It should be perfect. Josh studied the photo. Andrew was good-looking. Golden-haired, sleek, tanned and with the prosperous patina of wealth all over him.

Discreetly, Josh sussed out Meredith's place and then parked up well away from it under cover, avoiding the tourist hot spots, the campsites and hotels. He slept in the car overnight and breakfasted on the sandwiches Shauna had cut for him, then watched Andrew take his morning jog and worked out the best spot along the route at which to do it.

He waited out that day and another night, finished up the last of the sandwiches and the last drop of tea in the flask, then took out the holdall. He loaded the sawn-off, and when Andrew came jogging out next morning on to the track through the mist-shrouded scrub and gorse, he followed.

At the chosen point, Andrew paused, hands on knees. Josh could hear him breathing heavily.

'Hey,' said Josh.

Andrew turned, half-smiling. Saw the gun. The smile dropped from his face. 'What . . .' he started.

Josh fired. The sawn-off took most of Andrew Meredith's good-looking head away, and his corpse fell back on to the yellow gorse in a shower of dark blood.

Before Andrew even hit the ground, Josh was gone.

53

'How'd it go then, Josh?' asked Shauna when he came home.

She had the TV news on, and the newscaster was talking in solemn tones about two trains colliding somewhere abroad. Then they started talking about a shooting in the New Forest, the police were looking for leads. He went over and switched it off.

'Yeah, OK,' said Josh. He felt dirty, and sick.

'You won, didn't you?' It was a statement of fact more than a question. With that idiot Cloudy gone out of his life, Josh *always* won. He was king of the gypsy fighters, after all. Looked his opponent square in the face, battled it out like a man.

'Yeah,' he said, and went on upstairs to clean up.

It played on Josh's mind for days afterwards. Knocking someone out in the ring, that was one thing; doing strong-arm stuff on doors in clubs and sorting out bolshy gits in bars, that was OK. But this, blowing somebody's head off, taking their life, that was something else. He found it hard to sleep, and he was off his food. It surprised him. He was tough as old boots, usually.

'What's up with you, Josh?' Shauna asked him on day three. 'You're not right.'

They were having beans on toast at the kitchen table,

and baby Connor was in his high chair throwing most of his food on the floor and up the walls. Normally, this amused Josh no end, but today he was uninterested.

Josh put his knife and fork down and looked at Shauna. He had to talk about this to *someone*, or go mad.

'I've killed someone, Shaun,' he said.

Shauna stared at him. 'You what?'

'I've killed someone,' he repeated.

'What, in the fight you mean?'

'There was no fight.' He felt sick and he looked it, too. He had a gypsy's natural-born toughness; he was never ill. But when he'd looked at himself in the shaving mirror this morning, he'd hardly recognized his own face.

'I don't know what you mean,' she said, worried.

It all poured out of Josh then. About going to Dave for a job cleaning up the club, but it had amounted to much more than that. He told Shauna about Dave's relationship with Andrew, and the trouble that was causing, and that the trouble had to stop – or Philippa was going to crucify Dave in the divorce courts and he was going to be ruined.

'We agreed I'd do the hit,' said Josh finally, while beside them baby Connor gurgled and played with his dinner. Shauna was still as a statue, listening.

'He paid you? How much?'

Josh looked up at his wife and saw the ugly glitter in her eyes: *money*. That was what this meant to her, snatching someone's life away. It meant a pay cheque.

'More than I've ever made before,' he said. 'More than I've ever *seen*.'

'Josh . . .'

'It's upstairs. Under the boards.'

Shauna sprang to her feet and raced up the stairs. Josh grabbed the baby out of his high chair, wiped his chin with the bib, and followed more slowly, carrying Connor with him. When he got to their bedroom, Shauna was on the floor with the carpet pushed back and the board up. There were notes scattered all around her and piles more of them stuffed down in the gap under the floorboards.

'How much?' she gasped, looking up at him, her eyes alight with avarice.

'Five hundred thousand,' said Josh, thinking of Andrew Meredith's head blowing off his body in a meaty red shower.

'It's a fucking fortune!' she said.

'Yeah,' said Josh, and turned and left the room. He went downstairs, put Connor back in the high chair and sat there at the table with his half-eaten plate of beans in front of him. He pushed the plate away. Connor grizzled. Presently Shauna came back down and sat and looked at him.

'You feel bad about it,' she said.

'What do you think?'

She stretched across the table and grabbed his hand. 'Look, Josh. You did a job, that's all.'

'That's *all*?'

She was nodding. 'You did a job, and you're supporting your family with the money you've earned from it.'

'Blood money.'

'Don't look at it like that. We could buy a palace with five hundred grand,' said Shauna, glancing around their modest but ultra-clean kitchen.

'Yeah. I suppose we could.'

Shauna's voice was gentler, softer now. Almost hypnotic. 'We're all just passing through, Josh,' she said. 'Life is short. You didn't do a bad thing because that *man* was bad. He was a problem and you got rid of him. You did what you had to do.'

'Yeah,' Josh sighed. 'I suppose you're right.'

But deep down, he didn't believe it. What he *did* believe

195

was this: that the better part of him had died the night he lost Claire. And now? He didn't even know himself. Not any more.

54

'Happy then, Shaun?' Josh asked his wife.

It was two full years since Josh had fought Matty O'Connor. Two years since he'd lost Claire. Shauna had every reason to be happy, Josh thought. He'd bought this place in Henley-on-Thames, not a quarter of a mile from where Dave and Philippa Houghton lived, with a chunk of the money from the shooting. Cash on the table. The view from all the rear-facing windows was nearly identical to the view Dave and Philippa enjoyed.

Of course there was a small risk of flooding, the estate agent had been straight with them about that, but like Dave and Philippa's place the house itself stood up on a slight slope, so it was safe enough. The agent said that it certainly wasn't enough of a risk to deter anyone from buying such a beautiful house.

The place had everything. An indoor swimming pool. A gym for his training. Six bedrooms, four bathrooms, a kitchen you could play a game of cricket in and a lounge as big as a barn. It wasn't exactly *homely*, but Shauna was made up with it and had been eating into the money again as she furnished the place as grandly as she liked. Christ, she liked the high life, his wife. Before long they had interior designers poncing around the place as Shauna's vision of how they should be living took shape. All she ever seemed to do these days was thumb through copies of *Homes & Gardens*, exclaiming over sofas and footstools and all that shit, then poring over swatches of fabric and carpets.

Oh, and when their anniversary rolled round, Shauna made a huge fuss about it. He wished she wouldn't. For him, truthfully? It was just another year gone, with the wrong woman beside him.

Money was no object now; the sky was the limit. Since the big payout for solving Dave's problem, he hadn't done any more work of that sort. He didn't want to. Shauna had got a blond mink coat out of it and strutted around the bedroom wearing that and nothing else, a big grin on her face. But Josh felt sick to see it – luxury, bought with dirty money. He'd disposed of the sawn-off out in the Solent, tossing it into the waves from a mate's fishing boat, but he'd kept the other *yogger*, the Magnum, taped it ready-loaded to the inside of the wardrobe in their bedroom, for security. For himself, he'd rather fight an army hand-to-hand than fire a gun at them, but he had Shauna and the baby to think of.

Not yogger, he mentally corrected himself. *Gun.*

Shauna would rip him an extra arsehole if she heard him calling the gun that. But he missed the old language. Missed the old ways. And he knew that he'd trade all this grandeur, in the blink of an eye, for that brand-new van he'd bought for him and Claire to live in. He'd happily exchange all the posh dinner parties with their stuck-up neighbours for a single evening by the camp fire, cooking game caught fresh that day over an open flame while one of the old timers played a tune on the mouth organ.

Ah, shit. What was the use of even thinking about it?

Linus Pole's boys had solved the drugs issue in Dave Houghton's club and things were returning to normal there. As for Josh, he kept fighting, people coming at him with challenges at Linus's fairground, big bets being laid, and so he was quids in. He never lost. It didn't even enter his head that he ever would.

55

Months passed and still Josh suffered bad dreams over Andrew Meredith's death. He couldn't seem to shake off the night-time horrors. He would wake sweating, guilt scorching through him like molten lava. He'd killed a man for the worst of reasons – to get money to keep Shauna happy and their heads above water. He was cursed, bound for hell. He hadn't even had the decency to attend his own mother's funeral. And he should have. He knew that.

Without telling Shauna, he drove off one day and headed down to Winchester, to the big church where the gypsy graves were. Alone, he walked among the gorgi gravestones, the grey ones, the plain ones, until he reached the corner where his own kind was buried.

You couldn't miss it.

Gypsy families always paid out a fortune on honouring their dead. All the headstones here were lavish in the extreme; bigger, taller, carved out of black granite and with the names of the deceased etched in gold. Intricate carvings of horses and lurchers had been fashioned all around each loved one's name.

The flowers on each and every grave, although artificial, were replaced without fail every year with new ones, so the sun never bleached out their vivid colours of scarlet, turquoise, green, yellow or bright orange. All the gypsy families – Shauna's lot, the Everetts, Claire's kin, the Milos, and his own, the Flynns – were clustered together here, all the plots paid for, reserved. His own included. Mum had told him that once, long ago, when she wasn't off her head on the gin. She had been laid to rest here, beside his bully of a father. And one day Josh would rest right beside them.

He steeled himself and walked further, going in among the Flynn graves. Granny Flynn was there, and Grandpa, and their parents too; all his own kin – or jeal, in the old language of Cant. There was Dad, the old bugger. And there . . . oh Christ, there was his mother's grave. The stone he'd paid for was up. Josh looked at it and his eyes filled with tears as he thought of her miserable life and sorry end.

HERE LIES MONICA DELILAH FLYNN
MUCH LOVED WIFE AND MOTHER

He couldn't read any more, he couldn't even *see*. He stood there before his mother's fabulously carved headstone, with two rearing horses carved into the granite. Both the magnificent headstone and the big cluster of emerald-green fake carnations in the urn went out of focus as he cried. He cried for her and for his own life too, irretrievably ruined when he'd lost the girl he loved.

Then he became aware of someone standing right behind him.

He turned, half-blinded by tears and the low, stabbing sunlight, and squinted at them. Couldn't see them. It was the truth: he'd lost the girl he'd loved best in the world. Shauna would never compare with Claire. Much as he tried with her, and respected her because she was the mother of his child, he knew that she would never compare. *Never.*

'Fuck it,' said a sharp female voice. 'It's you.'

Josh blinked. And then he realized the person standing there was Trace Milo, Claire's sister.

56

'What the fuck are you doing here?' said Josh, swiping at his tears with embarrassment.

Blinking, he looked at Trace. Her mid-brown hair was tinted an unflattering pinky-auburn. Trace's expression had always been hard, and her eyes right now were blank of anything but hatred. She was wearing flared stonewash jeans and a black anorak trimmed with grey fur around the hood. She stood there and stared angrily at him, arms folded around herself for warmth as a biting wind whistled through the graveyard.

'You got some fucking balls, asking me what I'm doing here.' Her lips curved in a bitter smile. 'What about *you*, arsehole? What you doing here?'

'Visiting Mum,' said Josh.

'You left that a bit late.' Trace's voice was harsh. 'You didn't even attend her bloody funeral, did you? I come here every week. *Every fucking week.* And I've never once seen you here before. Couldn't be bothered, I suppose. Moved up in the world, aintcha.'

Josh couldn't say a thing to that. He *hadn't* come here as he should. He knew he should have visited, paid his respects. But the fact was, he *had* no respect for his mother. She should have protected him from his father, but instead she had stood by and watched. Only today had he been able to face coming to her grave. Now he felt wrecked and was wishing he hadn't.

'You visiting your folks then?' Josh nodded to where the Milo plots were.

'Yeah. That's what decent people do,' she said. Her eyes held his. 'She never came back, our Claire. Never got in touch, either.'

'I'm sorry.'

'Oh, you care, do you?' she sniffed.

'I looked for her. Went to Ireland. You know I did. I searched. But she wasn't there. You haven't had a letter? Nothing?'

'Not a fucking thing. Mum's never got over it, you know. She still clutches on to that fucking great wedding dress that Claire should have worn. Won't get rid of it. Shouts at Dad that they should have gone on with the search, they should have kept the muskras involved.'

Josh shook his head. 'Wherever she is, she don't want to be found. She's cut all ties, that much is clear.'

'Pretty damned clear you have too. Dad told me about finding you with that bitch Shauna Everett.'

Josh sighed. 'She ain't Shauna Everett no more. She's my wife. We've got a son.'

Trace was silent for a long moment. 'You poor bastard,' she said at last. 'I wouldn't wish *that* cow on anyone. But maybe you deserve her. Dad reckons it was that made Claire run off. You and that fucking Everett bitch.'

'Shut up, Trace.'

'What, truth hurts, does it?'

'It's *not* the truth. Me and Shauna happened after me and Claire split up, not before.'

'Yeah? Bollocks!' She stared at him with contempt. 'The pair of you? You fucking well *deserve* one another.'

As she moved away from his mum's graveside and stalked, her words echoed in his head and he couldn't shake them out of it.

57

Josh went on with his life, doing more and more lucrative fights, throwing challenges down and having them accepted, pulverizing every opponent who came at him. He won and won and won, but . . .

Claire was still missing. She'd never gone home.

As Shauna slept peacefully beside him, sometimes he would lie there in the dark and churn it all over. That fight with Matty O'Connor, and his *insane* insistence that Claire – gentle, caring Claire – should be there to see it. A night that should have been a triumph, and it was a total disaster. And then denying her the big wedding she wanted.

Stupid, stupid, stupid!

God, he'd loved her so much, and losing her had been like losing a part of himself.

He loved her still.

Shit, wasn't that the truth? He might have taken off with Shauna, he might be *married* to Shauna. As if she would ever let him forget it with all the anniversary bullcrap she insisted on. But he was still in love with Claire and that was his tragedy. Because she was gone and it was over. And he had a kid, now: he couldn't let his boy down.

He was too far along with *this* life to ever try to go back again and pick up the threads of *that* one.

Sometimes he dreamed of Claire running ahead of him

through meadows buzzing with bees and thick with wild flowers. Her blonde hair was bouncing like a beautiful banner of gold silk behind her. Her face was turning back toward him, a smile on her lips, her blue eyes alight with mischief, her laughter drifting to him on a warm summer breeze.

Catch me, Josh. Come on! Catch me.

But he never did.

And now he knew he never would.

58

Shauna opened the door one lunchtime, expecting the woman who would fit the blinds in her and Josh's bedroom, and found Jeb Cleaver standing there again. She thought maybe he'd got the message at last. But he bloody hadn't.

'What the *fuck*?' she asked, hand to her chest. 'Damn, you startled me.'

'Did I?' He was watching her with those dark steady eyes, lounging against her porch wall like he had all day for this.

'I'm expecting someone,' she said, hoping he'd clear off. 'Look, Jeb . . .' Shauna was looking past him. His shabby mud-spattered pickup was there, parked on her pristine driveway. She looked at his grimy old mac and workman's boots and suppressed a shudder.

'Yeah? Something you want to say to me, Shauna?'

She swallowed and said: 'Jeb, this ain't working. You coming here. We've had fun in our time, but now it's over. Truth is, I don't want to see you or the other boys around here.'

'Oh, you don't?' He was staring at her, holding her gaze. Shauna dropped her eyes first.

'No, I don't.' She felt a surge of anger. They'd *served* their purpose, the Cleavers. Now all she wanted was to cut loose.

'Suppose I want different?' Jeb said, and stepped forward and pinned Shauna against the wall. She couldn't move.

'Let go of me,' she said, her heart racing in her chest.

'Let *go*?' Jeb stared down into her face. 'You don't usually say that, gal. You're usually up for all sorts.'

'Well I'm not any more,' snapped Shauna. 'Look. I've got a husband now, a child. And I've . . . I've got a position to think of around here.'

'A position?' He let her go and grinned at that. 'Yeah, I know what *position* you like.'

'Look,' said Shauna, stung by his mirth. She was a member of the tennis club now, and active in local charities. She was doing stuff that counted, and people looked up to her for it. 'We're respectable people these days, me and Josh. And you? You fucking Cleavers? You're just like dogs after a bitch in heat, the lot of you.'

Jeb's grin dropped away. 'You think that, do you?'

Shauna nodded, holding his gaze with an effort. 'Yeah. I do. So leave me alone, will you? Just *piss off*.'

59

'The girls have invited me over,' said Shauna one morning at breakfast.

Josh looked up dully. Here he was with this stunning woman, his wife, and still he was dreaming night after night about a girl he'd lost, his first love. He straightened, poured more coffee. He'd wanted to tell her about visiting Mum's grave back in February and his talk with Trace, but he knew she'd get prune-faced and angry about it. She hated any mention of their old life. Baby Connor was sitting there, sprinkling the tablecloth and the floor with food. Then Connor bashed himself in the eye with a piece of toast and he let out a wail.

'What you done, you little jotter?' said Josh, not thinking, using the Romany word for 'monkey'. He scooped his son up in his arms.

'Don't be filling his head with all that old bollocks,' said Shauna.

'Ah, it don't hurt,' said Josh, smiling at the baby, rocking him.

'Yes it fucking does. I've told you.' She glared at him and then turned her head and yelled: 'Marta! Where the fuck is she . . . ?' Shauna leapt to her feet. 'Marta!' she bellowed again.

Now they had an au pair. A fucking *au pair*, thought

Josh, and not two or three years since they'd been living in trailers. Marta came clomping down the stairs. She was a big hearty Nordic blonde – not his type at all. Claire had been slight, dainty.

Fuck it! Got to stop thinking about her. This is my life now. This is the woman I chose.

He watched Shauna offload Connor on to Marta, who took him down into the play room and shut the door behind the howling noise of him.

'What girls?' he asked her when they were alone.

'The *girls*.' Shauna's dark eyes danced with excitement. 'You know Tanya, she asked if I'd be interested in doing the round-robin dinner parties? Well, her, and Chloe next door, and Philippa. These are the people we should be mixing with, Josh, and Tanya's invited me over for lunch with the girls tomorrow.'

His gypsy wife was becoming a lady who lunched. She was putting on an affected voice – when she remembered – and sounding her Hs. He found it false, stupid and wearing. Well, if it kept her happy. But one of those names had given him a jolt.

'Philippa? Not the same Philippa who's Dave Houghton's missus? But you hated her guts.'

'If she's willing to forget all that, then so am I.'

Josh looked at her sceptically. Shauna never forgot *anything*. And he didn't like Shauna getting up close and personal with Phil again. He'd actually been *pleased* they'd clashed when they first met, because it meant they wouldn't meet up, wouldn't talk. Now Shauna was going to be sitting across the lunch table from Philippa, and Shauna knew all about Dave and his little problem with the late Andrew Meredith, and that Josh had supplied the solution.

'Shaun, you know you've got to keep your gob shut, don't you? About . . .'

'About that?' Shauna lowered her voice. 'I know. You don't have to *tell* me. I'm not stupid.'

'All right then.' He wasn't happy, but then what else was new? Shit, he'd forgotten what happiness *was*. So what the hell. Who cared what she got up to? He'd be in Oxford tomorrow anyway, knocking the crap out of his latest opponent.

Shauna dressed very carefully for her lunch date. It was still warm so no doubt the girls would be eating outside on Tanya's patio. She selected her most expensive couture day dress, a beautiful short-sleeved shift in brilliant pillar-box red silk that suited her tanned skin and dark hair and eyes. She added strappy high-heeled sandals, red lipstick and lots of black mascara.

Then she looked at herself in the full-length cheval mirror in the master bedroom, turning, assessing. Yes, she was a bloody good-looking woman still, even if she was a mother. Men still showed an interest in her, but she didn't want anyone but Josh. This was the life she wanted now – prosperous, *decent*. Mixing with people with a bit of class about them. She loved it.

She frowned, thinking of her last encounter with Jeb. She had spelled it out for him this time, made her feelings completely plain. All that she'd been through growing up in the camp, and her doings with the Cleavers – she didn't want to think about that any more. And now Jeb had accepted that – it was weeks since he'd come sniffing around for the second time – life was going the way she wanted it.

But does Josh really want you? asked that tiny, niggly voice in her brain.

Yes. He wanted her. Sometimes. Not so often now. In the blackness of night, he wanted her and had her. There was wanting, the physical stuff, and there was needing, though. Did Josh need her? Did he crave her when they were apart? Did he truly, deeply, crazily *love* her?

Sometimes she caught him looking at her as if at a stranger. So did he love her? She lied to herself, told herself that of *course* he did, she'd given him a son; they were a family now.

60

Dressed and ready, Shauna kissed Connor goodbye and told Marta to take good care of him. She'd passed her test first time, so now she had a cute pale-blue BMW sports job to ride around in. She drove over to Tanya's, which was just down the end of the road but she wanted to make an entrance, to arrive in style in case any of the other girls should be at the front just parking up.

Disappointingly, they weren't, but there was a raft of other expensive sports numbers out on the drive. Shauna rang the bell and it was answered not by Tanya but by an unknown young white woman dressed in black.

'Hi,' said Shauna brightly. 'I'm Shauna Flynn. Tanya's expecting me.'

The maid opened the door wide and ushered her through the vast sprawling house.

'Mrs Prescott and her friends are on the terrace,' said the maid as she walked.

Terrace, thought Shauna. *Not patio.*

Another lesson learned. And why the fuck, if Josh was making so much dough these days, didn't *they* have a maid? Not that she'd entirely trust a maid to do the cleaning properly, of course.

Shauna fastened a broad smile on her face as she was shown out to where Tanya, Philippa and Chloe were seated around a marble table beneath the shade of a vast cream parasol. The patio – the *terrace* – overlooked the lawn, just like hers and Josh's did, just like Philippa and Dave's too, just like Chloe and Mike's. It ran on down to the river, which today glittered calmly, like a jewel in the hot sunlight. Last weekend the rain had come and the river had run fast. It had darkened and swollen and swished up over the lawns. Ten feet, then twenty. But then the sun had come out and the waters had receded again.

Now, the setting was idyllic. Perfect. But as she walked in, Shauna saw Philippa's lips tighten into a thin line. They hadn't met in quite a while, but straight away Shauna felt her hackles rise at the sight of the woman.

'Mrs Flynn,' said the maid, and pulled out a chair for her.

Shauna sat down directly opposite Philippa, Tanya on her left, Chloe on her right.

'You know Philippa?' Tanya asked her. She was a chirpy little brunette.

'Yes. We've met,' said Shauna, exchanging fake smiles with her beautiful blonde arch enemy.

'And of course you know Chloe, don't you,' said Tanya, pointing out the woman with the auburn bob.

'Hi, Shauna,' said Chloe with the languid drawling delivery of the comfortably wealthy.

'Of course I know Chloe, we're right next door to each other,' said Shauna, smiling even though Chloe never seemed that friendly. She never waved back when Shauna saw her out on the drive and waved to her. No borrowing cups of sugar off *this* lady.

The maid brought a starter – Caesar salad – and the girls started to eat as Tanya chattered on. Philippa was silent, sipping her wine, sending spiked looks across the table at Shauna.

'What we do is this,' said Tanya as the maid cleared away the plates and brought out the main course – thin slices of beef in a watery sauce, with minuscule portions of undercooked greasy carrots and broccoli. 'We go to, say, Phil's house, and she does the starter, then to Chloe's for the main, and, say, to yours for pudding. The husbands come too, of course. It makes a lovely evening.'

Shauna could just picture Josh in with this lot, he'd be like a roaring lion among a herd of timid gazelles. Spoiled, over-privileged women and their husbands, a bunch of air-conditioned arseholes who sat behind a desk all day, pushing pens on paper or shouting *buy buy buy*. Those men weren't *physical*, like Josh. They couldn't lift hay bales or lay a ton of tarmac in the burning heat of summer, or bench-press their own body weight down the gym like he could. You might as well cut their hands off, because they only ever used them to get their dicks out.

'It sounds great,' she lied. It was hot out here in the late Indian summer, and despite the parasol's shade she felt a bit sick, a bit queasy.

'Of course, Shauna's pretty new to all this,' said Philippa. 'Aren't you, Shauna?'

Shauna looked directly into Philippa's enormous blue eyes. *Oh really? You starting this again?*

'Meaning?' said Shauna, as the maid cleared away the remnants of their meal. No pudding this time; all the girls were watching their weight, particularly Chloe, who had pushed her food around the plate while drinking a bit too much.

'Oh, nothing. Just that maybe this is all a little too *civilized* for you, really.'

'Phil—' started Tanya.

'Tanya doesn't know your background, of course. Not like I do.'

Shauna looked at Tanya, then at Chloe. She thought of Josh, blowing Andrew Meredith's head off his shoulders at Philippa's husband's request. She was crazy-mad with that high-toned bitch across the table, but she was going to have to rein it in, be careful. 'I'm a gypsy,' she said. 'My husband's a bare-knuckle fighter,' she told Tanya. 'I think Chloe already knows that.'

'Oh yah. Sure,' said Chloe, her elbow slipping from the tabletop.

'Just thought you ought to *know*, Tanya,' said Philippa, her eyes glittering with malice as she smiled across at Shauna.

Shauna guessed that she wasn't going to be included in Tanya's round-robin dinner parties after all. She'd seen the shocked and – yes – disgusted look on Tanya's face. While Tanya walked out to Chloe's Porsche with her, there was a moment in which Shauna was alone in the hall with Philippa. The maid was in the kitchen, washing dishes. Shauna looked left and right, then she shoved Philippa up against the wall so hard that the blonde's head banged into the plasterwork. Philippa let out a cry. Shauna glared with feral hatred into the woman's shocked eyes.

'What the f—' gasped out Philippa.

'What the fuck is *this*, you cow. I know things about your family, your *husband*, that you wouldn't want repeated. I *know* things that would make these tarts shun you like a leper. So watch your fucking mouth or I promise you, you'll be getting all those expensive pearly-whites of yours back in an ashtray – and *then* I'll fill the "girls" in on all the grisly details about dear sweet Dave and the company he likes to keep.'

'I don't know what you're talking about,' said Philippa, but she looked shaken.

'No. You don't, do you. Ignorance is bliss. So keep that poisonous mouth of yours shut, or you'll be opening a can of worms you'll wish you hadn't.'

Shauna let Philippa go, turned and walked out to the BMW. 'Bye then, Tanya. Bye, Chloe,' she called warmly, and got into the car with her hands still trembling with rage and her guts knotted with tension.

That *bitch*.

Shauna knew she was going to have to work very hard with Tanya and Chloe to repair the damage done today. Well, she'd warned Phil now. But she was *furious*. Maybe a warning wasn't enough. So when she got home, she phoned the Cleaver farm.

61

'What the fuck's up with you then?' asked Bill Cleaver when he came out of the kitchen door and found Jeb standing outside, staring moodily into space.

One of their dogs, a big black Boxer, came sniffing around his leg and Jeb booted it. The dog cried out and slunk away.

'Nothing,' he said.

'Face on you like a cow's arse,' said Bill, picking up his stick.

'I told you, it's nothing.'

'You're not still mooning around over that Shauna bloody Everett, are you? Or Shauna *Flynn* as she styles herself these days. Christ, she's been gone over three years now – what the fuck's wrong with you?'

Jeb eyed his father beadily. The old fart would get a thump around the head if he wasn't careful. Yeah, Bill ruled the roost here, but Jeb was big enough now to give the cunt a pasting, and he *would*.

'Bitch thinks she's free of us all,' sniffed Jeb. 'Lording it in a big house with that Flynn git, she don't want to know her old pals any more. She's made that damned plain.'

It hurt him. He could scarcely credit it, but it *did*. He was soft on the bitch. And that – his own weakness for her – made him angrier still. Now she'd been on the phone to him, asking him to do a job on one of her snooty pals. She was using him. Keeping things on *her* terms.

'That's harsh,' said Bill.

'Harsh? It's out of the fucking question. She *owes* us. If it weren't for us, she wouldn't have Flynn. She'd still be wiping her arse with dock leaves back in the camp, and the Milo bitch would've had him. But is that cow grateful? She is not.'

'Damned right,' said Bill.

The back door swung open and Ciaran came out, followed by Rowan.

'What's this? Family conference?' asked Ciaran, looking from Bill to Jeb. He was the eldest son; he had to be included in everything.

Jeb looked at Ciaran with stark dislike. *Big-headed bastard*, he thought.

'Jeb's telling me the Everett girl's cooled on him,' said Bill with a black-toothed grin. 'And you two as well, I guess.'

'Well fuck it, I say,' Ciaran said. 'That one was always going to move on and up. I knew it the first moment I set eyes on her. She got that hungry look. The look that says, OK, this'll do for now, but soon? You can kiss my arse 'cos I'll be *gone*.'

Jeb looked sullen. 'Best fuck I ever had,' he said.

'And me,' said Rowan.

'Shit, *all* of us,' said Ciaran, and Rowan snickered. Even Bill raised a grin.

'It ain't funny,' said Jeb. 'All the stuff we done for that bitch. Now she's on at me to do *more* stuff, when not five minutes ago she's shouting in my face, telling me to sod off.'

Rowan held up his hands in a gesture of surrender. His younger brother was literally *steaming* with rage.

'You want a little advice from your old dad?' asked Bill.

'No. But go the fuck on anyway,' said Jeb.

'Who's making the rules here?' asked Bill, looking around at his sons in disgust. 'Her, or you? Listen. OK. Girl owes you. She owes us all, good fuck or no. Now she thinks she's too good for us?'

'So what do we do?' asked Jeb.

'Teach her a lesson. Bring her *smack* back down to earth. Let her know who's in charge here.'

'Yeah, fine. Suggestions?' said Ciaran, shoving Rowan as he continued to laugh.

'Woulda thought that was damned obvious,' said Bill. 'Way I see it, *he's* the problem. Josh Flynn. She's taken up with him and he's earning big and it's turned her head. Right round.'

'So?'

'So get rid of the son of a bitch. Hand him his arse cooked on a dinner plate. And then? Coast is clear. Do what you want with her.'

There was a loud silence as the three Cleaver boys looked at each other. Then Ciaran nodded.

'We'll do it,' said Ciaran. He looked at Rowan. Rowan was always his wingman, they worked well together. Jeb was too hot-headed to be relied upon in a tight situation, and it was clear his judgement was off where the Everett girl was concerned. He put a heavy hand on Jeb's shoulder. He was the eldest, he'd sort it out. 'I never did like that cunt Josh Flynn. Me and Rowan. It'll be a piece of piss. We'll set this right, Jeb. Don't you fret.'

'I'll do the job for her, the one she's phoned about,' said Jeb, brightening. 'That way she won't suspect a thing. Come as a big shock to her when Josh Flynn gets his, and serve the bitch right.'

'That's the ticket,' said Bill, and smiled.

62

The illegal bout in Oxford was set up in a big room where wedding receptions and wakes were held, over a public bar. People shoved back the chairs and laid their bets and soon a huge crowd gathered around the edges of the room. Josh faced a big blond-haired man called Don Swatley. He had a broken nose and KILLER tattooed across his huge hairy chest. The referee hit a copper pan with a ladle, and they were off.

The blond came in with a left, and then another, whacking Josh back a step. No one had told Josh the man was also a southpaw. This made things tricky from a defensive viewpoint. Josh flicked back a couple of staccato hard rights, then a piston-hard left flick. But the blond swiped in left-handed again, cracking Josh on the ear so that his head rung like a bell. Josh felt sticky blood flowing there, and thought *better wrap this up quick*.

The man was more powerful than Josh had expected. Supremely self-confident in his strength and ability, Josh realized he'd become too cocky for his own good. He turned up the heat as the crowd roared louder and louder, throwing out a flurry of vicious lefts to the ribs until the man's guard dropped. Then he went in further, pulverizing him until he started to weave and sag. A sharp hit to the temple sent the blond crashing to the floor.

The ref stepped forward and counted to ten. The blond didn't get up. So the ref lifted Josh's arm in the air and declared Fearless Flynn the winner. Josh stood there, sweat-stained and blood-soaked, and grinned around at the crowd in triumph. And it was then that he saw someone moving at the back of the room, someone he recognized.

63

After he'd washed up and claimed his winnings, Josh grabbed his sports bag and went downstairs, looking again for that familiar face. And Rowan Cleaver was right there, drinking scrumpy at the bar. Josh elbowed his way through the crush until he reached him.

'Thought it was you,' he said.

'Yeah, s'me all right, Josh Flynn,' said Rowan, grinning, and Josh thought that he'd had more than a couple of pints of that stuff, and it was strong.

'Surprised you came all the way up here for this,' said Josh, thinking of ordering a drink for himself and then thinking better of it.

Rowan was a giggling arsehole but he could also be a Trojan horse; the other Cleaver boys could be out in the car park, waiting to set upon Josh. Maybe they *did* still bear a grudge against him for stepping out from Cloudy's shadow. Who knew? So it was best to keep a clear head. It was the Cleavers who had always benefited hugely from Cloudy's insistence that Josh be the fall guy, so it was wise to be watchful.

'How's that sexy missus of yours?' asked Rowan, slapping Josh on the shoulder. 'Mrs Flynn now, eh? What a turn-up.'

'What?' Josh was wrong-footed. How the hell did

Rowan know him and Shauna were married? Granted, Pally might have gone back home and announced Shauna's pregnancy to all and sundry, but *marriage*? How could they know about that?

'Your missus! Shauna Everett who was. You got a family and everything I hear.'

'How did you hear that?' They knew about the baby too. This was odd. And worrying.

'Ah, ol' Jeb likes to keep in touch with her even now. Does little jobs for her – well, he did one just this week. Christ knows they been bedmates for years.' Rowan chuckled. It was an ugly sound. 'Although she told him to piss off the last time he called on her. That offended him. He was *hurt*. He got feelings, like everyone else. *Deep* feelings. So he spoke to the rest of us and we decided Ciaran and me, we'd meet up at yours and have a chat.'

'What the hell are you talking about?' Josh felt like his brain was spinning. Jesus! Shauna had been communicating with the Cleavers? With Jeb? *Bedmates?* This was crazy!

'Don't go thinkin' that we minded you winnin' that fight against Matty O'Connor,' said Rowan, calling to the barman for another. 'Shauna set us straight on that. She heard you and that cute Milo girl talking about it and she came and told us. So we made a *mint* on that fight.'

'Go on,' said Josh, trying to take this all in. Shauna. Back in the camp, she'd been listening in when he spoke to Claire about the match. And since then? She'd been meeting up with this fucking rabble.

The next pint of scrumpy arrived and Rowan supped it thirstily.

'You know what?' said Rowan, clapping him on the shoulder again.

'No. What?'

'Your missus was the best fuck any of us had ever had. Phew! What a girl. But God she was wicked. She didn't tell you any of this, did she? No, I can see from your face that she didn't. It was *her* who made sure Claire Milo cleared off. She asked us to put the shits up sweet little Claire, and Ciaran and Jeb did. Good and proper. Girl ran off. Did the dog, while we were at it. Put that fucker in the grave in that little church down near the camp, you know the one?'

Josh felt as if he was dreaming.

Rowan was saying that Shauna had been behind Claire going. Shauna had used the Cleavers to get rid of Claire, and she had been seeing Jeb since . . . for what? He couldn't even imagine. Visions of Shauna romping in *his bed* with Jeb Cleaver shot into his brain. His whole world seemed to spin on its axis then. This was *his wife* Rowan was talking about. The woman he should be closest to in the whole world. Yes, he was aware that Shauna had been wild in her youth. But *this* . . .

'What do you mean, a chat?' he said, his mouth dry as dust. 'What the fuck you talking about?'

'Jeb's been sweet on your girl for years. And she's liked it that way, know what I mean?' Rowan winked. 'Can't be doin' with people choppin' and changin' that way, our Jeb, and he's right,' said Rowan, taking a gulp of scrumpy and belching loudly. 'Loyalty's what counts in this world. Your Shauna, she thinks she can move on up and get rid of ol' Jeb, shake him off like a hound shakin' off a flea? She can think again.'

Josh thought of Shauna, back at the house.

We're going to yours . . .

He thought of baby Connor, the light of his life.

'Where's the bogs here?' he said to Rowan.

Rowan was draining his pint while pointing to the left of the bar. 'But don't you go wanderin' off now. You an' me, we're goin' to meet up with old Ciaran at your place and then your good lady is going to be *told* once and for all that she can't fuck with us Cleavers and get away with it.'

There was going to be blood. Drunk though Rowan was, Josh could see it, could feel it in the prickling of his skin, in a heightened state of awareness that was so much a part of his life as a boxer. Connor was there at home with his mother, unprotected. In danger. The rest of it, about Shauna? He couldn't think of that now. Later – if he was able – he would address that, make sense of it. But not now.

With every pulse in his body beating a sick tattoo, he hurried off in the direction of the men's toilets. When he was out of sight of Rowan, he surged off through the crowds and found a door that led through to a red-furnished snug. He went straight through there to the outer door and almost fell out into the night, glancing around him at the dimly lit car park. But there was no ambush. Not yet, anyway. He looked over to where his car was parked and half-started toward it, but then stopped. If they were so familiar with his wife, then they must know his car. Rowan could have fiddled with the brakes, done anything.

Christ! What to do?

Then a man came out of the snug door and Josh knew.

64

Josh left his car there in Oxford and bummed a lift from the punter who'd come out from the snug. The man chattered all the way to Josh's door, but Josh didn't hear a word.

'Look, shut your yap, will you?' said Josh when they neared his house.

All he could think was that Shauna was at home with Connor. Ciaran could already be there. And Rowan would have realized he'd been given the slip and would probably arrive soon, too. Christ knew what had been going on with Shauna and those arseholes, and right now he didn't even give a shit, he'd sort that out later, but *Connor* . . .

The man sent Josh a hurt glance. 'I'm doing you a favour here mate. I'm five miles out of my way.'

Josh looked at him. 'Sorry. But my head's throbbing like a bastard. You got any tools in this car?'

'Why d'you ask?' They were at the end of Josh's road now.

'Stop here, will you? That's close enough. I just want to borrow a spanner or something, that's all.'

Now the man was looking at Josh like he was mad. 'I got some stuff in the back,' he said.

'Good.' They got out, went round to the boot. Josh looked in the toolbox there and wished for the Magnum that was inside the house, out of reach. He selected the biggest monkey wrench, hefted it. It would have to do. 'Thanks, mate,' he said and trotted off into the darkness.

'I'll want that back,' the man said.

Josh ignored him. He ran on.

Shauna was passing through the hall to go upstairs and see to Connor because he was crying. Someone was leaning on the doorbell. Yanking the door open, she was ready to give whoever it was a piece of her mind. Some silly git out late selling door-to-door, probably. But the sight of Ciaran – huge and unkempt and standing there with one milk-white blind eye and one mean blue good one, a scruffy beard and – oh shit! – a shotgun pointing straight at her head was enough to make her heart turn right over.

'Christ!' she yelped.

'Hello, Shauna gal. Nice place,' he said, stepping over the threshold and into the hall, leaving the door open behind him.

'What the fuck do you want?' she said, backing up, rigid with fear.

'Just waiting for Josh to come home, that's all,' he said.

'You'll have a bloody long wait. He's out of the country.' Her voice shook.

Ciaran shook his head, almost smiling at that. 'Nah, he's up the road in Oxford. Rowan's up there keepin' an eye on him. Thought I'd come down here and then we'll both have a word with you.'

'We?' echoed Shauna, mesmerized by the gun.

'Yeah, me and Rowan.'

'Why do you need a gun, just for talking?' She couldn't look away from it. No one had ever pointed a gun at her before. It was terrifying.

'Well, it's a *serious* sort of talk,' said Ciaran.

Christ, what am I going to do? wondered Shauna. She

could feel the blood pounding through her veins. The baby was still shrieking upstairs. 'I have to go up to him. The baby. He's crying.'

'Let him cry. Let's go along the hall here.'

Shauna gulped down a breath. Tried to think straight. 'No,' she said. 'I have to see to the baby. Come on! What harm can it do?'

For a long time it looked like Ciaran was going to over-rule her. But then he nodded. 'Right then. But I'm coming up with you.'

Shauna turned and headed up the stairs, hearing Ciaran's heavy tread right behind her. If she turned, suddenly . . . but no, he could shoot her, maim her horribly. She couldn't take the risk. Up in the nursery, she hurried across to Connor, who was yelling fit to burst now.

'All right, honey, all right . . .' she crooned, as Ciaran loomed there, ugly and threatening.

Her legs shaking beneath her, Shauna went back to the door.

'Hold up.' Ciaran put the gun's barrels against her chest. She could feel the cold metal burning her skin through her thin top. She shuddered. 'Where you going?' he asked.

Shauna was finding it hard to breathe. 'The . . . the nappies, they're in the next room, I won't be a sec,' she said.

Ciaran didn't move. He was staring unblinkingly at her face. Then slowly he turned the gun aside.

Heart beating furiously, Shauna went out of the nursery and into the bedroom she shared with Josh. Aware of Ciaran following her, she went over to the wardrobe and made a great show of rummaging around in the bottom of it. Then she heard movement downstairs. She froze, looked back at Ciaran.

'That'll be Rowan, coming in ready for our talk with your old man,' he said, smirking.

Terror gripped her then. They were going to hurt Josh. She'd blown Jeb out and all her apologies after he'd sorted out that mouthy bitch Phil had fallen on deaf ears. This was the result. This was Jeb's revenge. Connor was still howling, screaming. The sound galvanized her, made her sharpen up. Made her quash the panic that was threatening to overwhelm her. Made her start to *think*.

They'll kill Josh and then they'll rape me, she thought. And Connor. Christ! Would they hurt Connor?

'Hurry it up,' said Ciaran.

'All right,' she snapped back, and then inside the wardrobe her groping hand found what she was searching for. She touched the end of the tape, yanked it back, flicked off the safety catch and turned with the ready-loaded Magnum in her hand. Ciaran's face froze and he started to raise the shotgun.

But Shauna fired first.

65

When Josh reached his driveway, he saw a dirty old pickup truck parked in the road outside, and that chilled him, creased his guts with anxiety. Silently he went up the drive. All the lights were on in the house, but he could hear no sounds coming from inside.

Shauna was in there with little Connor, the apple of his eye, already the spitting image of his dad. Not the au pair, she was off visiting relatives this week, thank God.

He passed the front door and went on round the back. He had the key. Going by the windows, he peered in through the film of net curtains and saw no movement inside, nothing. The TV was on in the living room, but there was no one in there and he couldn't hear the sound except . . . shit! That was Connor, crying. Josh walked on until he was at the back door, which led straight into the kitchen.

Quietly, his hand unsteady, he put the key in the lock and opened the door. Peeked inside. It was all lit up, but there was nothing, no movement. He stepped inside, turned right – and found himself staring straight down the twin barrels of a twelve-bore shotgun.

'Hello again, Josh Flynn,' said Rowan Cleaver with a drunken grin. 'Beat you back, didn't I.'

Rowan was standing in the doorway that led into the

hall, and he was so wide that he nearly filled it. Despite that big shit-eating grin he always wore, Rowan's manner, his stance, was terrifying. He was mildly drunk, yes – but still dangerous.

'Yeah,' said Josh with every appearance of calm, holding a monkey wrench in one hand and a sports bag in the other. *Where is Shauna?*

He could hear movement upstairs. Floorboards creaking. Faint voices. And Connor, crying loudly.

'Damn, you been avoiding me? That was neat, slipping out that way. You left your car there and hitched a ride with someone, didn't you?' Rowan laughed. 'You're a slippery one, aintcha? Now. That door you just came through? Open it again. Step back outside.'

Whatever they had planned, they were going to make it nice and neat, out in the garden. Josh's heart was thwacking against his chest wall like a jackhammer. Then it happened. Suddenly there was a huge thundering *crash* of sound from upstairs. Rowan half-turned, startled.

'What the *fuck*?'

Then there were rapid footfalls on the stairs and suddenly there was another massive noise, closer and louder than the first, and Rowan's head burst open like a smashed watermelon. The shotgun flew out of his hands and clattered down on to the kitchen tiles.

For a moment, all was stillness.

Blood dripped steadily, like a faulty tap.

Rowan's hand twitched, but there was no doubt; he was dead.

Then, slowly, Shauna appeared in the doorway, arms stretched ahead of her, both hands clasping the smoking Magnum. She looked down at Rowan's corpse and then over at Josh. Upstairs, Connor was still shrieking. Shauna started to shake.

'Oh my Christ,' she moaned, and stepped around Rowan's body and slumped into a chair, the gun still clutched in one hand.

'Shaun . . .' Josh could barely speak.

'Ciaran came to the door and barged his way in,' she said numbly. 'Connor was crying upstairs and I said I had to go up and see to him. I didn't think he was going to let me. But he did. I've seen the yogger up there so I got it out of the wardrobe . . .' She was babbling, half-crying with the aftermath of terror. She'd used the old gypsy word for gun and in her panicked state she hadn't even noticed. 'Josh, I was afraid he wouldn't let me go up there.'

Josh dropped the wrench and his bag and came over to her. He took the gun from her hand, put on the safety, laid it on the kitchen counter. Fell to his knees in the mess and the blood and hugged her. For that moment he forgot all he'd been told. She'd saved him. She'd saved them all.

'You did good,' said Josh. He was shaking too. 'You all right?'

'What the hell are we going to do with the . . . the bodies?' The metal stink of blood was hot and horrible in the kitchen. 'God, I feel sick,' said Shauna, and staggered to the sink and threw up.

Josh watched his wife and now Rowan's words came back to him. Jeb had been sneaking around here, maybe watching him go and then coming into the house and fucking Shauna. He thought of the baby, upstairs. *His* child here, while they were at it in the bedroom. Still, he had no doubt that Connor was his. Connor was the image of Josh, any fool could see that.

'You've had a shock,' said Josh. 'We both have.' He stood up, looking down at the corpse. Another one, upstairs. They were going to have to be smart here. Clean everything away. Do it just right. 'We're going to need bleach, and some of that stuff for the floors. Scrubbing brushes. Cloths. A tarpaulin, I've got one out in the shed. And their truck out front? I've got to get rid of that.'

'It's not just that,' said Shauna, wiping her mouth, flushing out the sink with fresh water.

'What?' His head was reeling. All that Rowan had told him about her. And all that had happened here tonight. It was too much.

'It's not just shock, Josh. Oh Jesus. Oh Christ what a day!' Shauna took a gulping breath and looked at him. 'I'm pregnant again, Josh,' Shauna told him. 'I saw the doctor late this afternoon. We're going to have another baby.'

66

They had done all they could. Cleaned the place. Stashed the bodies. Josh had taken Ciaran's pickup with Shauna following in her BMW and driven it off to the wilds and set light to it. Then they'd gone back home and looked for Rowan's truck. It *had* to be there. They searched up and down the roads and were exhausted, nearly sunk in despair, when finally they found it. That too they took off and destroyed, then they went home again.

Next morning they sat at the breakfast table. They'd managed coffee, but neither of them could face eating. Josh stared at Shauna bleakly. 'They came here to kill me, didn't they?' He stared at her face. 'But why? That's what I don't get.'

Shauna shrugged. 'Over you taking off and not going on losing fights for them, I guess. Those boys can sure hold a grudge.'

'What, after all this time?' Josh's eyes searched hers. Shauna was lying, snatching at straws to cover her own tracks.

The best fuck any of us ever had, Rowan had told him. *How's that sexy missus of yours?*

'People *do* bear grudges,' she said.

'Yeah. Maybe.' He stared at her. His wife. Yet she was a total stranger to him. He thought then of Connor, who was the picture of Josh at the same age. Yes, Connor was his. But now Shauna was up the gut again, and . . . *Christ*. He couldn't be sure this new kid was his. He doubted her now. Doubted everything.

Days later, when Josh was off down the gym training, Jeb Cleaver turned up at the door. He stood there, wide and tall. For the first time ever, Shauna felt afraid of him. Jeb Cleaver, who she'd been leading around by the cock for the best part of both their lives. Now he looked at her and there was something different in his eyes, something threatening. Thank God the nanny was out with Connor, and wouldn't be back for over an hour.

'What do you want?' she asked coldly, managing – just – to keep her voice steady. 'I told you: we're over.'

He's looking for them. For Ciaran and Rowan.

'You seen my brothers?' he asked, his eyes unblinking as they stared into hers.

'What?' Shauna gave him a blank look. Her heart was beating hard and she could feel a trickle of sweat worming its way down her back.

'Ciaran. Rowan. They went out a few nights since and they ain't been back.'

'What's that got to do with me?'

'Nothing,' he said. Staring at her like he wanted to pick her brains apart.

'I haven't seen them. Why would I?'

Jeb shrugged and smiled. It didn't reach his eyes. 'Can't run a pig farm with two men. Pa and me, we're fully stretched and here they are, going off on a bender or some such foolishness.'

'That's got nothing to do with me,' said Shauna.

'No, course. Only there's this, you see. We had all sort of

agreed between us that – painful but true – your old man should go.'

Now Shauna was really sweating. She could smell the fear on herself. She wondered if he could, too.

'You weren't going to play nice with me any more, that was plain. So we thought that you'd be nicer if you didn't have that fucking Flynn bloke with you. Ciaran and Rowan were going to do whatever needed doing, but they ain't been back home. We ain't seen them since they left that night. Ain't that funny? And I just seen Josh Flynn drive off, whole and well.'

'Well, they haven't been here. Maybe Ciaran and Rowan went on a real bender of a pub crawl. Maybe they got rat-arsed,' said Shauna. She gulped down a breath. 'It wouldn't be the first time, would it? Listen. I don't care where they are or what they're up to, *I* haven't seen them. And I don't want you coming round here, not any more. I told you. Take it in will you? We're finished. I'll pay you for any jobs you do, but that's it. All the rest of it? That's *over.*'

Jeb said nothing for a full minute. He just stood there, a half-smile on his lips, his eyes on her face. Then he reached out a hand, quick as a viper. He grabbed her throat and yanked her toward him. Shauna let out a half-strangled cry. She was nose to nose with Jeb now, her feet almost dangling off the floor. In panic, she grabbed the front of his coat, clawed at him.

'Now *you* listen,' he said right into her face. 'All right? They were coming here and now they're nowhere to be found? That's fucking odd, I'd say. But you know what? I'll tell you what, and you should be grateful for it, you scheming bitch. Fact is, I don't much care. That pair of whoresons have been kicking mc around for most of my life and so, who gives a fuck? Not me.'

Shauna tried to speak: couldn't.

'But you want to keep ol' Josh safe?' Jeb went on. 'You keep on being nice to me, Shauna. You be very nice indeed. Starting *now*. This ain't over – and you know what? It's *better* now, because it'll be just you and me, real cosy. No brothers to worry about. And if you think about changing that one more time, just think again, OK? Because I'll kill him. I'll kill Josh Flynn, I swear it. *And* the kid.'

He grabbed her chin again, looked into her eyes as he slammed the front door shut behind him. Then he pushed her ahead of him into the kitchen, hustled her over to the sink and leaned her over it.

'Jeb, stop . . .' she gasped out. *I'm pregnant. Don't be rough. Don't hurt the baby.* But the words wouldn't come.

'Shut up,' said Jeb, yanking down her pants, unzipping his fly.

Shauna shut up, let him do it, thinking of the baby inside her, knowing she couldn't fight this. She *mustn't*.

It seemed to go on for a long, long time. But it was only minutes.

When Jeb was finished, he pulled out of her, zipped up.

'Now!' said Jeb. 'You are going to learn your lesson and fall in line. You got that?'

Shauna turned, straightened, shivering with shock.

'Got it?' said Jeb, staring into her eyes.

'Yeah,' said Shauna. 'I got it.'

67

Seven months later, when the two eldest Cleaver brothers had rotted away almost to nothing, lying weighted down safely in the middle of the deep, wide riverbed at the bottom of the garden, there were big changes for the Flynn family. Josh started promoting as well as boxing; they moved house; and their daughter Aysha was born.

Aysha Flynn made her appearance in the world via a home birth, and Shauna was up and about within hours, making tea in her dressing gown in their brand-new kitchen while the dirty sheets whirled clean in the laundry room. Josh marvelled at her powers of recovery; she had babies like most women shucked peas. Shauna shrugged everything off; illness, concern, even her conscience.

But God how she loved her babies. He could see that, as she hefted Connor on to her hip in the upstairs nursery and cooed into the lavishly constructed cradle – new, not second-hand of course – containing the baby girl. Josh watched Shauna, saw her face glowing with satisfaction. She smiled across at him and then glanced around this beautifully furnished room in their new home, letting her gaze linger on the window where the sun streamed in like a blessing.

'A little sister for Connor,' she said to Josh. 'Life's just perfect.'

Josh looked at her. For Shauna, maybe it was.

But for him?

No.

It was far from that.

Now, when he looked at his wife and at the new baby – who was dark-haired and dark-eyed, like Shauna, and like *Jeb Cleaver* too – he saw lies. He saw secrets. His life had gone bad the instant he lost Claire, lost the happy Romany way of life he should have lived with her. And now, trapped with this manipulative woman he barely knew and certainly didn't trust, it was too late; there was no going back.

BOOK TWO

68

December 1999

Shauna Flynn looked around her vast sitting room. The fire was banked up and crackling cheerily against the winter cold, and she had just finished decorating a huge twelve-foot Christmas tree in tasteful tones of gold and silver. She'd had the decorators in recently, painting all the walls in neutral taupes and creams, so that in spring she could add primrose-yellow and soft sky-blue and sugar-pink cushions and rugs and paintings. In summer, she would accessorize with forest greens and lime and mint. But now it was winter, and she'd put red plaid throws on the huge cream sofas, and added scarlet rugs and a feature wall of deep berry-red around the fireplace.

She was made up with this house. She loved it. It was far better than the four they'd lived in since leaving the riverside place. They'd traded one in for another, climbing up the property ladder until now they were sitting on a goldmine. Their first real family home – the old one by the river – couldn't compare to this. And it had held terrible memories. She'd been glad to leave it. Every time she'd looked at it after that long-ago night when Ciaran and Rowan had come to call, she saw not a picturesque scene but something tainted and hateful.

This house looked out on to lawns and then to woodland. Although it wasn't far from that first house on the riverside, it was far enough. So she still kept her 'friends', such as they were – Chloe, her ex-next-door-neighbour, and Tanya. She still felt they just tolerated her, after all that bitch Phil had told them. But Phil was history. And ever since those days, Shauna had donated freely to all Tanya and Chloe's favourite charities, made herself indispensable to them as a fundraiser, made sure everyone saw what a good upright pillar of the community she was – so now she was in, she was a well-established part of their circle, and that was all she cared about.

Josh had upped the security here after a spate of robberies in the area. There was a state-of-the-art alarm system installed in this house, and electronic gates. Of course that didn't keep out Jeb Cleaver. Living the high life, enjoying her standing in the community, Jeb was like the evil fairy in Shauna's perfect tale of bliss. Over the years he'd haunted her. He called on her whenever he could, whenever he wanted to. Anytime Josh was gone – and he was gone a lot – Jeb was likely to show up. And then he expected sex. And she had to give out. Or else. She *had* to toe the line. He always casually dropped her kids' names into the conversation, and to hear Connor's and Aysha's names on his lips made her want to heave. She idolized her kids and she had to keep them safe.

Sometimes – this was the worst thing – she even enjoyed it when Jeb took her, and that made her feel disgusted at her own animal appetites. It was worse when he was slow about it, taking his time, really grinding away at her like he had all day. She couldn't stand it then, couldn't resist, because Josh had been neglecting her too long in that department. Sometimes it made her sick with rage that Jeb still had such a powerful hold on her. At those times, she thought of the Magnum tucked away upstairs in the wardrobe and wondered what it might feel like to blow his head to fuck, like she'd done with his brothers.

Josh was away fighting but he had promised he would be home on Christmas Eve. She still loved him, *lived* for him. But she knew it didn't cut both ways. She hated him leaving her, but he didn't seem to have any problem with it. Every time he went away on a bout or a promo tour of England or the USA with his team of boxers – who were mostly hard bastards from Linus Pole's boxing booths – she tucked little notes into his bag to remind him that she was here, at home, waiting. *I love you*, said the notes. *I need you. I want you.* Not that he ever did anything in return. He didn't even remember their anniversaries, the bastard, so over the years she'd stopped bothering with parties and gifts.

Now and then she wondered just *when* the rot had set in between her and Josh; and she always came up with the same answer: the night she shot Ciaran and Rowan Cleaver dead. After that, a void had opened up and she couldn't bridge it. The lack of sex between her and her husband crucified her. When they were first together, Josh hadn't been able to keep his hands off her. But she still loved Josh to bits. Nothing could change that. And if protecting his kids – and him – meant jumping Jeb Cleaver's stinking bones forever and a day, then she would continue to do it.

'Place looks a picture,' said Connor, coming downstairs and into the sitting room.

Connor was wearing tight jeans and a black leather bomber jacket over a plain white shirt. He flopped on to the sofa. Shauna smiled proudly at her beautiful adult son and felt a little cheerier. Connor himself was a real sight for sore eyes. He was big, nearly six and a half feet tall. He shared his father's athletic stature and rugged good looks. His hair was thick, tinted blond from the summer's sun, and his eyes were a clear, sharp grey – so like Josh's – that seemed to see everything. His face had strength but also sensuality, and he had a calm, commanding presence.

No wonder all the girls fall at his feet, Shauna thought, and her smile dimmed a little. Damned girls with their fluttering eyelashes and their wheedling ways. Ever since he was sixteen, Connor had been dating some, dumping others. She'd never approved of a single one of them. *Especially* not his latest, an uppity little cow of a hairdresser called Kylie Patten. He'd brought Kylie home a couple of times and Shauna had given her the cold shoulder. He'd brought a couple of others too, before this one, and she'd seen them off, of course. Skanky little bitches. But this one – Kylie, Christ what a sickening name – seemed to be hanging around longer than the ones before, and that concerned her.

Connor had brought in the Christmas tree this morning, having hauled it home from a nearby nursery. He and some of his mates with a van from the large and ever-expanding scrap and auto yard he ran had fetched it indoors, wedged it carefully into a bucket, given it a drink. Connor had even bought new decorations, expensive ones, showy ones, which Shauna loved. Give the girls something to talk about when they came over for lunch.

Shauna was completely settled into this gorgi way of life now; it was as if she had never known anything else, never lived in a muddy campsite or been from traveller stock at all. Her Everett ancestors had lived in the Irish Free State and they had roamed the lanes in horse-drawn painted trailers, repairing pots and pans, sharpening knives and selling woven wicker baskets. But none of that was for her. *This* was her life, the life of a lady who lunched, a society hostess. The past was done and she wanted to forget all that.

Now she was able to fully live the way she had always craved. She was still a member of the tennis club, she played golf with Tanya and Chloe. And if they ever talked about her behind her back as that jumped-up gyppo Shauna Flynn who was no better than she ought to be, then she'd yet to hear about it. Frankly, even if they did, she didn't give a fuck. Tolerating those two snobby bitches and sucking up to them over the years had been a small price to pay for moving in the social circles she wanted to. Tolerating the ongoing visits from Jeb Cleaver was another thing she just had to soak up. And she did. Josh didn't have a clue about that, and she was very careful to keep Jeb away whenever Connor or Aysha might be about.

Aysha.

It upset Shauna that Josh had never taken to Aysha the way he had to Connor. She didn't know why and she felt sorry for Aysh, who was moody and awkward whenever Josh was near, radiating general disapproval in the poor girl's direction. So Aysha had become a mum's girl, Shauna's creature, and Shauna knew just how to push Aysha's buttons, pulling her in for cuddles and saying, 'Who loves you, Aysh? Who'd do anything for you?'

Shauna smiled indulgently at Connor. Unlike his problematic sister, he'd been a good-natured baby, then a lovely kid. Now he was a stunningly handsome man with a strong look of his father about him. Connor was her prince, the pride and joy of her life. He'd set up the auto and scrapyard business with his mate Benedict, and it was a thriving *legitimate* business, a limited company.

Of course, a fair amount of ducking and diving also went on with him. When you'd had little in the way of real education – and Connor had never been a big one for school – the only way to earn really big was to be that much smarter and sharper than anyone else. And Connor was *sharp*. More so than Josh had ever been. Far too sharp to ever step into the ring himself, even though he did have the build for it. She didn't ask questions when he fetched home lavish items or bought himself a black Porsche to zip around the lanes in. It was always cash on the nail, a practice learned in the cradle. He was her boy and in her eyes he could do no wrong.

'Christmas lunch will be at two o'clock on the day,' she told him. 'As usual.'

'I know. You've *told* me,' he said, but he was smiling. He hauled himself back to his feet. 'Got some stuff to sort out. Benedict's going off his head over this millennium bug business. Thinks on the stroke of midnight on New Year's Eve every computer system we've got is going to crash. So I'll see you later. Oh.' He stopped and turned back to her. 'OK if I bring Kylie on Christmas Day? Her folks are away.'

Shauna felt her face stiffen. *No, it fucking isn't.* Then she got her smile back in place. 'Sure. OK.'

As Connor left the room, Shauna's smile vanished. Christmas was strictly a family time. There should be her, Josh, Connor and Aysha at the meal, and she wasn't getting outside caterers in like Tanya and Chloe would. Catch either of those two cooking a roast – they might break a nail! Shauna liked to cook the meal herself, because that was the only way it was done absolutely right. She would do turkey and all the trimmings. The Guinness-soaked home-made Christmas pudding was already prepared – it had been ready since October, along with the Christmas cake – and it was stuffed with silver coins to bring luck.

Not that they *needed* luck, not now. Josh was earning a huge wedge from the promo work and the fight game, and

Connor was earning well too. Aysha just flitted from job to job, but maybe one day she'd settle.

Through the big picture window she watched her son climbing into his car. Shauna waved and Connor waved back. Well, that was Christmas fucking ruined. She didn't want that little cow Kylie there, it would spoil the day. Kylie had been over to the house a couple of times already, whispering in Connor's ear, giggling, clinging on to him. She got on Shauna's tits. Just get shot of her, and they could all get back to normal, her family and her; that was all she needed, all she had ever needed. Just the family, at home here, together.

Shauna grew thoughtful. Jeb was still around, always loitering in the shadows – and if Josh didn't want her, then Jeb certainly did. She thought of Ciaran and Rowan, and what had happened on that long-ago night; and she could never forget Jeb's threat to Josh, and Connor and Aysha. He'd repeated it often enough.

And since Jeb was still about . . . well, maybe she'd make use of him again, get him to sort out a little something for her.

She went on about her day, plumping cushions and rearranging the pine cones on the mantelpiece. But Shauna didn't know that there were other things happening, far away, that would soon tear her world apart.

69

Baton Rouge, Louisiana

'Hey, you! Trailer trash!' yelled Stefan over the noise of Ricky Martin belting out 'Livin' La Vida Loca'.

Suki Vance turned. Bastard *always* called her that, and it stung. That or *white trash*. Either way, the name-calling hurt. She watched him now, clicking his fingers at her like she was a trained dog, that big grin on his face because he *knew* she felt that insult deep in her soul. And he loved it. Fat slimy SOB with his hair pulled back in a trendy pony-tail and his greasy face wreathed in false smiles as he greeted the customers.

Swallowing the urge to throw a bottle at his head, Suki gave him a questioning look.

'Do you think you could move it? Only, diner's open in an hour, and the speed you go, the customers are going to be in here and we're not going to be ready to serve them, and if we're *not*, then I'm going to peel your arse like a grape.'

It was too hot to move fast. But Suki dipped her head and picked up speed, polishing tables, setting the centre pieces and the napkin dispensers straight. A faint hot breeze blew through from the open front door. The back

250

one was kicked wide open and held in place with a stone, and the through-draught was heaven.

Suki's workmate Felice moved past, polishing, straightening, sending her a brief *Jesus, that fucker* look of sympathy. Felice reckoned that Stefan's cheerful persecution of Suki was his heavy-handed notion of flirtation, and that Suki had just better watch herself out the back in the storeroom or he'd pounce.

'If he pounces, that boy's gonna get my boot in his balls,' Suki told her. She might *look* all soft and fairy-dust blonde, she might shimmy around the place looking dangerously sexy in her lemon-yellow uniform and frilly white apron, but she was no pushover.

'Jeez, you think he's *got* some?' Felice laughed. Felice was all that kept her sane working in this shit hole. Felice was black and beautiful, and her default setting was happy.

Head down, do the work, then go home, thought Suki. It was her mantra. It got her through every day and right to the end of the week when sweaty Stefan put a brown envelope in her hand (and yeah, he tried for contact at that point, quite often, but she was fast on her feet and she always eluded him). Then she could catch the crowded bus back to the trailer park, get a wash down and change out of the hated lemon-yellow uniform, and fill Aunt Ginny in on her day.

Suki couldn't recall a time when she hadn't been dirt-poor, someone people looked down on. She couldn't even remember her mom and dad because they had died in a car crash when she was barely three years old.

Aunt Ginny had told Suki that she had been sitting on her mother's lap in the front seat, with her father driving, when an ancient Chevy swerved over the central reservation – its elderly driver had come from Jackson and fallen asleep at the wheel en route to visiting his daughter down in Beaumont on her birthday. The Chevy smashed into their car. The old man died instantly, and so did Suki's parents.

By some miracle, Suki herself had been thrown clear of the wreckage, and was found by a young interstate policeman, bawling her head off at the side of the road among the pink-wrapped and bloodstained birthday presents. Not a scratch on her. Lucky? Well, maybe. According to Aunt Ginny, Dad was Dave Vance, a carpenter, scratching around for jobs half the time, and Mom Josephine had been a high-school teacher who had become a full-time mother to her baby daughter. Her one, her only child.

Aunt Ginny had been a teacher too, bright just like her younger sister, but poor health had ravaged her career and her looks so she remained nothing more than a spinster living in a downtown trailer park, having little to do with the world. And then the accident – heartbreaking, devastating – and along came Suki, who would have been put up for adoption and passed through children's homes and taken for fostering, maybe adoption.

At that point, so her aunt told Suki – she had recounted this story to Suki so many times over the years that Suki felt she knew it by heart – Aunt Ginny had rallied herself, put on her best suit and scrubbed rouge on to her cheeks. She met with the social workers at the town hall and said *no*, there was *no way* her dead sister's child was going to live anywhere but with her. She was the child's godmother, after all. She was all the family the poor child had left.

So here Suki was. Trailer trash, just like Stefan said. She couldn't even remember the car crash in which she'd lost her parents. Ginny had told her about it when she was old enough to take it. And Suki guessed that it had been so traumatic that her three-year-old brain had simply stashed it somewhere under the heading *too bad to think about*. But still – she felt the loss of her parents all the time, like there was a gap in her life she ached to fill, and never could.

Now it was evening, the day's work over, and Suki and her aunt sat on the stoop watching the sun go down and contemplating life. They were putting off the hour when it would be bedtime because the nights were hot in the trailer but you didn't leave your windows open, because people would come in the night and take what little you had. There were good people on the park, some who could even be called friends, but there were others too, who would rob and rape and think nothing of it. So, overnight, you sweated and stayed safe.

'Good day, hun?' asked Aunt Ginny, sipping at her beer.

Suki thought her aunt looked thinner than ever in the evening's light, her skin waxy. There was a high spot of colour on each sunken cheek, but it didn't look healthy or good; it looked like the flush of fever.

'Got a few good tips,' said Suki. She had never mentioned Sweaty Stefan to her aunt, and she never would. Ginny would be worried, and she couldn't have that.

'Well save 'em up, gal, and you and me, we'll do the world cruise.'

'Will we stop in Barbados?' asked Suki. This was an old much-loved game of theirs, speculating over where the non-existent cruise of their dreams was going to take them. Suki knew she would never go anywhere; Aunt Ginny was growing frail and she couldn't leave her. She couldn't take her along, either, supposing she ever got together enough money to do a trip, which was doubtful. Aunt Ginny used to be tough, but she was growing less so day by day. No, travelling was just a dream, something to cheer the pair of them when they'd had a hard time of it. That was all.

'Barbados you say? Hell no. I hear Antigua's the place these days.'

'Then we'll go there.'

'I'd like to see England. They got a queen and everything. Palaces and stuff.'

'We'll do that too. In between cruises. In between sitting at the captain's table and eating with fancy cutlery. No more jambalaya on the bayou for *us*.'

'We'll flick peas at him.'

'They clap you in irons for things like that. Like in the pirate movies.'

'Then maybe not.' They were quiet, watching the sun sinking on the horizon, among floating bands of apricot and gold. 'England,' said Aunt Ginny quietly. She let out a sigh. 'Wouldn't that be something?'

'It would,' agreed Suki, with a lump in her throat. Aunt Ginny was the best of the best, she deserved good fortune. Without her stern and practical old spinster aunt, what would have become of her? Suki really didn't know. It frightened her to think of it.

'Listen,' said Aunt Ginny, rummaging in her dress pocket. She pulled out an envelope and handed it to Suki. 'You take this.'

'What is it?' Suki stared at it. Her name was printed on the envelope in Aunt Ginny's meticulously neat hand: *SUKI*.

Aunt Ginny was shaking her head, making *it's nothing* gestures with her hands. 'Open it when I'm gone,' said Aunt Ginny.

Suki felt her innards gripped by fear. She knew Aunt Ginny was failing, and so did Aunt Ginny. Suki thought her aunt must be so scared, and her eyes filled with tears at that.

'Now don't you go making a fuss,' said Aunt Ginny in a

scolding voice. 'We don't want tears, none of that. You stay strong, girl. You're twenty-three years old with everything ahead of you. Be grateful for that.'

'You'll outlive me,' said Suki, feeling choked with emotion. They both knew it was a lie.

'Happen I will,' said Aunt Ginny. 'But if I *don't*, you open that letter and read it, OK?'

Suki nodded. She was too upset to trust herself to speak. She'd already lost her mom and dad, and the thought of losing Aunt Ginny too terrified her. She put the envelope in her dress pocket and tried to forget about it.

More than anything, Suki wished she had the money to treat Aunt Ginny to something as luxurious as a world cruise. Maybe one of these days a miracle would happen and she *would*. Who knew?

But it was not to be. Aunt Ginny's chest finally gave out and she died six weeks later. She never saw England after all.

70

'You been on those bloody things again,' said Connor
when he met up with Joey Minghella at the Blind Beggar
in the New Year.

'What you talkin' about?' asked Joey, squinting at Connor
as they stood together at the bar getting the round in.

Connor gave his employee an old-fashioned look. 'The
bloody ecstasy, you twonk. Busy weekend?'

'Went clubbing, yeah,' said Joey.

Connor shook his head. Joey Minghella might *appear*
grown up, but his head was still somewhere up his arse. A
dazzlingly good-looking eighteen, Joey had been doing
drops for Connor, but now Connor was planning on dropping *him*.

He didn't like Joey, who had begged him for some work
until he caved. Joey was a waster from a family of them;
the kid was going nowhere. And the E was a problem. Joey
was dancing every weekend and by Tuesday – it was Tuesday now – he was ready to bite your head off and spit
down the neck end, the hangovers were so bad.

Having been raised by a man who made his living from
being fit and treating his body well, Connor despised
anyone soft enough to prop themselves up with dope.

Joey winked at the barmaid as she pulled their pints.

'Proper star, aintcha?' he said to her. 'You done that before,
I reckon.'

The girl smiled.

Joey's brown eyes were dancing around in his head like
pinballs. His dark curly hair was stuck up in all directions
where he kept dragging his hands through it. He'd be up
all night at this rate, Connor thought, shooting up again
and doing something fucking daft as usual. And tomorrow
he wouldn't even remember what.

'They'll wreck you, those things,' Connor told him.

Connor was finding everything bloody irritating today.
There he was, expanding the family fortune, keeping everything on track, and there was Dad, still boxing when he
should have packed it in five years ago. Mum moaned
about it, all the time. Connor loved his dad, but for fuck's
sake, why didn't he call a halt to it now? At least Josh had
never tried to encourage Connor to get into the ring. It was
a mug's game, getting knocked bandy day and night, in his
opinion.

He'd seen his dad come home bent double and bleeding
from fight injuries, stiff as a board for a week. He'd seen
the smears of blood in the sink where Josh had spit up
after taking bad kidney punches. No, he was never going
to be a boxer. Running the yard at a good profit and doing
a few iffy deals was about his limit.

'Ah, you're too bloody serious,' said Joey, thumbing out
notes and handing them over to the girl. 'Have one yourself,' he told her.

'Thanks,' she said, preening under the spotlight of his
attention. 'I will.'

They took the drinks over to their usual table in the far
corner by the fire. No one ever sat in the one particular
chair closest to the hearth except Connor; he was getting a
name around the area as a hard nut, someone you wouldn't

want to mess with. Everyone knew his father was a champion fighter with an eighty-four-inch reach, and the son was no less dangerous, built like his dad and cool to the bone.

Connor felt content in general with the way things were going. He liked working alongside his old mucker Benedict, who was a character who'd originally trained as an accountant. Benedict was always neatly suited and booted and *never* called Ben. He was also a neat freak, which tickled Connor, but his organizational skills and his flair for skirting the laws of the land really helped the business they were in.

Benedict also kept the books of some other businesses who practised on the borderline between bent and kosher – brothels pretending to be tanning salons or massage parlours or saunas; bars and pubs who got their stock off the backs of lorries fresh from the continent. He provided fake paperwork and references for people who needed to prove to banks that they had a reliable income before granting them a mortgage.

The deals were coming in nicely and the latest scam Benedict had cooked up was one where he arranged mortgages for people who didn't even exist; so far, he'd arranged twenty million pounds' worth of fake loans, so Connor and him had netted a commission of two hundred thousand. And the millennium bug that had scared everybody shitless before the New Year had never happened. So everything was sweet.

Kylie was proving a problem though. Mum always clashed with Connor's girlfriends, but she had *really* taken against Kylie. Mum had given her icy looks and acid remarks on Christmas Day at home, criticizing every word she said and acting as if Kylie ought not to be there. And then New Year's Eve came around and Shauna had thrown a special millennium party. Come midnight, there Connor was with his tongue halfway down Kylie's throat, with Mum looking daggers at the pair of them. Which meant that Kylie, rattled, had stepped up on the sofa in her six-inch heels – *Mum's sofa!* – and said they were getting engaged. Which was the first he'd heard about it.

'All the best,' said Joey, supping his pint.

Connor took a drink then set his glass on the table. 'So, you seen Tobias Wilkes then?'

Tobias Wilkes fronted a company for Connor and Benedict and had for quite a while been straight in his dealings with them. But then the wheels had come off in his marriage and the wife was suing him for divorce and threatening to skin him for every penny. He was hitting trouble, and because of that Connor had been watching his financial dealings very carefully. He had spotted what he feared; Tobias was skimming off the top and hoping he wouldn't notice.

'He's coming down here at eight,' said Joey.

Connor looked at his watch. It was quarter past. 'Then he's late.'

'Held up in traffic maybe.'

'Or just taking the piss,' said Connor. He lifted his pint and downed it in one long swallow. He stood up. 'Come on. If the mountain won't come to Mohammed, we'll take the fucker to him.'

They pitched up at Tobias's door and rang the bell. There were lights on, someone was in. Joey had been in the pub toilets before they left for a little livener, and now, to Connor's disgust, he was high as a kite. Joey hammered at the door.

'What you want?' came a trembling voice from inside.

'Tobias? That you? Open the fucking door,' said Connor.

There was the sound of a bolt being thrown back, and

the door opened. Tobias Wilkes stood there, a short and balding middle-aged man. He looked terrified, not the efficient businessman facade he usually presented to the world. He was scruffy, unshaven, and his shirt was soiled. A waft of sour whisky breath hit Connor. He'd been drinking hard, trying to give himself a bit of Dutch courage, and he was weaving on his feet. 'You were meant to be down the pub at eight,' said Joey, pushing in past the man. Connor followed more slowly. 'What you playing at? You know Mr Flynn wanted a meet.'

'What for?' Tobias smiled sickly. Connor saw there was nervous sweat on his upper lip. He knew what for. Tobias looked guilty as fuck.

'You been taking liberties with my cash,' said Connor as the three of them stood in the hall. Joey was dancing from foot to foot, coming in close to Tobias in a threatening manner.

Christ, how many of those damned things has he shoved down his throat this time? wondered Connor.

'No, I . . .'

'Ah, don't bother,' said Joey.

Without warning he pulled out a knife and smashed it into the man's right shoulder.

Tobias cried out like a stuck pig. Joey yanked the knife free, and blood flowed out from the wound and dripped down Tobias's manky old shirt. Joey came in close again, *too* close. This wasn't a murdering offence. Connor grabbed his arm and Joey's head turned. His eyes when they met Connor's looked wild, unfocused. For a minute Connor thought that Joey might even turn the knife on *him*, then the fog seemed to clear in Joey's drugged-up brain and he stepped back a pace.

'Argh! Don't. Don't!' yelled Tobias, sobbing. He was clutching at his arm, and his eyes were full of panic. Blood was spilling out, soaking his fingers in red. 'All right, I skimmed a bit. I admit it. I'm sorry. My old lady's going to have my balls on a platter over this fucking divorce and I was going to pay it back when I could, every penny!'

Now Connor came in close to Tobias. Wincing, bloody, Tobias staggered back against the wall as Connor loomed over him. Connor was big, powerful; Tobias was small and in shock.

'You'll pay it back on Monday,' said Connor, and even his *voice* struck fear in Tobias. Connor's voice was deep, resonant; it seemed to come from somewhere down in his boots. 'I'll call round and you better be here, with what you stole off my family, or you'll be fucking sorry. And you better start looking for another job, and consider yourself lucky I don't get *really* upset about this. I know you got troubles and I'm making allowances. But you take the piss any more and I *swear*, you're a dead man.'

'That told him,' said Joey, grinning as they went back down the path to the gate.

'Yeah. That told him.' Connor stopped walking and yanked Joey to a halt with a hand on his arm. 'And now I'm telling *you*. You're out, you fucking moron. Finished.'

'You what?'

'You heard.'

'But I—'

'Shut up. You're a fucking liability. I said all I'm going to say. You're *out*.'

71

Aunt Ginny's funeral was the saddest thing Suki had ever seen. It was all cut-price. There was only her, Sweaty Stefan and kindly Felice, plus the preacher and the pall-bearers in attendance. Aunt Ginny was ushered out of the world in a cheap casket without fuss, but there were plenty of tears. Suki howled the church down while Felice patted her back and cooed comforting words. When it was all over Suki said goodbye to her friend and Stefan chose his moment to step up.

'Sorry for your loss, Suki,' he said. 'I'm real sorry.'

He'd spruced himself up and the odour of his cheap aftershave was so pungent it was making her feel sick.

'That's kind of you,' she said.

'If there's anything I can do, name it,' he said, and hugged her while Suki stood rigid, hating the feel of his pudgy body against hers but too stunned and grief-stricken to even fend him off. And at least he was being nice to her for a change. Maybe he *wasn't* so bad.

'I'll walk you home,' he said, and Suki, dazed by grief, started walking.

But Felice was back. She'd seen what was happening as she went out the church gate and had turned right around and come back to the rescue. She eyed Sweaty Stefan with hostility.

'Suki don't need you to walk her home, Stefan. Although I'm sure she appreciates the thought. It's kind of you. But I'm going to do that,' she said.

He hesitated. Suki almost felt sorry for him, he looked so crestfallen. 'If you're sure . . . ?'

'Sure she's sure,' said Felice, hooking one arm through Suki's and hauling her away.

'Jeez, girl,' she said when they were out of Stefan's earshot. 'Wouldn't *that* be the perfect end to a perfect day? Sweaty Stefan rubbing his fat belly, his *buck-naked* fat belly, all over you?'

Suki burst out laughing at that; it was a laugh edged with hysteria.

'Now you settle down,' said Felice, squeezing her arm. 'Cry if you got to, but don't go doin' nothin' *that* desperate. Your aunt was a great old lady and she wouldn't want you mixin' with an arsehole like him.'

When Felice left her and she was home alone in the trailer, Suki went into Aunt Ginny's little bedroom and sat on the bed, feeling dismal. There was something slippery under her foot and she glanced down and then bent, picked up a magazine and looked at the cover. It was a cruise brochure, dog-eared and faded. She peered under the bed. There were stacks of them under there. Aunt Ginny had lain in here at night and dreamed of that life, cruising the world. A dream that was never going to be realized.

Feeling sick at heart, Suki stood up and went through to the kitchenette and poured out a big measure of Aunt Ginny's Southern Comfort, the one she kept over the sink for what she called 'medical emergencies'.

Well, this was an emergency all right.

But the booze made her feel worse, not better. She drank a bit more. Then the room began to spin so she went to her room and lay on the bed and clung to the thin mattress and followed Felice's advice. She cried hot bitter tears for the loss of the only person in the world who had truly loved her. She cried until finally she slept, and when morning came she was sore of eye and aching of head. Aunt Ginny was gone and she was utterly alone.

She slopped water over her face, towelled dry and dressed and pulled on her old but clean blue shirt-dress, and there protruding from the pocket was Aunt Ginny's letter that she'd got out the day before the funeral, ready to read. Only she hadn't been able to summon the nerve to read it. Not then. Now Suki sat on her own bed, her hair uncombed, her head throbbing like a brass band, and stared at it. She slit it open with one fingernail and pulled out the sheet of paper inside and began to read it.

Suki darling, look in the Mickey Mouse tin in the pantry . . .

She didn't get any further. The words blurred as the tears came again. Suki sat there, shoulders slumped, the note in her hand. With a sigh she staggered to her feet, feeling weak as an old woman, letting the note fall on to the bed. She went into the kitchenette and opened the door to the pantry, then she dragged the Mickey Mouse tin down from the shelf. She put it on the sink and prised the lid open. Inside, there was a stash of dollar bills. Quite a few of them. She took the tin into the bedroom, slumped down again, and turned it out and counted the notes.

There were five hundred-dollar bills in there.

And now . . . what would she do with that?

She looked out of the smeary trailer window. More trailers just like her aunt's were lined up out there. Trucks and flatbeds and ancient boats and other junk were piled up all around them. A mile or so up the way from here, there were grand old plantation houses surrounded by oak trees dripping with Spanish moss. Big-paddled riverboats were going up and down the Mississippi, taking people to other places. And beyond that . . . who knew?

Suki looked at the cash. Then she took out Aunt Ginny's note again and braced herself, dried her tears. There were more lines of writing, and this time Suki read them. When she'd done that, she just sat there and stared at the words. Then, shocked beyond belief, she read them again.

72

'Your mother fucking well hates me,' said Kylie one night after a marathon sex session in bed.

Connor grinned and lay back, hands behind his head, glowing with satisfaction.

'Don't take it personal. She hates all my girlfriends,' he said. It was a fact. Shauna was his mum, and all respect to her for that, but he knew what a cow she could be to anyone outside her precious 'family unit'.

'How many have there been?' asked Kylie, snuggling in against his chest.

'Five or six,' said Connor, thinking maybe forty. His girls never hung around for long. Shauna saw to that, and if he wasn't serious about a girl anyway – and he never had been – it didn't bother him. But maybe with Kylie things were hotting up a bit too much. And this 'engagement' thing . . .

'You did that just to get up her nose, right? The engagement announcement on New Year's Eve,' he said.

'Worked, didn't it?' Kylie smirked. 'Face like fury on her after that. Hey, we *could* get engaged, couldn't we.' She lifted her head, looked into his eyes. 'What d'you think?'

'Sure,' said Connor, thinking, *No way*. But then, it was just a ring. Nothing serious. It would keep her happy and when Kylie was happy, she put out like crazy. So why not?

Kylie let out a shriek of joy and got to work on him again. Later, she was going to give him some *very* good news.

Shauna stewed over the New Year's Eve event for a week. That little bitch! Jumping about on *her* furniture, announcing her engagement to *her* son. And grinning at her like that. *Mocking* her. Well, she wasn't going to get away with it. Shauna made a long overdue call, and within a day Jeb Cleaver was waiting to meet her in a barely used pub six miles down the road, well out of the way so that none of her usual associates would see them together. Shauna was groomed to perfection, and the sight of this apparently high-class woman alongside a tatty yokel was bound to attract unwanted attention.

'So,' said Jeb, getting a gin and tonic for her and a pint of real ale for himself. 'You got a job for me, yeah?'

'I might have,' said Shauna, and told him about Kylie and what a nuisance she was proving to be. 'I'm going to talk to her, but if she don't see reason, then you can try.'

Shauna looked at Jeb with thinly disguised disgust as he downed the ale in one and belched loudly. She was bound to him now. Jeb knew damned well that something had happened to Ciaran and Rowan at the hands of the Flynns, and he'd mentioned their disappearance lots of times, and said he was better off without them. Now Bill Cleaver was getting on and he had just the one son under his roof, so Jeb found himself more appreciated than before. Yes, Jeb might still puzzle over where Ciaran and Rowan had gone – but it didn't bother him one jot.

As for Bill, he was a drunk who had never been a good father to any of them. If he'd ever cared about why his other two sons had gone out one night and never come back, he'd long forgotten why. Jeb was in charge of the pig farm these days. He hired in casuals to pick up any slack, and on the rare occasions Bill got wistful about Ciaran and Rowan, Jeb shrugged it off, said they were probably out in New Zealand, herding sheep or fucking them, one of the two.

'What do I get out of this?' asked Jeb.

'I'll pay.'

'Pay me in kind,' said Jeb with a bullish leer. 'Come out to the pickup and we'll discuss it.'

'No. I'll pay cash. I'm just telling you now to make sure you're in, if the need arises.'

'Honey, things are *always* rising around you.'

Shauna thought this was so ironic. So fucking *sad*. Josh who she loved didn't want her. But this fucking low-life *oik* still did. 'I haven't got time today,' she told him.

'Suit yourself,' he said, and smiled.

73

Josh Flynn came triumphantly out of the ring waving his arms in the air and dancing from foot to foot, but inside he felt completely fucked. The minute he was out of sight of the raucous New York crowd, the bouncing and crowd-waving dropped from him like a cloak. He slumped into his dressing room and all but collapsed on to a bench there. The room was spinning, he was so exhausted.

'You did good,' said Benny, one of the older blokes from the gym he used when he was Stateside, who was acting as his second. 'Beat his arse like a real pro.'

'I thought he was going down in three,' said Josh. Everything hurt. He was used to that, but these last couple of bouts had felt hellish, overlong. He was in his forties now. His hair was turning grey and he had wrinkles around his eyes. Maybe he was, finally, getting too old for all this shit, just like his boy Connor kept telling him.

But bare-knuckle fighters didn't retire. They kept on fighting the next challenger, and the next, until they got knocked down and couldn't get up again and *had* to stop. Josh's opponent, a muscular black man eight years his junior, had hung on until round ten; he was a true street fighter, straight out of the Bronx, and wouldn't give up until his back smacked the canvas and he couldn't pull himself to his feet again without help.

'I just wanted to put the fucker down,' said Josh, still panting as Benny rubbed at his chest with a white towel. It soon turned red. He was scratched and cut and battered all to hell. The middle knuckle on his left hand felt sore as fuck; he'd busted that joint more times than he could count over the years, and now it ached every winter. 'Bastard kept coming.'

'You did him good.'

'Yeah,' said Josh, and the door swung open.

'Hey!' objected Benny, then he saw who it was and shut up.

Two men came into the room, both of them Latin-looking, one bulky, one slim and younger. Both were dressed in immaculate dark suits and crisp silk shirts and ties. It was Spiro and his younger brother Nikos, the Constantinou brothers. They were club owners and bare-knuckle promoters who'd been buying Josh drinks, taking a keen interest in him and his team of fighters.

'Josh, you did good, my friend,' said the biggest, Spiro, with a grin, coming forward and throwing his arms wide.

'Thanks,' said Josh, dragging himself to his feet and getting enfolded in a bear hug despite all the blood and sweat he was covered in.

'Everyone said you were good but they didn't say *how* good. Now we know. You'll dine with us tonight? Celebrate the win?'

'Sure,' said Josh, when all he wanted to do was go back to the hotel and fall into bed.

You had to do this stuff. He knew that. He was a promoter himself so he knew the score. It paid handsomely, but in return for all that loot you had to press the flesh, be entertaining, earn your crust. It wasn't enough to be a great fighter; there were other hoops to jump through, too. You had to keep influential people sweet or you wouldn't get a fight anywhere in the States, and the USA was where fighting paid the best because it drew the biggest, richest and most enthusiastic crowds.

'We have someone lined up for next month,' said Spiro, patting Josh's shoulder. 'A Mexican.'

'Mexican? They're all five foot nothing. Never seen a heavyweight Mex.'

'This one's a cross. Mexican mother, black dad. Big as they come but he was raised near Cancún and I tell you, they're *hungry*, these Mexicans. They keep coming at you. Terrific fighters. They never give up.'

Fucking *great*, thought Josh. Across the pond, he had a home waiting, a family. A wife. That *bitch*. He thought of the latest note Shauna had tucked into his bag. *I love you, Josh*. The notes irritated him to death. They always had. She was trying to control him, mark him out as hers even when he was a thousand miles away. He hated that, and he hated *her*.

Josh loved his kids but he'd got sick of Shauna soon as he'd heard all that she'd been up to, how she'd scared off Claire with her pet monkeys the Cleavers. That *cow*. He loathed her unpredictable rages, her soppy love notes, her stupid anniversary fixation and her determination to keep dragging them all ever upwards on the social scale.

It was getting bloody silly, the way she went on. Dinners and galas and charity launches and all that shit. Their marriage had been dead for years, and they both knew it. All he stayed for was the kids. Well, for Connor mostly. He wasn't even sure Aysha was his. How could he be, knowing Shauna? But he still felt protective of the girl, and guilty over his lack of true affection for her. None of it was Aysha's fault, after all. All he was waiting for was for Aysha to get settled into a career or a marriage, then he promised himself he was going to shut this thing down for good.

He still dreamed of Claire Milo sometimes, his lost love. He yearned for those times, when life had been so simple and *she* was there. But all that was so far in the past now that it was just that: a useless dream. That was all it would ever be.

'Get washed up,' said Nikos with a grin. 'We'll wait outside. And well done, my friend.'

74

Suki grimly stuck it out at the Baton Rouge café with Sweaty Stefan for a little while longer while she tried to digest it all. She pondered on the lie that had been her life, and thought of that *bitch* who had casually thrown her out with the trash. Then Stefan started in with the chocolates and flowers, and she thought, *Am I going to settle for this? Am I really going to sleep with this dickhead and probably marry him and have his kids?*

No. She wasn't.

She was still in shock over what she'd read in Aunt Ginny's note. Her kindly aunt had written it nicely, tried to soften the blow, but what it amounted to was this: her whole life up to this point had been nothing but bullshit. Her real mother hadn't been a teacher, her real father hadn't been a carpenter. Dave and Jo Vance weren't her parents at all. No – her *real* mother was up in New York, fancy-free and untroubled by the loathsome kid she couldn't wait to kick aside.

Suki didn't tell a soul except Felice that she was going. *Fuck* Stefan. She made her plans, then one day she locked up the trailer and got on the Greyhound bus and headed north. She was looking to hunt down this cold-hearted bitch called Claire Milo, who had dumped her as a baby on the Sisters of Mercy, and left her to fend alone.

*

'Thanks for goin' Greyhound!' the driver said as she and the other passengers shuffled off the bus after the long and exhausting journey. Over a thousand miles she'd travelled, passing through Alabama, Virginia, Maryland, and now here she was. New York. The Big Apple!

Already, Suki was missing Felice. But she'd made preparations for this trip, and she was planning to take her time over it. She had a Brooklyn apartment lined up, and a job; everything was in place so that she could settle here and spy out the land, track down that witch who'd abandoned her and give her a piece of her mind. All she had to do was go along to the real estate agent and collect the apartment key. *Then* she was going to visit that whore, who clearly didn't have a *clue* about what it meant to be a real mother.

The apartment was lesson one on New York living. She'd been sent photos of the place, and in the photos it didn't look too bad. Not a palace, but OK. When she unlocked it, she quickly saw that she'd been duped. Well, she was *used* to being duped by now, wasn't she? The apartment was north-facing, so the living room felt cold – it was *freezing*, this time of year in New York – and was permanently dark. The kitchen had about a year's worth of grime on every surface, so she had to take a whole day to clean it. The apartment was at the top of the building (she hadn't even considered this) with a lift that someday soon was due to be fixed according to a couple of the other residents, so she had to climb six flights of stairs when she got home at the end of the day, and she was worn out.

Lesson number two was the Sweaty Stefan situation, which she believed she had escaped. But no. When she started her waitressing job to pay the rent on the apartment while she sussed out her traitorous whore of a mother, she found that this new Sweaty Stefan was called

Mike Hodder, and the only difference between Stefan and Mike was the hair colour. Stefan's had been brown. Mike's was dyed yellow-blond. Both were greaseballs with wandering hands.

The other waitresses, who were experienced, older, hard-eyed and wary of Mike's overtures, watched Suki endure the pats, squeeze-pasts and leers for about a week and then one of them, Pammy, a red-haired middle-aged mother of three girls of around Suki's age, said: 'What you doin' here, hun?'

'What?' Suki stared at her over the griddle where she was flipping burgers. She wasn't bad at the job. She worked hard. And as for what she was doing in New York, that was *her* business, and she was going to attend to that real soon. So what was Pammy saying?

'Come on. Square peg, round hole, that's what I'm thinkin'.'

'Meaning *what*?' asked Suki. She felt irritable. It was smoking hot in the kitchen, she was sick of grease and burgers, and Mariah Carey was warbling grace notes out of the radio over the sink. Later, Suki would be up to her armpits in that same sink, washing dishes and cooking utensils. Shit, she *hated* this job.

Pammy hitched a hip on to the counter, slapped the tea towel over her shoulder and folded her arms. 'Meaning you're too pretty for this. You could work anywhere and do any damned thing you wanted.'

Suki stared at Pammy.

'Burger's burning,' said Pammy.

Suki got back to the burgers, flipping, flipping. The smell of greasy meat wafted up over her in a noxious cloud. 'Like what?'

'You could be in a top Manhattan eatery, girl. You could apply for host or maître d' and you'd get it. But at the very least you could wait tables there and meet a better class of people and *not* have to put up with Mike's crap.'

'You noticed that.'

'His tongue keeps hitting the floor every time you pass him by,' smiled Pammy. 'Little tip? Bend down to pick something up. He'll take the opportunity to brush up against you from behind. Then up you come, turn and give him an elbow in the nuts. Big apologies, then, "*So* sorry, boss, I'm so clumsy, did I hurt you?" He'll get the message.'

75

Aysha Flynn was twenty years old and bored to tears. Right now she had a job in a dental supplies depot, pushing invoices around on a desk and answering the telephone to clients, and she hated it. She hated her *life*. Living at home with Mum, who was forever ordering her to do this, to stop doing that . . . And then there was Connor, her older brother, who saw her as nothing but a nuisance, she knew he did.

As for Dad, well, he didn't want anything to do with her. He never had. He was all over Connor like a cheap suit, so what was wrong with *her*? She knew she'd been a pain in the arse in the past, playing up at school, refusing to study and so flopping at every exam, getting detention, once – famously – yanking one of her teachers' gym shorts up the flagpole by the front gate. She'd been glad to get out of that pest-hole and into work.

But work was so fucking *boring*.

She'd asked Connor if she could do anything around the scrapyard, maybe work in the office, but he'd turned her down.

'No fucking way,' had been his exact words.

Turned out, the only bright spot in her otherwise grotty life was Joey Minghella.

Joey was *so* good-looking. His parents were no-hopers, it

277

was true, but was that Joey's fault? His Italian grandpa and grandma had come over from Naples years back and set up a tidy fleet of ice-cream vans making a profit around the area, but when they went off to the great ice-cream parlour in the sky, Joey's dad had quickly run the business into the ground. Then he decided he'd rather sit on the dole than work. Since the day the vans went tits-up, Joey's dad Frank hadn't done a minute's graft, and he liked it that way.

But Aysha didn't care about any of that. She *adored* Joey. He was gorgeous. Very Italian in his looks. Dark-skinned, black-haired, with deep brown eyes that flashed with humour. She felt her stomach do backflips every time he came into view.

Aysha glanced at the wall clock. It was coming up to five. All afternoon she'd been glancing up at it, willing it to go faster, while she'd been filling out invoices for amalgam and cement and running round the place gathering orders together, ready to be shipped out by van to the local dentists.

'Right,' she said, the instant the big hand hit the hour. 'I'm off.'

She gathered up her bag and coat and almost ran out into the square. Glamour city, this place was. There was a petrol station over the road and a meat market right beside the dental depot, where flayed pigs' heads hung on metal hooks. Christ, she hated this place. There had to be *something* out there, something better than this.

Joey was waiting for her on the corner. He smiled at her. It was like the sun coming out, his smile. She loved it.

'Hi,' he said, enfolding her in a bear hug.

The other girls were coming out of the depot, looking over at her and Joey. She kissed him passionately on the lips, for their benefit.

'Wow,' said Joey, pushing her back a step.

'Pictures tonight?' said Aysha, thinking that being with Joey was all that kept her sane. It was a hundred times better than Mum's smothering brand of mother-love, Connor's disapproval, Dad's disappointed silence.

'Yeah. Oh shit. There's your brother,' said Joey, seeing Connor's Porsche turning into the square.

Joey backed quickly away, looking at the Porsche and wishing he had the dosh for a motor like that. Thanks to Connor fucking Flynn blowing him out, there wasn't much chance of that now. No need to tell Aysha that Connor had sacked his arse, though. 'I'll see you there,' he said to her. 'Seven-thirty.'

'OK,' said Aysha, and he was gone.

Connor parked the Porsche. Aysha went over, got in. She was taking driving lessons, and hoping to pass her test soon: then Connor could stuff his Porsche up his arse.

'Hello, Trouble,' said Connor, frowning. He always called her that. And actually, it suited her. *Truculent* was the word for Aysha. 'Did I just see Joey Minghella?'

'Yeah.'

'I don't want you hanging around with that waster,' said Connor, and started the car. 'Can we get that straight?'

Aysha looked at him. 'Why?'

'Because he's a pain in the fucking arse. Did some jobs for me, but he won't be doing any more. Just steer clear, OK?'

Aysha shrugged as if she didn't care. *OK.* But in her mind, the dream ran on, reel after reel of it, like one of those fabulous romantic old films. Her and beautiful Joey Minghella, kissing, caressing. And as for Connor telling her to steer clear? Aysha never followed any orders but her own. So Connor? He could go fuck himself.

76

On her day off, Suki went and stood outside the club where her mother had worked before she'd had a daughter and consigned her carelessly to the trash. It hurt Suki and enraged her, to think of anyone doing such a thing. To think that Claire Milo had cared so little for her that she was able to just toss her aside like that.

If I had a daughter, could I do that? she wondered.

No. Of course she couldn't. A mother was meant to *care*, wasn't she?

Suki stood out on the sidewalk and stared up at the sign over the big black double doors of the club. Sylvester's, the sign said. And there were big posters up showing a lush golden-lit interior, smiling hostesses bearing trays of drinks and wearing cute tight-fitting little outfits.

Her mother had probably been one of those girls, maybe a hooker part-time, who knew? Anyway, she was obviously a whore of some sort because she had given her child away and there was absolutely no excuse for that.

I probably cramped her style, thought Suki.

There was no chance that her mother would still be here, anyway. So many years in between. Suki fell back a step as the doors opened. Two meaty bouncers came out, pushed the doors wide, opening for the lunchtime trade. There was a glassed-in menu up on the wall; businessmen would eat in the club, entertain clients. As she stood there, a couple of wealthy-looking men went into the club and were greeted politely by the doormen. One of the doormen looked at her, no doubt wondering why she was staring, so Suki moved on. But not before she'd seen the sign pasted up above the menu board. Not before she'd glimpsed it and thought: *Shit! I could do that. Then I could* really *see this bitch close up.*

Yeah, but what if she was long gone?

Well, there would be nothing wasted; and Suki would be better off, so where was the harm?

The sign said: *Hostess Vacancies.*

77

To say that Kylie was surprised to get Shauna's invitation was an understatement. She knew how much Shauna hated her. She reckoned that Shauna would despise *anyone* who came within ten feet of her baby boy. But maybe the old cow was mellowing. An invitation to afternoon tea at the Flynns' place must be a sign of *something*.

When Kylie got there, and Shauna ushered her into the living room and seated her upon the sofa – *the same sofa* that she'd bounced around on at Shauna's New Year's Eve party – Kylie soon found out what this invitation was a sign of.

'How much to fuck off and leave my son alone?' asked Shauna, sitting on the matching sofa opposite and looking at her with blank dislike.

'What?' Kylie's mouth actually dropped open.

'You heard.' Shauna eyed the girl. Kylie reminded her a little of herself – she was tough, and bold. Shauna didn't want any woman like that hanging around Connor. If he ever got married – and she really hoped he wouldn't – then it would have to be to someone of *her* choosing, a girl who was soft enough to do as she was told by her mother-in-law.

'Right.' Kylie's mouth closed in a tight line. Then she said: 'Well, it might cost you dearer than you think.'

'Oh come on.' Shauna eyed her sceptically. 'You're not

about to pronounce your undying love for him, are you? Don't make me laugh.'

'No, what I am about to say is that I'm pregnant.'

That gave Shauna a jolt, but she hid it well. 'And you're trying to say it's his? I bet a tramp like you has slept with all sorts.'

Kylie's mouth tightened even more. 'Look,' she said sharply. 'It's Connor's. No one else's. You really want me to walk away? He'll never see his damned kid and neither will you, *Granny*.'

That felt like a slap in the face. Shauna's stare never wavered.

'Good,' she rapped out. 'He don't need that sort of distraction in his life, and *I* don't need some dirty bastard's spunk-bubble being passed off as my grandkid.'

'You fucking—' started Kylie.

Shauna stood up. 'Now, you know what? You've annoyed me. So I'm not paying. Not a single solitary bean. But listen good to me now, honey, because I won't be repeating myself. You *fuck off*. If I ever see your scrawny arse around my boy again, you'll be sorry.'

Kylie stood up too, gathered up her coat and bag, her colour high with temper. 'You know what? I feel sorry for him, having a cold, controlling bitch of a mother like you. But you don't scare me. I'll do what I bloody well like. *You* can fuck off.'

Shaking with rage, Shauna picked up the phone and tapped in the number. Bill answered, and he passed her over to Jeb.

'That job I thought might come up? Well, it has,' she said, her heart pounding hard.

She gave Jeb the details.

★

A week later, Kylie was getting into her car after leaving work at the salon when someone knocked her down with a punch to the jaw. While she was laid out on the road, dazed, someone in heavy workmen's boots kicked Connor's baby out of her. Then as Kylie lay there, cut, bleeding, her insides cramping with horrible pain, the man standing over her said: 'Shauna sends her regards.'

Then he walked away.

78

Aysha was *mad* about Joey Minghella. Every time she saw him she wanted to either throw up with nerves or grin like a Cheshire cat. Sneaking around with Joey was the best fun ever. Sometimes, when Connor didn't collect her from work, Joey walked her home, and they took detours along the way so that they could kiss. They kissed so much that her lips were sore.

'What's happening then, Aysh?' Mum would ask now and again, keen eyes fixed on her daughter's face.

'Nothing much,' she'd shrug, fizzing with excitement because tomorrow she would see Joey again. She was so happy she couldn't keep the smile off her face.

Shauna knew that look. She'd been like that herself, with Josh, in the early days. 'Is Aysha seeing anyone?' she asked Connor one day when they were alone.

'I saw her talking to Joey Minghella once,' said Connor. 'That's all.'

'That boy!' Shauna's lip curled in disgust. 'I don't like that family. Bunch of deadlegs.'

'I told her.'

'And she said . . . ?'

'She said sure, she'd steer clear. But you know Aysha.'

Shauna did. Aysha went her own way and bollocks to everyone else. 'Keep an eye on her,' said Shauna.

'Always do,' said Connor, sighing. His mother was forever running everyone's lives for them, and it was fucking tedious.

'Oh, come on!' said Shauna, seeing his expression. 'I've a right to know what my own daughter's up to.'

'Yeah. Sure,' said Connor. 'I'll keep a watch on her, OK?'

Shauna couldn't believe how fast the years had passed. Her son was getting little alley-cats pregnant and her daughter Aysha was a full-grown woman, and now Shauna was well into her middle years. She was noticing the odd wrinkle or two, the stray grey hairs in her once magnificent dark mane that she got coloured out at an expensive salon. It was an adjustment, and she supposed women who were blissfully happy in their marriages handled it pretty much OK. But when you suspected your husband was happiest when he was away from you – and he was away a lot, mostly in the States – then it got difficult. You began to see a long tunnel stretching ahead, with old age and death at the end of it, and what was there to sustain you?

Your kids, that was all. Shauna had a lot invested in them. She *adored* them. And that was sad, too, because knowing that proved that she had nothing else. She thought that this was the situation: Josh was happy enough to go on with it all because he had kids off her.

But this was her life now. It would have to be enough. And there was always Jeb, lurking in the background. If she craved sex, she could turn to him – and shamefully, she often did. She was never going to be free of him; after everything that had happened, they were linked and could never be separated. He'd seen to Kylie and she had paid him, in cash and in kind. That was what her life amounted to now.

79

Suki was still spying out the land. She'd walked past the club many times among the hustle and bustle of New Yorkers on the sidewalks. She found that she rather liked New York, the yellow cabs thronging the streets, the noise, the sheer liveliness of the place. After the trailer park, it felt like heaven. Like things were happening, all around her, for the first time ever.

She must have hovered outside Sylvester's a dozen times before she summoned the nerve to actually walk through the black doors and speak to one of the big muscle-bound men there.

'You know the advertisement? The one on the wall?' she asked one of them, who was smiling at her.

'Ah sure do,' he said, aping her accent. 'Where you from, honey chile?'

'Baton Rouge,' she said.

'Phewee! That accent's to die for. You sound warm as molasses, baby doll. You really do.'

'Thank you,' said Suki. 'Um. The job? I'd like to apply, if I can.'

Now his colleague came over. He was smiling too. Suki had that effect on men, in general. She was used to them staring and acting the fool around her. Look at Stefan. Look at Mike.

'Come on up to the office, I'll see if the boss is home to visitors today.'

Suki went in, gazing around at the club. It looked elegant and expensive, and there were girls up at the bar chatting and laughing, all of them squeezed into tight costumes in various colours. A brunette in scarlet. An ash-blonde in cool primrose-yellow. An ebony-skinned stunner in bright Caribbean lime-green. They looked gorgeous.

She followed the doorman upstairs and at the top he knocked at one of two closed doors, and opened it. 'Hey, Donna? Got a lady here wants to apply, if you'll see her?'

Donna, thought Suki. Not Claire. If Claire had once been one of the girls downstairs, she'd have been out of the job long since. Only the young and glamorous could hack that. Or maybe she hadn't been one of the girls at all. Maybe she'd been a cleaner. Or worked in the kitchens. Or behind the bar. Suki itched to ask either the man or the middle-aged woman behind the desk if Claire Milo was still here. If she *wasn't,* no matter. Suki would just go right on searching until she found her.

'I'm open for business,' smiled the woman, and the man ushered Suki inside. 'Come in, do. Sit down.'

Suki sat. She looked at the woman. She was mid-forties, with an air of efficiency, and she wore a bright-red jacket that clashed with her big mop of dyed auburn hair. Not a looker; mouth too big, eyes too small. But she had a real friendly aura about her.

'You done hostess work before?' she asked Suki, pulling out forms from drawers and selecting a pen from a pink pottery tub of them on her desk.

'Waitressing, mostly,' said Suki.

'Nothing wrong in that,' said Donna, getting to her feet. 'Here. Fill this in, we'll see how we go, OK?'

Donna left the room, closing the door after her. Suki

looked at the form and sighed. What was she doing? Did she *seriously* want this job? No, she didn't. But she wanted to be here, she wanted to soak up the atmosphere of the place; to *feel* it. It was like walking in her treacherous mother's footsteps. So she picked up the pen and started writing.

When Donna came back ten minutes later, Suki had finished filling in the application form.

'Oh, that's fine,' said Donna, going around her desk. She didn't sit down, but reached out a hand, indicating that this little meeting was at an end. 'Thank you for coming by. I'll take a look, and then I'll be in touch, OK?'

Suki nodded. What if she *didn't* get the job? She'd have no excuse to come back here again.

'Do you know a woman called Milo? Claire Milo?' she blurted out, coming to her feet.

Donna looked at her sharply and Suki quickly went on: 'She's a friend of my mom's, and Mom thought she worked here once, a long time ago, at this club. She wanted me to give Claire her regards, that's all.'

Donna nodded. 'Claire Milo don't work here,' she said.

'Oh! She doesn't? Mom must be mistaken.' Suki felt her heart sink. Of course Claire Milo wasn't here any more. It had been lunacy to think she would be.

'No, your mom's right in a way, Claire is *here,* but she don't *work* here, not as such.'

Suki was flustered. What the fuck? She couldn't understand what Donna was saying to her.

'I'm sorry. I don't know what you mean,' she said, feeling like an idiot, a bright blush creeping up over her cheeks.

But Donna only smiled. 'I mean that Claire Milo *owns* Sylvester's. She don't work in it.'

80

Aysha didn't know how to tell Joey the news. Over a year now, they'd been dating, mostly in secret. There'd been quite a lot of heavy petting. Then he'd started asking for oral, which frankly made Aysha want to puke. She felt guilty about that, and he sulked.

So a couple of times they had actually done The Deed. It felt very strange, and the first time had been painful, but Joey had said, panting and pushing at her, wasn't this great? So she agreed it was, although she couldn't see how, and she wished he'd wear a condom because she was worried that she'd fall for a baby – and what a shit storm *that* would cause. Dad hated her anyway – it seemed like he had been mean to her just about forever, so cold and dismissive – and *that* would put the tin lid on it.

But Joey said wearing a condom was like scratching your toes with your fucking boots on, so she hadn't insisted. And then it happened a second time and although it was less painful, again he didn't wear a condom.

'Well, if you won't suck me off, the least you can do is throw me a fuck,' he told her when she finally summoned the nerve to tell him she hated doing oral and *detested* getting a gobful of cum. It was *horrible*.

So she had thrown him a fuck. She was terrified that if she didn't, some other girl would, so she did it. Twice. And now she had something to tell him and she didn't know how, so she just blurted it out.

'I think I'm pregnant,' she said.

Joey was without a job, although he said he was looking, but she didn't really believe that any more. She'd passed her driving test but still didn't have a car. She'd swapped the dental depot for a job in a travel agency. Trouble was, she hated every second of it. But she was earning, contributing to the family pot. She liked that feeling, and maybe she could even prove to Dad she wasn't a complete waste of space.

'You're fucking *what*?' said Joey.

'Pregnant,' said Aysha, her heart beating hard in her chest.

He was looking angry, like *she* was the one in the wrong. This was going to start big trouble with her family, she knew that, and what she needed from him was reassurance; she needed him to tell her it was all going to be OK.

'What the *fuck*?' He'd stopped in his tracks and was pulling his hands through his dark curls and staring at her like she was crazy. 'How the hell . . . ?'

God, is he really going to say that? Aysha wondered. *Is he really going to ask how it happened, when it's bloody obvious?*

'We had sex, you didn't wear a condom, and now I think I'm pregnant,' said Aysha.

'Christ!' He turned around, walked away, walked back. Stared at her face. 'You *think*?'

'I'm getting a test kit today.'

Aysha hadn't seen the red flag flying for two months now. Soon, she was going to *have* to tell her mother, and that was going to be hard. Even harder? Her father. He was going to be mad as hell and even more disappointed in her than he normally seemed to be. *She* was the one who was going to have to face the music on this, and here was Joey, acting like a twat, like it was all about *him*.

'For fuck's sake,' said Joey, and kicked a tin can across the road in fury. 'Then bloody do the test, will you? Hurry up, this is fucking killing me.'

Aysha went to the chemist. Hoping against hope, she did the test. It was positive.

'I'm sorry, Joey,' she said when she told him later in the day that it was confirmed. Then wondered why the fuck she was apologizing, because *he* was responsible for this, not her. She felt tears fill her eyes.

'No, hey . . .' He was patting her shoulder, alarmed by the onset of tears. 'This is my fault. I should have taken better care of you, I see that.'

This would be one in the eye for fucking Connor Flynn, thought Joey.

In fact – now he'd had the chance to cool down a little, to just take it all in – he thought that this could all work out just fine.

'What are we going to *do*?' asked Aysha.

'Simple,' said Joey with the dazzling grin that always melted her heart. 'We'll get married.'

81

The job fell into Suki's lap. She was amazed – she'd seen the calibre of women working at Sylvester's – and she felt at once triumphant and anxious as she stared at the letter of acceptance that came not a week after she'd gone to the club.

For days she'd chewed over what Donna had told her, about Claire owning the joint. Maybe Claire came from a wealthy family, and the business was in their blood. Maybe she'd got pregnant outside wedlock and her well-to-do folks had been appalled and prompted her to give the baby away. Suki wondered what she would do, in the same situation. But really she already knew the answer to that. She would *keep* her baby, if it took her last breath to do so. No way would she ever abandon her child, like Claire had done to her.

Or maybe Claire was a hard-faced career woman. She ran the club, after all. Maybe that was it. She'd got herself pregnant and that had been inconvenient, not part of her plan, so she'd jettisoned her daughter like so much flotsam.

Christ, who knows?

Suki was wearing herself out playing guessing games, and in the end she just had to shut down. When she actually met the bitch, when she confronted her, *then* she would get her answers.

She'd thought that once she started work at the club, she'd be sure to see the owner. She was disappointed to find it was Donna who met her, showed her around, introduced her to the other girls and handed her the soft pink velvet costume she would be shoe-horned into every day. Donna taught her the moves the girls performed as they ferried drinks between the bar and the clients, helped her perfect the 'dip' until she had it just right. No mention was made of Claire Milo and Suki didn't enquire; it would look too weird if she mentioned her again. But she did ask one of the other girls – Vicky, a chatty and glamorous brunette who always wore a scarlet costume – if Claire lived over the shop.

'She does,' said Vicky. 'She's got an apartment on the second floor.'

Then one evening Suki was crossing the club floor. It was a busy night, the place was heaving and there was a three-piece band playing bluesy numbers. A woman came in – middle-aged, blonde, and went over to the bar. Suki was there, giving the barman an order. Donna was standing talking to the barman, and when the woman tapped her on the shoulder she turned quickly, then gave a grin and hugged her.

'Claire! You had a good trip?'

'It was a nightmare! Too much traffic, and when I got there they started trying to up the price.'

'You didn't let them, though?'

'Hey, do you *know* me? Have we been introduced?' Claire laughed. Suki stood frozen, shocked. She was standing two feet away from her mother. And . . . the woman sounded *English*, not American. 'Good to be back. See you in a bit,' she said, and went off up the stairs.

Suki took the order from the barman and delivered it to the far table, chatting to the clients, smiling, doing her job, while all the time she was thinking, *My God, my God! That was her.*

She didn't see Claire Milo again that night, or the next day. Suki felt like her whole being was electrified with awareness; Claire Milo was here, in this building. That *bitch* was here. She waited all day, and then the evening shift was due to start and she took her chance and crept up the stairs. Donna's office door was ajar, and she could see Donna in there, her head bent over papers, making notes. She crept past. Then past another closed door. And on up the stairs. At the top of the flight was another door.

Christ, I can't do this . . .

She steeled herself and knocked on the door. She gulped, nervous. Her palms were damp. Her heart was beating madly. No one answered, so she turned and started off down the stairs again. Then she heard the door open. Suki stopped, glanced back over her shoulder.

Oh shit!

'Hello! Can I help you?' asked Claire.

Suki took a breath and started back up. At the top, she came face to face with the woman who'd given birth to her. She stared at her. Claire Milo was shorter than her, and dainty of build. She had an air of energy and purpose about her. She was wearing a peacock-blue satin dressing gown. Her hair was cut in a shoulder-length bob and expertly coloured a subtle pale blonde. Her face . . . she had a kind face. Big almond-shaped periwinkle-blue eyes that twinkled with warmth. That was a surprise. She was smiling now, looking expectantly at Suki, not having a damned clue who she was.

'Taken a wrong turn?' asked Claire. 'If you're looking for Donna, her office is down there on the left.'

'I'm not looking for Donna,' Suki managed to get out. 'I'm looking for you.'

'Me? You're new, aren't you? What can I do for you?' Claire was half-smiling, half-frowning.

'You can tell me why you threw me away,' said Suki.

Claire's smile froze on her face.

Suki felt it all blow up in her head then, erupting like lava. 'Don't you get it yet? Can't you see the similarity?'

Claire was staring at her as if she was mad.

'What sort of *mother* does that to her child?' demanded Suki. 'Tell me, you bitch. Because I would *really* like to know.'

Claire's eyes widened. Then her mouth clamped shut – and she slammed the door closed in Suki's face.

82

'You're *what*?' asked Shauna.

'Pregnant,' said Aysha.

They were in Shauna's beautifully appointed and recently refurbished kitchen that looked out over the long driveway to the gates and the road beyond. As Aysha said it, Shauna sat down on one of the button-backed cream leather bar stools, all the wind knocked out of her.

Damn.

Of all the possible futures she had envisaged for her only daughter, getting banged up and dropping that waster Joey Minghella's kid was the one she had feared the most. She'd tried to get her daughter mingling with a better class of people. She'd imagined Aysha marrying a lawyer maybe. A doctor. Even a surgeon. That would be one in the eye for the girls at the tennis club. But *this*?

'Is it Joey's?' she asked, numb with shock. She wished Josh was here. But Josh was still over in the States, making money. *Bloody* Josh. But maybe it *wasn't* Joey's.

'Of course it's Joey's,' said Aysha, taking the other bar stool and going red in the face. 'How can you ask me that?'

'Sorry,' said Shauna sarkily. 'It's just that I hoped it could be someone else, that's all. The postman or the milkman. The *dustman* would be an improvement on Joey fucking Minghella.'

Aysha sat down and looked across the bar top at her mother. 'Don't be like that. I love him, Mum.'

'He's easy on the eye, I'll give him that,' snorted Shauna. 'Not that he'll stay that way when Connor gets to hear about this.'

'I don't want him hurt!' Aysha burst out.

'Have you told Joey about this? About you being up the duff?'

'Yeah, I have.'

'And he's run a mile?'

'Of course not! He wants us to get married. We're *going* to get married.'

'Your father,' said Shauna, 'is going to be very disappointed in you.'

'Oh come on, Mum!' Aysha beat a fist on the counter in exasperation. 'That's nothing new, is it? He's *always* been like that with me, and you know it! Besides, I'm not his little girl any more, *or* yours. I'm a woman. I love Joey and I'm fucking well marrying him. There's nothing you can do about it.'

Shauna was still sitting at the kitchen counter an hour later when Connor came home. Usually, she would have the evening meal simmering on the stove by now. Connor looked around the kitchen, but there was no sign of any food coming. Shauna just sat there, staring at the counter.

'What's up?' he asked.

'If I tell you, don't kick off.'

Connor stiffened. He'd had a whole day of aggravation: lots of late-payers to be chased, and Kylie had dumped him over the phone, telling him in tears that she was sick of him *and* his fucking family, then ringing off. He wasn't *too* bothered, but she'd kept the ring that'd cost him one boring afternoon's browsing around jeweller's shops and a hefty seven hundred pounds. Now, something else. This day just kept getting better and better.

'Why should I kick off? What is it?' he asked.

'Aysha . . .' Shauna was shaking her head.

'What about her? She OK?'

'She's pregnant. And it's Joey Minghella's.'

Connor sat down on a bar stool. 'You're fucking kidding me.'

'No, I'm not. Silly little fool thinks she's in love with him. They're going to get married, she said.'

'He's a dosser. He's useless.' Connor recalled Joey's knife attack on Tobias, who was a cunt but hadn't deserved *that*. He'd been happy to kick Joey's unstable arse out the door. Now here the little bastard was again, lingering like a bad smell.

'I told her,' said Shauna.

Connor stood up, began pacing restlessly. 'This ain't happening,' he said.

'Really? Looks like it is.'

'No,' said Connor, and headed for the door. 'Never in a million bloody years.'

'Connor,' said Shauna.

'What?' He stopped in the doorway, turned back.

'I just wondered. How's Kylie? Haven't seen her lately.'

Connor was still for a moment. Then he said, stony-faced: 'Mum – fucking well butt out of my love life, OK? I'm not ten. And for your information – Kylie is history,' and left.

Shauna felt grim satisfaction. *Something* had worked out, after all.

83

That bitch is going to fire my arse now, thought Suki as she stomped back down the stairs, hardly caring whether Donna heard her this time or not. She was shaking with emotion, shuddering with rage. She knew how this would go: Claire would tell Donna to get rid of her, and that would be the end of it.

She carried on doing her job, knowing that at any moment she was going to be collared by the manageress of the club and given the order of the boot. She waited a whole week for the axe to fall, but it didn't happen. She didn't see Claire down on the club floor, either. Then one evening when the place was busy, Donna called her to one side.

'Claire wants to see you in her office,' she said.

'Oh. Right.'

Suki went up there, past Donna's little office and into the bigger one, the *owner's* office. Claire was sitting there behind a big walnut desk with a tooled red leather top, her hands folded in front of her. She stared up at Suki as she entered.

'Come in,' she said. 'Sit down.'

Suki sat and crossed her legs, one foot twitching like a metronome. Unblinking, she gazed back at the woman who had callously abandoned her all those years ago. Left her newborn baby on the steps of a convent. If not for Dave and Josephine and Ginny Vance, what would have become of her? She couldn't believe anyone would be so callous. So *cruel*.

'My God,' said Claire, and her voice trembled.

'What?' Suki was steaming mad with this woman. This *bitch*.

'You look like me,' said Claire.

Suki shrugged her shoulders. She wasn't going to make this easy for her. *Fuck* her.

Claire took a deep breath, moved her hands. They shook, Suki noticed without sympathy.

'How did you find me?' asked Claire.

'My aunt died. Well, not my aunt, was she? But she died. And then I read the note she left me, explaining things. You dumped me with the Sisters of Mercy in New York.'

Claire shook her head. 'That was Gina. She took you there. She used to be manageress here. She tried to talk me out of giving you away, but in the end she could see that it was no use, I just couldn't cope. You know, I always thought,' said Claire. Then she stopped, took a breath. Started again. 'I always thought that if I ever saw you again, you would look like . . . like them.'

Them? Suki wondered what the hell Claire was on about. 'Where's my father?' she asked, her eyes hostile. 'Didn't *he* want me either?'

'What?'

'Who is he? Where is he?'

Claire was shaking her head now. 'Wait. Stop. You don't understand.'

'So *explain* to me. And what do you mean – "them"?'

'I had you,' said Claire, and her voice was so low that Suki had to lean forward to hear the words. 'I had you right here. Upstairs. Gina was manageress, and Sylvester owned this club. They were my friends. When he died, he left the club to me.'

'What, am I his then? This Sylvester? Is he my father?'

Claire shook her head. 'God, this is hard.'

'It's hard for *you*?' Suki let out a sour laugh. 'What about me?'

'I've never spoken about this. Not before. I didn't think I would ever have to.'

'So who knocked you up? Who was it? You said *them*. Christ! Was it a threesome or something?'

'Suki.' Claire paused. 'That's a pretty name.'

'Yeah. My mother gave it to me. My real one. The one who cared for me. Not you.'

Claire flinched at that. 'I'm glad someone cared for you.'

There was such heartfelt sincerity in Claire's face and voice when she said that. Suki felt her throat close. *No*. She was not going to cry. She *refused* to.

'Good job someone did, yeah?' she snapped.

Claire nodded, looked down at her hands and then up at Suki's face. 'The fact is, Suki, that I was raped.'

Suki felt her breath catch in her chest. 'You *what*? But . . . by who?'

'That doesn't matter. Not just one. It was two men.' Claire paused, gulped down a breath. 'I was a virgin when it happened. It was shocking. Brutal. And when I found I was pregnant with you, I just . . . panicked. I was horrified. Terrified. I wanted to deny it was even happening, and when you were born . . . it was just a nightmare. I couldn't even look at you. Couldn't bear to.'

Suki stared at Claire. She couldn't think what to say. The anger drained out of her like water from a bath and left her chilled. Claire had painted a brief but ghastly picture of awful abuse, and it knocked Suki sideways.

'Oh God,' said Suki, and stumbled to her feet.

'Suki . . .' Claire stood up too, her eyes filling with tears. 'Wait, don't—'

But Suki had already blundered to the door and gone.

84

Joey Minghella had been pissed off, naturally, when first he heard that Aysha was in the family way, but he could see now that there would be advantages to this. He told Dad his news. Frank Minghella was lying on the sofa watching the racing in trousers, braces and a vest on a warm spring Saturday afternoon. Like Joey, he quickly figured out the wider implications.

'You got a good deal there, son,' he said, a blue cloud of cigarette smoke surrounding him as he reached for another can of beer from the six-pack on the floor. He scratched his fat belly luxuriously and winked. 'Flynn lot are loaded. You'll be on a damned good thing if you can get her up the aisle.'

Joey looked at his dad. Marital advice from Frank Minghella wasn't all that. Frank's own wife and the mother of four boys – of whom Joey was the eldest – had gone out to the shops one day and never come back. Nobody had been even faintly surprised. Frank was idle, Joey knew it. Idle, dirty, always on the scrounge for handouts. But Joey thought his dad was right about this being a good thing.

'I've asked her to marry me,' said Joey.

Frank snapped the tab off the beer then paused, looking up at his son. 'She say yes?'

'Damn right,' said Joey. Girls worshipped him, he was so good-looking. Damned *sure* she'd said yes.

'Then the world is your oyster, boy, and good luck to you.' Frank took a swig of beer and belched.

Joey went off down the pub to meet his mates that night in a good mood. Granted, he wasn't keen to get married – what bloke in his right mind was? – but it would work out fine. Connor Flynn couldn't go on bypassing him for jobs or treating him like dirt if he was his brother-in-law. This would turn the tide. The work would come back his way, the sun would shine, Aysha would drop the kid and she could look after it, no way was *he* turning into one of these 'New Man' types and changing nappies and crawling out of bed to give the little bugger feeds. He could carry on clubbing, popping some E – he'd be able to afford all he could handle when he hooked up with the Flynns. Everything would be just fine.

That's what he *thought*, but when he was walking across the pub car park heading for a relaxing evening, a game of snooker, a few beers, he was grabbed from behind and hauled around a line of cars, out of sight.

'What the fuck?' he demanded, his voice high with fear.

His attacker flung Joey away from him, into the bushes. The thorns scraped at Joey's arms and he let out a yell then bounded back to his feet, spinning around to face whoever had jumped him.

Fuck! It was Connor Flynn. Joey half-started forward, then thought better of it.

Connor indicated he should go on, approach. 'Oh, you want some of this? Come on then, you little bastard.'

Joey felt sick with fear, but he thought of Dad's words of wisdom. Connor couldn't hurt him. If he did that, then it was Aysha who would feel the pain of it. The Flynns seemed a tight-knit family, unlike the Minghellas, who didn't much care if they saw each other from one year to the next.

'Christ, you nearly gave me a seizure,' he said, grinning past his nerves. He didn't *think* Connor would hurt him, but he wasn't sure. Connor was as big as a truck and packed with muscle. If he hit you, he'd knock you clean into the middle of next week. His dad being a pro boxer, he had probably taught Connor how to hit for maximum damage.

'Damn, wouldn't *that* solve all our problems,' said Connor. 'You little prick, is this true? You got Aysha up the duff?'

Joey swallowed hard. He was going to have to choose his words with care and he knew it. 'Yeah. It's true. We're in love, Connor. We got carried away. I'm sorry. But I want to do the decent thing by her. I want to marry Aysha.'

'Sure you do. You'd be on a bloody good squeeze, wouldn't you? Marrying into the Flynns.'

'It's not like that,' said Joey, although it was.

'Then what *is* it like?'

'I told you. I love her. Really.'

Connor stepped forward and loomed over Joey, who forced himself not to back away. The look in Connor's eyes was terrifying.

'I ought to beat the shit out of you, you little tosspot,' he hissed.

'Go on then!' snapped Joey, bracing himself for it. If Connor battered him, this was going to *hurt*. But Aysha would see him as a fallen hero; she would be furious with Connor and firmly on Joey's side.

Connor stared at him coldly. Then he shook his head. 'No. You don't get me that easily. But you know what, prick? You better behave your fucking self. You better treat Aysha like a queen. Because if I hear you've stepped out of line, trust me, one way or another, I'll be coming for you.'

85

Claire was in her office with the radio playing a Bon Jovi track when Suki came back days later and knocked on the door.

'Can we talk?' she said.

Claire looked up at Suki – *her daughter* – and thought that she looked strained. And no wonder. All this was as big a shock to Suki as it was for Claire herself. Claire had been talking to Donna about Suki in the meantime, asking what she thought of her.

'She's a real hard worker,' Donna had told her. 'And popular with the other girls. No bitching, nothing like that. She's fitting right in, no problem.'

'Of course we can talk,' Claire told Suki.

Suki came in, closed the door behind her, took a seat.

There was an awkward silence.

'I don't know where to start,' said Suki, her eyes probing Claire's face.

'Me neither,' said Claire.

'I . . . I had no idea it would be something like that. I thought I was a mistake you wanted to brush aside. I didn't realize it was *that*.'

'How could you?' said Claire.

Suki's eyes were suddenly brimming with tears. 'And

you were a virgin? That's awful. You must have been so frightened.'

'I was.'

'Did you know them? I mean . . .'

'Can we not talk about them?' said Claire with a shudder. 'Their name was Cleaver. That's all I can say. Later maybe I'll tell you. But for now . . .'

'No. Sure. I'm sorry. God, I'm so sorry,' said Suki, the tears spilling over. She wiped at them irritably. She sniffed. 'I just wanted to say, look – I'll leave. You don't have to see me or speak to me. I understand now. I really do. And I won't stay.'

Claire's eyes were filling too. The girl's sincerity moved her. This whole thing was too much. She thought of her own family and how over the years she had blocked them from her mind because she had to do that, had to keep them safe. Now here was Eva and Pally's grandchild, and Trace's niece, part of their family. And it was so tragic. They would never know her, or she them. Suki got to her feet.

'I'm sorry – real sorry – that you went through that,' she gulped. 'I truly am. And please believe me when I say that I wish you well.'

'Suki . . .' Claire started, getting up.

'It's OK. Goodbye, Claire,' said Suki, and she left the room.

Suki was at her apartment a week later, doing the hoovering and wondering where she was going with her life. She'd left the club, and she knew she had to find another job soon, to keep a roof over her head.

She almost didn't hear the knock at the door over the roar of the Hoover. When she did, flustered and hot, she opened it and got a shock to see Claire Milo standing there holding a paper bag. She stared in surprise, and Claire gave a tentative smile.

'I brought Danish.' She held up the bag. 'Can I come in? And will you *please* come back to work?'

86

Another fight, another victory. Josh was getting tired of it all, but it paid, and paid in bundles. The Greek boys, the Constantinou brothers Spiro and Nikos, had become firm friends of his, and they came on back to congratulate him after the fight. They'd won big again. He was cut, bleeding, aching. Tomorrow all the bruises would come out. He was thinking about going home, to England. Thinking about seeing Connor. And . . . yeah, all right, Aysha too. But . . . there was Shauna.

'Come on, we'll go out and celebrate your win,' they said.

'Guys . . .' started Josh. He didn't want to go anywhere, not tonight. He wanted to fall into a nice big soft bed, and sleep – that was all. Maybe he really *was* getting too old for the fight game. But as usual they jollied him along.

'No arguments! Come on, get washed up and dressed.'

'They're in,' said Vicky, Suki's friend, who was a gorgeous and very loud native New York brunette.

A ripple of interest went up from the other girls. Suki too. She was happy to be back in the club among all her pals, and . . . she couldn't believe Claire had come and begged her to return. But she had. And she loved it.

Suki was learning more about her mother day by day,

learning that everyone here loved and respected her, that she was The Boss, but a kind and benevolent one. She was learning that Claire was quiet, but not shy; strong as iron, but never aggressive. That she was admirable, likeable, with a quick smile and a gentle way with anyone in trouble.

She was so happy to be near to Claire. Grateful, too. She thought that a lesser woman would have turned her back on her for a second time, but Claire was something special. Her *mother* was special, she had to correct herself over and over. Not Claire. Her *mother*. Her mother had extended a welcoming hand even when Suki's very existence must have brought unbelievable pain to her. That took both grace and guts, in Suki's opinion.

'In? Who?' asked Suki.

'The Greek boys. Spiro and Nikos. You seen them yet?'

Suki shook her head. She had never set eyes on the Constantinou boys and she was curious.

'What are they like?' she asked Vicky.

'They're big players. Rich enough to indulge themselves. The oldest one, Spiro, is kind of cute I think.'

When their shift started, Suki circulated with her tray and was kept busy for the first half an hour; then she took a moment at the bar and had a look over at the Greeks on their table right beside the stage. One was big and hooknosed. Spiro. The other one was small, slight, and smiled a lot as Vicky and one of the other girls brought drinks to the table. That was Nikos.

There was another man at the table with them who didn't look Greek though. He was big, even sitting down. He had close-cropped mid-brown hair feathering into grey, and a strong-boned face that was arrestingly handsome. There was a tough, very masculine look about him, and a cut over his brow, like he'd been in a fight. When the man turned his head she could see that his eyes were pale, maybe grey. She could see suffering, and sweetness, when she looked into those eyes. He was staring at her, frowning.

When she smiled at him, he just looked back at her, his expression blank. It made her feel nervous. So she moved away, went back to her tables.

87

Josh felt like he'd taken a punch straight to the gut.

Claire?

She was *there*, standing over by the bar, wearing a shell-pink costume. Her hair was as it had always been, blonde, lustrous; her eyes were blue and her impish smile was just the same.

It was her. It was his Claire, the same Claire he had walked through the meadows with . . .

It gave him such a jolt it made his head spin. He reached for his glass of Bushmills single malt and emptied it quickly, then took another look. No. It wasn't Claire. Claire would be in her forties. *This* girl was in her twenties. But she looked so like his lost love.

'Excuse me,' he said to his hosts, and stood up and walked over to the bar, his eyes searching. She was gone.

Fucking hell, he thought. Now what was happening? He was getting punch-drunk, that's what it was. Seeing old flames when they weren't there at all. Imagining things. This was what every boxer feared; that he would get punchy in the head and start seeing gremlins crawling out of the wallpaper. A lot of people said the greatest, Ali, had got Parkinson's from brain damage sustained in the ring.

It's happening to me, he thought. *I've got to give this fucking game up.*

He would go home. Retire. Live a life of ease and luxury. Which ought to make him feel happy and relieved and hopeful. Only it didn't. It just made him feel depressed. Yes, there was Connor. But also he had a wife he hated, and Aysha – and his doubts over her parentage had never left him, much as he had tried over the years to set them to rest, to be kind to her as a true father should be.

'Can I help you, sir?' asked a female voice beside him.

He turned. It was her. She was looking up at his face and he thought again, *Oh Claire, it's you, it's you at last.*

He had missed her, longed for her so much. Settled for a poor second-best with Shauna, who was a treacherous bitch.

But it wasn't Claire and he wasn't punch-drunk. This girl was American, with a southern twang to her accent. Now he could see the differences. This one's face was broader; she was more inclined to smile, she didn't have Claire's quiet, calm demeanour. She had a mole on her left cheek and Claire didn't. He stared down into those blue eyes and said the only thing he could think of.

'You're extremely pretty.'

She looked uncertain for a moment and almost seemed to sway back, away from him as if he might be a lunatic or something; he knew his sheer size was intimidating. But then her mouth turned upward in a smile. She had pretty teeth, small, well-formed. She looked into his eyes and then raised a hand to the cut over his left eye, brushed against it very gently.

'What happened to you?' she asked.

'I was in a fight,' he said.

'You shouldn't get into fights. It's not a good idea.'

'It's what I do.'

'What does that mean?' She tilted her head, curious.

'I'm a boxer.'

'Get out of here!' Her smile widened.

'It's true.'

'Did you have a fight tonight?'

'I did. What's your name?'

'It's . . .'

Claire. She's going to say Claire, and then I'll know I'm lying spark-out on the canvas and I'm dreaming this . . .

'Suki Vance,' she said.

'You remind me of someone I knew a long time ago.'

'Do I?' Suki looked at him curiously. 'What's her name?'

'Claire. Claire Milo.'

Suki stared at him.

'I lost her years ago, back in England. We were engaged.'

Now Suki was eyeing him with suspicion. 'Your name's not Cleaver, is it?'

Josh stiffened in surprise. 'What the . . . no, it's not. How do you know that name?'

Suki was backing away from him. 'Nah, forget I said anything. It's been nice meeting you, but I have to get on.'

'I'm Josh Flynn,' said Josh, holding out a hand, willing her not to go. He was watching her face with acute curiosity.

Suki eyed his hand for a moment. It was big and scarred, the knuckles scraped. Then she shook it. 'Hello, Mr Flynn,' she said, and hurried away.

As soon as she could get free, Suki went up to Claire's office.

'Claire? Claire!' she called, rushing in. 'Mom' was beyond her, for the moment. It was all too new, too strange.

'Hey, where's the fire?' Claire laughed, looking up from what she was writing.

Suki threw herself into a chair and stared at her mother. 'There's a man down in the bar says he knew you years ago.'

'Right. Who is he then, this mystery man?' Claire was still jotting things down, barely paying attention.

'His name's Josh Flynn. And he's a boxer. He says you were engaged.'

Claire dropped the pen. She looked at Suki and all the colour left her face, just drained out of her, leaving her deathly white. She started to shake.

'Jesus! You all right?' Suki hurried around the desk and clutched at Claire anxiously. The physical contact felt strange – but also kind of nice. 'Do you know him then? Is it true?'

Claire shrugged Suki off and stood up, her knees trembling. 'Show me,' she said.

'There. There he is, with the Constantinou brothers. You see?'

Claire came down the stairs after Suki and stopped dead. The noise of the club in full flow was cut off from her all of a sudden. Time stood still as her eyes found him. It was *Josh*. Older, yes. But the same. *Her* Josh. She put a hand to her mouth in shock. Suddenly there were tears pouring down her face.

'You want to come over with me? Say hello?' said Suki, watching her mother with concern. She was frightened Claire might pass out; she looked dazed, shaken.

Claire could only nod. She followed Suki across the room, weaving among the packed tables, dodging hostesses hurrying around with trays of drinks and empty glasses. Spiro looked up. Then Nikos. Finally, Josh. He saw Suki standing there. Suki stepped aside and they were face to face, Josh and Claire.

Josh slowly stood up. Claire was standing right there in front of him.

'Hey, what's this?' joked Spiro. Then he saw the tears

staining Claire's face, her stricken expression, and his smile dropped away. 'What's going on? You two know each other?'

'Yeah,' said Josh, his eyes never once leaving Claire's face. 'Yeah, we do.'

'Josh,' said Claire, and then her tears became laughter. 'Oh Jesus! *Josh!*'

They moved together then. Claire threw herself into Josh's arms and he lifted her clean off her feet, spun around with her, kissing her beloved face, crushing her against him.

'I can't believe it, I can't believe it,' he was saying over and over in a choked voice. 'Claire. My darling, my Claire.'

Spiro looked at Suki, who was standing there grinning and blinking back tears at the same time. All around them, people were staring, forgetting their conversations, smiling, watching Claire and Josh together. Something big was happening here, something *momentous*.

Then Josh set Claire back on her feet. He swiped at his eyes. Couldn't believe it. He was crying.

'Where the fuck have you *been*?' he asked her, cupping her face in his hands. She was shivering with emotion. 'What did you do, where did you go? No! Don't worry, it doesn't matter. You're here now. You're here.'

And he kissed her, Claire who had danced through the meadows with him when they were young, Claire who he had lost but finally, miraculously, found again.

88

Claire took some days off and she and Josh spent time together, just walking, eating together. He showed her around the grand Waldorf Astoria and took her up to his hotel room. Kissed her. Claire quickly pulled away.

'Josh . . .'

'Yeah, honey?'

'There are things about me you don't know,' she said, looking troubled. She nodded her head toward the bedroom. 'I mean, I'm not sure I can . . .'

Josh's eyes were intent on her face. 'You've been married, I suppose?'

Claire shook her head.

'But the girl. The one who looks so like you, I thought that was your daughter.'

'Suki? She is.'

'Yet you're still nervous about sex?' he asked gently.

He looked at her, trying to read her mind. So she'd had an illegitimate child. He wasn't worried about that, why should he be? But she looked closed off from him all of a sudden, and that disturbed him.

'I got married,' said Josh. 'Can't say it's been a happy marriage, but I've got two kids. Connor. And Aysha.'

'I'm sorry if you're unhappy,' said Claire.

'I married Shauna Everett.'

Claire's face was blank with shock.

'She came away with me the night you disappeared. Pushed herself in, really. And I was so fucking upset at losing you that I let her. Then she got pregnant with Connor, and it was a done deal, I had to marry her.'

'Good God.' Claire stared at him in horror. 'So she got what she wanted after all. She wanted you – and she got you.'

'I wanted *you*. I never wanted her.'

'I need to explain things to you,' said Claire. 'Can I do that? Tomorrow, over lunch? Suki will join us and then you might understand.'

'Sure.' He was hurt. She was saying no to making love with him and he didn't understand why. But he could wait. God, he'd waited long enough, a little more time wouldn't hurt him. 'Claire?'

'Hm?' She was cuddled in against him and he was holding her tight.

He lifted her chin. 'Whenever you're ready, OK? And even if you never are, that won't change how I feel about you. That's the truth.'

Claire's brow cleared and she smiled sadly up at him. 'You're such a sweet man, Josh Flynn,' she said. 'You always were.'

'So kiss me,' he said, and she did.

Josh booked them a table next day for lunch at his hotel and Claire joined him there at one o'clock. She came into the restaurant alone. He looked around. 'Where's Suki?'

'She's coming for the pudding course, she thought we'd need a little time to chat first.'

They settled at the table and Josh ordered wine. Then the waiter left them the menus and departed. They stared at each other across the table. Josh held out his hand and smiling, Claire took it.

'This has been a strange time for me,' said Claire. 'I've only recently found Suki, and now you show up here too.'

Josh frowned. 'What does that mean, you "found" Suki?'

Claire took a breath and then she told him that she had given Suki away shortly after her birth, but that Suki had tracked her down.

'What, you didn't want her? Why was that? Were you having trouble making ends meet?'

The wine waiter came back, poured a little into Josh's glass. Josh nodded, and he poured more and left the bottle.

'I'm going to need this,' said Claire, taking a gulp of the wine. 'No, I wasn't having money troubles. I had a good job at the club, and marvellous friends around me. But Suki . . .' Claire shook her head. 'Oh, Josh, I hate to even talk about it.'

The waiter came back and took their order. Then Josh looked at Claire. 'Go on,' he said.

Claire started to speak. She told him about all that had happened on the night she vanished from his life. About Ciaran and Jeb Cleaver and Shauna coming up to her in the lane. Them killing Blue and burying his remains in the church in the dell. The rape inside the little church that she had always loved so much. The threat from Shauna that she would join Blue and all her family in death if she didn't clear out and never come back. The fact that the brutal rape she suffered led to her giving birth to Suki. Running away, first to Ireland and then to America, terrified for her life.

Josh listened throughout. Their meal arrived and neither of them ate a thing. Claire kept talking. Finally, she fell silent.

'Say something,' she said when he sat there, stunned, appalled by all that he had heard.

'*She* did that to you. Shauna. Set those Cleaver bastards on you?' he said. He wanted to hit something. He was incandescent with fury. From what Rowan Cleaver had told him, he thought they'd just thrown a scare into Claire; not that they'd *raped* her.

Claire nodded.

'Holy *shit*,' said Josh, and drained his wine. Ciaran was dead and out of reach. But *Jeb* wasn't. 'I'm going to kill that low-life son of a bitch,' he said.

Claire looked alarmed at that. She caught his hand. 'No! If you do anything to him, then Shauna could find out. She'd know that *you* know. And how could you have heard that, except from me? Promise me you won't start anything? You have to promise me!'

Josh shook his head.

'Please!' said Claire. She was thinking of Eva, Pally and Trace.

He looked at her. 'You're still frightened of her? Even now?'

'She threatened my parents, and Trace. She *meant* it. Please promise.'

'All right. I do.'

The waiter came over, looked at their untouched plates with concern. 'Is everything all right with your meal?' he asked.

'Yeah, it's fine, just take the plates away, will you?' said Josh.

'I'm sorry,' said Claire. 'This must be such a shock to you.'

'Christ,' he muttered, his brain spinning.

Josh was thinking that Shauna's evil truly knew no bounds. She'd shoved Claire aside and railroaded him into marriage. She'd got her way. But then – Shauna always did, didn't she? He thought of Claire standing in his suite upstairs, looking nervously through the open door at the bed there. Then he thought of all she'd been through.

'God, I'm sorry,' he said, choked with emotion. 'I should have been there to protect you. I was an arsehole. I was stupid.'

'You were young,' said Claire. 'Look – here's Suki.'

Josh stood up and somehow smiled, greeted Suki. But his head was still full of what Claire had told him, and his heart was consumed with loathing for his wife – and the Cleavers.

89

The three of them meeting up for lunch became a regular thing. Every week, Josh Claire and Suki met and talked and laughed, and Josh began to think that Suki was like another daughter; she was the image of her mother and she was a charming girl, ebullient, very American and forthright. And Suki liked him.

Claire and Josh had regained all their old closeness, but still sex was off the agenda, which was fair enough, he thought; she had good reason to be wary of the whole idea.

One spring day after meeting Claire and Suki for lunch in a recently opened diner that was getting rave reviews, Josh walked a couple of blocks and then hailed a cab back to his hotel. When he got to his room, a telephone call came through. It was Shauna.

'Hi,' he said, wondering how he could sound so normal when in fact his whole world had been turned arse-backwards. This *bitch* and her low-life mates had hurt Claire. He'd disliked Shauna for a lot of years, detested her domineering ways and her scheming and her poncey aspirations, but now all that had turned into stark, black hatred.

'Josh, can you come home?' she said.

'Why? What's up?'

He didn't *want* to go home. He wanted the next day to pass quickly so that he could see Claire again.

'There's been trouble. I've been putting off telling you this. Didn't want to bother you.'

'What?'

'It's Aysha.'

Josh's attention sharpened. 'Aysha? She all right?'

'Josh, I hope you're sitting down. She's pregnant, and it's Joey Minghella's.'

Josh flopped back on to the bed. 'Fuck's *sake*,' he said angrily. 'You kidding me?'

'You need to come home, Josh. We have to talk about this.'

The thought filled him with dread. He didn't want to leave Claire. He was worried that if she was out of his sight he could lose her again. 'Yeah. Sure.'

Christ! Of all the times for Aysha to get herself in trouble. There was a bout planned for next Saturday, but he was going to have to cancel. Then he thought again of Claire with her gentle blue eyes, the love of his life. If he got involved with her now, this was how his life would be: he would be torn in two, ripped in half between his family in England and his lover in the States. Wanting to be with her, *needing* to be there for his kids. But he *was* involved with her. He couldn't help that.

When Shauna got off the phone, he called the club, wanting to speak to Claire, to explain. But she was out, so he left a message with Nick the barman and arranged for a flight out next day, back to the UK.

90

Connor collected his dad from the airport, hugged him warmly, took his bag.

'Your mother told me the news about Aysha,' said Josh as Connor drove them home in the Porsche.

'I'm fucking furious about it,' said Connor. 'That bastard Joey Minghella, what a prize *he* is.'

'Whole Minghella family's a washout.'

'She's besotted with that cunt. What can you do?'

'You had a word with him?'

'Several.'

'And?'

'And he swears he's in love with her and wants to do the right thing.'

'What do you think?'

Connor'd had the week from hell. The metal compactor at the yard had broken down and that was going to cost a mint to fix or replace. Costly car parts had been going missing. And the strangest thing had happened to him when he was in the shopping mall. He'd seen Kylie passing by, and called out to say hi. She'd looked at him wildly, then hurried on past. Surprised by her reaction, he'd caught up with her, stopped her with a hand on her arm.

'Hey, Kylie. You OK?' he'd asked.

But Kylie glared at him. 'Ask your bitch mother and her pet ape,' she snapped, and dashed off.

Connor didn't think he *would* mention Kylie to Shauna. Truth to tell, he'd been relieved to see the back of her, and if Mum had whispered something in Kylie's ear, he didn't really care that much. But what was that thing about a pet ape? What did *that* mean?

'Joey thinks he's hit pay dirt, don't he,' said Connor to his dad. 'He's been trying to get on to the family firm for ages. Now he's succeeded. If he's one of us, he'll get the cream of the jobs and plenty of perks, that's his thinking.'

'Well, he's fucking spot on there,' said Josh grimly. 'If he's Aysha's husband, we *have* to see him right.'

'It bloody galls me to have to say it, but that's a fact. She's so charmed by that imbecile that she'd cut us all dead if we took against him. But I've warned him – if he steps out of line just once, that's it. Game over.'

Shauna and Aysha were waiting for them at home, in the living room.

'Hi, babes,' said Shauna, standing up and kissing her husband on the cheek. He stiffened, but somehow managed to hug her. This was his wife, the mother of his children; and she was a monster.

'Hiya,' said Josh. He tried to catch Aysha's eye, but she was looking at the floor, her face petulant. All these years he'd doubted she was his, and he knew it had hurt her, but he couldn't seem to help it.

'Aysha,' he said softly. She looked up. 'You OK?'

Aysha nodded, bit her lip. Then she blurted out: 'I'm sorry, Dad.'

'Come here,' he said, and Aysha ran into his arms and started to cry.

'I'm so sorry,' she wailed, knowing she'd let him down.

Josh hugged her tight. If he had been here more, not so

dazzled by the Stateside money and razzle-dazzle the Greek boys had tempted him with, maybe this situation with Joey Minghella could have been avoided. It was obvious that his family needed him. Not so much Connor, but Aysha obviously did. He was painfully aware that he hadn't been warm toward her, growing up. Desperate for male affection, she had flung herself at that twat. Was this *his* fault for being such an absent, uncaring father?

But Claire . . .

He wanted to be in New York with her. He didn't want to be here. But he *had* to be. He glanced at Shauna. His wife, who had done such evil to the woman he loved. Quickly he looked away.

'Don't cry,' he told Aysha. 'It's not the end of the world.'

'I've let you down. I know I have.'

'You can say *that* again,' muttered Connor.

'Hey!' said Josh sharply.

'Damn it.' Then Connor relented. 'All right. There's nothing we can do about what's happened.'

'We've got a lot of planning to do,' said Shauna.

'What?' said Josh, pushing Aysha gently away. He could barely stand to look at Shauna, he hated the sound of her voice.

'The wedding. July or August would be good. Before she starts to show too much.'

Josh looked at Aysha. He clasped her arms in his hands and gazed into her eyes. 'This what you want?' he asked.

Aysha nodded, eyes red with tears.

'Then we do it. Now dry your eyes, this is an occasion to celebrate. You're going to get married, and you're going to be happy.'

Trouble was, he didn't believe it. Any more than he believed he could sort out the mess his life had become.

91

Claire looked for Josh the next night, the next, then the one after that. The Greek promoter pals of his, Spiro and Nikos came in, but he wasn't with them.

She had too much pride to ask the Constantinous about him. She was afraid of the disappointment, the anguish, they would read in her face when she spoke his name. She knew what they'd say, anyway. She was pretty sure he'd gone back to England, back to his family, to his ghastly witch of a wife and the kids he'd given her.

So she worked. She ran her club, juggled the staff rota because half of them were off with the flu. She chatted to the clients, got on with her life and tried hard to forget him. But she couldn't.

'All men are bastards,' said Suki, hurting for her mother.

'Josh isn't,' said Claire, but she was frantic.

Time wore on and Claire tried to put Josh to the back of her mind. Clearly, he wasn't coming back so she had better just try to forget him. *Again*. Meanwhile, Suki found a better apartment a little closer to the club. She furnished her new home with pieces from vintage stores, tried to make it look good, although it wasn't exactly Park Avenue. Claire and Vicky – Vicky lived just over the Brooklyn Bridge – came to help her decorate.

There was a tiny roof terrace at Suki's new place and sometimes in the evening she would sit out there and drink a glass of wine and smoke a daring menthol cigarette with Claire, although neither of them really liked the taste. Suki told Claire about Aunt Ginny and what a rock she had been to her. She said that she wished Aunt Ginny could see her there, the cool city sophisticate. Ginny would laugh her socks off at the sight. She would cheer and say, *You go, girl!*

Then one day Claire got a call from England: it was Josh. He told her about Aysha.

'Why didn't you tell me you were going?' she demanded. She was fuming mad at him. And damned glad he'd called her, all at the same time. 'You *bastard*.'

'Hey! I did. I had to go, quickly. You weren't in, I left a message.'

'I never got it.'

'Nick the barman. He said he'd tell you.'

'Nick's been off sick. Got a dose of that thing doing the rounds. I thought you'd bailed. Gone back to Shauna. How is she, by the way?' she said with a hint of acid in her voice. That *bitch*.

'Who gives a fuck how she is? I had to be here for Aysha. Not *her*.'

'Then that's OK.'

'I'm sorry you didn't get the message. I love you.'

Claire melted. 'I love you too. Oh, for God's sake, Josh!' Her voice was full of tears. 'I don't want to waste any more time.'

'Neither do I.'

'Please hurry home.'

'I will.'

92

Over the months that followed, Josh found himself flitting back and forth across the pond, torn in two between his duties to his family and his love for Claire.

'It's OK,' Claire told him, but he knew it wasn't, not really, and that she was afraid one day he'd go back and never return. 'I understand you've got to be there sometimes. I *know* that.'

He tried to reassure her. Slowly, they got back the physical bond that had once drawn them so close together, and she would endure his kisses and caresses, but balked at going further, refused to spend the night with him, and that frustrated him.

One day he took her into the bedroom of his hotel suite and showed her the bolster running down the length of it that he'd placed there. Claire looked at it, then at him.

'Boxing's all about discipline,' said Josh, pulling her close to him. 'You see that?' He pointed to the bed. 'You can sleep with me. And I won't cross that middle line. You know me. Do you believe me?'

Claire gazed into his eyes. 'Yes. I believe you.'

'Stay with me tonight then. Please.'

So Claire stayed, and Josh didn't cross the middle line.

★

331

All too often, Shauna was on the phone to him, summoning him back to England to get his morning suit for the wedding fitted, and asking for his help on cooked-up household problems. A radiator off the wall. A bust boiler. She even wanted his advice on the bloke who trimmed the hedges, because he'd just hiked up his prices.

'Fire him,' said Josh coldly. 'Get another one in.'

'Yeah, but you know how it is with these people,' she wheedled. 'They see a woman on her own and they take advantage.'

Josh wondered who the fuck would have the balls to take advantage of Shauna Flynn. He also wondered if Jeb Cleaver was still on the scene. Shauna was a highly sexed woman and had to be getting her kicks somewhere, as she damned sure wasn't getting a thing off him. Probably she had Jeb round there fucking her while he'd been away earning their money, the filthy mare. *He* didn't want her, the very idea made him want to puke: he wouldn't fuck her with someone else's dick, much less his own. And Jeb Cleaver? He promised himself that one day soon, when all this business with Aysha had died down, he would sort that bastard out quietly, once and for all.

'You have to come back,' she said, over and over. 'The suit needs altering, and that takes time, and the wedding's not far off now and Aysha will want you to look your best . . .'

Shit. 'All right,' he said, aware that she was yanking his chain. He knew – and of course Shauna knew it too – that he hadn't been a great father to Aysha over the years. So he had to do the wedding stuff, see her off into married life in style. 'I'll be back Tuesday, OK?'

She was satisfied with that. And as he put the phone down, he thought: *Now I've got to tell Claire.*

And so it went on, Josh coming and going, Shauna

complaining, Claire often in tears as he left her, the pressure building so high that sometimes he thought he was going off his head, wondering what time zone he was in, wondering which way was up.

93

When Aysha came downstairs dressed in her bridal gown on her wedding day, Josh could hardly draw breath.

'You look beautiful,' he said honestly.

Aysha did. She had dark gypsy colouring, black hair and a stunning figure – which was not yet too obscured by the bulge of the baby she was carrying. Shauna had moved heaven and earth to make this wedding happen exactly as she wanted, mercilessly bullying florists, photographers, priests and caterers. There had been tantrums along the way, and tears and screaming matches, but somehow all that had passed and now here they were, on Aysha's big day.

'It doesn't show too much, does it?' Aysha asked her dad anxiously, coming down into the hall and picking up her bouquet of long-stemmed white lilies from the hall table.

Josh just shook his head; he was too choked to speak. The poor little bitch couldn't help what had gone on between her parents, could she? Aysha looked like an angel in a white chiffon scoop-necked gown, cut in the high-waisted Empire style to help conceal her pregnancy. The gown had long sweeping sleeves and a trailing crystalled hem that pooled behind Aysha like a glittering waterfall. Her hair was piled up on top of her head, and her make-up was subtle but flattering.

'You look wonderful too,' she told him. Josh had the stature to carry off a morning suit.

There in the hall, with the sunlight streaming in through the windows and lighting this vision of bridal loveliness, Josh looked at his daughter and said: 'You're sure now? Really sure?'

Aysha nodded. 'Dad . . .' she said, then stumbled to a halt.

'Hm?' Josh was smiling at her.

'I . . . I know you've never liked me very much, and—'

The smile slipped from Josh's face. 'Aysha—'

'No! Let me finish, because I don't think I'll ever have the nerve to say this again. I *know* you've never loved me like you love Connor, and I wish . . . I just wish I knew what I'd done to cause that, to make you hate me . . .' Aysha stopped speaking, then half-smiled shakily and dabbed at her eyes. 'Shit, I'm going to ruin my mascara.'

Josh felt like crying himself. Poor bloody Aysha! She was ignorant of all the crap that had gone down before she was born, she couldn't know that she could easily be Jeb Cleaver's daughter – or *any* of the Cleaver boys, or maybe even Bill the dad's, the filthy old bastard – and not his.

'Honey.' Josh caught her shoulders in a gentle grip and looked her dead in the eye. He'd raised this girl, but he knew he'd caused her pain with his attitude toward her. 'You've done nothing wrong. You hear me? *Nothing.* And you know what? Looking at you here, today, I couldn't be prouder. You . . .' He swallowed hard and forced out the words he knew she needed to hear. 'You're my daughter, OK? And I love you.'

'I love you too, Dad,' said Aysha, blinking back her tears.

'*Kushto bak*, my darling girl.'

Aysha grinned at that. He'd used the old Romany words, meaning 'good luck'.

'Good job Mum didn't hear you say that,' she told him, and he laughed.

'Yeah,' said Josh. They might be Romany, but Shauna never liked to be reminded of it.

Josh hugged her, careful of her veil. Then he drew back. 'Well then,' he said, and held out his arm.

Aysha tucked her hand under his arm and Josh, smiling, led her out to the waiting Rolls-Royce.

Shauna was already inside the church, up at the front. The priest was waiting, ready. The organist was playing 'Jesu, Joy of Man's Desiring'. She had said hello to Frank Minghella and to his latest girlfriend, a blowsy old tart with frazzled hair and bad teeth, and to his waster of a son Joey and the best man, a skinny, pimply little runt of a boy who must be one of Joey's younger brothers.

God, these people are going to be our in-laws, she thought.

Shauna deliberately hadn't invited any of her upmarket friends such as Tanya and Chloe to this. She thought of what that bitch Philippa Houghton would have made of this shindig, and shuddered. Not that Phil was a problem any more. No way would she want the people she mixed with seeing the rabble across the aisle. She'd come a long way in her personal life, and she'd done that by becoming a shrewd judge of occasion. The low lifes on the right-hand side of the church were all toffed up in cheap too-short skirts, orange fake tans and fascinators. Not one decent hat between the lot of them – and the clothes! The last time Shauna had seen such a load of old tat she'd been passing a recycling bin. And the men were little better, all of them badly groomed, wearing cheap shiny suits and stinking of stale sweat.

Shauna's outfit could never be compared to those worn by the women over there. Her dress suit was a lovingly cut and beautifully draped rose-peach Yves Saint Laurent, and her hat was Philip Treacy. She knew she looked damned good, and so did Connor, who was acting as an usher today, along with a couple of Minghella brothers.

Because the Flynns had more or less lost touch with their family from way back, there were no bridesmaids or pageboys. But that was OK. Shauna was only sad – and furious – to think that Aysha was going to link their family to a bunch of no-hopers like the Minghellas. Well, they wouldn't have to see much of them, she supposed. She would make very sure of that.

Then the organist launched into 'Here Comes the Bride', and everyone was standing up. Shauna glanced back. Josh was looking a million dollars as he led their daughter up the aisle. Her Josh. Her heart felt like it was going to burst with pride then. All these years, and he was still with her.

Pity he don't love you though, whispered a voice in her head.

But there was no time to dwell on that today. Her daughter was getting married.

'Dearly beloved,' started the priest, and then he said the words that would bind Aysha to Joey Minghella for life.

94

A week later, when Aysha and Joey had gone off on honey-moon – paid for, of course, by Josh – to the Seychelles, Shauna took the opportunity to have a word with her husband.

'Listen,' she said as they sat in their palatial living room. 'I've been thinking.'

'Oh?' Instantly Josh was wary. He'd been downstairs in the basement gym all morning. It was kitted out with speed-balls, skipping ropes, heavy bags, light bags, a big mirror for shadow boxing so that he could improve on his ducking-and-diving technique, weights and a rowing machine. It was a refuge, away from her. After a gruelling three hours in there, he'd showered – and now she'd taken her chance to corner him.

'You don't have to go back to the States, do you? You could organize some more bouts here. All that travelling, and what's it for? We've got plenty of money, you could earn enough here to keep us in clover.'

The hopeful expression in her eyes might once have made him feel bad, but not any more. The truth was, he *wanted* to go back to the States. Claire was there. Here, with Shauna, he felt stifled. Miserable. Over there he was a free man again, in control of his own life, happy with the woman he loved.

'I suppose I could,' he lied.

'Yeah! Course you could. It would be great, having you home again.'

Shauna was grinning from ear to ear, compounding Josh's dread. This bitch had forced him into marriage, used sex to gain control over him, and finally bound him to her with iron threads by giving him Connor. As for Aysha, well, who knew? Now he felt he'd never be free of Shauna. But he wanted to be.

'The Poles still in the fight game?' she asked.

'Linus has retired. But his nippers have taken it over, they'll still be setting up bouts,' he said, feeling his heart sink to his boots. He hated the idea. It brought it all back, being here. Those fucking deadbeat Cleavers. Shauna's part in all that had happened to Claire. Everything.

'That's it then. Get in touch with them and see what you can get sorted out, all right?' she said happily. Then her voice grew wheedling. 'At least wait to see Aysha get back from her honeymoon, will you? She'd love it if you were here.'

'Yeah,' said Josh. 'I will.' For a couple of weeks, he'd do it. Longer than that? Forget it. He had to get back to Claire. She was right. They shouldn't waste any more time.

To keep Shauna quiet, Josh went reluctantly over to the Pole place, where he found that Bubba, Linus's eldest boy – with a huge gut straining against his red braces and a waxed moustache just like his dad's – was interested in getting Josh back inside the ring for some English matches, soonest.

'My dad spoke very highly of you, Mr Flynn,' he said respectfully. 'Said you were an iron man, a fearless fighter.'

'I could be looking for some local stuff about now. But I'm not over here for long.'

'For you? Damn sure. You're still the heavyweight champion, still the king of the gypsy world.'

As two weeks stretched into a month, with Shauna inventing one reason after another for why he should stay, Josh fought four times in England. His last English fight, a twenty-rounder, was set in an open-sided farm building, with oil barrels marking out the four corners so that the roped-off ring measured twenty foot square. Extension cords dangling off the beams powered bulbs to shed light on the proceedings. The barn was packed, the summer heat inside it oppressive. People were staggering on hay bales to peer over the top of the crushing throng as Josh and one of the Pole cousins, Darnley Jones, squared up to each other.

Josh toyed with Darnley for the first round, got his measure in the second and third, then laid him out flat on the floor in the fourth.

The match was over.

Josh shook the referee's hand and got a pat on the back and a large wad of cash from Bubba Pole.

'I never seen anyone take down Darnley fast as that,' said Bubba. 'He's like a brick-built shit house, our lad. You done good.'

Josh went off to his corner, where the second he had hired for the night attended to him.

There was barely a scratch to show for the encounter. Experience outweighed youthful enthusiasm now: Josh assessed each opponent, sought out their weaknesses, and exploited them. Let them tire themselves out, then he'd move in for the kill. After the fight, he was escorted over to the farmer's house, where the man's wife cooked him bacon and eggs before showing him to the bathroom so that he could shower and make himself presentable.

Searching for his shower gel in his bag, he found a note from Shauna.

I love you, Josh, it said.

Instantly Josh was grinding his teeth in fury. Christ, she was a grown woman, not a clingy girl. What the fuck did she keep doing that for? He thought of Claire and felt such rage bubbling up inside him that he felt he wanted to just kill that slag wife of his and have done with it. He tore the love note up and flushed it down the loo. Then he went back out to the farmer's kitchen and thanked the family for their hospitality, and said goodnight. He stepped outside, breathing in the cooling night air, and got the shock of his life.

'Josh? Josh Flynn?' asked a quavering voice.

'Who the fuck's that?' It was hard to see clearly by the porch light. The man standing there looked like a blob, a pale face, nothing more. Could be anyone.

'It's me,' said the man, stepping forward so that the light caught him.

'Christ,' said Josh. It was Pally, Claire's father.

95

Josh's first thought was that Pally had aged, drastically. But then, hadn't they all? Time skimmed by, and suddenly you were a father with two kids and a wife who made your skin crawl. But Pally looked *ill*. He looked as though something was eating him up from inside. Weight had dropped off his frame, making it narrow, and his eyes had dark blue shadows beneath them.

'I heard you was coming here to fight. Hoped I'd catch you,' he said. His breath sounded wheezy, like he was nursing bronchitis or something. 'I've something to show you.'

Josh frowned. Pally didn't only look ill, he looked *vague*, as if he was only half-aware of his surroundings and what he was doing.

I ought to tell him about Claire, thought Josh. But he had sworn to her that he wouldn't tell anyone where she was or what she was doing. He had promised on the Sacred Heart. And truth to tell, he thought this was a can of worms best kept shut. Too much time had passed now. It was no good to start everything up again, and maybe place Claire or her folks under threat.

'You're a busy man, but I hope you'll have time for this. Come. I've something you should see. Something you should *know*.'

Pally started walking. Josh felt half-inclined not to follow.

He wanted to get home, fall into bed. But there was something about Pally's manner that had him hooked. He followed.

Pally drove them in his battered old Jeep. Neither of them spoke. It was very dark out in the country at night, no street lights, but Pally knew his way and Josh looked ahead as the headlights cut through the blackness. He realized that he knew this route. He knew where Pally was taking him.

'Pally . . .' he started, dry-mouthed, wanting to insist that he turn this bloody thing around.

'Nearly there,' said Pally, and pulled off the lane and down a dirt track.

Josh knew this place so well. It was in his blood. He'd grown up here, on this site, with Claire and her parents Eva and Pally just over the clearing, and Cloudy Grey and Shauna's lot, and his old drunk of a mother, God rest her.

Before Pally reached the clearing into the campsite itself, he pulled the Jeep off to the left. They bumped along over open meadow, the lights tilting crazily up ahead in the gloom, until they saw a small gathering of people standing beside a barrel-top wagon. Pally clamped on the handbrake but left the engine running and the lights on to highlight the scene.

'You should see this,' said Pally, and climbed shakily out of the Jeep. 'Come on.'

The small group of people beside the wagon were turning, looking back in the glare of the headlights. Josh thought he saw Trace, Claire's sister. And that looked like Claire's old Aunt Lil, her mother's sister. Pally's brother too, he thought he recognized. No one else. At least, no one that he could *see*.

He climbed out of the Jeep and approached the group.

They watched him in silence as Pally grabbed a tilley lamp, opened the door of the wagon and ascended the steps. Josh followed. He had to bend nearly double inside, he was too tall for these old things. Pally hung the lamp on a hook and suddenly Josh could see what was in here.

It was a *corpse*.

'She passed three days ago,' said Pally.

Oh shit, thought Josh. Now he knew what was eating Pally up; it was *grief*.

He found himself staring down at a little old woman on the narrow bed. It was Eva Milo, Claire's mother. She could almost be asleep, but she wasn't. Her face was serene and white as parchment. Her thin wrinkled arms were folded on her chest, and she was dressed in a plum-coloured crushed-velvet dress with a pearl necklace at her throat. There were gold hoops in her ears. Her white hair was carefully coiffed, and someone had dabbed a little rouge on her lips.

But it was what Eva was clasping to her that caught Josh's attention and made his breathing stall. She was hold-ing a white dress, billowing and huge; it was spread out over her waist and legs like a vast white blanket. It glowed with pearls and glittered with crystals in the lamp light.

Josh felt the blood turn to ice in his veins as he looked down at Claire's mother.

'Is that . . . ?' he started, then found his throat was too dry, he couldn't get the words out.

'Claire's wedding dress,' said Pally, nodding. 'Eva kept it all this time, in here in its plastic wrapper. She said one day Claire would come back and she would want it.' Pally's tear-filled eyes met Josh's then. 'Eva kept the dress, in case. She wouldn't let anyone touch it, not even when she was so ill this past six months or so. Claire would come back, she said. But Claire never did.'

'Pally, I'm sorry.' He had to tell the poor old cunt right now, that he'd seen Claire, that she was alive and well. But he *couldn't*.

'Your girl, your Shauna. She wanted Claire out of the way so she could get her hooks into you, isn't that so? She wanted it, and she got it. You might ask yourself about that. Shauna was in real tight with Jeb Cleaver once, did you know that?'

'No,' he said. He felt a shiver clutch at his vitals. 'I didn't know that.' He *did*, he knew it damned well, but he wasn't going to discuss any of that shit with Pally. He thought of the other two Cleavers, Rowan and Ciaran, both of them dead at Shauna's hand.

'Think about it,' said Pally, and unhooked the lamp and indicated that Josh should open the door.

Out in the fresh air, Josh stumbled down the steps in a nightmarish daze and watched as Pally followed.

Pally paused on the steps, blew out the lamp. Someone in the watching group – Josh thought it was Trace, Claire's sister – moved. Close by, someone started playing a melodeon, a mournful sound in the still of the night.

'You want me to do it, Dad?' Trace asked.

Pally didn't reply. There was a liquid glugging as Pally fiddled with the lamp on the top step, and the sharp chemical scent of paraffin hit Josh's nostrils.

Jesus, he's going to . . .

'Goodbye, old girl,' said Pally, and a match flared and then the long chiffon folds of the wedding dress erupted in flames.

Josh had a horrifying sight for a moment – the dancing fire in the foreground and the dead old woman lying there at the back. Then the flames roared higher, and he couldn't see a thing. Black smoke billowed out and the heat blazed fiercely. They all had to step back, it was searing. There came a smell of cooked meat and Josh found himself holding his breath in case he threw up.

The barrel-top wagon and its contents burned briskly, and soon the flames went dancing away into the night sky, carrying Eva Milo's poor tormented soul up to the heavens. Josh looked around for Trace, Claire's sister, but she was gone.

96

Josh crawled into bed at gone one in the morning. Shauna stirred, turned toward him.

'I've missed you, Josh,' she said, and he saw the glint of her eyes in the moonlight.

Josh's mind was a whirl, trying to sift through all he'd heard and seen tonight. 'I've only been gone a few hours,' he said.

'Not just tonight. Before. When you were away so much in the States. I hate it every time you go there. I miss you.'

Well, I don't miss you.

'You smell smoky,' she said, sniffing his shoulder.

'Do I? Don't know why.'

Pally's words were echoing around his head. *You might ask yourself about that*, he'd said.

'That right, you were in tight with Jeb Cleaver?' he said. He couldn't help himself.

Shauna was silent. He couldn't even hear her breathing. Then there was movement, and she switched on the bed-side lamp. The room filled with light. Josh screwed up his eyes, wishing he'd said nothing. He was tired and he needed to sleep. But the thing had been circling in his brain ever since Pally had uttered the words; he couldn't get it out of his head. He'd been so dazed by it all, so shocked. He'd never confronted her about any of this shit.

Anything for a quiet life, that was him. But now he felt he *had* to speak.

'*What?*' she said, sitting up, staring down at him.

'Jeb Cleaver. You and him had a thing going.'

'Who told you that?'

'It don't matter who told me. *Did* you?'

'This is *bollocks*! I think we went on one date, back in the day. *Years* ago. He spent the night chatting to his mates while I played the juke, bored out of my skull. Then he cut up nasty 'cos I wouldn't go out with him again. I wouldn't even let him in the trailer, locked the door on him, and he was there for nigh on an hour, knocking and shouting. I s'pose you were out fighting or you'd have seen. You'd have certainly heard. He left a half-eaten box of chocolates outside. And he kicked old Sand, our dog. I must have been mental to go out with him even once. But I was young and stupid. And it was just one date – God's truth, Josh – then never again,' lied Shauna, thinking *Shit! How had he found that out?*

Josh was silent, taking it in, thinking that she lied so easily. It came naturally to her.

'Josh, you have to believe me,' Shauna said in exasperation. 'It was nothing. Now, who told you?'

But Josh turned his back to her. 'It don't matter. Turn the light out, will you, Shauna. I'm done in.'

Josh couldn't sleep, not after that. As the luminous dial on the bedside clock read 2.05 a.m., in his mind's eye he saw the flames of Eva Milo's funeral pyre. Pally's devastated face swirled in front of him as the man set light to what remained of his wife and to his daughter's wedding gown, and sent them on their way together.

Now he was starting to see the whole picture. Shauna had been more tied in to those Cleaver bastards than he had ever known, and they had grabbed Claire, killed her dog, raped her, told her to go and never come back – on *Shauna's* instructions.

The clock dial showed 3.14 a.m. when he started remembering the older Cleaver brothers, Ciaran and Rowan, coming into the kitchen at their old house overlooking the river. They'd brought shotguns, looking for him, intending to maim or kill him; 1978, that was the year – he'd never forget it. Shauna had saved him that night, no doubt about that. And the awfulness of what him and Shauna had to do afterwards – clearing away the bodies in the dead of night, praying that no one would see them at their grim task. Then sitting in the kitchen afterwards, exhausted, blood on the walls, blood and brains on the floor. It all had to be cleaned up, cleared away.

But Shauna saved me.

The memory was lodged there, at the back of his brain. He'd come in the back door that night, and Rowan Cleaver had been waiting for him at the door that led into the hall, holding the shotgun.

Josh looked at the illuminated dial on the clock again: 4.35 a.m.

And here was a strange thing. Their younger brother Jeb had never come back at the Flynn family, never pursued the matter of his two missing brothers. Or *had* he? Had Jeb – who had already done vile things for Shauna – had he come back here while Josh was away, made a deal with her?

Josh thought he had.

What he *also* thought was that Shauna had probably kept – and still kept – Jeb at hand to do any dirty work for her. And he shivered in alarm as he thought of poor old Pally and Trace and – *Jesus!* – Claire, over there in New York. One thing he was certain of: Shauna must never, ever know about him and Claire.

Rikker dovo adrée tute's see, he thought in his old Romany tongue as he drifted off into a restless sleep.

Keep that a secret.

97

'I'm going back to the States,' said Josh at breakfast a few days later.

They were alone in the kitchen, him and Shauna. Connor was in London at the flat he kept there, and Aysha was out for the day with her husband.

'*What?*' demanded Shauna, dropping her knife and fork with a clatter. 'Do you have to?'

'Come on, Shaun. You know the pay's better there. The crowds are bigger. It makes sense.'

'No it *don't*,' said Shauna. 'We need you here, Josh. Your family needs you.'

Josh said nothing, carried on eating. His family didn't need him. His *kids* didn't, anyway. Connor was a coper, he'd handle anything. And Aysha? Poor little cow, he felt bad for her. But they had both said their piece on her wedding day, and that had cleared the air. Now she was a married woman with a kid of her own on the way. As for Shauna . . . well, he wanted to be away from her. The further, the better. He wanted to think all this shit through, without her nagging at him. And he desperately needed to see Claire.

He couldn't even look at Shauna now. Because of this woman, he'd lost his true love. And because of her love of money he'd killed a man, been untrue to himself.

Committed to her, *tied* to her by Connor's birth, he'd

tried so hard to give her everything she wanted. But really he'd always known that nothing would ever be enough for her. He'd got a fortune for what he'd done in the New Forest – but it had eaten into his soul, killing Andrew Meredith. He'd crossed a red line that day, gone against his own instincts, and it was all *her* fault. *Everything* was.

'Is this about some bastard telling you crap about me and Jeb Cleaver?' she asked, her eyes alight with fury.

'No. It ain't.'

'You've been in a funny mood ever since you came back from the States.'

'No, I'm OK.' Josh pushed his empty plate aside and picked up his coffee cup.

Now Shauna's eyes filled with tears. Her lips trembled. 'Don't you love me any more, Josh? You used to love me . . .'

'Don't give me that bullshit, Shaun. I'm just going where the work is, that's all.'

'Then . . . I could come with you,' she said.

Holy shit.

The thought of this poisonous bitch getting anywhere near Claire again . . .

'No. Not a good idea. I'm going, and I'm going alone, OK?'

Josh stood up, went over to the sink and threw the coffee in there. He couldn't drink it. He felt suffocated, like he was drowning; his throat was closed.

It's her, he thought. *Christ, I've got to get away.*

'I'm off out,' he said, and headed for the door. 'Jobs to do.'

Behind him, he heard his wife start to cry, huge theatrical sobs – the kind she was best at.

*

It was only when he was on the plane back to the States that he felt he could breathe easy again. Shauna had crushed the life out of him in those final days back home, and her screams and wails of protest had gone on right up to the wire. He watched an in-flight movie, a murder mystery, and his mind drifted; he saw again the flames of the gypsy burial, Pally's bleached-white face, Trace looking at him with hatred – and why wouldn't she?

'More coffee, sir?' asked the hostess, and he nodded. She refilled his cup. The drone of the plane's engines was soothing, reminding him that he was leaving Shauna far behind.

Shauna.

His wife.

Mother of his children. Well, *child*, anyway.

She'd wanted Claire gone, and Claire was gone. She'd dated Jeb Cleaver. They'd been lovers and she probably still saw that low-life cunt.

All this time he'd spent with Shauna, but did he know her at all?

She'd decided he was going to be hers, he knew that. And when he'd told her way back in the seventies after the Matty O'Connor fight that it was finished with him and Claire, she had seemed . . . what? . . . surprised? Wrong-footed? It was so long ago, but he could still remember the oddness of her reaction. And that was because she'd already seen to Claire.

I'll be yours, Jeb, only do this one thing for me . . .

Josh could almost hear Shauna saying that, her honeyed words concealing the bitter lake of bile floating underneath them. He looked out at clouds stained pink with the light of the dying sun. He sipped his coffee and looked out at the beauty of the world and was glad to be away from her, glad to be going back where he truly belonged, with Claire.

When he reached his hotel and unpacked, there was another note in his bag from Shauna.

I love you, Josh. Hurry back.

He crumpled the note, an expression of disgust on his face, and tossed it into the bin.

98

Josh went straight to Sylvester's to see Claire. All the girls were in, working hard in their saucy corseted costumes. Spiro and Nikos Constantinou were in too, at their usual table by the stage. No act on yet, just the sound system on and Cher hollering 'Believe'. The Greek boys stood up and grinned when he appeared. They greeted him like an old friend, slapping him on the back, calling for champagne to celebrate.

'Where you been? *Yassou*, Josh. We've missed you,' said Spiro.

'*Yamas*,' said Nikos, and they all clinked glasses and drank.

'In England. Daughter's wedding. Had a few fights. Time goes. You know how it is,' said Josh, sitting down, glancing over at the bar, looking for blonde hair and that sweet smile. He drank their champagne and they said they could have some more fights coming up soon, was he interested?

'Of course,' he said, although he wasn't, not really.

More and more he was getting tired of the fight game. The poundings he took were telling on his body; he didn't recover so fast from them these days. He liked the fitness regime and he kept to that, although it was punishing. But fighting now? Maybe he'd lost his edge. His ribs had been broken and strapped up over and over. His knuckles were scarred. His nose was crooked, broken long ago by a pile-driving right-hander.

Maybe he'd finally had enough. Everything had changed since the old days. He had money to burn, he had offshore accounts in fake names – the Greeks had told him how it was all done – and he had cash tied up in property and shares, *also* under false identities, quite a few that Shauna didn't know about, so *sod* Shauna and her grasping ways. If what he allowed her to know about wasn't enough for her, then she could go fuck herself.

He drank, and listened without interest to the female act who came on to the stage to enthusiastic applause. All the time, he was looking for Claire or even Suki. But neither seemed to be here. Later in the evening, he went up to the bar and he saw another girl, a tall brunette, that he'd once before seen Suki chatting with.

'I'm Vicky, sir,' she said, smiling. 'Can I help you?'

'Remember me? Josh Flynn? You seen Suki?' he asked.

Her eyes took on a guarded look. 'Who?'

'Suki. Pretty blonde. Is she coming in tonight?'

'I can't discuss that with you, sir. Club rules. If there's anything I can get you . . . ?'

'Yeah, you can tell me if the owner is in. Claire Milo.' What was Vicky playing at? Of course she recognized him, he'd been in and out of the club many times with Claire and Suki.

'Sorry, sir. I don't think she is.'

'Saw you talking to Vick,' said Spiro when he went back to the table.

'She's a lovely girl. But I was looking for Suki, or for Claire, the owner.'

'Look – she's right over there.'

Josh turned in his seat, and there Claire was, just coming

down the stairs from the offices. He felt his heart falter in his chest as she stopped at the bottom of the stairs and talked to Vicky. Then she looked over to where he was sitting and her eyes met his. The smile died on her lips and she turned away.

Josh went over there, caught her arm.

'Let go of me,' said Claire.

'Claire, for fuck's sake.'

'I thought I could cope with this but I can't. You going back there again, back to *her.*'

'I didn't go for her, I went for Aysha. God, are you jealous?' Josh laughed at that. 'You don't need to be. Don't be stupid.'

'No? Well, she clicks her fingers and you run back there like a fucking lapdog,' snapped Claire. 'I hate her! God, Josh, will you leave me alone? You're making me crazy! I don't even recognize myself any more.'

'Claire . . .'

'No!' she shouted. Heads turned. Claire took a breath and looked him straight in the eye. '*Leave me alone. OK?*'

99

Josh was in despair. Claire was hopping mad at him. She hadn't even given him a chance to break the news about Eva's death. He had never seen his sweet-natured Claire lose it like that. He was feeling the pressure, and now he realized that Claire was feeling it too, badly. But he'd done as she asked: he'd withdrawn, left her alone, hoping she'd cool off, hoping this wasn't going to be the end of things between them.

Miserably he moped about the sidewalks, strolled in Central Park, where the leaves were turning russet and gold, and starting to fall. He went down the gym and trained, but for the first time in his life he didn't feel like making the effort. What was his life, really? It was a pitiful lie, a half-life caught between two continents. And if Claire gave up on him, he was well and truly fucked.

One afternoon he took lunch in a diner and walked back to his hotel. Went up to his suite and lay on the bed. The bolster down the centre seemed to mock him. Nah, she wasn't coming back. He'd blown it. He picked the bolster up and lobbed it across the room.

'Fucking *thing*,' he shouted, and then there was a knock at the door.

'Ah, sod it,' he moaned, rolling to his feet and going to the door, expecting housekeeping wanting to tidy the room.

Claire was standing there, her face set with determination.

They stared at each other and then Claire said: 'Well? Are you going to ask me in?'

Josh stood back from the door. Claire walked in and he closed it and stood there leaning against it.

'I'm glad to see you,' he said after a long pause. She was here. She still looked mad enough to spit, but she was at least *here*.

Claire turned and looked him dead in the eye. 'All right, let's get this out in the open,' she said. 'I *am* jealous. It cuts me to the bone every time you go back there. It hurts me so much I can barely stand it. Because it's to *her*. And she destroyed my life. Do you understand that? She ruined everything for me, and it's a miracle I ever got back on track again, a fucking *miracle*. But now what do I find? That the one person who caused me so much pain still has power over me. Because she has *you*.'

Josh was staring at her, open-mouthed. 'Christ, Claire—'

Claire held up a hand. '*Don't* give me all that old bollocks about you staying for the kids. The kids are *adults* now. So what's really going on here? Are you enjoying the thrill of it, having two women on the go? Is that it?'

'Claire . . .'

'If it is, just tell me. She *robbed* me of a normal life, Josh. I hate her guts. And how you can stand to be in the same house as her is beyond—'

'I'm getting a divorce,' said Josh.

Claire stopped talking. Looked at him.

'You heard right,' said Josh. 'I've had it with her. I've seen Aysha married, that was all I wanted to do. Now I can draw a line under it, and get out.'

'Am I supposed to believe that?' said Claire. She was walking around the suite now, agitated. She went into the

359

bedroom, saw the bolster on the floor. 'And *this* bastard thing,' she said, and kicked it.

Josh started to smile.

'Don't fucking *laugh* at me,' she warned.

Josh looked at her; small, dainty, gorgeous. He loved her so much, even when she was in a rage. 'Or what? You're going to sort me out, are you?'

'Yes! As a matter of fact, I bloody am,' she said, and threw off her coat. Then she unbuttoned her blouse, pushed down her skirt, stepped out of it. Kicked off her shoes. She looked at him fiercely. 'I am going to *do* this. I am *not* going to let that cowing *bitch* win even though she's not even here. I won't *have* it.'

Josh stared in amazement as Claire undid her bra and threw it on the floor. She stepped out of her panties, and chucked them aside too. Then, stark naked, she lay down on the bed.

'So come on then,' she said. 'Get over here, Josh Flynn, before I lose my nerve.'

Josh went over to the bed and looked down at her. He thought he had never seen anything half so beautiful. She was quivering with anxiety. On the nights they'd spent together so far, she had been decorously attired in night-dresses. He'd never seen her fully naked before. She was so lovely and he didn't want to hurt her. 'You're sure? Really?' he said.

She nodded.

Slowly Josh undressed. When he was naked too, he got on to the bed beside her, kissed her shoulder. Claire moaned and turned to him, curling in against him. He kissed her mouth then trailed hot kisses down over her collarbone to her breasts, taking each hard nipple into his mouth, not hurrying. He knew he couldn't rush this, he daren't. Then on and on, down over her belly to the golden triangle of her bush, parting the opening with his fingers and then letting his tongue probe there until he could sense her relaxing, could feel her fingers twining into his hair and hear her gasping breaths growing quicker.

'Oh God, oh Josh,' she groaned, opening herself up to him. 'Don't stop, please don't stop . . .'

He didn't stop until he felt her shudder, felt the strong pulses of her orgasm go quivering through her entire body, heard her unstoppable cries. Then he moved between her legs and eased his erect cock into her, so gently, feeling her warm wetness and steadying himself, thinking that he had to make this last, this was heaven. He felt an instant's resistance when she stiffened and might have pushed him away, but he stayed there inside her, filling her but not hurting her, and she relaxed again.

'I love you,' he murmured against her mouth. 'I've always loved you and I always will.'

Her eyes opened and stared into his. A tear slipped from her eye. 'We've lost so much time,' she whispered.

'We're here now,' he said, and moved in her, feeling that this was blissful, this was all that he wanted in life now; making love, proper love, to this woman. 'My beautiful brave girl,' he said, brushing her tears away.

Claire held him tight as his movements grew faster, and when Josh came in her, letting out a triumphant shout, it felt right, like this was what always should have happened and now, finally, their lives were coming good. They were together again.

100

'Dad ought to be giving it up by now. Don't you think?' said Aysha.

Mrs Aysha Minghella was sitting on the edge of her father's desk in his study, one long leg swinging back and forth, her expression troubled.

Connor Flynn, seated behind the desk, looked up at his little sister, thinking that the suntan suited her and noting how huge the bulge of the kid – his niece or nephew – was. She looked ready to drop, but apparently that wasn't due to happen until around Christmas. All of which should have, *would* have delighted him, if only she hadn't hooked herself up to that Adonis-like prawn Joey.

'Give it up? Nah. Not very likely to happen,' he said.

Aysha's dark eyes bored into Connor's. 'Why not? It makes sense.'

'Dad don't see it that way. You know what he's like. He loves the ring. And, be fair, he can still punch the crap out of men half his age.'

'It's a shame he has to spend so much time away from home.'

'Well, he does a lot of business over in the States with the Greek lot.'

'Mum never goes with him.'

'So what are you saying, he shouldn't take the best-

362

paying jobs around, should turn the American lot down flat?' Aysha fell silent. Connor looked up at her. His sister was like a dog with a bone on this subject. 'He's got to do it, Aysha,' said Connor. 'Mum's OK with it, so why aren't you?'

Aysha didn't think that Mum *was* OK with it. Talking to Shauna this morning, she'd got the distinct impression that the rift she had always felt between her parents had long since become a huge yawning chasm.

'I just worry, that's all. He's not *young* any more.'

'He's not old, either.'

Aysha looked at Connor in exasperation. He was so sensible, so reasonable, so bloody *rational*. The grown-up one who calmed things down, took the long view, *never* freaked out over their father getting pounded to hell in the ring. She swung her feet to the floor, stood up, stretched. Her spine crackled with tension.

'How's married life then?' asked Connor.

'Peachy,' said Aysha, and smiled.

She loved Joey, even if their honeymoon *had* been a bit of a washout. She'd been suffering from morning sickness and feeling unwell and unattractively bloated, and she had to admit to herself that he hadn't been very sympathetic. He'd complained, said it was his frigging *honeymoon,* and if a bloke couldn't fuck his wife then, when could he? He had joked that maybe she was frigid. That had cut her to the quick. She certainly hadn't ever enjoyed sex very much. So maybe he was right; maybe she was.

The honeymoon had opened her eyes, just a bit. But then all men were selfish bastards when it came to getting their end away, weren't they? The accusation of frigidity hurt her. And some of his habits were annoying. She wished, for instance, that he would close the bathroom door whenever he took a shit instead of leaving it wide open. She wished he wouldn't spit on the pavement when he was out with her, and maybe take her to a decent restaurant now and again instead of a procession of skanky old two-for-one-deal pubs.

But then, he was a rough diamond, she told herself, and what else could you expect from him when he'd been dragged up by fat, idle old Frank Minghella? She would work on Joey's bad habits. Things would get better.

She wished he'd start to shift himself a bit more, actually *do* something now that they had a baby coming, maybe stop the clubbing at the weekends. But you couldn't change people overnight. It was nice that Mum had cleared a space for them to move in here, at home. Joey didn't have much money – none of his family did, apart from what they got off the dole and the few under-the-counter jobs they managed to pin down – so it would have been hard for them to get a place otherwise. Now, they didn't have to worry. They lived here. She wished Connor would push something Joey's way – let him help out in the yard, which was turning into a gold mine, maybe – but she knew Connor didn't like Joey. Maybe Connor would mellow, in time. She hoped so. After all, Joey was her husband now.

'And the kid?' Connor indicated the bump. 'All OK?'

'Absolutely fine,' said Aysha. 'Everything's fine.'

101

Joey Minghella was cock of the walk; he was happy. He had a beautiful wife, a sprog on the way, he lived in a fucking great house and the Flynns could no longer look down their noses at him because he was now one of them.

'So how about a job now I'm your brother-in-law?' he said to Connor one day as they stood in the kitchen.

'What sort of a job?' Connor asked. He hated the little tit, but this was Aysha's husband.

'Deliveries. This and that. Like I used to do for you. Or anything. I don't mind.'

Connor eyed Joey with dislike. The business was doing well and the work was almost entirely legitimate these days. He was expanding, too – in the process of buying up another yard, with Benedict's help. They'd splashed out on new signage, new lorries. Things were on the up. But the thought of Joey hanging around at work as *well* as around the house was a pain in the arse. Connor could never forget that Joey was far from reliable. He liked the drugs too much, he was too hair-trigger in temperament. And – worst of all – he had fucked Connor's sister and got her railroaded into marriage.

'Aysha would like it,' said Joey with an angelic smile.

'Fuck what Aysha would like,' said Connor. 'Get work if you want, but you won't get it with me – clear?'

★

Joey was fuming at the way Connor dismissed him. He hadn't expected things to pan out like this, or he would never have bothered marrying Aysha, he'd have just legged it. The pay-off was supposed to be loads of dosh from work shoved his way, a nice big pile of it to stash away for his own personal use, buy plenty of E, hire a prossie or two because for sure Aysha wasn't up for it; his wife had turned out to be a chilly bitch. But that wasn't happening.

'I'm part of the family now,' he moaned to his dad when he went back to the estate to visit. Dad had his feet up in front of the TV as usual, watching the racing. 'And the fuckers are treating me like dirt.'

'Ah, don't worry about it,' said Dad through a blue fug of cigarette smoke. 'They'll get used to the idea.' He glanced up at his son, who was pacing around the grubby carpet. 'Get Aysha to put the screws on, that'll do the trick.'

'Tried that. She's had a go. No result. That Connor? He's an obstinate sod. He won't let bygones be bygones,' said Joey moodily. A job in the yard would have been good; there would have been plenty of chances to pocket stock and sell it on at a good profit.

'One of the blokes down the club said there was something going,' said Dad.

Joey looked at his father. When he wasn't draped over the sofa, drinking beer and smoking fags, Dad sometimes frequented the local working men's club – which was a laugh, because Dad had never done a stroke of work in his entire life.

'Oh? What is it?'

'Clearing gardens.'

'Fuck off.'

'No – pay's handsome. Big houses, people with more

money than sense. Old dears left in bloody great mansions when their husbands have fallen off the twig, they got cash to burn.'

'Fucking hard work, that,' said Joey.

'Nah, not really. You can doss off as much as you like, take it nice and slow and easy. Longer the better, really. Charge by the hour, not the job. Ups the pay.'

Joey went off down the club that night and – sure enough – he got himself a job. He was still signing on the dole, of course. But so what? Big bloody deal.

102

'I can't believe this,' said Claire.

She was snuggled in against Josh's big naked hard-muscled body in the hotel bed and she felt like she must just die of pleasure. He was here. He was back. Then the doubts set in and again she stiffened. He would leave her again. He *had* to. He had family back there. Kids. And a wife. Christ – *Shauna!*

'What?' asked Josh, his eyes on her face. 'What is it?'

'You're going to leave me.'

'I'm right here.'

'Part of you's always over there, though.'

'Claire,' said Josh, stroking a big hand down over her face. 'I love you. And I meant what I said. I'm getting a divorce.'

Josh lay back with a sigh. His marriage had been one long dry desert but this was an oasis of calm happiness. Shauna was a fucking monster, he could see that now. She'd battened on him like a leech and sucked him dry. He'd never felt this good, not for *years*. Not since he'd last been with this same woman.

'God, this is so scary,' said Claire.

'What's scary? We're happy and we're together,' he said. God, his poor girl. She'd had such horrors done to her, and yet here she was, still strong, still coping with life. He admired her so much for that. She was a true Romany. A survivor. And she was whole and well, and with him at last.

Claire was thinking that she'd had a fearsome enemy in Shauna, and she had escaped her by the skin of her teeth. If Shauna ever found out about this, they would suffer. *She* would suffer. And she had a family of her own to protect. Her mum and dad. Misery-guts Trace her sister, who she loved and missed every day. And now she had Suki, too.

'What's up?' asked Josh, feeling the shiver run through her. Her body, pressed so close against his, was making him grow hard again.

'Nothing,' she said, and sighed and pushed the whole thing aside. 'Kiss me,' she murmured against his mouth, and he did, and she reminded herself she was happy *right now*, and that would have to be enough.

103

Joey was on the dole but Job Seeking, which was a laugh. He turned up at one or two interviews, slouched in the chair, made himself look unemployable, and then went on his way. What paid better and suited him best were the occasional under-the-counter jobs his mates down the club could pass his way, all undeclared, cash in hand, and topped up by the steady trickle of benefits from the DSS, courtesy of the great British taxpayer.

He got a job clearing an old lady's garden. She was a sweet thing, brought him out lemonade when it got hot and ushered him into her vast barnlike kitchen when she had to pay him. Cash in hand, of course. He charged her twenty quid an hour, but slipped in an extra half hour here or there to see if she'd complain. She didn't, so he slipped in a few more.

He chatted to her, found out her background. She had no kids except for a daughter in New Zealand, and that was great because there would be no one poking their noses in and keeping an eye on what he was doing around the house. The old lady was vague, emptying her purse on the worktop and asking how much did she owe him today? And he saw the bundles of twenties in there. Shit, she really did have cash to burn. So he added on a bit, and again – she didn't notice.

He suspected the old dear was losing her marbles, and that was confirmed to him when one day she took off to see a specialist with a hospital volunteer and forgot to lock the doors or set the house alarm. He was there in the garden, just pottering around, no need to exert himself . . . and then she went out, and would be gone some while, so he went indoors and had a look around.

It proved well worth the bother. There was a large bundle of cash upstairs in a wardrobe, hidden under a pile of mothballed clothes. He pocketed about a third of that, left the rest. And on the ground floor, tucked under the stairs, was a safe. Her husband had been an industrialist, he'd owned a factory, so there must be a good pile of wedge sitting in there, Joey was sure of it. But he couldn't crack safes. Wouldn't have a clue where to even begin.

So he went back to the club and talked it over with a couple of his mates.

'She must know the combination,' said one of them, ordering a whisky chaser to go with his beer.

'Yeah, she must,' said the other. 'Just get it out of her, that's all.'

Joey looked at the pair of them. Suddenly he wasn't sure about this. 'What, *beat* it out of her?' he asked.

'You say the poor old cunt's doolally, she'd probably just tell you it if you slapped her around a bit.'

Joey eyed them dubiously. This was getting a bit heavy, and he didn't like it. Nicking the old girl's cash was one thing, but beating the crap out of her?

'Nah,' he said. 'Think I'll leave it.'

'Up to you,' said his mate.

'Yeah,' said the other one.

104

Days passed in a contented haze, blending one into another. Josh and Claire took a leisurely lunch together and then strolled over to Turtle Pond in Central Park. After that, they went back to the hotel and made love all afternoon. They lay there as evening drew in, wrapped in each other's arms until Josh stirred himself enough to ring down for room service. Then they showered together, kissing and caressing all the time, and emerged to eat. They drank wine, then fell into bed. Josh had never slept so well in his entire life. All the torment he'd felt, all the doubts and suspicions over Shauna, fell away from him and he was happy, spent, exhausted.

When he awoke in the morning to make love to Claire all over again, he knew that this was something beyond special. He watched her lying there dozing, her mouth open a little, her breathing gentle, her hair spread out silky and corn-gold on the pillow.

Claire, he thought, and got a flashback of her running, young and untroubled, ahead of him through the wild-flower meadows, her hair flying, her eyes teasing as she glanced back at him.

Catch me, Josh.

He'd never caught her then, but now – at last – he had. His heart lurched in his chest every time he caught sight of her. When she was away from him, he felt bereft. Lonely. This was deep, enduring love and now he'd rediscovered it he was never going to let it go.

She stirred, her eyes flickering open. They gazed up at him and her arm came up, her fingers brushing through the hair at the nape of his neck. He bent his head and kissed her. Thought of her mother, Eva, the funeral pyre . . . *I have to tell her.* But Claire was so happy, so content, that he couldn't bear to ruin it for her.

Soon though, he thought. *Soon, I will have to tell her.*

'Wake up, sleepy head,' he murmured against her mouth. 'We've got a busy day ahead.'

'Doing what?' She yawned.

'Let's rent a place together,' said Josh.

'*What?*' Claire shot up in the bed and stared at him, blinking in surprise.

Josh shrugged. 'We can't be spending all our time in hotel rooms or at your place at the club. I could rent us a really nice place. Bigger. Better. In your name, not mine, I don't want you worrying that I'm going to fucking well abandon you or some crap like that. I'll set up a standing order paying the rent into it every month. So come on. Let's go shopping for what this lot call real estate. What do you say?'

'I don't believe this.'

'Believe it. It's true.'

Claire let out a squeal and threw her arms around him. 'I love you!' she shouted.

'I know,' he said, laughing.

105

Shauna nearly threw a fit when two uniformed police came knocking at the door. Her first thought was *Josh. Something's happened to Josh.* Her second was that somehow they'd found out about her killing the two Cleaver brothers all those years ago. Or the other things. There *were* other things, bad things, and the police on the doorstep brought them all crashing to the front of her mind.

'What the hell?' she asked them.

She was alone in the house except for Aysha, who came lumbering, large with the baby, into the hall and stared at the two coppers on the doorstep.

'Is Mr Minghella in? Mr Joey Minghella?' asked one of them.

Aysha went white as a sheet. 'Why?' she asked. 'What's going on?'

Shauna put a comforting arm around her daughter's shoulders. 'I'm sure it's nothing,' she said, giving them her most penetrating stare. 'Why do you want him?' she asked.

'We want to talk to Mr Minghella in connection with a serious incident. Is he in?'

'No, he's not. He's gone over to see his father,' said Aysha. 'He's my husband.'

'Can we have his father's address please?'

Aysha reeled it off. 'What's all this about?' she asked.

'Nothing to concern yourself with, Mrs Minghella. We need his help with our inquiries.'

It was only later, when they'd pulled Joey in, that Connor drove Shauna and Aysha down to the police station and the true facts of the case came out. A Mrs Rothstein's neighbours had told them she had a gardener called Joey Minghella so the police needed to speak to him as soon as they could because something awful had happened. Poor Mrs Rothstein had been the subject of a robbery, in the course of which she had suffered a stroke and died.

That evening, Shauna phoned Josh at his New York hotel, but they said he was out. Could she leave a message, they would make sure that Mr Flynn got it.

'Tell him to phone me back, it's his wife, it's urgent,' said Shauna.

'Your number?' asked the receptionist, who had seen Josh going through the lobby many times with an attractive middle-aged blonde woman.

Shauna told her. Then she sat down in the living room with Aysha, who was in tears, and wished to God she had a normal husband like any other woman – a stockbroker, a lawyer or even a fucking road sweeper – and not one who kept disappearing off the face of the earth when he was bloody needed *here*.

Josh and Claire had a lovely day together, hunting for the perfect apartment.

'So I'm going to be your mistress,' said Claire.

'Don't say that. That's not how I think of you. You're what you've always been: the woman I love.'

They found the perfect apartment at East 76th Street, on the Upper East Side – a vast place lit by vivid sunlight and with a panoramic view of the park and the New York

City skyline beyond it. Josh put down a retainer, and they went back to the hotel to celebrate over dinner. When they got there, the receptionist discreetly said to Josh:

'Mr Flynn, your wife called.' The woman did not so much as glance at Claire, but Claire felt her cheeks burning all the same.

Josh felt his happy mood evaporate. *Aysha?* he thought. *The baby?* 'What did she say?'

'She said you were to phone her, that it was urgent.'

'I'll do that. Thank you,' said Josh, and in silence he went with Claire over to the lift and up to the room. He sat at the desk in the window, and dialled out. Claire went into the bathroom. He knew she couldn't bear to listen to him talking to Shauna.

Claire sat on the edge of the bath while Josh's voice droned on in the sitting room. When he stopped speaking, she came out. Josh was sitting there at the desk, staring out of the window.

'Josh? What is it?' she asked.

He half-turned in the chair, held out a hand. Claire went to him and he pulled her down on to his lap with a sigh. He looked like he had the weight of the world on his shoulders and she felt suddenly afraid.

'Josh?' she queried, linking her arms around his neck and gazing into his face.

'I'm sorry, babe. I have to go back,' he said. 'Family trouble.'

'Bad?' she asked. She felt crushed. He was about to abandon her. Once again.

'Pretty bad. I have to be there.' His grey eyes held hers. 'You do understand?'

'Yeah. Sure,' she said with forced lightness, thinking of her, his wife, *Shauna*.

He'd said he was going to get a divorce, but she couldn't dare believe that. Was this the way it was going to be for them, like, forever? Snatched moments of happiness, and then he'd go and she'd have to wait and wonder if his guilt was so bad about his family over there that he might not come back this time, or the next, or the time after that?

'Go,' she said firmly, and kissed him, keeping the worry out of her face, smiling, trying not to let any of it show. 'You have to go. Sort it out. Then come back to me.'

106

'Where is the little arsehole?' asked Josh when he and Connor got indoors. Connor had picked him up from the airport as always, and said little on the way back except that the shit had hit the fan, and why had his sister been so *stupid* as to marry such a low-life creep?

How do we know who we're going to fall in love with? thought Josh. Once, he might have called Aysha stupid too, but that was before he'd met up with Claire again. He felt a wash of shame sweep over him at the situation. He hated it here now and he wanted to be back in the States, with Claire. Not here, sorting out yet another mess. Seeing Shauna again, bringing back all the doubts, all the unanswered questions, all the bone-deep loathing he felt for her and which he could now barely conceal.

Shauna was there, sitting in the living room next to a pale-looking Aysha.

'I'll take your bag upstairs,' said Connor.

'Thanks.' It struck Josh then that he was going to have to sleep in the master suite, in the same bed as Shauna. If he took the spare room, there'd be hell to pay and she'd never stop pecking his head over it. Christ, he'd become so far removed from her that it filled him with horror, the thought that she might reach for him in the night.

Shauna stood up, came over to him, kissed his cheek.

He forced himself to kiss her back, without warmth. Then Aysha levered herself to her feet and came over. 'Daddy!' she said, and hugged him; but she didn't cry. She seemed too shocked for that.

'It's all right,' said Josh. 'We'll work this out. Where is Joey?' he asked as Connor came back downstairs and stood beside him. 'They let him out, didn't they? He was just helping with inquiries?'

'He's over at his dad's place, but I had a word with him before he went,' said Connor. 'The thick little fucker. He set it up then got cold feet. He was doing garden clearance at this old lady's house. Talked about it with two of his mates down the club, told them the old woman had a safe under the stairs and money all over the place in the house. They broke in and started slapping her about to get the combo out of her, and then she goes and drops dead with fright. One of the neighbours mentioned the gardener Joey Minghella and bob's your uncle, here we are.'

'He wouldn't have hurt the old woman,' said Aysha.

Josh shook his head. 'Aysha. He *killed* the poor old tart, doing what he did.'

'I know, but—'

'You still defending that tosser?' asked Connor. He twirled a finger around on his brow. 'You're *mental*.'

'None of this would have happened if you'd given him some work,' said Aysha.

Connor eyed her with disbelief. 'Oh, so this is my fault? Jesus, Aysh. That bloke's a liability. Face it.'

'So what's happening now?' asked Josh.

'Joey mugged his two mates off to the police,' said Shauna. 'Said he was the innocent party, that he'd only mentioned he was working there to them, nothing else. They'll go down for manslaughter at least, no doubt about that. The muskras . . .' Shauna paused, a brief look of disgust crossing her face. She corrected herself. 'I mean, the *police* pulled them in. They're nicked – and they never did crack that safe open.'

'So Joey's out,' said Josh.

'He's out on bail. Cost us a fucking fortune,' said Connor.

'I'd better get over there,' said Aysha, awkwardly bending to snatch up her cardigan and handbag. She felt ill with the baby, this was all she needed. Her family were right. Joey *was* a fool. But she loved him. 'He'll be upset.'

'You want me to drive you?' asked Connor, concerned.

'What I want, Connor, is for you to leave me alone,' she said, brushing past him and vanishing into the hall. 'This is all on *you*,' she added, and the front door slammed behind her.

107

Aysha went outside and started up her BMW. 'My Heart Will Go On' by Celine Dion roared out of the speakers and irritably she flicked the thing off. *Fuck* romantic songs and *fuck* romance. She could barely get behind the ruddy steering wheel; she was massive, she felt sick and fearful, and bloody Joey was playing them all up. She was starting to feel that the whole bloody marriage thing was just too much *fucking* trouble.

She drove over to the estate and parked the car outside the house, behind Joey's old beat-up Ford with its boom box in the back. Joey loved music, the louder the better. He was still like a teenager in that respect.

In a lot of respects.

She got out. There were kids zipping up and down the street on skateboards, and they eyed her car with interest.

'Anything goes missing on this bloody thing and you'll pay for it,' she snapped at them, and they grinned.

'Keep an eye on it for you for a tenner,' said one, a carrot-topped porky kid with eyes like a riverboat gambler.

'Five,' said Aysha.

The kid spat in his palm and Aysha shook on it and passed over the cash. She went up the concrete pathway to the house. Joey's dad's rust heap of a car was parked up on the long grass in the front garden, beside an old pink sofa with the springs hanging out. The nets up at the windows were coffee-brown, and the front door was so badly scraped that it was impossible to tell the colour. The wood around the battered faux-brass letterbox looked scorched. She knocked on the door.

'Who is it?' roared a male voice after a pause. She could hear the telly going.

'It's me. Aysha,' she shouted back.

There was a scrabbling sound and then the door opened. Joey peeked around it, then quickly pulled her inside. 'Don't stand out there shouting the odds,' he said, yanking her after him into the dingy sitting room.

Joey's dad was on the sofa in front of the telly, dressed in his usual uniform of vest and brown trousers. Some daytime show was on but she could barely see the screen for the cigarette smoke in here. The room stank of fags, booze and male sweat. Aysha wrinkled her nose and tried not to breathe.

Ten, twenty years' time, is this Joey? Is this what I'm going to end up with?

As soon as the thought crossed her mind, Aysha hated herself for it. Yeah, Joey came from a bad family. That wasn't his fault. It didn't mean *he* was bad, did it? She loved him. He was handsome and . . . but Jesus. This business with the old lady. He couldn't really have been involved in that, could he? He was going to be a father soon. She needed a man. Not a fucking delinquent.

That was exactly what he looked like right now, standing there in his dad's house with his hands stuffed in his jeans pockets and his eyes on the floor. He looked like a boy, scared when he'd been caught raiding the biscuit tin. Aysha thought of the men in her own family, rugged, big, tough. That they would ever be involved in anything as shabby as this was out of the question.

'What happened, Joey?' she asked him flat out. 'What *is* this about the old lady who died?'

'Fuck it, Aysh, I don't want to talk about it,' he said.

'And what are you doing here? We should be at home.' She couldn't stand this place, or Joey's low-life father. Truth was, it frightened her to see it and she avoided it whenever she could. Joey seemed far more comfortable here than he ever did at home with her folks. Maybe this was where he really belonged.

Joey was avoiding her eyes. His dad coughed loudly and reached down, popped open another can of beer, his gaze fixed to the telly.

'Joey?' persisted Aysha.

'I got some stuff upstairs, I stopped over to pick it up,' he said.

'Does that matter? When all this shit is going on?' demanded Aysha.

'Look, I gotta . . .' He hiked a thumb at the open door-way and then left the room.

Aysha followed him as he went up the stairs and turned left. He opened a door and went into a poky grey room with a disordered bed and a thick layer of assorted crap all over the floor. He picked up a black bin bag and started throwing open drawers, emptying T-shirts and underpants into it.

'What are you doing?' asked Aysha. 'I thought you brought all your stuff over to the house.'

He shrugged. 'Some of it got left in the rush,' he said.

'Joey, for God's sake! Why are you doing this now? Haven't we got enough trouble, without you faffing about rearranging your fucking underwear?'

'Look.' He turned to her and his dark eyes were full of anger. 'Listen, all right? I gotta take off for a while.'

'You what?' She couldn't believe what he was saying to

her. 'But Connor stumped up bail for you, you can't just . . .'

'Christ, you don't know a fucking thing, do you?' he yelled suddenly.

Aysha flinched. He'd never shouted at her before. Not once. 'Then tell me,' she said. 'Is it true about you and the old woman? That you set it all up?'

'No! I was just shooting the breeze with my mates, telling them what I saw, that's all. It was fucking stupid of me, I admit that, but that's *all* I did.'

'Well, that's OK then. You made a mistake, but you weren't involved in any nasty business . . .'

'Aysha. For fuck's sake, get real! I shopped them to the Bill. The coppers pulled me in for it, some neighbour told them I was doing the garden for the old bint, and . . . I made a deal with them. It was all my fault, I admit that. But beat up the old bird that way? I wouldn't do that. So . . .' He paused, zipped up the bag.

'So what, Joey?' Aysha felt numb. She was heavily pregnant with his child, and here he was, getting involved in sick-making stuff like this.

'I dobbed in my mates,' said Joey. 'I had to, or I'd have done time too. I still might. Some. I don't know. But I told the Bill all about them, what they had planned, and that I'd had nothing to do with it.'

Jesus. He wasn't just a low-life juvenile, he was a grass too.

'OK. So . . . we can make this all right, can't we?'

'You must be bloody joking!' He laughed, a mirthless horrible sound.

'Well, they're inside, aren't they, and—'

'Sure. *They* are. But their fucking *families* ain't. And now they're going to track me down and kill me like a dog. Dad's had threats against me put through the door. And worse. Shit in a bag. A fucking burning rag last night. You don't know what you're talking about. Aysh, I got to clear out. Let it all die down.'

Aysha thought of the scorched letterbox downstairs. This was serious. The whole house could have gone up in flames.

'But you're skipping bail. Connor will lose his money. The police will be after you too. And the baby . . .'

'The baby, the baby!' he mocked her in a high-pitched voice. 'Christ, listen to yourself! You don't have a fucking clue about anything, sodding Princess Aysha, spoiled-rotten little rich girl.'

Aysha felt the colour leave her cheeks, felt the room tilt and sway. She clutched at her belly. She was carrying his child, and he was going to leave both her and the baby behind. And for how long? Was she ever going to see her handsome, feckless husband again?

Joey picked up the bag and swung past her out the door, along the landing. Aysha followed, grabbed his arm. 'Joey, don't,' she pleaded.

'Shut up, Aysh, I'm going,' he said.

'No!' Aysha yanked him back, hard, and he shoved her.

As she tried to regain her balance, Aysha's foot slipped from under her and then, almost in slow motion, she felt herself tilt sideways. She clawed at the wall, but it was no good. With a faint cry of horror, she toppled down the stairs. She felt a crashing pain in her knee, her elbow, her neck, as the world spun around her. Then blackness grabbed her and everything was gone.

108

The atmosphere in the house was so stifling that Josh escaped to the pub down by the river as soon as he possibly could. He couldn't stand being around Shauna any more. Couldn't even bear being under the same roof as her.

Fuck, what a mess.

The kids, the house, everything . . .

What a bloody *mess*.

He ordered a pint and then stood at the bar drinking it and thinking of Claire so far away. Claire had been good about this, although he could see it troubled and hurt her. She had said, 'Yes, Josh, of course you have to go, I understand, and don't worry about a thing. I'll sort out the removals and get settled in the new place, you come straight there when you get back and I'll be waiting, OK?'

He couldn't wait to be with her again. And then . . . when all this muck and fuddle died down with Joey, he was going to sort this properly. Get rid of that cow Shauna. Yes, the kids would be knocked to fuck by it, he knew that. But at least Connor and Aysha were adults now.

'Josh? That you?'

He turned. Standing there was a short seventyish man with a wrinkled-monkey face. He was smartly dressed, prosperous-looking, with a tan and a shiny bald dome of a head.

Josh had hoped never to see him again. But here he was: Dave Houghton. With less hair and more lines on his face. Instantly into Josh's mind came the image of Andrew Meredith falling back with his brains spraying out in a crimson fountain. He swallowed hard as bile rose in his throat, and held out a hand. Dave shook it.

'How are you, Josh? Christ, you look bloody well,' said Dave with a smile.

'How are you, Dave?'

'Nowhere near as good as you. What you on, fuckin' hormones or something?' Dave patted Josh's washboard stomach. 'Still keeping up the fitness malarkey then?'

'Sort of,' said Josh. Yes, he was still fit, and finding Claire again had knocked years off him. He felt like a twenty-year-old when he was with her. Then he came back to England, saw Shauna, and felt a hundred.

'How's the family? How's that lovely Shauna?' asked Dave. 'What'll you have, Josh?'

'No, I'm fine,' said Josh. He didn't want to linger here chatting to Dave. It brought it all back, and he didn't want that. 'Shaun's great,' he lied.

'And your kid? Boy, wasn't it?'

'That's right. And a girl too. Yours?'

'Both doing fine. Married now, the eldest is coming to lunch in a mo, you want to join in, you're welcome.'

'No, thanks, got things to do,' said Josh quickly. 'How's Philippa?' He'd hated the woman, thought she was a high-toned bitch, Shauna had been right about that. Took one to know one, he supposed. But he had to be polite.

'Oh.' Dave's face fell. 'Poor old Phil.'

Josh stared at the man. 'What?'

'Well, she died,' said Dave.

Josh froze in surprise. 'She what? But she was no age at all. What happened?'

'It was tragic.' Dave's voice was suddenly choked with emotion. 'Bloody awful, I'm telling you. I went out to work and came home and the house was empty. Kids away at school, Phil would always be home cookin' the evening meal. Well, opening a bloody packet and shoving it in the microwave, anyway. Hopeless in the kitchen she was, really. But there was nobody there.'

'So . . .' prompted Josh.

'I searched the place from top to bottom. Nothing. Then I went out in the garden and had a look all around. Still nothing. So I goes down by the river and looks there. You know how slippery the banks are, we were always warning the kids about not playing too near. And that's where I found her.'

'What, in the river?' Josh felt his stomach gripped by something. Maybe fear. He was Josh 'Fearless' Flynn, but yes, all at once he felt frightened. Like someone had just walked over his grave.

Dave was nodding. 'Yeah, there she was. All tangled up in the weeds and the willow roots, or the current would have taken her further downstream. Staring right up at me, she was. Drowned, poor old Phil. Dead as toast.'

'Christ. I'm sorry,' said Josh.

'Tragic, yeah? She must have got too near the edge and just lost her balance. I couldn't get over it for a long while. Shook me right up.'

'That's awful.' Josh was remembering how much Shauna had hated Phil. And now she was dead. 'When was this?' he asked, although he really, really didn't want to know.

'Late autumn I guess – 1978.'

Now Josh thought of Shauna coming back from lunch with the 'girls' and saying, *That cow Philippa, Dave Houghton's wife? She told the others I was a gyppo, the mouthy cow. Christ, I hate her guts.*

Then Dave turned a little, elbow on the bar, and his face lit up. 'Ah, here she is,' he said, stretching out a welcoming arm.

For a moment, feeling he was in a nightmare, Josh expected to see Phil, white as a bloated maggot and covered in fronds of stinking grey weed, come stumbling on dead legs across the bar toward them.

But the woman who joined them wasn't Philippa, dead *or* alive. It was a tiny, pretty young Malaysian woman who looked at Dave with adoration as he slipped his arm around her shoulders.

'Josh,' said Dave proudly. 'This is Wi Lin.'

So not *that* broken-hearted about poor old Philippa then. Josh wondered if Dave still had male lovers, too. He supposed he did. But what the hell. Who cared?

Josh stayed there for another few minutes, then left Dave and his new love to it.

109

Not wanting to go home yet, Josh went over to his mum's grave, feeling reluctant to do it but thinking that for once he should pay his respects. He half-hoped he would see Claire's sister Trace there and have a word. On the night of her mother Eva's gypsy funeral, she had vanished too quickly for him to talk to her, but maybe today she might stick around.

She wasn't there.

So he drove back to the camp, near to where Pally had taken him to see off his old lady into the next world. The dogs came out straight away and started barking. Then Pally appeared at the door of his trailer, still looking like death warmed up. He saw Josh and came over. Josh got out of the car. The dogs sniffed around him, then went away.

'You back? Thought we'd seen the last of you,' said Pally.

'I wanted a word with Trace,' said Josh. 'She in?'

Trace came out into the trailer doorway. 'She's in,' she called down. 'What you want, Josh?'

'Can we talk?' he asked.

She shrugged. 'What's to say?'

'Please. Five minutes.'

Pally looked between the two of them and then wandered back to the trailer door. Trace came down the steps, passing her dad with a brief pat on his shoulder. She approached Josh and stood there looking at him expectantly.

'Five minutes then,' she said. 'Let's walk.'

Trace and Josh went out of the camp and down the dell by the line of poplars, toward the wildflower meadow and the disused old church beyond. Two of the lurchers followed, romping around in the long grass playing tag. The sun shone down. It was heaven, like he had once known with Claire.

'So speak,' Trace said after a while, halting and turning to look at him with stark dislike.

Josh stopped walking too. Above them, skylarks whirled in the sky, singing – a tinkling waterfall of wild joyous notes. The sun beat down like a blessing. But in his heart there was only darkness.

'What do you know about Shauna and Jeb Cleaver?' he asked her.

'What?'

'You heard.'

Trace was nodding slowly. 'Didn't think you knew about that. What's she told you?'

'That it was one date, then forgotten.'

Trace rolled her eyes and blew out her cheeks. 'My arse. They were an item for like, *forever*. You didn't notice of course. Besotted, weren't you – with Claire. I thought at the time – so did Claire – that the whole Jeb Cleaver thing was for your benefit. Make you jealous. Or try to. Didn't work, did it? You didn't even bloody notice.'

Josh looked at Trace. She was not pretty. Claire had always been the attractive one. Even now, Claire had kept her looks. But Trace hadn't and she'd become a plain middle-aged woman, thickening around the middle. 'What did you think, about Claire vanishing like she did?'

'Who knows? Maybe they done away with her.'

'They?'

'Shauna and Jeb Cleaver.'

'Is that what you think?'

'Maybe. *You* ought to know what Shauna's like, she's your missus, ain't she. So who knows? Claire's dog vanished too that night. Blue. Good old dog, he was. Gone like he'd just disappeared into thin air.' Trace looked at Josh sharply. 'Shauna's lot were rotten, you know. Dark and bloody dangerous. They were into curses and black magic, things to do you harm. My Nanny Irene had some powers in that direction too, but all she ever did was help and heal people. She's dead now, God rest her.'

'Yeah? I'm sorry to hear it.' Josh looked over to the little church. His and Claire's special place. Shauna and that wicked fucking Cleaver bunch had ruined it now, for both of them. He thought about it. He *had* to say it now. Claire's mum and old Nanny had died without knowing, he couldn't let that happen again. 'Listen. Trace. I want to tell you something. And I want you to pass it on to Pally. Gently, mind. Careful how you tell him.'

'What is it?' Trace was frowning.

'Claire's alive. She's well. I've seen her.' Josh thought then of his promise to Claire. But for fuck's sake! He couldn't let poor old Pally go on without knowing she was all right. The man had suffered enough.

'Where?' asked Trace.

'I can't tell you that. But she's fine. Tell Pally that.'

Trace nodded and her eyes were full of tears. 'Jesus! Really?'

'Really. But keep it between the two of you, OK? No one else must ever know. Promise me.'

'Yeah. OK. I promise.'

110

When Josh got home, all hell was breaking loose.

'Christ, where have you *been*? It's Aysha,' said Shauna, shrugging on her coat in the hall as Josh came through the front door. She looked wild with worry.

'What's happened?'

Connor came through from the kitchen. 'She's had a fall over at the Minghella place,' he told his father.

'Shit. Is the baby all right?'

'We don't know. They've taken her straight to hospital. Come on, I'll drive.'

At the hospital, they had to wait an hour and a half until they could speak to a doctor. They sat in a grey-painted waiting room in grim silence, while a TV warbled away in a corner and a scrawny mother with a fretful yelling five-year-old sat opposite.

'Jesus, this is fucking terrible,' wailed Shauna. 'Shouldn't Joey be here? Or that useless bastard, his dad?'

The scrawny mother shot Shauna a look. 'Can you not talk like that in front of my child?'

'Shut your cunting face,' advised Shauna. 'Or I'll rip your fucking tits off.'

'Mr Minghella?' asked a white-coated blonde woman of middle years, appearing in the open doorway.

Thank God for that, thought Josh, standing up, seeing that World War Three was about to break out between Shauna and the woman with the kid. He stared at his wife with contempt. She might style herself as a society hostess these days, but she could still have a wicked tongue on her, and she wasn't afraid to use it. Claire wouldn't talk to a dog the way Shauna spoke to some people.

'I'm Josh Flynn, Aysha's father. Her husband isn't here. Is she OK? Can we see her?'

'Is the baby all right?' asked Shauna, coming to her feet.

'Come into my office,' said the doctor, and Josh, Shauna and Connor trailed after her into a poky little room with a depressing view of a dark central courtyard.

The doctor moved behind the desk and sat down, indicating that they should sit, too. None of them did. Josh's mouth was dry as he said: 'Is Aysha all right?'

'She has some nasty bruising.'

'And the baby?' asked Connor.

The doctor pursed her lips. 'I'm sorry. I'm afraid we couldn't save it.'

Aysha was propped up in bed in the middle of a busy ward with several other women, looking almost as pale as the thin hospital pillows. When she saw Shauna and Josh, she started to cry.

'Oh, Mum,' she sobbed, and Shauna hugged her tightly.

'There'll be other babies,' said Shauna. That *fucker* Minghella.

'No! No there won't.' Aysha pulled back from her mother's embrace. She grabbed her father's hand, squeezed it. Connor came to the other side of the bed and kissed his sister's cheek.

'Where *is* Joey?' asked Connor, thinking that when he

got hold of that git he was going to pull his guts out. He should be here, with his wife.

'He ran off,' gulped Aysha, rubbing her eyes with a tissue. 'He fingered his mates for that job with the old woman who died. Their families are out to get him, so he said he had to go. I tried to stop him. Told him he had responsibilities, now he was going to be a father.'

'Aysha,' said Shauna, her eyes dark with concern. 'Don't . . .'

'You want the truth? I was in his way, so he pushed me down those stairs and killed his own baby. He could have killed me too, but he didn't care about that. All he was thinking about was running away, saving his own skin.'

'We'll find him,' said Connor.

'No,' said Aysha, casting a desperate, tear-sodden glance at him. 'Don't you get it? I don't want him back. I *hate* him. He murdered my baby and he as good as murdered that poor old woman too. I don't want him anywhere near me. Not now, not ever.'

111

'I can't come home yet,' said Josh quietly on the phone as he sat in his study back at the house. And saying it made him realize all the more where his heart truly lay now. *That* was home, New York, with Claire and her daughter. This was just a remnant of a life. But it was one he couldn't abandon yet, much as he wanted to. He might not have planted the seed that grew into Aysha, but he was all the father she had, and she needed him.

'Is Aysha all right?' asked Claire.

'She fell down the stairs.' He couldn't bring himself to say that tosser Joey had pushed her. It was too painful to talk about. A grandchild, a new life full of promise, smashed and dead. 'She miscarried.'

'God, I'm sorry.'

'So you can see why I can't come back yet. Soon. Not yet.'

Claire was silent for a moment.

'Claire?'

'Is this the way it's always going to be for us?' she asked in a small voice.

'No. It isn't. As soon as I can, I'm going to do it. Get the divorce rolling. I can't go on like this much longer. I want to be there, with you, but I'm tied here. Once I can get a divorce through, things will get easier. The kids are grown, they'll understand. I expect it'll be a rough ride for a while, but they'll come round.'

'I can't lose you again,' said Claire.

'Don't say that. You never will. I'm coming back, just as soon as I can. I told you. When I have this sorted, we'll be together and nothing is going to stand in the way of that, I promise you. On my life.'

'The new place is beautiful,' said Claire wistfully.

'I can't wait to see it again. And you.'

'I love you, Josh.'

'I love you too,' he said, and hung up.

Claire stood alone in their lovely apartment, where the sun flooded in and lit the whole place. Slowly, she replaced the phone on its cradle and looked around at her new home. *Hers and Josh's.* Suki's too, whenever she wanted. Only Josh wasn't here, with her. He was thousands of miles away, with his family. With that awful bitch Shauna who had hurt her in so many ways. And maybe this time the pull of his kids would be too strong. Maybe this time, he wouldn't come home to her. She sat down on the couch, bathed in warm sunlight, her heart as heavy as lead, and wept.

112

Something changed in Aysha when she lost the baby. Within a couple of weeks she was back on her feet, but now she looked at the world with hostile eyes.

Josh and Connor went over to the Minghella house to try and find out what had happened with Joey. Old man Minghella looked like he'd done ten rounds with Sugar Ray Robinson, he was so cut and bruised. He had nothing to tell them except that Joey was gone and he didn't know where.

'I ought to beat the shit out of you,' said Josh, dragging the smelly useless old cunt off the couch and staring into his eyes from inches away.

'Don't, don't!' Frank shouted, trembling. 'They already done it, them bastards. Don't hit me no more. I told them and I'm tellin' you. I don't *know* where he went.'

'I want to divorce him,' Aysha told Shauna one day in the kitchen.

'You can't,' said Shauna. 'If we don't know where he is or what he's up to, how is that possible?'

Aysha's eyes hardened and her mouth was set in a grim line.

'Then I'll change my name by deed poll. I don't want to be a Minghella any more. I'm going to change my name back to Flynn.'

And that's what Aysha did. Once again she was Aysha Flynn, but an Aysha Flynn who was marked by life. The carefree and in love Aysha Flynn was gone. Now she was a blank-faced woman who eyed the world with dislike.

She caught Connor in the yard office one day. His mate Benedict was in there too, but she ignored him. Men! She detested them now. 'Connor, I'm going mad with nothing to do. Give me a job in the office sorting the paperwork or something, I don't care what.'

'Jesus. All right then,' said Connor.

Anything to keep her happy. And it would be good to have her here in the yard where he could keep an eye on her. Aysha wasn't herself. More and more, she was reminding him of Mum – and not in a good way. Mum was a control freak and she could be scary. Her rages were legend and she bore grudges like, forever. When she got hopping mad and she stared at you with those dark, rock-hard gypsy eyes, you knew you were in deep, deep shit. Aysha was starting to get that same look, and he didn't like it.

'This is nice,' said Shauna to Josh one evening as they sat together watching telly.

'What?' Josh had been gazing at the screen and not seeing it. Thinking of Claire. Wondering how long before he could get back to her.

'This. You and me here, together.' Shauna looked at him. She could see he was distracted, maybe a bit bored. Josh was a man of action; slumped on a sofa wasn't him, not at all. 'You've not used our gym lately.'

'Yeah, I have.'

What was she, his keeper? He had the gym in the basement here, but he preferred to go to the local public one because it got him out of the house and away from her. And on his way out yesterday, he'd passed a messy old pickup truck parked at the end of the road. Sitting in the cab was a big bloke with a scruffy beard. He looked sort of familiar. Jesus! Was that Jeb Cleaver?

Well, let the bastard have her. They deserved each other.

Josh still liked to train. It helped him relax, clear his mind. Helped lift some of the stress he was under right now. Sometimes his chest felt unbearably tight, he was so strung out. Worried about Aysha. Hating Shauna. Fretful over Claire, who he knew was missing him badly. Unable to see her, speak to her properly. It was all getting to him and he wanted to be *gone*.

'Any fights lined up? Bubba Pole might have something for you.'

'Too much going on at the moment for that.' Truthfully, Josh felt that if he started fighting here again then Shauna would take it to mean that he was staying. And he wasn't. He absolutely bloody *wasn't*. He would probably get back in the ring again soon – he always did, fighting was his life – but for now he felt too scrambled to seek out fights, here *or* across the pond. Aysha was just getting back on her feet again with Connor's help, and Josh felt that within a couple of weeks he might be able to make a break for it.

He looked at his wife. She was watching him with bright-eyed interest, a fake smile on her face. She was still a handsome woman, Shauna. Kept herself smart, svelte. Went to dance classes with her stuck-up mates who actually looked down their noses at her, probably still laughed at her behind her back, called her pikey and gyppo. Not that she gave a fuck.

Shauna still had a little of that dark-skinned and flashing-eyed gypsy thing going on. Lots of men still gave her the eye. But Josh knew her secrets now. She was a cold, hard, merciless bitch. Josh wished that she would run off with one of the men who admired her – with Jeb Cleaver, for instance, or *any* bastard – and make all this easy for him. But she wouldn't, of course. Once Shauna had you and the lifestyle you could provide for her, that was you done for. You were *hers*.

If she knew what I was up to, she'd fucking kill me, he thought. That sent a chill up his spine. Set him thinking about the meals she cooked him. Shauna was a terrific cook, most gypsy women were. He always enjoyed the famous Shauna Flynn Full English, bacon and mushrooms and stuff – mushrooms could kill you, couldn't they? Deathcaps could, for sure.

And Claire. Christ, Shauna must never find out about Claire. He worried about having told Trace, but he was just going to have to trust her and Pally to keep their gobs shut. They *had* to.

Shauna gave him a smile and turned her attention back to the TV show.

Josh was still watching her, thinking of her shooting the two older Cleaver brothers dead.

Of Philippa Houghton, drowned.

Claire's dog Blue, killed. Shauna had been there, watching that.

And Claire. Raped and terrified, running for her life, her family threatened.

It was hell now, being in the same house as Shauna. At night he slept side by side with her, and thought that if she knew, if she *knew*, then there would be ructions. And what if he talked in his sleep? Said Claire's name out loud?

One night he woke up and found himself face to face with Shauna in the moonlight, and her dark eyes were wide open. She was awake, and she was watching him. It was such a shock to see her right there in front of him that he almost shrieked like a girl. Somehow he stopped himself. He got up, fetched a drink of water.

'You're restless, honey,' she said when he came back to bed.

'Yeah, bit of indigestion,' he said, lying down again, turning his back on her.

He hadn't touched her in years, and if she made overtures to him, he always turned away. He tried to get back to sleep again, but he couldn't. His chest was tight as a drum. His heart was racing.

Christ, I have got to get out of here.

113

'What do you think?' asked Claire, leading Suki and her friend Vicky through the new apartment, room by room. The large sitting room was sunlit, glorious with its fabulous Park view; there were two bedrooms, a super-sized bed in each; a dressing room with ample allocated space for shoes and bags; a bathroom with a bath easily big enough for two.

'It's like the bridal suite in a five-star hotel,' said Vicky. 'It's fantastic.'

Suki thought so, too. No thrift-shop finds in here, no vintage. It was all modern, classy, brand new. 'It's lovely, Mom.'

'So where's Josh?' asked Vicky.

'Business. England.'

'Shame. He coming back soon?'

'Very soon, yeah.'

'Is he paying for this? This is big bucks,' said Vicky.

'It's in my name,' said Claire, feeling put out. Vicky might be Suki's best friend, but she could be abrasive; and money was her god.

'Even better. Then if things get a little tired and he moves on, you keep the gold mine.'

The thought of Josh 'moving on' made Claire want to cry. Already she missed him like a limb. 'Is that how it is? With you and Spiro?' she asked, her voice cold.

'Hey, no offence! Spiro's paying my rent right now. Buying me things. This dress. This bag, that's a Chanel.'

'It's beautiful,' said Suki, who didn't really care about bags. *Or* dresses. She knew Claire didn't either. What Claire wanted was Josh here, with her. That was all. Cuddles and commitment. Suki envied her mother that. She herself had no boyfriend, no one she cared about like Claire cared about Josh. There'd been a few casual dates of course, but nothing serious.

Vicky flicked a perfectly manicured nail at the gold double C on the black quilted leather of the bag. She looked at Claire. 'Can I ask you a question?'

'Sure,' said Claire. 'Have a seat.'

They all three sat down on the couch.

'It's occurred to me . . .' Vicky paused. 'Look, don't shoot the messenger, Claire, but hasn't it occurred to you that he might be *married*? All this running back to England looks sort of suspicious and I—'

'He is married,' said Claire. 'You mean Spiro hasn't told you? I'm sure he knows.'

'You're kidding me.'

'Sadly, no.'

'Well fuck me.'

'He's going to divorce her, first chance he gets,' Suki chipped in, feeling defensive of her mother.

Vicky gave a sharp sigh. 'Christ! *That* old line.'

'It's the truth,' said Claire.

'I hope you're right.'

'I am.' Claire swallowed hard. 'He's having troubles back there right now. His daughter's lost a baby and his wife needs him there.'

'How long's he been there?'

'About a month.' *Or more . . .*

'But, Claire . . . *you* need him here.'

'Look,' snapped Suki. 'She *knows* that. But she can't put pressure on him, not now. He's having enough of that at home.'

'This wife . . .'

'Shauna,' said Claire, hating even to say the name.

'He still got time for her?'

'He hates her. He wants the marriage done,' said Suki.

Vicky looked at Claire. 'Is that the truth? Or just a line he's spun you?'

'No. It's the truth, Vick. It really is,' said Claire.

'Well, we got to get him back here then,' said Vicky.

'Oh yeah. Easy.' Claire sighed. She felt like she was losing the fight; that Shauna was winning.

'Girl – when you got influence, you have to learn to use it,' said Vicky with a smug smile.

Vicky had a word with Spiro that day, and Spiro made a few calls. Then in the evening, he rang Josh.

'How are you, Josh?' he asked.

'Fine. You?'

'Fine, fine. My friend, have I got a fight for you! It's all lined up, you got to come! Next weekend. Big prize money. What do you think?'

It was a get-out clause and Josh felt bad but he grabbed it. He told Shauna that night, and the kids the next day. He slipped an old mate from the pub a tenner and called Claire from the mate's house. He was getting paranoid about Shauna maybe listening in to his calls if he made them from home.

'I'm coming back on Tuesday,' said Josh, and he grinned as Claire whooped with delight.

'I can't wait!' she said, laughing. 'Oh Josh, I've missed you so much.'

'I missed you too. Tuesday. My flight leaves Heathrow at eight thirty in the morning, and I'll be at JFK at eleven-o-five.'

Josh put the phone down. She was still laughing for joy, and he was grinning like a schoolboy.

114

Dad was gone again, and Mum was in a foul mood. All as normal, thought Connor. He dropped Dad at the airport to catch his flight then came back to the family home. Mum was in the kitchen, knocking the fuck out of some steaks with a tenderizing mallet. Aysha was in the sitting room. He opted for the sitting room. Mum's bad moods were as infectious as rabies, and he didn't want to get too close.

'She's gutted he's gone away,' said Aysha, putting her magazine aside when Connor came in.

Thump!

The steak was getting a right battering out there. Connor sat down beside his sister.

'Maybe she clings on to him too hard, you thought of that?' said Connor.

'He can't seem to get away fast enough, that's for sure,' said Aysha. She looked at Connor. 'D'you think they're in trouble? Their marriage, I mean?'

'What makes you say that?' He'd thought it for *years*. To him, his parents had always been a mismatch – Shauna so fierce, climbing ever upward on the social scale, and Josh the gentle giant who – it was obvious – yearned for the simpler days of his youth. Josh, it seemed to Connor, had always been true to his roots, even when Mum had been stuffing him into a dinner jacket and hawking him around at society bashes.

'I dunno. Just a feeling I suppose.'

'Women's intuition?' He smirked, thinking fondly of the times Josh had sat him down as a boy and as a teenager, telling him tales of the old gypsy settlement, the church in the dell, the Cleaver pig farm up the road. Sometimes Josh had used the old Romany words to him, and spoken in the language of Cant. Yeah, Dad was a real genuine Romany rye – a true gypsy gentleman.

'Don't knock it. I *am* a woman.'

Connor nodded. She certainly was. He'd never tell her, but since parting company with Joey Minghella – and losing the baby – his little sister had turned into a hard-faced knockout, she'd developed a style all her own. She usually wore black. Her dark hair was cut into a severe chin-length bob. Scarlet lipstick, black mascara. High heels. No longer a girl, that was for sure. A woman. Every time she was in the office, his mate Benedict nearly had a seizure.

'What do you think of Benedict?' he asked her.

'Who?' She squinted at him.

'Benedict. Come on.'

'Why does he have to be called *Benedict*?' asked Aysha. 'It's a bit affected, don't you think? Why not plain Ben?'

Connor shrugged. 'He likes Benedict. And come to that, it suits him.'

'He's a bit up himself. Dresses like a fashion plate. In a scrapyard, I ask you. *And* he's a neat freak. You seen his desk? All the pencils in line. Pitiful.'

'Benedict's OK. He just likes things orderly. He's been great in the business, he got all the licences straight, gets the ads word-perfect in the trade mags, he even sorted out how to isolate the precious metals from the catalytic converters. He says you ignore him.'

Aysha shrugged. *So what?* She'd noticed how attractive Benedict was, of course she had, she wasn't a *nun*. But God! Did she really want to start all that again?

'You're not . . .' Connor started, then hesitated.

'What?'

'You're not still hung up on that berk Joey, are you?'

Aysha's lips grew thin. 'I don't give a fuck about Joey Minghella.'

That was true. Granted, Joey was the most beautiful man she had ever seen and she had loved him, wanted him. But all that had come to an end when she'd seen his true colours.

'Well thank God for that,' said Connor.

Shauna came in, wiping her hands on a tea towel, her face like thunder. 'You two going to give me a hand out here?' she snapped, and turned on her heel and walked back into the kitchen.

They exchanged a look, stood up and followed.

115

'I'm happy you're back,' said Claire, snuggling in against Josh as they lay in bed together.

'Me too,' said Josh.

He'd come through the door and instantly they were kissing, caressing each other, hungry for love, desperate for it after their too-long separation. They fell on to the floor in the hall in a tangle of arms and legs, laughing, kissing, tugging each other's clothes off until finally Josh could thrust his cock into her warm, waiting body and know he was truly home again.

Afterwards, they went into the bedroom and fell into bed and hugged each other.

'I've missed you so much,' said Claire. 'I was so sorry about your daughter's baby. That was awful.'

'She's a tough girl,' said Josh, thinking that once that hadn't been true. Now, it was. Aysha seemed to have grown a hard shell over the hurt of the miscarriage and the disaster that was her brief marriage to Joey Minghella.

'It must have been horrible for all of you. How did her husband take it?'

Josh filled Claire in on the story about Joey, the gardening job and his two pals getting banged up on a charge of manslaughter. He told her about Joey grassing them up, and the families baying for Joey's blood.

'So he legged it. Aysha tried to stop him going, and he shoved her arse-backwards down the stairs and that's how she lost the baby,' Josh told her.

Claire hitched herself up and settled on Josh's chest, looking into his eyes. 'He sounds like a complete bastard,' she said.

'He's a worthless son of a bitch. We all tried to tell her. We all warned her off. She wouldn't listen.'

'Strange, the people we fall in love with.'

'Yeah,' said Josh as their eyes met. 'Very strange.'

She was smoothing her hands over his big muscular chest, sending ripples of pleasure through him.

'I don't want to go back there,' he sighed. 'Christ, I *never* want to go back there! I want to stay here, with you.'

'I know,' she said.

Claire sighed too. He was married to that despicable whore, they had a *family*. She still sometimes felt a sense of shame at what she was doing, making hot and almost demented love with a married man. All the trauma of that long-ago rape was forgotten when she was with Josh. Now, he came through the door and right away she couldn't *wait* to feel his naked skin against hers, to marvel at his hard, lean boxer's body, to get him inside her. She loved him.

'Get this one fight out of the way, then I'll do it. OK?' said Josh. 'I'll start divorce proceedings.'

Claire's hands stopped moving. 'Really?'

'Yeah.' Josh's light-grey eyes were serious as they stared into hers. 'It might get messy,' he warned.

'I know.'

'But it will be worth it. And I'll keep you out of it, don't worry about that. Totally. I'll just say irreconcilable differences. You won't be mentioned or known about. OK?'

Claire nodded and dropped a kiss on to his chest, feeling both excited and scared. Shauna would kick and scream against a divorce; Claire knew it. Possession was Shauna's middle name; she wouldn't let go of Josh easily.

'Claire.' He couldn't put this off any longer. He *had* to tell her now.

'Hm?'

'I have some sad news for you. I'm sorry,' said Josh.

'Oh? What is it?' Claire's eyes were anxious.

'I'm sorry, honey. Your mum . . . she passed.'

Claire stared at him. Suddenly she gave a sob. 'All these years,' she gasped out. 'I missed her. I wanted to tell her where I was, that I was OK. But I was *scared*, Josh. I was scared of Shauna and scared of *them*. Of what they might do. And now it's too late. She's gone.'

'I know.' He cuddled her. 'Shh, baby. And listen – I told your dad and Trace that I'd seen you and that you were fine. I didn't tell them where you were, nothing like that. But after Pally lost Eva, it seemed only fair to give him some comfort.'

Claire looked at him. 'You broke your promise.'

'I know I did. And I'm sorry.'

Claire lay down, holding him tight. 'I'm still scared of her. Of Shauna. I shouldn't be. I'm a grown woman now. But when someone does something like that to you . . .'

'Yeah. I know.'

'It haunted me, Josh. For a long, long time.'

'I know. But, honey, I'm here to protect you now. You're safe. I'm going to get the divorce done and then I am never, ever going to leave you again.'

116

Aysha found that working in the scrapyard was no more exciting than the dental depot or the travel agency, but Connor and Benedict found her administrative experience helpful and it was soon agreed that she should become a director of the company like them, which pleased her.

This cold November morning, the blokes out in the yard whistled when she drove in and parked up. As usual, she ignored them, passing by the piles of old motors, the crane with its motor roaring and the huge crusher, then past the line of big steel containers and the dumpsters. She went over to the Portakabin that served as the office, tried the door. No one in yet. Breath pluming out in the frosty air, she rummaged in her handbag for the spare, ignoring the catcalls and lewd suggestions still coming her way, then unlocked the door and went in.

It looked like nothing, this little place, but it was neat inside. Everything tidy, with a small electric heater to warm the place up on cool days. She flicked it on to high. Then she went to her desk, took off her coat, hung it up, put the coffee on to percolate. She sat down and saw that the dopey office junior they'd hired last week and would probably fire *next* week had left the adverts that should have gone out yesterday in the in-tray, undone.

Aysha stood up, went to the filing cabinet: it was locked.

Her irritation with the world in general exploded then. She threw her arms in the air and yelled: 'Christ alive! Who do I have to fuck to get anything *done* around here?'

'Me,' said a male voice behind her. 'If you absolutely insist.'

Aysha whirled round, a hand to her chest. Connor's mate Benedict was standing there in the open doorway.

'Shit! You startled me,' she said.

Benedict smiled and closed the door. 'Problems?'

'Adverts haven't gone out. Last night was the deadline.'

He went over to his desk. Hung up his coat, sat down. 'I'll phone them, see what I can do.'

Aysha was embarrassed that he'd seen her outburst. She could feel her face going an unflattering shade of red so she busied herself with the coffee while Benedict talked to the editor on the phone. He was a charmer on the phone; she'd heard him in action, forming close relationships with trucking companies, car dealers and other yards. Even when regular punters off the street came in looking for spares, he was helpful, pointing them in the right direction when they were searching for engines, alternators, power-steering pumps or even just a second-hand headlight.

Finally, he replaced the handset and looked at her.

'Sorted,' he said. 'We're late, but there was a bit of wriggle room, so the ad's in.'

'Thanks,' she said, putting a mug of coffee on his desk and hurrying back to her own. 'The filing cabinet's locked.'

'Always is, overnight.' Benedict held up a key.

Aysha got up, went over to his desk and snatched it out of his hand. Or tried to. Benedict hung on to it. She widened her eyes at him. *What the fuck?*

'I've got a spare, if you want one,' he said.

'Thanks,' she said, and stood there tapping her foot in

annoyance while he searched in the desk drawer and found it, handed it over.

She went back to her own desk, unlocked the filing cabinet and sat down. Glowered at Benedict. Smooth bastard. He smiled back, serenely.

117

Shauna had chewed it over in her mind until it drove her almost crazy. Sometimes, your gut told you things. You just *felt* that something was wrong. She might have moved on up, but she was still Romany, and her senses were sharp. She thought she was right about this.

She didn't want to be right. She'd had Jeb watching Josh when he was over here, but he hadn't seen a thing out of order. Nothing suspicious. Still the feeling persisted – that Josh was *up* to something. And so she was going to have to *prove* that she was wrong. Now, to do that, she was here at lunchtime in the middle of town, getting a professional involved.

Christmas was coming round again soon, there was tinsel draped over the till and out in the streets of London all the decorations were alight and glowing. But Shauna was full of gloom.

She was meeting up with Lesley Deveney in a busy coffee shop off the Strand, full of yummy mummies and their howling brats and gangway-filling double pushchairs. It was raining outside and all the windows were misted up. She arrived first, ordered a cappuccino and waited for a quarter of an hour. No sign of the bloke. A forty-plus woman came in, straight shoulder-length dark hair, a plainish face, intelligent down-slanted dark eyes with big bags underneath them. She was dressed in a black jacket, a crisp white shirt and skin-tight jeans. She walked over to Shauna's table.

'Excuse me, are you Mrs Flynn?' she asked. 'I'm Lesley Deveney.'

Shauna nodded. 'I was expecting a man,' she said.

'I get that all the time. Trust me, I blend in better.' Lesley was used to this sort of mix-up. But she was the best. Dickhead Dandridge, her business partner, never missed a chance to sideswipe her with a sexist remark – but that was because he knew she was a better detective than he would ever be.

'Sit down,' said Shauna, and held up a hand. The waitress came over. 'What'll you have?'

'Whatever you're having,' said Lesley, taking a notebook and pen out of her large black leather tote bag.

'Two cappuccinos,' said Shauna, and the waitress hurried off.

'Mrs Flynn, would you like to fill me in on the details?' asked Lesley, taking off her jacket and draping it over the back of the chair. 'Thanks,' she said, as the waitress came back and put the coffees on the table.

Shauna waited a beat until the waitress departed, then she said: 'I think my husband could be having an affair.'

Those bright dark eyes held Shauna's. The pen hovered over the notebook. 'Based on . . . ?'

'Based on a feeling.'

'Your husband's name . . . ?'

'Josh Flynn. He's a bare-knuckle fighter.'

Lesley wrote that down. 'You got a picture?'

Shauna did. She handed it over. Lesley stared at Josh.

'Striking-looking guy,' she said.

'Yeah. He is.'

'And . . . ?'

417

'And what?'

'And what makes you think he is having an affair?'

Shauna told her about all the trips to the States. That Josh had seemed moody and withdrawn when he was here, but he'd had a call saying there was a fight on in New York and he'd perked up, looked happier straight away. And he'd nearly *run* out the door to get to the airport.

'And there's fuck-all happening in the bedroom. I mean, *nothing*. Not for quite a while.' Like, *years*.

'Maybe it's just the prospect of the fight that's cheering him up,' said Lesley, sipping her coffee, her eyes on the photo.

'He could find fights here, in this country,' returned Shauna. 'But he don't seem interested in doing that any more. He wants to be there.'

'You think that's it? An affair?'

'I do think that, yes. And I want to know the details. All about it. Who the woman is. Everything,' said Shauna. *And then I'm going to kill the bitch.*

'New York? That's going to cost.'

Shauna gave a tight smile. 'You're mistaking me for someone who gives a shit. I want to know everything about this cow who's fucking my husband. And when I catch up with her, she'd just better fucking well watch herself.'

'Where does he stay when he's out there?'

'Waldorf Astoria.'

'And what then?' Lesley was writing things down in shorthand.

'What?'

Lesley shrugged. 'If we find you're right. Divorce proceedings?'

Shauna sipped her coffee and shook her head. She'd fought so hard and done so much to achieve her perfect family unit with Josh. 'I dunno. If he comes to heel, maybe I'll forget it. Forgive him. Take him back.'

Comes to heel. Like a dog, thought Lesley. She didn't envy Josh Flynn right now. She certainly wouldn't want to be in his shoes when the brown stuff started flying with wifey here. Lesley found she didn't like Shauna at all; but she was paying. What else mattered?

'I'll head back to the office, get you a quote worked out,' said Lesley, quickly draining her cup and standing up, gathering up notebook, pen and photo. She put on her jacket.

'Soon. I want to get on with this,' said Shauna.

'I'll be in touch today,' said Lesley. 'Without fail. Good-bye, Mrs Flynn.'

118

Everything was running like clockwork at the yard now and money was pouring in the door. Dividends were distributed lavishly from the auto parts trade and the scrap business and other income streams, so Aysha was able to buy herself a diamond-studded Rolex Oyster as a pre-Christmas present and to rent a small flat in Kensington.

'That's some watch,' said Benedict when she came into the office and flashed the thing about. Connor wasn't in.

'You like it?' Aysha twirled her wrist around so the diamonds caught the light.

'I like it,' said Benedict, coming around the desk and grabbing her hand, pulling her closer. He looked into her eyes. 'I like you, too,' he added.

Aysha hadn't really even looked at a man since the disaster of her marriage to Joey Minghella. But Benedict? He was hard to ignore. He was big, solid. Not handsome, exactly – but he was a beautifully groomed hard man who could obviously handle himself, like Connor, like Dad. He dressed well, to impress. Always smelled nice. He had thick straight black hair and dark sexy eyes. But she'd *done* all this shit. One minute they were charming you into bed – and anyway she was useless at all that sex stuff – then they were taking you for granted. And next thing? They were kicking you aside like you were rubbish.

'Thanks,' she said, and snatched her hand away. But her heart was beating a little faster, and she wished it wouldn't. This was a bad idea. Mixing business with pleasure couldn't be good.

'Don't you like me?' He gave a lopsided smile. 'Maybe just a little, uh?'

'I don't even *know* you.'

'You've been careful about that,' he said.

She had. From the outset she had thought that yes, he was a very attractive man, and she had a weakness for them. They were as seductive as chocolate, as addictive as crack, the ones who could pull women easily. So mostly she tried to avoid the office whenever she knew for sure Benedict would be there. In fact, she wouldn't even have come in today at all, if she hadn't been looking for Connor.

'Benedict, listen – this is business,' said Aysha. 'You've got a possessive girlfriend who'd tear my guts out if she knew there was anything going on with you and me. So, it's business only, my friend. Let's just keep it that way.'

'What, you mean Bev?' Bev was a hard-eyed blonde who ran a couple of massage parlours; she'd been into the office a couple of times to see Benedict. 'That party's more or less over.'

'Oh sure.'

'It is. Because I've met someone else.'

'Oh? Who?'

He gazed hard into her eyes. '*You*, you daft mare. So business only? That's what you want? Really?'

'I do.'

'You've been married. To that tosser Joey, Connor told me the worst bits. Not his fault. He didn't want to tell me, I prised it all out of him. Connor was in torment over the whole thing. He was concerned for you. Told me to be really careful what I said to you, that you were on a knife-edge.'

'That's all history,' she said. 'Marriage? Sod that. Never again.'

'Bad, uh?'

The worst. 'Pretty bad, yeah.'

'Maybe next time will be better.'

'Benedict, there's not gonna *be* a next time.'

He gave her a glinting smile. 'Shame,' he said, and turned back to his desk.

119

When Lesley Deveney got to New York, she booked into a hotel not too far from Josh's own gilt-fronted palace on Park Avenue. Her place was plainer but a hell of a lot cheaper. She settled in and then went out and walked a block to the Astoria, then she sat in the reception area with a copy of the *New York Times*, drinking coffee. Jet lag was setting in and she needed the coffee just to stay awake, but she still looked around her with interest at how the other half lived.

This was quite some hotel. Big chandeliers and acres of glossy marble. Huge potted palms and someone tinkling a tune on a grand piano. Classy waiters plying you with drinks, spruced-up bellboys zipping here and there with guests' bags and suitcases piled high on golden trolleys, while the richly dressed clientele sauntered through en route to a late lunch or some high-end shopping.

After about an hour and a half, Josh Flynn appeared, stepping out of the lift and walking across reception and out to the big revolving doors. He was a good-looking man, if your tastes ran that way. Powerful. Sexy. A real silverback of a guy. Lesley hopped to her feet when she was out of his line of sight, chucked the paper down and hurried after him. Outside, the doorman pulled over a cab and she heard Josh say an address on East 76th Street to the Indian driver.

She flagged down her own cab and gave the man the same address. When they got there, haring through the teeming streets, she paid the driver and got out and looked around, hoping to spot Josh.

He was nowhere in sight.

'Fuck,' she muttered, and walked over to the building he'd asked for. She peered into a brightly lit hallway. It was clean, and empty. She pushed the door lightly, but of course it wouldn't give. There was an intercom system on a brass side panel beside the door. She looked at the names there, pulled out her notebook and jotted them down. *W. Humbert, I. Patton, J. Cleeve, F. Barlow, C. Milo, P. Schuster.*

Six large apartments in there. It was a smallish brownstone building, not tall but old and lavish. There was a bell for the doorman but she didn't want to risk him being the protective type who would alert anyone. So now all she could do was wait until Josh came back out. She found a diner over the road where she could keep an eye on the street, ordered fruit juice and a hamburger with fries – she was famished and feeling stuffy-headed, the precursor of a cold. You fed a cold, right? And starved a fever.

Eventually, she got tired of hanging around and gave it up. It didn't look like Josh was going to come out. Whoever lived there, whichever apartment he was visiting, it was clear he was going to stay the evening, and probably the night too.

So why bother with the hotel?

Simple. Shauna Flynn was the possessive sort who would be phoning, keeping tabs on him. Lesley bet she was one of those emotionally blackmailing bitches who put those twee little notes in the poor bastard's suitcase, that sort of thing. Reminding him of who he belonged to. Yeah, like a dog.

Hey, Rover! Heel!

Yawning, sneezing, she went back into the street and hailed a cab, thinking that it wasn't very likely that Josh would stay overnight visiting a male friend, unless he was *that* way inclined. She was starting to think that Shauna was right. One of the residents in that building was a woman, and Josh Flynn was fucking her.

Big surprise.

In this job, every day of the week Lesley was on the trail of treacherous wives, cheating husbands. Nothing shocked her any more. She viewed the human race and its foibles with curiosity but detachment. Catch her getting involved with anybody, no way was she going for any of that shit. She did the job, took the money. None of it was any skin off her nose. Thinking she'd start again tomorrow, she went back to her cheap, charmless hotel, fell on to the hard mattress of her bed, and was asleep in minutes.

120

Lesley crawled out of bed at eight the next morning, feeling rough. She was still jet lagged and on top of that – this happened a lot when she travelled on planes, and everyone had been coughing on the flight – she had the itchy throat and thick head that told her that yes indeed, a cold was on its merry way, and it was going to be a bad one.

Still, she showered, dressed, had a room service breakfast, checked the contents of her tote bag – camera, notebook, pens, cash and cards – then went out and hailed a yellow cab and took up her station once again in the diner opposite the apartment block Josh had gone into last night. She ordered a coffee and an oversized cookie, and watched, and waited.

Christ, they were *never* coming out of there, she thought when it got to eleven and still no sign. She left the diner – there was a limit to the number of coffees any girl could drink before nature called, and what she didn't want to happen was Josh coming out of that building with her in a rest room somewhere, missing the show. She sauntered about on the busy sidewalk outside, her head feeling achy and her limbs tired, thinking *oh come on, come on.*

She waited until nearly half past twelve, and there he was – at last! – coming out of the block. Her heart skipped a beat. Bingo! It was him. Wearing last night's clothes. And, better yet – there was a sweet-faced blonde woman with him, a real honey, a bit too old for Lesley but definitely her type if only she could afford the upkeep on anything as gorgeous as that. The blonde was dressed in dark jeans, boots and a turquoise wool coat.

The couple started walking off along the sidewalk, arm in arm, and Lesley scrabbled in her bag and pulled out the Pentax. She focused. They looked happy. Well, she was about to put paid to *that*. She fired off as many shots as she could, and then they were behind a delivery lorry which had just pulled in to the sidewalk.

Fuck!

Lesley ran a few steps to get past the lorry, bumping into New Yorkers who said: 'Hey, watch it!' and 'What you doin', you crazy broad?'

She didn't even hear them. She was totally engaged with her quarry. Josh was just emerging from behind the lorry with his lover on his arm. Lesley started shooting again, but she couldn't get a decent shot of their faces, so she moved on, forging through the crowds. There was traffic all over the place, horns honking, it was mad here in New York City. And then *yes*, that was it, there was the shot that showed them for what they were. Josh was leaning down and kissing the woman, with her craning her neck up to receive his kiss.

The camera whirred, capturing shot after shot.

Gotcha, gotcha, gotcha!

121

'Hiya, darling,' said Shauna when she phoned through to Josh at his hotel in New York. She was getting impatient with the whole thing. That fucking Deveney woman had been quiet as the grave for *days*. What the hell was she paying her for? Meanwhile, Shauna was calling Josh herself, putting out feelers. And she was going to put a rocket up Lesley Deveney's arse next time she deigned to call.

'Hi,' he said.

'Everything OK?'

'Yeah, fine. You?' asked Josh.

He was looking at Claire standing there, wearing just his white shirt, over by the window. It was way too big for her and the sunlight was making the thing transparent. She was so gorgeous.

Won't be long, he mouthed. She smiled. He felt bad, talking to Shauna with Claire standing right here. Guilty and awkward and pissed off. He hated all this. And again, she'd slipped a note into his case. *Love you, babe.* He'd dumped it straight away.

'How are you getting on over there? Training hard?' asked Shauna.

''Course. The fight's on Friday.'

'You found a gym all right then, after the other one closed? Or is there one in the hotel?'

'Yeah, I'm sorted,' said Josh, getting irritated.

Claire was unbuttoning the shirt, her eyes holding his.

'Miss you,' said Shauna.

Ah shit, thought Josh. As soon as this fight was over, that was it. Finished. The kids were just going to have to suck it up.

Claire slipped the shirt off and let it slither to the floor. Naked, gorgeous, she lifted her arms, displaying her fabulously full tits with their shell-pink nipples. All the while, her eyes held his.

Josh watched her and felt himself grow hard as rock. He shook his head at her, but he was smiling.

'Kids OK?' he asked. It was all he could think of to say.

The kids had their own lives now, just like he had his. Only Shauna was sitting back there in her grand house, expecting the world – the family – to revolve around her like she was the fucking queen or something. And it didn't; not any more. They had all moved on, and somehow she just hadn't noticed, or she hadn't wanted to. Shauna was clinging on to a forgotten past, clinging on to *him*, and now it had to stop.

'I miss them,' he said, as Claire sauntered over to where he stood.

'They miss you too. You'll be back in time for Christmas though, won't you?'

'Shaun, I dunno . . .'

'I really don't know why you have to keep going back to the States. I told you – there are fights to be had here, Josh. You know that's true.'

'Shaun . . .' He was so tired of hearing this.

'Or is the truth that you'd rather be there, than here with me? Is *that* the truth, Josh?'

Stop it, he mouthed, but Claire was tugging at his belt

now. He turned away, making a *no, not now* gesture with his free hand. Claire paused, smiling into his eyes.

'Josh, is there someone else? Are you cheating on me?' said Shauna.

Christ, he thought, winded by the suddenness of the accusation. With Claire standing right here in front of him. He felt almost like Shauna had X-ray vision, could see inside the room, right now.

'Shaun . . .' he started.

'I know what you did, don't forget that, Josh,' said Shauna.

What?

Josh stared at the phone. 'What the fuck does that mean?' he asked Shauna.

'Andrew Meredith. That little job you did for Dave Houghton in the New Forest. You killed Andrew. Dave paid you to do it. You can't have forgotten.'

Christ, was she talking about *blackmailing* him? Saying, stay with me or I'll shop you?

Claire, sensing something was wrong, was frowning up at him but he was barely even registering her presence. He put his hand over the mouthpiece. 'Give me a minute, can you?' he whispered.

He saw the puzzlement in her eyes but she left the room without argument, snatching up his shirt and disappearing into the bathroom. Josh turned his attention back to his wife.

'Listen, Shauna – I know what *you* did too.'

'Meaning?'

Josh lowered his voice. 'You shot two of the Cleaver brothers dead, Shaun. You forgotten that?'

'Hey – you helped me out with that, have you forgotten *that*, you bastard? I saved your fucking life, incidentally. You ought to be thanking me. Instead, you're flinging that back in my face and fucking off to America. *We* put them away. You and me. *Both* of us.' Now she was shouting down the phone at him. 'So you start that shit with me and we'll go down together. They can find whatever's left of the Cleavers and I'll be done for, but you know what, Josh? You will be too, because I'll sing like a fucking canary.'

Josh was silent, his mouth suddenly dry.

The venom in this woman. The *hatred*.

'What did you do to Claire?' he burst out. He was sweating now. He was Fearless Flynn and he was scared of no man. But this madwoman on the end of the phone, whose voice pierced his brain like knives? Yes. Right now, she scared him.

'What?' That stopped her in her tracks.

'Claire Milo. She vanished the night we left the camp. You know that. You hated her because she was going to marry me. Did you do something to her? Or was it your fucking boyfriend Jeb Cleaver?' Josh *knew* what she'd done. He shouldn't be saying this, baiting her, but the words were pouring out of his mouth like a collapsed dam, he couldn't help it.

'What the f—'

'And Philippa. Dave's wife. You hated her and – surprise, surprise – she's dead, did you know *that*? I met him in the boozer and he told me. She drowned in the river. Was that you too, you poisonous *bitch*?'

There was total silence.

Josh was breathing hard. He closed his eyes, steadied himself. Shit, he had to stop this. Had she hung up?

'Shaun . . . ?' he said at last.

'If you're screwing some little cow over there, you're going to be *sorry*,' she said.

The chill threat in her voice made his flesh creep.

'Bye, Shaun,' he said, and slammed the phone down.

He was shaken. Stupid, she was thousands of miles away. But he'd felt her presence like a curse, right here with him. Drawing in gulps of air, he went over to the window, stared out at the skyscrapers, standing hazy in the weak late-afternoon sun. Then someone slipped their arms around him from behind and he recoiled in shock.

'Josh? Honey, you OK?'

It was Claire, and she was watching him with concern.

Josh drew her close against him. 'She thinks something's going on,' he said in the warm circle of her arms, crushing her to him in a bear hug.

'Well,' said Claire against his chest, alarmed at the shivers she could feel coursing through him. She felt scared for him, and for herself, too. Shauna – even at a distance – still put the shits up her. 'She doesn't *know* that, does she. You can sue for divorce like you said and put it all behind you. It's going to work out. You'll see.'

But Josh couldn't believe that. He clung to Claire, loving her for her efforts to calm him. It was as if she was the strong one and he the weak, all of a sudden. All he wanted now was to get in the ring on Friday and win the fight, then he would get back to England and sort this mess out, once and for all.

122

The fight was set up in one of the Constantinou brothers' venues. There must have been a thousand people crammed in there, and to hell with fire regs. Spiro and Vicky were in, sitting in the front row with Suki and Claire. It was hot as hell in the club, and the ring was brightly lit. There were huge banners up, red on black, shouting *THE VIKING v THE KING OF THE ENGLISH GYPSIES*.

'I don't want to be there,' Claire had said to Josh. She hadn't seen him fight since 1975 and she wanted to keep it that way.

'Don't feel you have to, OK? But I'd like you to come,' he said.

So – reluctantly – she'd agreed to be there. But when Claire saw Josh come into the ring with Spiro's younger brother Nikos acting as his second, and when she saw the height and the mountainous width of the blond Icelander he was to fight, she wished she hadn't.

It was too late now. Always one for a theatrical flourish, Spiro had hired two bikini-clad blondes with huge plastic tits and no hips to hold up the round number signs, and he had encouraged Josh to have FEARLESS picked out in big gold letters on the waistband of his red silk shorts. A bow-tied referee was in there, saying he wanted a good clean fight, no holding, no low blows, and were they ready? This wasn't regular boxing, all gloves and gum shields; this was bare-knuckle and brutal. The fight wasn't ten rounds and then stop and if both were still standing, score on points; this was fighting each round up to twenty, or even beyond that – until one of them dropped.

Josh nodded, bumped his fist against the other fighter's hand, and then the bell rang and they were off.

Josh started pounding lefts into the Icelander's midriff, then the Icelander shot out a perfect right cross to the chin that sent Josh skidding back on his heels into the ropes. Josh shook his head to clear it and then he stormed back in, throwing six, seven, eight jabs. The blond Icelander retaliated with another right cross that clunked against Josh's skull like a sledgehammer.

'Jesus!' muttered Claire, Suki on one side of her, Vicky on the other. They all held hands and watched with bated breath.

'He barely felt it,' Vicky told Claire over the roaring noise of the crowd.

'How can you say that?' Claire shot back. 'Christ, *I* felt it.' She was getting flashbacks to that night when Josh had fought Matty O'Connor. This was *horrible*.

But Josh was ducking and weaving his way back in again, landing punch after punch, sending a brisk middle-knuckle shot into the Icelander between his lips and his nose. The man staggered back, blood dripping. He shook his head like a wounded ox, but charged in again and was met by a bull-hammer blow between the eyes from Josh's left hand.

The Icelander reeled back and went down. A massive roar went up from the watching crowd. Josh was the favourite, everyone wanted him to win, and this looked like *it*.

But the Icelander was tough, just like Spiro had promised. He pulled himself back on to his feet and came storming in at Josh again, landing wild punches, holding on to Josh when his own feet went wobbly beneath him, pounding away at Josh's torso.

The referee pulled the Icelander back.

'No holding!' he bellowed.

As the referee yanked the Icelander back again he took another swing, landing a right punch to the bone behind Josh's ear before he could get his guard up.

'Dirty *bastard*!' shouted Spiro, leaping from his chair.

Josh was staggering on his feet all of a sudden. The Icelander came in fast, punched Josh hard on the left cheek and then the right. Josh stepped back, unsteady, and swung a right but missed and overbalanced. He went crashing on to the mat.

'Josh!' Claire was on her feet.

A roar went up. The favourite was down. The referee held the blond giant back and started the countdown.

'One! Two! Three!'

Josh wasn't moving.

'Get up. *Get up!*' Vicky was yelling in Claire's ear.

'Four! Five! Six!'

Jesus, he's out for the count, thought Claire, hugging herself with anguish, watching Josh laid out there. Everyone in the room was shocked. The favourite was down!

'Seven! Eight! Nine!'

'Get up, Josh, you bloody fool!' roared Spiro.

'TEN!'

The referee grabbed the Icelander's arm and yanked it into the air.

'The WINNER!' he yelled, and the Icelander went prancing around the ring to catcalls and boos and a meagre scattering of cheers. His corner was alive with celebration. Everyone in Josh's was still and shocked. Josh was spark out on the canvas. Nikos ran over to slap his face, then dab him with water.

'Shit, I hate this,' said Claire, trembling.

Suki hugged her mother. 'He's fine, he just took a bad knock,' she said.

Nikos was there, kneeling beside Josh.

'Why isn't he getting up?' said Claire.

Now Nikos was calling the referee over. The man went, and bent over Josh. He was patting Josh's face, and his expression was worried. He straightened up and gestured to someone outside the ring.

'God, I've got to . . .' said Claire, and ran forward and ducked under the ropes. Someone caught hold of her.

'Let go of me!'

Seeing something in her face, the man let her go. Claire ducked under the ropes and went and knelt by Nikos at Josh's side. He lay on his back and it was almost like he was asleep. Nikos looked at her.

'Took a hard punch,' he said, but he looked yellow-pale and sick with shock. 'He'll be fine.'

'Josh! Wake up,' she said, her guts creased with horror. This was what she had feared the first time she'd seen him fight. Now it was all coming true. 'Come on!'

The referee was at the side of the ring talking to Spiro. The Icelander had stopped prancing around and was now standing still, looking down at Josh lying there. The referee came back.

'They're sending for an ambulance,' he told Claire.

Oh Christ. This was serious. This was an illegal fight, and they were actually going to let paramedics in here? Risk prosecution?

'Just a precaution. He'll wake up in a minute,' said the referee, patting her shoulder.

The room had fallen silent.

Claire was weeping, hugging Josh to her, clutching at his bruised and bloodied hands. 'Wake up. *Please* wake up,' she sobbed.

But Josh did not respond.

123

The phone was ringing beside the bed. Shauna woke up with a start, dazed from sleep, and switched on the onyx-based bedside light, one of a very expensive pair she'd gone to huge trouble to source. She snatched up the phone.

'What?' she mumbled, running a hand through her hair, looking around the big master bedroom, coming back to herself and the reality of her situation.

Josh was in New York. Aysha was at her place in Kensington. Connor was in town too, at his Notting Hill flat. She was alone here, in this big house in Henley-on-Thames that once had so delighted her. The hours she had spent on doing the fucking place up, bossing around interior designers until they got the look of it *exactly* right! But now it was little more than a mausoleum, a sad reminder of what had once been a happy family home.

She thought of her last conversation with Josh. She was sorry she'd said all that now, in the heat of the moment. Afraid she'd pushed him even further away from her.

How much further away could he be, Shaun? she wondered. *He's not even in the same country as you any more. And you think he's fucking some other woman.*

Someone was talking on the other end of the phone. A foreign accent, speaking English. She let out a sigh, paid attention.

'Sorry, what?' she asked. 'Who is this?'

'Mrs Flynn, my name is Spiro Constantinou, I am a friend of your husband's. I'm phoning from New York.'

'He's never mentioned you.' *But then, when has Josh ever mentioned anything about his life over there?*

'I am afraid . . . I am afraid I have some very bad news.'

'Oh?' Suddenly Shauna's mouth was dry. 'What's happened? Is Josh all right?'

'He was in a boxing match tonight.'

'He told me there was a big fight coming up. Is he OK?'

'He was knocked out in the ring, Mrs Flynn. Taken to hospital.'

'But he's OK?'

'Mrs Flynn.' Spiro paused, seemed to take a breath. 'He had a bleed on the brain. They operated but they couldn't save him. I'm sorry. He didn't come round again.'

'He . . .' Shauna was shaking her head, over and over.

'I'm so sorry, Mrs Flynn. Truly I am. Josh is dead.'

BOOK THREE

124

Shauna phoned Connor first. She didn't know what else to do.

Josh, dead?

She couldn't take it in.

Connor picked up, sounding bewildered, snapping out of sleep to a waking nightmare.

'Connor . . . it's your dad. I just had a call from the States. He's *dead*. He took a punch in the ring and now he's dead.'

Shauna started to cry.

'*What . . . ?*' Connor's voice was thin with shock. 'Mum, you're sure?'

'A friend of his called. Spiro somebody. I've got his number here.'

'Tell me.'

Shauna gave him the number and Connor rang off.

Numb, Shauna replaced the phone on the cradle. She looked around the room and barely saw the costly Osborne & Little drapes at the windows, the plush watered-silk red buttoned sofa at the end of the bed that so beautifully matched them. The chandelier, the fitted wardrobes, all the *stuff* she had set such store by when all she had ever really wanted was Josh, right here with her.

She had lost him years ago. She knew that.

And now, she had lost him for good.

Josh, dead?

She let out a howl of anguish and the tears started to fall. Maybe she could have got him back, made it all good again. Now . . . She couldn't. There was no coming back from this. Josh and the *bloody* fight game.

'*Noooo!*' she wailed, hitting the pillow, wanting to hurt somebody or something, to take her own pain away.

Now the fucking phone was ringing again. She picked it up. Swallowed. Swiped at her eyes.

'Connor? That you?'

'It's Aysha.' Aysha's voice was thick with tears. 'Connor just called me. Told me the news. Jesus, Mum, this is so awful . . .'

'Can you come over?' Shauna's voice was pitiful, child-like. Not like her voice at all.

'I'll be right there. Just hold on.'

Hold on to what?

Aysha rang off and Shauna replaced the handset again. It rang immediately.

'Connor?' she asked.

'Yeah, Mum. I got hold of this Spiro person. I'm sorry. He said they did everything they could for Dad at the hospital, but . . .' His voice trailed away.

'Oh God, oh God,' moaned Shauna.

'I'll come over,' said Connor and put the phone down.

Shauna sat up in her palatial bedroom with a dead phone in her hand, crying her eyes out. Her children were coming. But . . . ah, Christ . . . Josh was gone.

125

The morning after the fatal fight, Claire sat in the living room of the apartment she had shared with Josh. She sat on the couch in the room where the light flooded in, while Suki made her coffee she didn't drink, and offered her food she couldn't eat.

'Spiro has phoned the family,' said Suki, choked with tears and watching her mother with concern. 'Josh gave him his home number in England ages ago.'

'Oh. Right.' Of course. *They* were Josh's family, those people over there – that bitch Shauna and his kids. Not her.

'Everyone's very upset,' said Suki.

'Yeah. Sure. Of course they are.'

'I wish you'd eat something. Some toast?'

Claire shook her head. She'd had him back. At last. And now, it was too much: she'd lost him forever.

'Let me run you a bath. Get these clothes off you.'

Claire looked down at the dress she'd been wearing when Josh died; it was her favourite colour – turquoise. There were small smears of his blood on it. She was never going to wear that colour again. From now on it would be black, or nothing.

'OK,' she said, although she didn't want to, because when she took this ruined dress off it was cutting ties with the life she'd known with him. All that ended right now. Somehow, her life was going to have to go on, without Josh.

Maybe she wouldn't let it.

Suki went and ran the bath, and then she came back and took Claire's hand and led her into the bathroom. As sweetly as if *she* was the mother and Claire the daughter, Suki removed Claire's clothes.

'Suki, can you get rid of that,' said Claire, indicating the dress. 'Please?'

Suki nodded. She opened the door and threw the thing outside, closed the door again. Then she helped her mother into the bath, sat her down, took up the sponge and the soap and washed her clean, while she sat there with tears streaming down her face.

'What will happen now?' Claire managed to ask.

Suki swallowed hard. She'd loved Josh too, in her way. So much. They'd grown closer and closer over the past few months, and to think of never seeing him again was devastating.

'They'll fly him back to England. Back to his family.'

'I'm his family.' A flare of anger ignited in Claire's gentle blue eyes. 'Me.'

'No. I know you loved him very much,' said Suki. 'But he belongs back there, with them now.'

'I just think I'll wake up in a moment, that it will all have been a bad dream,' wailed Claire.

'I know.' Now Suki was crying too. Christ, this was awful. 'But now you have to let him go.'

'I don't want to,' said Claire with a heavy sigh, the warmth of the water and Suki's gentle touch soothing her, just a little. But the thought of him going back to Shauna, that cruel heartless *bitch*, made her choke with rage. 'He was going to divorce her.'

Josh might have had the best of intentions, but Suki

thought he was tied in to his English family too tight to have ever got away. But she didn't say that aloud. Let her mother cling on to any illusions she had.

'Come on, let's get you out now.'

Claire lay back, shook her head. 'Leave me here a moment, I'll have a soak,' she said.

But Suki had seen the bleak look in Claire's eyes.

'You soak,' said Suki, taking a seat on the toilet. 'I'll sit here, OK? Keep you company.'

When Claire finally got out of the bath, Suki dried her, wrapped her in a warm bathrobe, then fed her a little soup as tenderly as if she was a baby. Still she felt no better. If she'd had a gun, she would have finished her life right then. Sooner or later, Suki was going to have to leave her, and then Claire thought that maybe she would go up on to the roof and just let herself fly down into the street below, end this anguish. Then she caught herself. If she did that, Suki would be alone. She had a daughter. And she couldn't bear to cause her pain.

Suki stayed. Days and nights passed, Claire didn't know how many and she didn't even care. There Suki was, preparing food which Claire only nibbled at. All she could think about was Josh's body travelling back home, back to England where his family – where *that vicious cow* – would be waiting for him.

And what about her?

What did she have left?

Only memories.

She went to the wardrobe where Josh's things hung. Fingering the jackets, the shirts, she hugged them to her and smelled the faint scent of Josh's skin still on them. Cried wrenching tears over the loss of him, when their future had held such promise.

'What should I do with those?' asked Suki, finding her there in the wardrobe sobbing her heart out. 'Do you want me to sort that out for you?'

Claire drew back, closed the wardrobe door, shaking her head.

'No. Not yet,' she said, and went back to bed.

126

Connor was passing through the hall at Shauna's place when the phone rang. He stopped, picked it up. His eyes fastened on the Christmas tree in the corner – a modest one by Mum's standards, only twelve feet high and sparkling with gold baubles. It seemed to mock him. All the family Christmases! How could any of them have known that last Christmas was going to be Dad's final one with them?

'Hello?' he said.

'Could I speak to Mrs Flynn?' asked a female voice.

'She isn't here at the moment.'

In fact Shauna was upstairs, in bed. It was one o'clock in the afternoon, and all Shauna seemed to want to do since she'd heard the news about Dad was sleep. Christmas was cancelled. Connor and Aysha had moved back in after they'd got the news although neither really wanted to. Mum was a dictatorial pain in the arse at the best of times, and these were the worst. And soon they'd have Dad's funeral to face. It was a fucking nightmare.

'I'm her son. Can I help you?' he asked.

'No, I'm sorry. This is a confidential matter, I need to speak directly to Mrs Flynn.'

'And who are you?'

'Lesley Deveney. If you can get her to call me when it's convenient? Here's my number, in case she's mislaid it.'

Connor jotted the number down as Lesley reeled it off.
'You can't tell me what this is about?' asked Connor.
'No. Have her phone me, please.'
Lesley hung up.

When Connor woke Shauna at two o'clock with a cup of tea, he handed her the scrap of paper with Lesley's number on it. 'This woman called. Lesley Deveney. Said she had to talk to you, no one else.'

Shauna sat hunched in bed, her eyes sore from weeping, every muscle aching, and looked dully at the number on the paper. She recognized it as the detective's office number. A laugh that was little more than a croak emerged from her mouth.

'What?' asked Connor, watching his mother's face.

'It's nothing,' she said. She'd been mad as hell a couple of weeks ago, wondering when Lesley was going to give her an update. Now – too late – here Lesley was, no doubt about to say she was sorry to hear about Josh, because she had been out there in New York, she must know what happened.

'Drink some tea,' said Connor, going to the window and opening it, letting in some fresh air. 'Can I get you anything else? You hungry?'

'Nah. Where's Aysha?'

'In the kitchen. Look, I'm going out but she'll be up in a tick.' He came back to the bed and dropped a kiss on to her cheek.

'Quite a rota you got going on, the pair of you. Make sure Mum don't top herself or something, that it?' Shauna almost smiled.

'You wouldn't do that,' said Connor. 'You're tough.'

But I've lost everything. I've lost Josh. 'Yeah, that's me. Hard as nails.'

'Drink your tea,' he said, and left the room.

Shauna took a sip of the tea. It was nice, hot and strong. Then she picked up the phone and dialled Lesley, who picked up straight away.

'This is Shauna Flynn,' she said.

'Hello, Mrs Flynn. I'm sorry, I've been off with a rotten cold or I would have called you sooner . . .'

'That's OK. We've had a family bereavement,' said Shauna. 'My husband died. Maybe you know that? You were supposed to be in New York watching him.'

'Jesus.' Lesley paused. 'God, I'm sorry. No, I didn't know he'd died. It must have happened after I came back. That's shocking.'

Now, Shauna thought it was all beside the point anyway. All her suspicions, none of that mattered any more. 'If you send me the bill, I'll settle up,' she said. All she wanted was to tie up any loose ends and forget it.

'Well, the thing isn't quite finished yet, Mrs Flynn.'

'Yeah, it is. My husband's dead, didn't you hear me? Whatever he did prior to that, what does it matter now?'

'You seriously feel that way?'

'Right this minute? I do. Yes.'

'Because I got some pictures. I'm sorry. Maybe I'm being insensitive and, if I am, I apologize. Maybe under these circumstances you don't want to see them.'

Do I? Shauna wondered. She thought of Josh, being untrue to her. Cheating on her. There was still a flare of deep indignation at the thought of it. She'd been through so much to get him. To make him *hers*. And even with him dead, the thought of any possible infidelity on his part was beyond toleration. She couldn't have it. Not now. Not *ever*.

'Was he . . . ?' she started, then found she couldn't even say it.

'Yes. I'm afraid so.'

'All right,' said Shauna, feeling her heart shrivel to nothing in her chest. Ah God, it was true then. He *had* been deceiving her. 'Can you come over? Say, at three?'

127

Connor went home to his flat, throwing the post on to the kitchen table and making coffee. He checked his phone for messages. Benedict had called a couple of days back. That was OK, he'd phoned his mate from Shauna's place this morning and explained what was happening.

Christ, Dad was dead.

He couldn't take it in. All the times Connor had said to him, *Please, Dad, give up the fight game.* Why had Josh never listened? If he had, he would have been alive today.

'Ah *fuck*,' said Connor.

It was awful, thinking he was never going to see Dad again in this world. He was relieved to be away from his mother's black well of grief and depression for a while, although he felt bad about that. Shauna was his mum but she was also a colossal pain in the arse, always kicking off and seeing doom in every situation. In a black mood, she sucked all the life out of everything around her, including him, including Aysha.

Then the doorbell rang. When he opened the door he found Aysha standing there.

'Thought you were babysitting Mum?' he asked as she came in.

'I was. But she told me to piss off out of it. She's getting up.'

'She's getting *up*?' Shauna had seemed like she was *glued* to that bed.

Aysha nodded. 'She's got someone coming over, and she said to me, "Go out, do something, I want a private word with this person." So I have been dismissed.'

'Who is it? Life insurance or something?' Dad had been worth a packet. They all knew that.

'I asked. She wouldn't say.' Aysha sat down at the kitchen table and started rummaging through his mail, the cheeky mare. Connor swooped in and gathered it all up, took it over to the worktop. 'How does she seem?' he asked, getting out another cup, slopping coffee into it.

'I dunno. You know what she's like. If there's one thing Mum loves, it's a crisis so she can do her "woe-is-me" act. Oh shit.' Aysha put her hands over her eyes. 'That sounds cruel. But you know what a drama queen she is.'

'Yeah, I know.'

'She seemed to be livening up a bit though.'

'Well, thank fuck for that,' said Connor.

'It's hit her like a sack of shit, all this with Dad,' said Aysha, looking mournful. 'You know that old saying? There's always one that kisses, and one that turns away? That was them, I think. She kissed, and he turned away. I've thought for years that there was something wrong between them. Something *off*. There was always tension in the house, didn't you feel that?'

'I don't know.' Connor shrugged. He'd thought Aysha was ignorant of the cracks in their parents' marriage. Clearly, she wasn't. 'I suppose you get used to it. It becomes what's normal. That feeling of always being on a knife edge.'

'So you *did* feel it. You're not dead from the neck up after all,' she said, and even raised a smile.

'I've been worried about you, Sis. Benedict's been worried about you too,' said Connor.

'Oh really.'

Connor shrugged. 'He likes you.'

'I know that.' *I like him too. Too much.* Aysha sipped her coffee. 'He's all right, I suppose.'

'Ah-*ha*!' said Connor.

Aysha gave him a small, sad remnant of her usual cheeky grin. 'Don't get excited! Just pour some more coffee and shut up, OK?'

Aysha stayed for an hour, drinking too much coffee. Then she stood up. 'Christ, Connor, I feel wrecked. I'm going home, have a shower, get cleaned up. I'll catch you later.'

But when Aysha got back to her own flat, her refuge from the madness of the world, she had a shock: her husband Joey Minghella was there, sitting on the front step, waiting for her.

128

Some days after Josh died – how many? She didn't know – Claire got up, was spoon-fed soup, and *really* wished that Suki would fuck off and just let her be.

But Suki remained.

'We'll go walk in the park today,' she said, dressing Claire in jeans and a top.

'No,' said Claire.

'Yeah, we will.'

Claire was unresponsive but Suki's will was strong. They went for a walk in the park. Snow was falling, light as kisses. The sun shone but the air was frigid. Kids played. Life was going on even if Josh was dead. When they got back to the apartment, Claire went back to the wardrobe again, opened the door, and felt panicky as she inhaled the faint but slowly vanishing scent of him. He was going from her, her long-lost and re-found Romany love, the king of the gypsy fighters. She should have been his queen, but life had played cruel tricks on both of them. And this time, he would never be coming back.

'All right. Get rid of his clothes,' she said, heartbroken, and closed the door.

129

Lesley Deveney stood in the sitting room of Shauna's place and thought, *Wowser, look at this!* Shauna was just as she remembered: hard-looking, with piled-up and dyed black hair. She had darkly outlined and very penetrating eyes that seemed to skewer you. She was expensively dressed – and this place looked like it was worth a fortune.

Shauna sat down opposite and said: 'All right, what've you got then?'

Lesley laid her briefcase on the Italianate glass and marble coffee table between them and unlocked it. She took out a large envelope and handed it to Shauna.

'I was sorry to hear about your loss, Mrs Flynn,' she said.

Shauna said nothing. She flipped the contents of the envelope out on to the table. There were seven eight-by-ten black-and-white photographs in total, and in each one . . .

She took in a gasping breath. 'Oh Christ,' she moaned, putting a hand to her mouth.

'I'm sorry, Mrs Flynn,' said Lesley, meaning it. She didn't like this woman, but it was a horrible blow, all the same, this on top of her bereavement, and she did feel sympathy for her.

Shauna stared aghast at the prints. In each one of them, walking among crowds of tourists and New Yorkers, she could see the tall figure of Josh arm-in-arm with a pretty blonde woman in a mid-toned coat, boots and jeans. They were smiling at each other, and in one of them Josh was bending a little and *kissing* the bitch on the lips.

Shauna's breath caught for a second time.

That looks like . . .

'But . . . that can't be . . .' she started.

'What is it?' asked Lesley, alarmed by Shauna's sudden stillness.

Fuck! Shauna couldn't speak. She sat there and stared, shaken and disbelieving. Her mouth felt dry as ashes and her heart was beating hard against her ribs. It was true. All her suspicions, all her feelings, she'd been right all along. He'd been having an affair. But it was worse than that. It was a thousand times worse. Because . . . that was *her*, the Milo bitch. She looked again, wondering if she was going mad, if she was *imagining* Claire Milo's face – but she wasn't. She knew she wasn't. Claire was older, sure. But it was *her*. Somehow – Christ, *how?* – Josh had been reunited with the cow.

No, she thought, *it can't be.*

Claire Milo had hardly aged at all. The years had been good to her.

'But . . . I know her,' she said.

'You do?' Lesley was surprised.

'From a long time back.' Shauna was still staring at the photo of her husband, *her husband*, kissing Claire Milo. The Cleaver boys had killed the dog and had a real fuck-fest of a time with Claire, and she had run. Of course she had. And now it was obvious she'd run far: to New York.

Josh had been over there so much. Had seemed so happy to go. And *this* was why. How long had this been going on, her husband and that fucking no-mark Milo bitch, laughing at her behind her back?

'Can I get you something, Mrs Flynn? Water or any-thing?' Lesley asked in concern.

Shauna was shaking her head, over and over. All right, she had suspected. But here it was, proven. Her husband had cheated on her. And he'd done it with Claire Milo, who should have been *gone*.

'I don't know,' she said, dazed, shocked beyond belief.

'Well, I'll leave those with you for now. You know where I am if you want to get in touch.' Lesley stood up. 'Once again, Mrs Flynn – I'm sorry. I'll see myself out.'

Shauna sat there, barely noticing her going, staring at the evidence of her husband's betrayal.

Josh looked so happy in these shots.

So carefree.

Because he wasn't with me.

Because he was *with her*.

She was still sitting there looking at the photos when Connor came back.

'What's this?' Connor asked, coming into the sitting room, looking at the shots over his mother's shoulder. Then he focused. 'What the hell . . . ?' He came around the couch, sat down beside Shauna, picked up first one print, then the next, then the next. Then . . .

'What the *fuck*?' he asked, staring at the picture in which Josh was kissing the unknown woman, who was very pretty in a non-tarty way – a smallish pale blonde, with big eyes and a broad smiling mouth.

'I was having your dad followed in New York,' said Shauna.

Connor stared at her face. Her expression was blank, closed-off.

'He was having an affair over there. With *her*. It's some-one from his past. He knew her years ago. I know her, that *bitch.*' Shauna almost spat out the last word. 'I thought he was up to something and I hired a private detective to find out.'

'Christ.' Connor looked again at the prints. 'I can't believe it.'

'Believe it. There's the proof.'

Fury was gnawing at Shauna. How did Claire fucking Milo have the *gall* to go near Josh again? Josh was *hers*. Hadn't she learned her fucking lesson? No. She hadn't. Shauna gathered up the prints, stuffed them back in the envelope.

'What are you going to do?' asked Connor.

Shauna thought about that. Josh was gone, out of her reach. The Milo clan weren't, though. And *that* little cow . . . 'I want to know where she's living, what she does. What sort of low-life *whore* goes around stealing another woman's husband!'

130

The fates had been unkind to Claire Milo. All that time apart from Josh, and now he had been snatched away.

'We should have grown old together,' she cried to Suki. 'This shouldn't have happened.'

'I know,' said Suki, thinking that it was beyond sad.

Sometimes in the weeks after Josh's death she had truly thought that her mother was going crazy. She had seemed either dazed or hysterical, one or the other. Weight dropped off her; she had no interest in food, the New Year festivities, she had no interest in *anything*, it seemed. The club ran on, thanks to Donna's good management, but Claire didn't go there as she used to, chat to the clients, help out behind the bar.

'These things take time,' Donna told Suki when she expressed her worries to her. 'Just be there for her. Support her. Claire's a strong woman. She'll pull round.'

But Suki was starting to wonder if that was going to happen. She'd heard of people dying of a broken heart, and was starting to fear that's what was in store for her mother. Sometimes people just lost the will to go on.

I can't lose her, thought Suki in desperation.

'Come on, let's go out,' she said one morning.

'You go,' said Claire.

'No, we'll *both* go. Come on. Get your shoes on.'

'Oh Christ,' said Claire, groping for her shoes but wanting nothing more than to crawl back into bed, to be left alone. Josh was gone, what the hell use was anything else to her?

'Don't give me that,' said Suki. 'You think Josh would want you like this? He'd expect you to be strong, *fearless*, just like he was.'

'You don't know a damned thing about Josh,' Claire burst out, hurling her shoes at her daughter. 'How *dare* you tell me what he would want? He's . . .' Claire started crying. She shook with tears.

Suki dashed over and held her tight. 'Hush,' she said, crying too. 'We're going to get through this. Together, OK? We've lost him, but we still have each other and we have to hold on to that. All right?'

Claire was nodding. 'Yeah,' she said wearily. 'All right.'

Then a letter arrived from England.

131

Shauna met up with Jeb Cleaver in their usual spot – the sad-looking country pub that never had many patrons. Over the years, they'd met there many times. Jeb got the drinks in and then they sat at a corner table well away from the handful of other lunchtime drinkers, and Shauna ploughed straight in.

'You let me down,' she said with barely repressed fury. He was well overdue a bollocking, and she was in just the mood to give it.

'What?' Jeb stared at her.

'This.' She threw the envelope containing the prints down on to the beer-stained table.

Jeb picked up the envelope, shook out the prints. Looked at them.

'That's Josh Flynn. And that . . .' He squinted at the print. 'Do I know her?'

'You bloody ought to, since you had your cock stuck up her last time you met.'

'*What?*'

'Although I grant you it was a long time ago. That's Claire Milo. Remember her? Remember what we did that night? You were supposed to have seen her off once and for all. And now what do I find? My husband was in New York, kissing her in the fucking *street*.'

'Holy shit,' Jeb said, staring at the woman's face. He nodded slowly. 'Yeah. That's her, all right.' He looked up at Shauna and grinned. 'So hubby's been playing away, yeah? Bet *that's* bit you up the arse.'

Shauna gave him a freezing look.

'Hubby's dead,' she said.

'He . . . you *what*?'

'He died during a fight in New York. I thought he was up to something more over there, and I had him followed. The detective took these shots of him and the Milo bitch before he died.'

'So, you want me to shake up her old dad, Pally? Eva's gone, but there's still him,' he said thoughtfully. 'And the sister, Trace.'

Shauna considered it. But no: it was *Claire herself* she wanted to see suffer. She found she didn't care about the others any more.

'No. What's the fucking point?' she said.

'Well ain't this a day for surprises.' Jeb downed his pint in one long swallow. 'You not bothering to kick someone's arse, given the chance? Amazing, I call that. Another?' he asked, pointing to her untouched gin and tonic.

Shauna shook her head and he went off to the bar. When he came back, he was smiling.

'What?' demanded Shauna.

'So what I'm thinking is this: he's gone. Forget all this business with the Milo cunt, she don't matter any more. What matters is, there's nothing standing between you and me now, is there. Nothing at all.'

'You what?' Shauna was staring at him.

'It's a goer, ain't it? You, me? What do you say?'

Shauna picked up her gin and tonic and flung it in his face. Then she stood and hurried out of the pub while he spluttered and swore behind her. She got out her car keys.

Jeb caught up with her and dragged her to a halt with a rough hand on her arm.

'Get the fuck *off* me,' said Shauna, rounding on him in icy rage.

'Too high and mighty for me, are you? That what you think?' He was wet through with gin and his face was screwed up with anger.

Shauna wrenched herself free of his grip.

'Just *fuck off*, will you, Jeb?' she snarled. 'You've let me down badly. You've screwed up. And I'm sick of seeing your ugly mug hanging around me. As for me cosying up to you now Josh is gone? The idea is laughable. So why don't you just fuck off!'

She went to her car and got in while he stood there staring after her. She roared away and still Jeb stood there. Years, he'd been Shauna Flynn's puppet, doing her dirty work, cleaning up her messes. And *still* she treated him like he was rubbish. Like he wasn't good enough for her.

Well fuck it, he thought in fury. If she thought she could treat him this way then she was wrong. Josh Flynn might be gone, out of his reach, but she still had her kids, didn't she.

Her *precious* kids.

132

'What the fuck do you want? How d'you know where I live?' Aysha demanded when she found Joey on the doorstep.

Joey was still the Byronic dark-haired charmer even if he was dishevelled, his clothes creased and dirty. Looked like he'd been hiding out somewhere, maybe on the streets. He pushed himself to his feet and gave her that same old smile, the one that said, *Hey, you'll forgive me because I'm so cute, you know it.* It was the fail-safe Joey Minghella charm offensive smile, the one that always made her drop her drawers in the past even if she *was* a frigid bitch, according to him.

'I followed you a couple of days ago, from your mum's place,' he said. 'She still the same mardy old cow she always was? Jeez, what a ball-breaker that woman is.' He gave her a pitiful look. 'It's the Christmas holidays, Aysh. Thought I'd come see you.'

Aysha couldn't believe he'd have the gall to show up. All the local faces were out looking for him and so were the police. And yet here he was. Handsome as ever. And now it had no effect on her at all. Except that she was annoyed. No, she was *enraged*, because if there was one single thing she didn't want on top of Dad dying, it was this – Joey *fucking* Minghella coming back.

'Christmas is over. It's the bloody New Year now, haven't you noticed? I've got nothing to say to you,' she said, and pushed the key in the lock and went inside, trying to slam the door closed behind her. But Joey pushed hard, and Aysha was forced back. He came in, gave her that same glinting smile.

'I don't want you in here,' she said through gritted teeth. 'Just fuck off, Joey. Get *out*.'

'Jesus, is that any way to greet your husband?' he said, coming in close to her, shoving her back against the wall. He was so close she could feel his breath on her face and it didn't smell good.

'You're not my husband,' she said.

'Yeah, I am.'

'Haven't they caught up with you yet, you miserable useless fucker? Haven't they gutted you like you deserve?' she spat out.

Joey's smile dropped. 'Now that's not nice.'

The door swung inwards. In his haste to get inside, Joey hadn't properly closed it.

Benedict was standing there. 'Aysha? What's going on? You didn't come in this morning, so I came over to see you're OK.'

'Nothing,' she said, but she had never in her life felt so glad to see anybody.

Joey looked back over his shoulder. 'Piss off, pal. Just shove off out of it. This is husband-and-wife stuff.'

Benedict was quiet for a beat. Then he said: 'Like when you shoved her down the stairs so she lost your kid? You mean *that* sort of stuff?'

Joey spun away from Aysha with frightening speed and launched himself at Benedict, punching him hard in the jaw. Benedict reeled back against the wall. Aysha let out a yell of protest.

'I *told* you,' said Joey, wagging a finger in Benedict's face. There was blood dripping down over Benedict's pristine suit from a cut on his lip. 'I *told* you, pal. Fuck *off*. Or you'll be sorry.'

Joey turned back to Aysha, grabbing her upper arms. 'And *you*, bitch, why you talking to me like—'

There was a sharp *smack* and Joey's eyes turned up in his head. He slumped against Aysha, his grip loosening, then he crumpled to the floor at her feet. Aysha, shaking, her heart beating crazily, watched him fall and then looked at Benedict, who was standing there with a cosh in his hand.

'Damn,' he said, touching his lip and wincing. 'Should have used the bloody cosh first.'

'Yeah. Maybe that would have been better,' said Aysha, her voice breathless.

'You OK?'

'Fine,' said Aysha, but her legs were like jelly. She stared down at Joey, who looked to be unconscious. 'What the hell are we going to do with him?' she asked, rummaging in her bag. She found tissues, handed them to Benedict. He dabbed at his lip.

'Let me make a call,' said Benedict, and went through to her sitting room and picked up the phone.

Aysha stood there, staring down at her husband. *Jesus, was I mad? What did I ever see in a loser like him?*

Now Joey looked pitiful. A scruffy overgrown boy. She could hear Benedict talking on the phone, then he came back out into the hall, stuffing the tissues, stained red, into his pocket. His split lip was still seeping blood.

'Open the door, I'll pull him,' said Benedict.

Aysha opened the door. Benedict got his hands under Joey's armpits and dragged him out, bumping him down the front step and leaving him on the cold pavement.

'What, we're just going to leave him there, spark out?' asked Aysha. Not that she cared, but he could have a head injury. She thought of Dad, dying from a punch to the head, and shuddered. All right, Joey had treated her like dirt, but she couldn't be so callous as to let him lie there and die, all alone.

'He won't be there for long.'

'Oh?'

'Someone's coming to clear the rubbish away,' said Benedict. 'The family of one of the blokes he shopped.'

'Jesus.'

'Let's get back inside,' said Benedict, seeing that a car was moving at the top of the road. He took her arm, ushered her into the flat.

'Let me get that stain out of your suit before it dries,' she said, leading the way into the kitchen.

'Fuck the suit,' said Benedict, and pulled her to a halt, turning her and kissing her. '*Ow*,' he said, pulling away sharply.

Aysha stiffened in surprise. Then she started to smile. 'Hurts a bit, yeah?'

'Bastard smacked me right in the gob,' said Benedict, getting the tissues out again and dabbing at the cut. His eyes met Aysha's. 'Shit. I may have to get a little inventive here. Kissing may be temporarily out of the question.'

'Right.' Aysha's smile faded. She liked him so much. Fancied him, too. But . . . 'I don't want to disappoint you.'

'How could you do that?' he tugged her into his arms.

'Easily.'

'How? Come on, talk to me. Don't keep it all inside, that's not good for you.'

Aysha hitched in a breath and spat it out. 'Look. I'm not very good at all the sex stuff. I just don't get it. I'm sorry.'

She felt a hot blush of shame as she said that; she was a failure as a woman.

'Well, perhaps you've just never had the right bloke to do it with.'

'Joey said—'

'Joey? That gormless fucker? Look. He's history,' said Benedict. 'So let's see, shall we? Where's the bedroom?'

133

'Oh God. Oh Jesus *Christ*,' said Aysha, laughing and naked and breathless an hour later.

'I never knew you were religious,' said Benedict, lying back equally naked in Aysha's big double bed, hands behind his head, looking very pleased with himself. He turned his head and smiled into her eyes. His lip was swollen and looked painful, but he didn't seem to care. 'Frigid, yeah?'

Aysha shook her head. She was still laughing, still fizzing with desire after the first ever climax of her life. 'I didn't realize.'

'Realize what?'

'He was always in too much of a hurry. And too fucking clumsy.'

'And now, as I said, he's history.' Benedict propped himself up on one elbow and looked at her. 'You're a beauty, Aysha Flynn. I've always thought it.'

'Yeah? Well, you've looked better.' Aysha touched a gentle hand to his cut lip. All that time with Joey, she had thought the lack of chemistry was *her* fault. She smoothed a hand over Benedict's chest. And Joey had never made her laugh in bed. He hadn't even made her *smile*. But Benedict had made her laugh, made her scream in orgasm, made her feel full of joy. And since Dad's death? She truly hadn't ever thought she'd laugh again.

471

'Since the first day you came into the office, I've wanted this,' he said.

'I thought you were a flash git,' she said. 'A real office-wallah.'

'Charming.'

'And Joey turned me off men.'

'Guessed as much.'

Aysha's face grew serious. 'What do you think they'll do to him?'

'Honey, it's best not to ask questions like that. You won't like the answers.'

Aysha cuddled in against him. 'This is so nice,' she said, and her hand wandered down and smoothed over his cock.

'I've created a monster here, haven't I?' Benedict laughed. 'Give me a few minutes, for God's sake.'

'OK,' she sighed and lightly slapped his chest. 'Then I wanna see some action, buster – all right?'

Lesley Deveney got a call from Shauna Flynn. A day later, she was on a flight to the States, to see what she could find out about Claire Milo, the woman in the photos with Josh. Josh usually stayed at the Waldorf Astoria, but he had visited overnight at the brownstone apartment block on East 76th Street. So Lesley loitered outside there, looking at the list of residents on the entry phone system. W. Humbert, I. Patton, J. Cleeve, F. Barlow, C. Milo, P. Schuster.

C. Milo.

This time, she rang the bell for the caretaker and a smiling grey-haired black man came to the door wearing crisply pressed khaki coveralls.

'Help you, ma'am?' he asked.

'I'm looking for a friend of mine,' said Lesley. 'This is her. Claire Milo.' She got out the clearest photo of the blonde's face. The caretaker looked it over, thrusting out his lower lip as he thought it over. 'She does live here, right?'

He tapped the brass plate bearing the residents' names. 'Sure she does. Real nice lady. That's her, C. Milo, right there.'

'OK if I go on up?'

'You'd be wasting your time.'

'Meaning?'

'Your friend's stuff's still here, but she ain't. Last I saw of her, her daughter Suki – sweet girl – told me she was taking a vacation. Had a bereavement, I was told. Had some hard thinking to do and some things to sort out.'

'A vacation to where?' asked Lesley. She'd come all this way, and the Milo woman had gone somewhere else.

'England. That's what I heard.'

Fuck it.

134

On the morning of his father's funeral, Connor rose early. He couldn't sleep. He'd loved Josh so dearly that this was going to be a very hard day for him. Mixed in with his grief over losing his dad was something horrible, deeply distasteful. The thought that Dad had been playing away. He still could scarcely take it in. But the photos were concrete proof. And if Josh had been cheating, then he'd been more unhappy than any of them could ever have known. Connor hated the thought of that, but it was something he'd always been aware of at gut level. Josh had been looking for something else, something more than his wife, his family, could give him.

Connor showered, shaved, dressed and then sat at his kitchen table drinking coffee. Soon, he'd collect Aysha and go on over to Mum's place in Henley and together they would attend the burial near Winchester. Josh would be laid to rest beside his Romany parents in the Flynn family plot.

It was still so hard to take in the fact that Dad was gone. Every time Connor allowed himself to dwell on it, he felt choked up, unable to function.

Connor glanced up at the kitchen clock. It was time. He straightened his black tie and checked his Hugo Boss suit was dust-free in the hall mirror; then he took a breath to calm himself, and left the flat.

It was awful. Winter was gripping the countryside. The day was black as Satan's arse, cold rain swooshing across the graveyard and wind seeping into every exposed pore. Inside the church it was cheerless and the ceremony seemed to go on forever; outside, as the mourners assembled beside the family plot in readiness for Josh 'Fearless' Flynn's burial, the sleety rain came down even harder.

Shauna seemed calm, but Aysha was in tears. Benedict was at her side, supporting her, holding an umbrella over her to shield her from the worst of the weather.

So that's happened at last, thought Connor, watching his sister and his partner from the other side of the grave as the priest said the last words of blessing for Josh's eternal soul. Well, this fucking awful day was yielding some good news after all. Aysha and Benedict? He'd always felt they'd be good together. When Connor questioned Benedict about his cut lip, Benedict told him about Joey showing up; they'd had a ruck but he'd dealt with it, and Connor was pleased about that, too. Fucking little weasel had finally got what he deserved.

Now the ceremony was over. The priest hurried away and the mourners were picking their way over the tussocky mounds of grass toward the gravelled pathway leading to the lych gate, all of them hunched against the probing wind. Connor turned away from his father's grave, anguished, and then he saw something that made him freeze to the spot.

There was a middle-aged blonde woman dressed in black, standing out by the lych gate, her gaze fixed on Josh's grave.

It was *her*. It was that bitch, Claire Milo.

He stared, thinking it couldn't be. But it *was*. The shoulder-length bobbed pale hair billowing in the breeze. The big eyes. Fuck's *sake*, it was her, the woman in the photos with Dad. He moved forward then and her eyes drifted away from the grave and fastened on him, standing there, staring right back at her. Any minute, Mum was going to see her and there'd be hell to pay. He surged forward, making his way toward her. She saw him coming and turned on her heel and started to hurry away.

Yeah, bitch, you can run but I can run faster.

He couldn't get over the fucking *nerve* of her, showing up here today. He jogged through the groups of mourners, passing Aysha, who looked at him in surprise. Once he was out on the pavement, he caught sight of her, down the road, getting into a car. He started to run. He wasn't going to lose her now. He ran full-pelt to the car and got there just as the engine was starting. It was a big black S-Class Merc and there were tinted windows so all he could see in the back of the car was an outline, a pale face turned upward to stare at him in alarm. Another one too. There was someone else in there with her.

Yeah, be afraid. I'll throttle the life out of you if I get my fucking hands on you, you cow.

He wrenched at the door handle but it was locked. He pounded on the window and she shrank back as if he was a madman. At that moment, he felt like one. She was here, besmirching his dad's memory, reminding him that Dad had a secret life, one Connor had until recently had no clue about. Then the other passenger leaned forward, said something to the driver. He floored the accelerator, and the engine roared into life.

The Merc swung out and was gone.

135

'What were you doing, earlier? You were hurrying, what for?' Shauna asked him when he met up with her a few minutes later.

'Thought I saw someone I knew. An old mate of mine.' He couldn't tell his mother that Dad's bit of fluff had pitched up here, today of all days.

'Let's get back to the house, it's fucking freezing,' said Shauna, shivering.

All the mourners were getting into their cars. Shauna got into the limo, and Connor sauntered back to where Benedict was unlocking his BMW, Aysha at his side.

'It went off OK then,' said Benedict. 'Sad day. I'm sorry, mate. It's awful.'

'What were you running for?' Aysha asked Connor. Her face looked bleached white with grief, her eyes dark and intense, just like Mum's.

'I'll tell you later,' said Connor, and hoped that she'd forget it, hoped that this was a one-off and that Claire Milo would *never* dare show her face around his family again.

136

'See this?' said Connor.

It was days after Dad's funeral. Connor had thought it all through over yet another long sleepless night. Finally he'd contacted Mad Dog Cunningham, one of his and Benedict's street boys. Mad Dog was so named because he had bulging Marty Feldman eyes that swivelled wildly in his head like a hound with rabies. Connor had torn his father's image out of one of the shots the private dick had taken, and given Cunningham what remained of the print. A nice, clear shot of the blonde woman.

'So who's the skirt?' asked Mad Dog.

'Her name's Claire Milo. I saw her the other day. Maybe she's here, in London, maybe at a hotel, or maybe she's renting somewhere. Put the word out. Find her.'

'Bit old for you, I'd have thought.'

Connor gave him a look.

'No offence. Know you got an eye for the blondes. I'll pass the word along.'

'Yeah. Good. And less of the fucking lip, OK?'

Connor called in on Mum next day, see how she was doing. Shauna seemed OK. Today, she seemed more angry than grieving.

'That bastard. I can't believe he'd do that,' said Shauna

as they sat in the kitchen having coffee. 'A hole-in-the-corner affair. It's so bloody *sordid*.'

Ah, fuck. Connor had been wishing she wouldn't mention it. It pained him. He couldn't take sides, not against Dad. He'd always looked up to his father, the king of the gypsy fighters. And now the poor bastard wasn't here to defend himself.

'Cheating on me with that dirty *bitch*,' Shauna spat. 'That fucking Milo cow. After all these years.'

Connor still couldn't bring himself to tell Mum that the Milo woman had been at Dad's funeral. Mum would kick off in spectacular style, and her temper was something no one would put a match to without standing well back first.

'You got nothing to say about it?' Shauna demanded.

'What the hell can I say, Mum?' Connor burst out in exasperation. 'It was a fucking shock. Didn't seem like Dad at all. But he did it.'

'I got a call from Lesley Deveney this morning. The detective.'

'And?'

'She went back out to the States to find her. That whore.'

'Right.'

'She's left her place. According to the doorman the Deveney woman talked to, she's over here.'

'Right.' Somehow, Connor kept his face expressionless. Of *course* the Milo woman was here. He'd seen her, with his own eyes.

'If I ever see her scheming face, I'm going to rip it off,' said Shauna. 'I'll tear her bloody blonde hair right out of her fucking stupid *head*.'

'She won't come near,' said Connor. 'She must know what our reaction would be.'

'She better not.'

'She won't.'

But she'd been at the funeral . . .

'I hope he rots,' Shauna spat out.

Connor shook his head. 'No. You don't mean that.'

'He *betrayed* me, Connor.'

Connor stood up. He couldn't take this.

'I'll catch you later,' he said, and left.

He went to Aysha's place, and wasn't too surprised when Benedict opened the door to him.

'Hi,' said Benedict, in jeans and shirtsleeves, toast in hand. 'Aysh!' he called out. 'It's Connor. Come in, mate.'

Connor went in. Aysha was in the kitchen, having breakfast. She gave her brother a peck on the cheek. 'You want tea? Toast?' she offered.

'Nah. I came by because I have something to tell you.'

'Oh? What, then?'

'Maybe you'd better sit down for this.'

'Blimey, this sounds bad,' said Aysha, frowning.

'What's this about?' asked Benedict, following him in.

'It's about Dad,' said Connor, and he pulled out a copy of one of the photos of Josh and Claire Milo, snapped right there in the New York street. He put it on the worktop in front of Aysha. Benedict looked over her shoulder at the print. Aysha stared at it. Slowly, she sagged back on to a kitchen stool.

'Oh God,' she said faintly.

'But – fuck it – that's *Josh*,' said Benedict.

'Dad was having an affair with this woman. Claire Milo. When he was in the States.'

'I don't believe it,' said Aysha. But really? She did. And she thought it explained a *lot*.

137

Jeb Cleaver was still furious. He stalked around the farm in the icy downpour, doing his work with the hogs, giving his old dad nothing more than the bare minimum of conversation. He couldn't shake off the rage he felt at Shauna's nerve. So the bitch thought she could just dump him, did she? Chuck him, as if all these years meant nothing at all. Damn, she'd got that wrong. Hadn't he been her helper, her bedmate, through all their lives? He had. And now she thought she could call it off, just like that?

Big mistake.

Jeb had waited so patiently, too. One day Josh Flynn was bound to leave her, he knew. She was a strong woman and some men couldn't hack that. *He* could, of course. He knew how to master her. But Shauna had run Josh Flynn ragged, Jeb had seen it all happening from the sidelines. Poor cunt hadn't had a leg to stand on. She'd ruled the roost, had him firmly under the thumb.

And now Josh was dead.

Which *should* have left the way clear for him.

Jeb trudged through mud and rain, fed the pigs, watched them grunting and shoving each other to get to the feed. So the father was gone, out of reach. But that still left the son, didn't it. That still left the sexy dark-haired daughter. Shauna lived for her kids. Lived *through* them. If anything should happen to them, wouldn't she be in a tear then? Wouldn't that break that ice-cold heart of hers?

He toed one of the big sows with his mud-spattered boot and she grunted and turned with a snap of her jaws. He jerked his leg back with a grin. Fucking pigs'd eat the lot. Meal and fruit and ale waste, any damned thing. Even people – if they stood still long enough.

138

Connor hated to do it, but he'd had to put Aysha in the picture. If the Milo woman was still hanging around – and she might be – then he didn't want Aysha being approached by some stranger and mocked for her ignorance. Within a week, Dad's will was going to be read at the solicitor's up West, yet another fucking dreadful thing to look forward to.

After Connor left Aysha's, he did something he'd been wanting to do for a long, long time. Now Dad was gone it seemed appropriate somehow. He drove down to the gypsy camp where Josh had lived as a young man.

Josh had often talked about this place to his son – never in front of Mum and never to Aysha, though. He'd told Connor how he'd got started in the ring when he'd lived here. The place was a good *tan*, Josh had always said; that was the Romany word for a stopping place. He had told tales of his long-ago manager Cloudy Grey, of an old dere-lict church, and of a tribe of deadbeat pig farmers called the Cleavers who had once lived not far from the site, where a little circle of eight trailers were parked up well off the road down a bumpy gravel track. And about Linus Pole, his old mucker with the funfair business, who'd helped him as a fighter.

The campsite backed on to woodland and then on to

open fields – *puvs*, Josh had always called them, and Connor thought how little he knew of his Romany heritage, and it was sort of sad. But then, Shauna had never wanted to be reminded of any of it. And whenever Josh had used those old words, she'd always yelled at him, told him to speak the cunting Queen's English.

Connor paused in the lane, looking down the track that led to the site, and then he put the car in gear and drove on until he reached a place where bill boards were up saying *Fun's the game and Pole's the name!* He turned the Porsche in off the road and inched along a rutted track, hoping he wasn't going to fuck the Porsche's suspension. When the track opened into a clearing with trailers, he stopped the car.

Five big dogs ran out, barking. He stayed put, as Dad had told him he always must when approaching a camp. *Stay where you are,* Josh had always said, *and they'll come out to see what the noise is all about. If they want you to come further, they'll call off the dogs. Don't go wandering in there on foot unannounced, though: the dogs are there to stop you and they'll happily do it by tearing a good-sized chunk out of your arse.*

Not that Connor had ever been within a mile of any place like this, not until now. Shauna had seen to that.

A couple of men emerged from one of the trailers, followed by a girl of about eighteen with a dark-haired baby crying on her hip. They stared over at Connor's car, then one of the men gave a whistle and the dogs fell back, slinking off into the undergrowth as quickly as they had appeared.

The man who'd called off the dogs, a big middle-aged beer-bellied type wearing braces that strained over his shirt-covered gut, came over. Connor wound down his window.

'What you want then, boy?' the man asked him. His face

was reddened from the outdoors life, his eyes watchful but benign. He wore a large handlebar moustache.

'I'm looking for Mr Bubba Pole.'

For a moment it looked like Connor was going to be told to piss off, then Bubba's face cleared.

'Well, you found him.' Bubba squinted at Connor. 'And . . . you couldn't be Josh Flynn's kid, could you? I got a good memory for faces. I saw you when I came out your dad's place once for a chat on business. Although you've grown up a damned lot since then.'

'Yeah. That's me. I'm Connor.'

'You're welcome here, Mr Flynn.'

A dark-haired boy of about twelve with light-blue eyes came running up and threw his arms round Bubba. Bubba smiled down at him. 'This here's Archie, my youngest.'

'Hiya, Archie,' said Connor, reaching out a hand. Archie shook it, solemnly.

'You got a big family, Mr Pole?' Connor asked.

'Archie's one of six.'

'I like your car,' said Archie, his gaze running over the Porsche like he was in seventh heaven.

'Archie do love a nice car. You in the boxing game then, like your dad?' asked Bubba. 'Come on in, don't sit there. My old lady's gonna cook you something.'

Connor got out of the car. Archie was still standing there, his eyes saucer-like and one hand stroking the Porsche's gleaming paintwork. 'Get in, have a try-out,' said Connor.

Archie dived into the driving seat and grabbed the steering wheel, beaming from ear to ear.

Connor drew Bubba to one side. 'Mr Pole . . .'

'It's Bubba, Connor. Our families go way back.'

'Bubba. I'm sorry. I've got sad news.'

Archie was going *vroom vroom* and taking sharp corners at the wheel of the Porsche.

'What is it?'

'It's Dad, Bubba. He died in the ring while he was over in the States. Took a bad blow and never came round.'

Bubba's eyes filled with tears. 'Jesus, no.'

'The funeral was a few days ago. I'm sorry, I realize I should have told you this sooner, given you the chance to come and pay your respects, but . . .' Connor hesitated, sighed. Shauna, Aysha, him – they had all been shattered by Josh's death and by the news of his secret life – and none of them had been thinking straight. But he couldn't tell Bubba that.

'It's all right, I understand. When my dad Linus went, I didn't know my own arse from a hole in the ground. Ah, that's terrible sad news.' Bubba swiped at his eyes. 'He was a fine man, your father. A legend. Beat the shit out of every fighter I ever put up against him – and we had some fantastic talent, I can tell you.'

'He was a great dad,' said Connor.

Bubba looked at Archie, who looked set to stay behind the Porsche's wheel all day if he could. 'Come along, Arch, get out of the man's car. Let's go see your mum and get him some food and drink.'

'No, let him sit there, he's fine,' said Connor. 'Bubba? You know anything about a Claire Milo?'

'Sure I do. That was Pally's girl, she vanished years back. Moved on somewhere, I guess. She was going to marry your father, and then it was all off.'

Connor was quiet, absorbing this. Then he said: 'You know anything about some people called the Cleavers?'

'I know they're arseholes,' said Bubba. 'We got an agreement – they leave us alone and we don't bother them.'

'Someone mentioned them to me,' said Connor.

'Yeah? Well, that someone ought to be more careful of who they mix with. They're pig farmers up the lane. Wife took off years ago, then the two eldest boys. Now there's only Jeb and his dad Bill there, but they ain't friendly.'

'You think I could speak to them?'

'I think you'd be crazy to try,' said Bubba. 'Now come on in and forget them, for the love of God.'

139

A week later, Connor put on his black suit, Turnbull & Asser white shirt and black tie, and then he drove Mum in the Porsche to the West End offices of their family solicitor for the reading of the will.

They sat in a dark-toned waiting room with comfy low seating and two over-large ficus pot plants. Pink copies of the *Financial Times* were laid out on a coffee table in front of them. Mum was still in the black of mourning. She was pale but crisply groomed, her eyes dark-shadowed and without expression.

Aysha arrived ten minutes after they got there, letting in a gust of cold air with her. She looked washed out, depressed. Connor reckoned that not even Benedict could cheer her up on a day like this. The receptionist offered them all coffee or tea, but they refused.

'I'm sure he won't be much longer,' said the smiling girl, who was used to a procession of grief and misery passing through.

The outer door opened again, admitting another blast of chilly air, and then closed. None of them took any notice. Two women crossed to the desk. The receptionist smiled at them.

'We're here for the reading of Mr Flynn's will,' said the older one.

Connor, Aysha and Shauna looked up. The older woman had bobbed blonde hair and a neat figure clothed in a crisp black trouscr suit. Beside her stood a younger woman with long pale-blonde hair. She was wearing a neat boxy black jacket and a matching slim-fitting skirt with a kick-pleat at the back. She wore killer black stiletto heels and Connor couldn't help noticing that her legs went right up to her armpits.

'If you'll take a seat, Miss . . . ?' said the receptionist.

'Claire. I'm Claire Milo and this is my daughter.'

The older woman turned toward the seating area. Connor was struck by two things before hell erupted – that his father's mistress was prettier than his brief glimpse of her at the graveyard or in the photographs had suggested. And her daughter was a beauty. Her eyes were huge, and they were the clear pale powder-blue of the Man City strip, set under finely arched brows. Her lips were full. There was a Marilyn-type mole, a beauty spot, on her left cheek.

'You fucking cheeky *bitch*!' erupted Shauna, springing out of her seat, her hands forming claws, her nails needle-sharp. Claire cowered from her.

'Excuse *me*,' started the receptionist in alarm.

'You bitch, you fucking *cow*!' said Shauna, launching herself at Claire.

'What the hell . . . ?' Aysha burst out, also jumping to her feet.

The receptionist was on the phone, half out of her seat, talking rapidly.

'Mum! Fuck's sake!' Connor was up too now, grabbing his mother around the waist while her hands flailed inches from the Milo woman's face. Suki backed up, alarmed.

Shauna looked demented, like she wanted to kill Claire Milo with her bare hands.

'Let me fucking *go*!' Shauna was screaming at him. 'I'm going to *flatten* the cow.'

'Sit *down*, for God's sake,' said Connor to his mother. 'Christ, is this really going to help anything?'

He couldn't believe the woman had summoned the nerve to show up here today. He turned angry eyes on her and her daughter while holding on tight to Shauna. 'What the *fuck* are you two doing here?' he demanded.

Claire, visibly shaken, her eyes still on Shauna, gulped and said, 'I got a letter asking me to attend the reading of Josh's will. I'm sorry. I didn't mean to upset anyone . . .'

'You *what*?' roared Shauna. Claire flinched. 'Don't you say his name, don't you bloody *dare*! If you didn't want to cause upset then you shouldn't have been fucking my husband, you low-life *cunt*.'

'Sit down,' said Connor, manhandling his mother back on to her seat. 'Come *on*. This ain't helping. Aysha, sit down. And you.' He looked at the younger blonde. 'Whatever your fucking name is . . .'

'It's Suki,' she said shakily.

'Like I care. Sit *down*.'

'What's going on here?' asked a hefty, sharply suited and red-faced man, coming thundering down the stairs and into the reception area. It was the family solicitor, James McCready. He looked around at them all.

'Nothing,' said Connor, staring at the row of seated women. Aysha looked shocked. Suki's eyes were wide with fright. Claire was trembling but standing her ground. Mum looked like she was going to explode. 'Nothing at all.'

'If there is going to be any trouble, I won't go on with the reading,' said McCready.

'You *bitch*,' said Shauna, still looking daggers at Claire.

'I'm not here to cause trouble,' said Claire. 'This is what Josh wanted. That's the only reason I came here, to respect his wishes.'

Shauna looked set to start again.

'I have to warn you,' said McCready, puffing himself up.

'There won't be any trouble,' said Connor, glancing over at the white-faced receptionist then looking at his mum. 'Sorry. It's all fine now. *Isn't* it?'

Shauna just glared at him.

'Then . . . if you would all like to come upstairs . . . ?' said McCready uncertainly, and turned and led the way.

On entering the office, Connor was careful to place the Milo woman at the far side of the room on his left, then Suki, then he seated himself, then Aysha, then Shauna. Better to keep a *big* distance between Shauna and the woman Josh had been having his torrid affair with. Shauna still looked ready to rip Claire to pieces. All Connor wanted to do was get this done and get the fuck out of it.

With calm descending – and God knew how long it was going to last – James McCready quickly attended to the reading of Joshua Flynn's last will and testament. In measured tones McCready told them all that Josh's will had been made out a year ago. In it, he bequeathed the million-pound-plus family home to his wife Shauna, and a hundred thousand pounds to each of his children, Connor and Aysha. To Claire Milo, he left five hundred thousand pounds so that she could live in comfort in the future.

'He *what*? I'll contest that,' shot out Shauna when McCready read it aloud.

'That is your right,' he said.

'She's nothing but a *whore*. I'm going to pull all the hairs out of her lousy crab-infested *twat*.'

'Mrs Flynn, please moderate your language.'

'Yeah, Mum, shut it,' said Connor.

'Dad left her *how* much?' said Aysha faintly, looking across at Claire as if she was the stuff of nightmares.

'Five hundred thousand,' snapped Shauna, putting a shaking hand to her brow. She glared at Claire and at Suki. 'But she's not having it. She's not having a *bean*. I swear it. She's not having a penny, over my dead fucking *body*.'

McCready was folding the will. His job was done.

'Come on,' said Connor. 'Let's go.'

They all piled down the stairs and Connor ushered his mum and sister out the door. As he went to follow, Claire Milo caught his arm.

'What?' he snapped.

'Ask your mother about the Cleaver boys,' said Claire, her eyes holding his, her mouth trembling. 'Ask her about what they did to me and to my dog Blue. Just ask her.'

When Connor had dropped off Aysha at her place and driven over and parked the Porsche on the driveway of the Henley house, he followed Shauna inside. She led the way into the kitchen and started making tea.

'That Milo woman said something odd to me,' he said, pulling out a bar stool and sitting down.

'That fucking mare! Well, what? What did she say?' Shauna flung off her jacket.

'As we were leaving the solicitor's, she said to ask you about the Cleaver boys.'

Shauna's face took on a hard scowl. 'What about them?'

'She said something happened. Something with her and her dog.'

'What the fuck's she talking about? They're just pig farmers. They live up the road from the site where your dad and me lived years ago. He was always babbling on about the great life we had there, I suppose he must have mentioned them to you?'

'Yeah. He did.' Connor didn't tell her he'd been down there, looking at the campsite, the funfair. She'd only hit the roof. Shauna Flynn thought herself – and her son – far too good for all that now.

'Great life, my arse. It was a shit hole, and I was glad to get out of it.' Shauna turned away, busied herself with the tea.

140

Some days after the reading of Dad's will, Claire's words were still playing on Connor's mind. No good asking Mum about it, she'd made that plain. So he drove out again, past the campsite and on to the Cleaver house, passing Bubba Pole's site as he did so.

He parked near the farmhouse, and walked up. At the rusted, ruined gates, he hesitated. It was shady here; the temperature felt ten degrees colder than it did half a mile along the road. The house seemed to *loom*, as if inviting him to come closer. And if he did? Well, then it would just open the door (and its hinges would creak like a coffin lid, he knew it) and swallow him whole.

The place looked bleak. For the first time he noticed a jokey statue of two mating pigs perched above the porch. A dog was barking inside the house, a big one. He stepped forward and then a voice behind him said: 'What you doin' here?'

Christ! He hadn't heard anyone approach. He turned quickly, nearly overbalancing on the rutted entrance and going arse over tit. He righted himself and stared at the man who'd appeared there. The man was not tall, but he was *big*. He was solid, wide, with sloping shoulders and a bull neck. He was dressed in an old mac and heavy mud-coloured work boots. He had dark hair turning white and a matted grey beard. And he was staring at Connor with tiny, hostile eyes.

And . . . *oh shit* . . .

Connor felt his bowels turn to liquid. Felt his head go light.

The man was carrying an axe.

'You want to tell me what you're doing here?' he repeated when Connor didn't answer. 'I'm Jeb Cleaver and I'm *not* at home to visitors.'

Connor had never seen any of the Cleavers before, but now, standing here and confronting one of them, he could see that it was lunacy to think you could talk reasonably to these people, ask them about Claire or Blue or any of that stuff.

Connor opened his mouth to speak. Say something about his car stalling, breaking down, any shit he could think of. But he was here now. And this was not a horror movie, this was just two men facing each other in broad daylight.

'I'm Connor Flynn,' he said. 'My dad used to live up the road on the campsite.'

Jeb Cleaver was silent a while, looking him over. Then he started to smile.

'*Are* you, by Christ,' he said, and then he came forward fast, raising the axe.

Shit, thought Connor, backing up.

'You know what I'm going to do to you?' said Cleaver, swinging the axe in his hand. 'I'm going to send a few choice pieces of you back to your mammy in a carrier bag, how's *that*?'

He lunged forward. Shocked speechless, Connor dived behind the gate and the axe swiped down, steel flashing, and hit the post, splitting it in two.

Connor stumbled back, looking around for something,

anything, to defend himself with. Jeb Cleaver was laughing like a mad man, bringing the axe up again, ready for another swing.

Then a dusty dark-blue flatbed truck came shrieking around the corner of the lane, roaring like its exhaust pipe was nothing but a memory, shattering the silence. It screeched to a halt outside the Cleaver house. Bubba Pole emerged from behind the wheel, and three men hopped down from the back of the flatbed.

'How do, Jeb?' asked Bubba cheerily, coming around the front of the truck.

Jeb went still. He lowered the axe. The three men came closer to him. They were each holding a baseball bat.

'My friend, you got lost, yeah?' Bubba said to Connor. Then he turned and spoke to Jeb. 'This is a mate of mine, he was looking for my place, we saw the silly fucker miss the turn and shoot past. Sorry to disturb, Jeb.'

Jeb Cleaver said nothing. He eyed the three men with the bats, idly swinging the axe as he did so.

'Let's go then,' said Bubba, the smile slipping from his face as he addressed Connor: 'Come along, let's sink some ales.'

Connor somehow got his feet moving. His heart was thwacking away against his ribs like he'd just run a mile. He passed close by Jeb, thinking, *He's going to swing that fucking axe and take my arm off.* The blade glinted wickedly, the steel honed to a slick sharpness. Connor somehow walked back to the Porsche and got in. He saw Bubba climb into the pickup, and then the three men hopped aboard and the engine revved. Connor started the Porsche, reversed in the Cleavers' muddy drive, and shot back to Bubba's place, and safety.

★

'What the fuck you doing?' asked Bubba as they sat in his trailer half an hour later.

Connor was silent. He'd drained a whisky and he felt steadier now. He couldn't believe what had just happened. That mad bastard had meant to *kill* him.

'Fucking good job young Archie saw your Porsche go past the drive,' said Bubba. 'He do like a nice car, that boy, and he ain't forgotten yours. Came straight in and told me you passed by.'

'He was going to use that fucking axe on me,' said Connor.

'Nah, he was just teasing with ya,' said Bubba. 'The Cleaver boys always did have a strange sense of humour.'

'No, he meant it.' Connor had seen the blood lust in Jeb's eyes.

'Why would he do that?'

'Christ knows.' Connor was shaken. He was a tough nut, but an axe attack wasn't something you just shrugged off.

'Look, you got out – by the skin of your teeth, but you got out. No harm done. So leave it, Connor. Stay away from them; they're bad news. Curiosity killed the cat, remember? And if you ain't careful, next time it will kill *you*.'

141

Mad Dog Cunningham came by to see Connor one lunch-time, when Connor was grabbing a sandwich at his flat. Out of the window, Connor could see rain falling in a steady downpour from leaden skies. He thought that he was lucky to be alive, after his visit to the pig farm. He kept turning it over and over in his mind. Jeb had mentioned Shauna, as if he was looking forward to exacting some sort of revenge on her – like, for instance, chopping her son into neat bite-sized chunks. So Connor decided that he was going to call in on Mum and ask her some more hard questions. Not that he was looking forward to it. He guessed he wouldn't like the answers, even if he managed to get any.

Then the bell rang and he opened the door. There was Mad Dog, his pinball eyes swivelling with excitement.

'Know the Milo skirt you asked me to track down?'

A picture of Claire Milo sprang into Connor's mind. So did one of Suki, her daughter. Blonde hair. Long legs. That mouth . . . shit, she was hot as hell, that girl. And strictly off-limits. 'Yeah.'

'Well, you ain't gonna believe this . . .'

Shaking with rage, Connor paid Mad Dog and then left him outside the flat. He got in the Porsche and drove through the rain to where Mad Dog had said. Then he parked the car, went in through the lych gate and strode over to Josh's grave. It gave him a chill, coming back here. The AstroTurf covering the newly dug plot was gone and in its place the soil piled up on the grave was a raw dirty orange. All the floral tributes had been removed. No headstone yet, of course. You had to let the ground settle before you did that. Once it did, Dad's monument would be installed, and it would be as costly, as magnificent, as any of the other gypsy family ones here.

On her knees to one side of the grave was Claire Milo's daughter, Suki.

Connor paused a few steps away, thinking he was going to kill her, coming here to his father's last resting place. Shauna had been furious in the solicitor's, and he felt that same fury now, felt that the woman shouldn't be here, that he was going to obliterate her and her mother, strike her memory from the world so he could forget all this shit, all this bollocks about his dad being a player. Then maybe he could remember Dad as he *should* be remembered; as Josh Flynn the devoted Romany family man – and not as a cheating son-of-a-bitch adulterer.

Suki Milo wasn't wearing the heels today. Same black suit, but no heels. Practical flats.

As he drew nearer he could hear her crying, loudly. Her head was in her hands. Her shoulders were shaking.

Oh yeah? Well, I'm going to give you something to cry about.

Connor moved in. She hadn't even heard him coming. Didn't have a clue. He could strike her dead, and she'd never know.

'What the *fuck* are you playing at, coming here?' he said.

Her head whipped round, blonde hair flying limply in the cold breeze. Her hands dropped to her side. Her face was wet, her eyes red. She swallowed hard, then said: 'I didn't . . . I mean, I couldn't . . .'

The fury grabbed Connor, red rage descending. He took her arm roughly, hauled her to her feet. She staggered and gave a cry of pain as his fingers dug into her flesh. Her knees were muddy. Her face was pale and shocked.

'I *said*, what the fuck are you doing? You're not welcome here.'

She was still crying, shedding huge helpless tears.

'Shut the fuck up with the crying, OK?' he demanded, shaking her.

'You don't understand,' she managed to choke out. 'He was almost like a father to me, he really was . . .'

'Don't you fucking dare say that. He was nothing to do with you. He wasn't yours, *or* your mother's. He belonged to his family and he belongs to us still.'

'He loved my mother,' she said.

'No he didn't. He *knobbed* her, you stupid cow, that's all.'

'No . . .' She started crying harder.

'Oh, for fuck's . . .' Connor stared at her in exasperation. He was still holding on to her arm, and his grip was crushing. Well, good. He hoped he'd hurt her. Cow *deserved* it. Now he let her go with a contemptuous flick of the fingers but she just kept right on crying and sank back down on to her knees beside Josh's grave.

'I never had a father, but Josh was as good as one to me,' she gasped out. 'He was a lovely man. It's just *tragic*.'

'Get up,' said Connor.

She didn't get up.

'I *said*, get up, bitch,' he said, and yanked her back to her feet again. She stumbled, fell against him, clutched at his jacket to keep her balance.

'If my mother found you here, she'd tear you to bits,' said Connor.

She was crying again. But there was a glint of defiance in her eyes when she looked up at him.

'You and your bully-boy family, you might have frightened my mother in the past, but you aren't going to frighten *me*, OK?'

Then she was off again. Crying and crying and crying.

Connor stood there, breathing hard. Suddenly the rage drained out of him. For the first time in his life he was undecided as to what to do next. He had never hurt a woman, wouldn't dream of it; and Josh had always told him to take care, because Connor was big and he knew the damage sheer size could do. And now the fucking rain was coming down harder, drenching both of them.

'*Shit*,' he said with feeling.

Suki just stood there and cried.

He grabbed her arm again. She winced but said nothing.

'Come on, let's get in the fucking car,' said Connor, and led her away, out of the lych gate and over to the Porsche.

What the hell am I doing? he wondered.

But he opened the passenger door and pushed Suki Milo into the seat and shut the door after her. Then he went round to the driver's side and got in, out of the pouring rain.

142

The rain was coming down even harder now, battering the roof of the car. And *still* she was crying.

'*Shit*,' muttered Connor again, and he lunged for the glove compartment.

She cringed away from him and howled louder.

'Oh for fuck's . . .' He popped open the compartment and snatched out a packet of tissues. He tossed them in her lap. 'I was just getting these out. That's all. I'm not going to hurt you. Even if you *are* asking for it.'

Suki hitched in a breath, looked down at the tissues, swiped at her eyes. With trembling fingers she started picking at the cellophane, but she was shaking so hard with the cold that she couldn't get the pack open.

'For God's *sake!*' Connor snatched it off her, opened it, tossed out a couple of tissues.

'Thanks,' she mumbled, dabbing at her face.

Connor flicked the rain out of his hair, rubbed a hand over his face. Wondered what the fuck to do now. He stopped moving when he realized she was staring at him.

'What?' he asked.

'Nothing.' She gulped, wiped her eyes again.

'No, come on. What?'

'You look a bit like him.' Her eyes filled with tears again. 'You look like Josh.'

'I said shut up with the crying, didn't I?'

Her accent came as a surprise. American, and with a real southern twang to it. Yet this was Claire Milo's daughter, and Claire was English. How did that work? And he was *nothing* like Dad, not really. No way would he have tolerated Mum's mouthy dominating bullshit for so long.

'I'm sorry.' She sniffed, wiped her nose. 'I know how it must seem, to you. That my mother's some sort of awful scarlet woman . . .'

'You mean she's not?' Connor demanded through gritted teeth. 'My dad was married, with kids. You think that was the right thing she did, go with him when she knew that?'

She heaved a sigh. 'Look. They were together before . . . then they split up. Once they met again in New York, it was a done deal.'

'Dad was *married*,' said Connor.

'Yeah. To a woman he didn't love. That he'd *never* loved.' Suki was shivering now. 'It's cold,' she moaned, clutching herself.

'Oh, for fuck's . . .' Connor switched on the engine, flicked on the heater.

'Thanks,' she said faintly.

The roar of the heater filled the car. The rain hammered on the roof.

'He was so unhappy with her. With your mother,' she said.

'Don't you fucking dare,' said Connor, although he knew it was true.

Suki was staring at his face with those big baby-blues. 'Don't you know what happened? Didn't he ever tell you?'

'Tell me what?'

'That your mom drove mine out of town.'

'What does that mean?'

'It means she scared her to death, left her with no choice but to run away.'

'How? Your mother don't seem the type to frighten *that* easy.'

'Maybe she isn't so much *now*. But then? She was just a girl and she was terrified. Your mother had some bad friends. Scary ones.'

'Such as . . . ?' What a load of bullcrap this was.

'The Cleaver family. Do you know them?'

Oh fuck. Into Connor's mind flashed an image of Jeb Cleaver, coming at him with the axe raised, a crazed glint in his eye.

'You want to know what your sainted mother did to mine? Really?' said Suki.

'Yeah, I do. I won't *believe* it, but tell me anyway.'

'First they killed her pet dog, Blue, and threw his body into a tomb in front of the altar of a little disused church near the camp where she and Josh grew up. Then two of the boys from the Cleaver clan raped her, right there in the church. And me? I was the product of that rape. One of them was my father, and I don't even know which one. She gave me away as soon as I was born. Couldn't stand to look at me. When I first met up with her again – not so long ago – you know what? She couldn't even bear to be near me. And no wonder.'

Connor turned toward her, actually *looked* at her. What the fuck was she saying? Big pitiful blue eyes, a face soaked in misery. Pale blonde hair, wet and trailing down over her coat, which was too thin for this sort of weather. Knees all muddy from kneeling in the wet dirt by the grave. Long bare legs almost blue with cold. She looked a fucking mess. And – shit – she also looked sexy as hell. He'd thought it in the solicitor's office and he thought it again now. Damn, she was *hot*.

And now she was spinning this tall tale, and expecting him to believe it. *His* mother, instigating a rape? In tight with the Cleavers? Then a thought occurred to him. A bad one, because he was finding her so fucking beautiful he could barely take his eyes off her.

'Hold on. You're sure about that? You couldn't be anything to do with my dad?'

Suki shook her head. 'What, you think I could be *his* child? I wish. I really do. But no. Mom was a virgin when she broke off her wedding to Josh all that time ago.' She sighed. 'He was great. I—'

'Look, shut up, will you?' he cut in, irritated with her, and irritated by the fact that he'd just felt a very male reaction to a woman when for one horrific moment he'd wondered if she could be his half-sister.

But tales of dog-killing and churches and gang rape? It was all too much to take in. And it was *bollocks*. He snapped on his seat belt. 'Where are you staying?'

'The Royal Garden,' she sniffed. 'It's in Kensington.'

'I'm going that way, I'll drive you back,' he said. 'Put your seat belt on. And keep away from here in future, you got that? And tell your fucking mother too. She ain't welcome.'

'Yeah,' she said tiredly. 'I get the message.'

143

Claire was waiting for her when Suki got back to the hotel.

'I was worried. You've been gone so long,' said Claire, anxiety plain in her eyes.

'I took a taxi down to Winchester. I went to see Josh's grave. I wanted to go there, just once, on my own, say my goodbyes. And his son was there. Connor.'

Claire's eyes widened in alarm. She touched Suki's arm. 'Are you all right? He didn't hurt you?'

'No. He didn't. It was raining. We talked in his car.' Suki thought of Connor, of his barely repressed fury, of his very handsome face that reminded her so much of Josh's.

'Suki, please stay away from him. I don't know what he's capable of, but I know his mother and, believe me, she'd stop at nothing to do us harm.'

'I know.' Suki sat on the couch, drew her mother down beside her. 'Mom, I told him what happened to you. And his mother's part in it.'

'Oh God.' Claire put a hand to her mouth. 'You didn't.'

'Yeah, I did. I'm sick of them painting you as the villain of the piece. You were the *victim*, Mom. They hurt you, and it was all *her* work.'

'And . . . did he believe you?'

'I don't know.' Suki shook her head tiredly. 'I don't think so. But at least now he *knows*.'

Claire eyed her daughter's face. She hadn't told Suki, but she'd been so scared to come back here. Terrified. She feared Shauna, knew what she could do. When she'd got the letter from the solicitor, she'd agonized over it. She was frightened to come back, but she owed it to Josh to be there for the reading of the will. So she'd shown up, done what was expected of her. She hadn't *wanted* to. The whole experience had been fraught, bringing back hateful memories.

'Your dad and your sister still live at the camp, don't they?' asked Suki.

A shaft of pain lanced through Claire at Suki's words. Mum wasn't there, not any more. She was dead. It hit her again, the anguish of that cold hard fact. But her dad was still there. Trace probably was, too.

'Maybe,' said Suki tentatively, 'you can visit them? See them again? Wouldn't you like that?'

Claire bit her lip. She would *love* to see Pally and Trace again, but she was fearful. They must hate her for abandoning them as she had. They knew nothing of Shauna's threats. It must have seemed to them that she'd just kicked them coldly aside, and she didn't anticipate a warm welcome. Added to *that*, she still felt it was safer for them if she didn't go near. She knew all too well the kind of low lifes Shauna mixed with, and they could be watching Claire's movements even now.

No. It was safer to let Shauna think that Claire was totally detached from her family. That way, they were protected.

'I'm not going to see them,' said Claire.

'But, Mom . . .'

'No,' said Claire, her voice edged with steel this time. 'Now drop it, will you? Come on.' She forced a smile. 'Let's raid the minibar. You look like you need a drink.'

Suki accepted a measure of whisky from her mother, and Claire poured one more for herself. They sat in silence on the couch, sipping the warming alcohol, Suki thinking about her unknown grandfather and her aunt, wishing so much that she could meet them. Then she thought of Josh's witch of a wife in the solicitor's office, the harshness of her voice, the viciousness of her gaze, the way she had come at Claire, shrieking, her nails ready to rake the skin off Claire's face.

Aysha, Josh's daughter, had eyed them like they were the worst kind of scum. And Josh's son, Connor – who looked so like Josh – he had stared at them both like he hated their guts. Suki shuddered at the memory. Somehow, Connor's reaction had hurt the worst. And yes, maybe she'd found him scary, but she had also found him devastatingly attractive; every nerve in her body had felt sensitized when he was near her.

Probably she had told him more than she ought to. Maybe he would talk to his mother about what she'd said. And if he did . . . what the hell would happen then?

144

Having dropped off Suki at her hotel, Connor called Mad Dog. He told the swivel-eyed gink to keep an eye on the Milo women, make sure they didn't go near the family, check in with him now and again, let him know what they were getting up to.

'Consider it done,' said Mad Dog Cunningham.

'It better be,' said Connor.

When Connor got to Mum's, he found Shauna in the kitchen, sitting at the coffee bar. She'd taken up the fags in earnest since Josh's death, and she was puffing away beside an ashtray overloaded with stubbed-out filter tips. A half-cup of espresso was at her elbow.

She looked rough, edgy. Not like she needed espresso. She looked like she needed to calm down, quick. Her dark hair, usually so neatly groomed, was all over the place, as if she'd been dragging her fingers through it. Her eyes were fixed and manic as she took another deep drag of nicotine.

'That bitch,' she said the minute he came into the room. 'That cowing *fucker*.'

'Thought you'd kicked the habit,' said Connor, sitting down opposite. She'd smoked before, sometimes – thin cigars at Christmas, the odd cigarette when she was feeling tense – but now she was dragging that shit into her lungs like she wanted to start something down there, something black and terrible.

'Taken it back up,' she said with a tight, bitter smile. 'What you been doing?'

He looked at her and wondered if he knew her, if he had *ever* known her, his mother. Suki's words were dancing in his head. A brutal rape. Killing the dog. Claire, running for her life. And his mother at the back of it all? Could any of that be true?

'Work,' he said. No way was he telling her what he'd really been doing. She was jittery enough as it was; mention the fact that he'd just driven the girl back to her hotel and Shauna would hit the fucking roof. And somehow . . . he didn't want to tell his mother where Claire and Suki were staying. He didn't know why, but he didn't.

'I'm glad you called in,' she said, exhaling sharply so that two plumes of smoke came down her nostrils.

Dragon Lady, he thought. She looked fearsome. Christ, *he* wouldn't want to cross her. Once Shauna Flynn had it in for you, your goose was well and truly cooked. Uncomfortably, that made him think again about Claire, and what had – according to Suki – happened to the woman all those years ago. If Shauna had really been involved in that, how could he feel anything but disgust for her?

Almost against his will, his mind turned again to Suki, Claire's undeniably gorgeous daughter. Keep thinking *those* thoughts about the American girl, and there would be trouble.

'Listen. I've been hearing some crazy things,' said Connor. 'About Claire Milo.'

Shauna's face grew still. Her eyes flicked down and she stubbed out her cigarette, hard. 'From who?'

'That don't matter. But I was told she was raped, and

her dog was killed. By some people called the Cleavers. And that you had a hand in it.'

Shauna let out a bark of laughter. 'That's total *bollocks*. She just broke off her engagement to your dad and took off. Now we know she went to America. Who's been telling you all this rubbish?'

Connor ignored the question. 'I went out to the Cleaver place a while ago. Just looking around. With Dad gone, I wanted to see where he grew up, just look around the area. Anyway, I pitched up at the Cleaver place.' He paused, stared into her eyes. 'One of them – said his name was Jeb – came at me with an axe.'

Shauna's face grew still. 'You *what*?'

'He said he was going to send bits of me back to you in a carrier bag. Serious. Dad's mate Bubba Pole saved my arse.'

'*You what?*'

'It's true.'

'That *bastard*!'

'About Claire Milo . . .'

'She was a milksop little cow, Claire Milo. A real gutless wonder,' said Shauna, suddenly ashen, her manner distracted.

'She vanished that night, didn't she? The night you and Dad left the site.'

Shauna's dark eyes fastened on his. 'I don't know a thing about any of it,' she said. 'All I know is your dad was all I wanted, always.'

If he believed nothing else, Connor certainly believed that. Mum had verged on the obsessive about Dad.

No wonder the poor fucker ran for the hills. Got tucked up again with a sweet little honey like Claire Milo.

He shouldn't even be thinking that. But what he *was* thinking about now was Kylie, his ex. Stopping her in the shopping mall, and her looking scared and saying, *Ask your bitch mother and her pet ape*. What the fuck? Who was this 'ape'? Was it – could it be – Jeb Cleaver? And had Jeb and Shauna fallen out over something? Was *that* why he'd swung an axe at Connor while mentioning his mother?

Christ! What the hell had she been up to?

'Anyway!' Shauna drew a breath, swept a long-nailed hand across the marble worktop between them as if drawing an invisible line. 'Forget that shit. What matters is what I want to talk to you about now.'

'Oh?' Connor eyed his mother.

'Yeah.' Shauna reached into the drawer under the worktop and pulled something out that shocked Connor to the core.

'Christ,' he said as Shauna pushed the thing toward him.

'Don't tell me you ain't seen one of *these* before,' she said.

'What the . . . ?'

Connor stared at the big Magnum pistol. He looked up at his mother's eyes and she was smiling. She looked *mad*.

'Take that,' she said. 'And kill that bitch Claire Milo. *And* her runt of a daughter.'

145

There was a long, chilling moment of silence. Then Connor spoke.

'I'm not killing anyone,' he said, pushing the gun back toward her. 'Are you off your fucking head?'

The smile dropped from Shauna's face like a discarded mask. 'I'm your *mother*, Connor Flynn. And I'm telling you to do it.'

Connor stood up so suddenly that he knocked over the bar stool. He didn't pick it up.

'*No*,' he said.

'What, you ain't got the balls for it?'

'I'm not doing it.' Connor flicked the thing back across the countertop. 'Get it out of your head. It ain't going to happen.'

Aysha came by late afternoon after work to see how Mum was getting on. Poor bloody Mum, talk about everything kicking off. Aysha herself was in a state of bewilderment. Everything was so new with Benedict, breathless and wonderful, but she could hardly allow herself to be happy when poor Dad was lying dead. She'd loved her dad and they'd finally found an uneasy sort of peace between them after all those rough years. Josh had clearly had issues with her, but when she'd suffered through Joey's shit and through the trauma of losing her child, Dad had really come through for her. He'd been so good to her when she'd lost the baby. It was beyond sad that he was gone, when they could have grown so much closer. Mum was numb with grief, and now there was all this other stuff, terrible stuff, about this other woman being involved with him. How could she believe any of that?

But it was true.

Awful though it was, it was a fact. The money didn't matter, of *course* it didn't, but it was a bitter blow all the same. Five hundred thousand pounds would keep that Milo bitch in clover for the rest of her life. That was family money. Money Mum should have to keep for her old age. Or to squander. To do whatever she liked with. Instead, it was going to be wasted on that horny cheating bitch and the girl with the legs and the fucking blonde hair that Connor hadn't been able to keep his eyes off. Aysha felt rage grow as she thought about it. The front of those mares, turning up at the solicitor's office like that.

'Mum? Where are you?' she called out, letting herself in through the front door.

She went straight to the kitchen, but Shauna wasn't there. Then she went into the sitting room. Shauna was standing in front of the big picture window, her back toward Aysha. She was looking down toward the woodland beyond the garden.

'Mum? You all right?' said Aysha, coming up alongside her. Her mother was still dressed in funereal black, still deep in mourning for Josh.

'Oh! Hi, doll, didn't hear you come in, I was miles away.'

Aysha joined Shauna at the window. 'Pair of magpies.' She pointed out the two black-and-white birds, chittering and chasing each other around on the lawn.

'Death birds,' said Shauna.

Aysha was starting to wonder whether the doctor ought to give Shauna something, perk her up a bit. She seemed very down, very remote. Again Aysha felt that uncomfortable stab of guilt at her own newfound happiness. What did her mother have now? She wasn't that great-looking any more. Her face was harsh and lined, her hair dried out from years of chemical dyes. Now there were grey roots showing, and Shauna didn't even seem to care.

'I'm nipping down the shops, you want to come?' said Aysha.

Shauna shook her head.

'Can I put some tea on for you? Make you a sandwich? What you eaten today, anything?'

'I can fucking feed myself, Aysha, don't fuss,' said Shauna.

Aysha thought that Shauna was looking thinner by the day, but she didn't snap back.

'It's no good upsetting yourself like this,' said Aysha. 'I know it's been hard, Dad going like he did, and that bloody woman turning up.'

Shauna turned her head and her penetrating eyes stared into her daughter's. 'You don't know shit, Aysha. He was mine. *Mine*. And she's robbed me of that.'

'I know. And I'm sorry.' Aysha came to Shauna and put an arm around her shoulders. 'I'm so sorry, Mum.'

Shauna's stare held Aysha's. 'It's a pity your dad never loved you,' she said.

Aysha blinked. 'What?'

'He never did.' Shauna shrugged, her face full of sadness. 'Doted on Connor, of course, but you? Seemed he could never take to you.' Shauna pulled Aysha into a hug. 'But *I* love you, don't I. I've always been there for you. You know that. I'm the only one who's been a proper parent to you.'

It had never been said out loud before. Aysha stood stiffly in her mother's embrace. She could feel the bones on Shauna's back, she hadn't been eating well at all.

He never loved you.

Christ, that hurt.

'If there's anything I can do,' said Aysha, a shake in her voice. 'You know you've only to ask and I'll do it. You know that. Anything.'

Shauna pushed Aysha back a step and again her eyes bored into Aysha's. 'There might be something,' she said. And then she smiled.

146

Claire woke up and wondered where the hell she was. She was staring up at a ceiling, and she could hear the background hum of an air conditioning unit. She sat up, panicking, thinking *Josh . . . ?* And then it all came back, hit her like an express train. Josh was dead. She was never going to see him again. She'd crawled off the couch, having drained a whisky from the minibar, and she'd come in here to the bedroom, thinking, *Just a little nap.* Then she had fallen straight into a deep sleep.

She looked at the digital display on the clock by the bed; it said four-thirty in the afternoon. Yawning, she went to the bathroom to shower, then pulled out clean underwear and clothes, and got dressed. Combed and dried her hair. Then she saw the note on the table.

Gone out for a walk. Back soon. S.

Benedict took the call at the scrapyard office. 'Hi, Benedict? It's Mad Dog. The young one's walking around the pond by Kensington Palace.'

Benedict stared at the phone. 'What? Who is?'

'That girl who was with Claire Milo – Suki. Connor said I was to keep an eye out for both of them, and that's what I'm doing. I can't reach him right now on his mobile, and he said it was important, so here I am, giving you an update. Pass it the fuck along, will you?'

'OK.' Benedict put the phone down and dialled Connor's home number. The answering machine kicked in, and he left a message telling Connor what Mad Dog had just told him. As he did so, Aysha came into the Portakabin.

'Hiya sweetie,' she said, and listened to what he was saying.

'Hi, babe,' said Benedict, kissing her cheek when he'd finished speaking.

She watched as he hung up the phone. 'Anything exciting happening?'

'Nope. You know where Connor is?' He eyed her with concern. She looked distracted and pale. Not herself.

'No idea. Why?' Her gaze was still fixed on the phone.

'Oh, it don't matter. You OK?'

Aysha seemed to shake herself then. 'Yeah. I'm fine. Damn. Listen, I forgot something down the shops. I'll catch you later, all right?'

'Fine,' said Benedict, wondering what the fuck was going on with her.

Aysha drove over to Kensington and parked up in a tiny square behind the High Street. She locked the car and walked briskly over to the gardens. She passed the Palace and the statue of Queen Victoria, and walked on, over to the pond.

At first, she couldn't see Suki. There were people feeding the swans, people jogging, people on bicycles, people walking their dogs, a bloke with a traffic cone set out so that he could practise his fly-fishing technique with rod and line. All the while she was asking herself, *Where the fuck is she? Did that moron Cunningham get it wrong?*

Her heart was thudding in her chest so hard that it frightened her, but she had to keep a clear head, she *had* to do this. And then she saw her, sitting on one of the benches, staring out over the water. She was right over the other side of the pond, but she was there. It was her. Aysha quickened her pace.

Connor got home late afternoon and the light on his answer phone was blinking. He clicked *play*.

'The girl Suki is walking around the pond in Kensington Gardens,' said Benedict's voice. 'Mad Dog said you wanted to know her movements.'

Connor heard Aysha's voice in the background. 'Hiya sweetie,' she said.

'He couldn't reach you, so I'm passing this on,' said Benedict. The time of the message was three forty-five.

Connor deleted it. So what? He was still reliving his conversation with Mum in her kitchen, the shocking moment she'd shoved the gun toward him.

Fuck me! She'd really expected him to do it.

Mum's state of mind was troubling him more and more. He groped for his mobile and found the battery flat. Then he picked up the landline and dialled Shauna's number. It rang for so long he nearly put the phone down. Suddenly she picked up.

'Mum? You OK there?'

There was a long silence. 'Oh, it's you,' she said.

Jesus! He'd refused to kill two innocent women and now he was being given the cold shoulder over it.

'You all right?' he asked.

'I'm fine now. Aysha's been in to see me.'

'Right.'

'She took the gun, Connor. Which is more than you had the nerve for. She took it, and she is going to do it.'

147

Connor hung up straight away. Oh Christ. Aysha had been there in the Portakabin, she had heard Benedict giving out Suki's whereabouts. He had to get there. But he knew he would never make it in time. *Suki is walking round the pond in Kensington Gardens.* Rush-hour traffic. The roads were crazy right now. His sister was about to commit murder and get herself sent down for life on their crazy over-controlling mother's say-so, and he *couldn't get there in time* to stop it.

Trying not to panic, he phoned Mad Dog.

'Yeah?' asked Mad Dog, yawning on the other end of the phone.

Connor told him what was happening.

'Get over there, see if you can stop her,' he said, though he knew Mad Dog lived in a shit-hole cellar squat in Hammersmith, which put him further away than Connor. But what else could he do? Phone the police? Connor debated with himself for long, painful seconds, then decided against. Aysha was carrying, and that was serious. The police would come down too hard on her. So he ran out to the Porsche, got in and drove like a fury.

He parked the Porsche in a back street and ran along the High Street and then into the park, feeling sick with fear for Aysha and red rage at Mum's stupidity, his heart nearly bursting out of his ribcage as he ran like the wind.

There ahead of him was the pond. People. Lots of people, and that meant witnesses. For fuck's sake. As he ran closer he was looking left and right. He could see Mad Dog coming past the statue of Queen Victoria, spotting him, slowing down, then stooping forward, hands on knees, trying to get his breath back.

Connor couldn't see Aysha. *Or* Suki.

Christ! Where are they?

Frantically he scanned the crowds.

Old ladies with pooches on leads. A man practising fly-fishing. Kids screaming and yelling, out from school, on the loose at last.

Where the hell are they?

Then he saw Aysha. She was standing beside a bench, pacing back and forth, fury and nervous energy radiating from her like a furnace. Her mouth was moving and she was carrying a large holdall.

For Christ's sake Aysha, don't.

And where was Suki?

Maybe he was too late. Maybe Aysha had already done the deed somewhere *close* to the pond. Back in the trees? Connor hit the brakes as he drew close. Aysha was looking at him now, her mouth opening in a silent O of surprise. And . . . ah shit, there was a woman on the bench, her back turned toward him. The same too-thin coat, the long pale blonde hair lifting in the breeze. She was sitting there and . . . *oh fuck* . . . when he stepped around the bench and looked, he knew Suki's beautiful face would be shot away; she would be dead.

But he hadn't heard gunfire. He'd been running hard, focusing on just getting here and stopping a disaster. No one was turning, pointing. No horrified passers-by were

reacting. There were no screams. But now Aysha was looking in her bag . . .

'Aysha,' he gasped out, and crossed the final distance
between them. He stepped around the bench and looked
down at Suki.

She looked back at him.

She was alive. Big eyes. Sexy mouth. She was OK.

'*Fuck* it,' he said, his breath coming out in a whoosh of
relief. He turned back to Aysha, whose hand was now
reaching inside the bag. He grabbed her arm.

'Don't,' said Aysha, through clenched teeth. Her face
was set, determined.

'Don't *what*?' he said. 'Don't stop you doing something
that's going to ruin your entire fucking life? *Give* me that.'

Connor turned his body into hers so that they were
shielded from view. He grabbed the gun from the depths
of the bag and tucked it inside his coat.

'What's going on?' asked Suki, standing up.

'Nothing,' said Connor firmly, turning toward her. He
glanced at Aysha. 'Go on home, Aysh. I'll sort this out.'

'She was apologizing for her mother,' said Aysha, trembling, her face a mask of disgust as she looked at the
American woman. 'Saying she understood how upset I
was. Then trying to *justify* it. Saying how unhappy Dad
had been, married to Mum.'

'Go home,' repeated Connor.

'Mum wanted me to do it,' said Aysha, her voice barely
more than a whisper.

'I know that, Aysh. She asked me first. Now fuck off
home and don't be a div. She's just using you. That's all
she ever does. And it ain't worth it.'

Aysha gave Suki one last look and walked away. In the
distance, Mad Dog was watching. Connor gave him a nod,
and he walked off.

Suki was staring at Connor.

'What was that about?' she asked. She was very pale. 'Was she . . . was she going to do something? She kept looking in the bag. And she seemed hyped.'

Yeah, he thought. *She was going to kill you. And incidentally, she was going to fuck up her whole life too.*

'It was nothing,' he said.

'Right.' She was staring at his face. Not believing a word of it, he could see that. She stood up, edged away from him. 'I'd better get back to the hotel.'

148

Connor watched her go. She walked fast, glancing back a time or two. She was cutting across the park, past the fly-fisherman, past an elderly couple walking a fat Pekingese dog.

He followed more slowly, calming down after the stress and exertion. Fucking Mum, what was she thinking? But he knew the answer to that; she wasn't thinking at all. She was in revenge mode, and when Shauna got like that, any damned thing could happen.

Connor hadn't actually decided to go into the hotel, but having followed Suki back to the High Street, he went in, past the smiling top-hatted and red-coated doorman. He found her sitting in the reception area beside the big plate-glass windows that looked out on to the busy streets where black cabs, motorbikes and open-topped tour buses whizzed past night and day. It was starting to rain again.

She looked up when he came in, and visibly flinched. He walked over, looked down at her. She looked pitiful, small and vulnerable. He sat down opposite. They eyed each other silently.

'Are you here to finish what your sister started?' she asked unsteadily, when the silence had stretched on for too long. 'Why are you following me?'

I'm fucked if I know.

The gun was right there, in his pocket.

Then Connor said: 'You're shaking.'

Suki gulped down a breath. 'That's because you're scary.'

Finally Connor said 'Fuck it,' and stood up. 'Come on,' he said.

'What?' She stared up at him in alarm. 'What are you going to do?'

'I said come *on*. We're going to the bar. I don't know about you, but after all that, I need a bloody drink.'

'How did she meet up with him?' asked Connor as they sat in a corner of the hotel bar fifteen minutes later. 'I know they were together years ago, but in New York? How did that happen?'

'You don't want to know, do you? Not really.'

She'd slipped off her coat. Connor was drinking Johnnie Walker on ice, she was sipping a Bloody Mary. Suki thought that this was surreal, sitting here with Josh's son. Her nerves were still jangling from her meeting with Aysha. She knew Aysha had been trying to work herself up to something, something *bad*. She just didn't know what. And now she was here, with Connor. He was even more frightening than his sister.

'If I didn't want to know, I wouldn't ask,' said Connor.

'It must be horrible for you. A shock. I do understand that.'

'Answer the question.'

Suki took a swallow of her drink. Then she said: 'He was friends with the Constantinou brothers. They're club owners, boxing promoters and regular clients at Sylvester's, the nightclub Mom owns, the one I worked in. I don't think I'll go back to that. Maybe Mom won't either.'

'Now you've got all that cash to spend?'

'Mom didn't ask for that, or expect it. She didn't *want*

that.' Suki gazed at him. 'I think she wanted to come back not only to honour Josh's wishes but maybe to confront old demons. To look your mother in the eye in the solicitor's office and say, *Fuck you.*'

'She'll take the cash though.'

'I know how disgusting all this must seem to you.'

Connor took a gulp of the whisky. 'What sort of nightclub?' he asked.

'What, you think we're strippers, parading around stage wearing a G-string and a smile? I told you: Mom is the owner, and I serve drinks at tables. Nothing too shocking.'

'You said you only met up with her recently.' Connor's interest was piqued. 'How come?'

Suki explained about her life in the trailer park with Aunt Ginny and the shocking letter she'd read after Aunt Ginny's death, revealing the fact that Dave and Jo Vance hadn't been her *real* parents at all.

'It took such balls for Mom to come back here, you know. She's still scared of your mother, but she faced her down and I'm proud of her for that. I told you they killed her pet dog Blue, right in front of her? Slit the dog's throat, then threw his body into a tomb.'

'You did.'

'Yeah, but did I mention that they did it while your mother stood by and watched? She said the same thing would happen to Mom and her whole family if she didn't leave town. And then Jeb and Ciaran Cleaver took it in turns to rape her, right there in the goddamned *church*! They tossed the dog's body into the grave of a woman called Polly James – she's buried just in front of the altar.'

'Are you making this up?' asked Connor, although he didn't think she was.

He had a sickening feeling that she was telling the absolute truth. His mother! All right, she was a bitch. He *knew* that. Interfering in his love life, warning off his girlfriends, controlling Aysha to the point where she'd been about to commit murder, dominating Dad and making his life one long caged misery. But orchestrating a rape? Overseeing the slaying of someone's pet dog?

'I'm not making *anything* up!' She looked at him, indignant. 'God, why would I want to? One of those awful bastards was my father. A *rapist*. It's not something to be proud of, is it? You know what? Josh really disliked your mother. I'm sorry, but it's the truth. We saw it on his face whenever she phoned him. And she used to put little notes in his bag. He hated that. He said it felt like she was clawing at him, manipulating him, saying *You're mine.*'

'Waste of time, as it happens,' said Connor. Shit, the things she'd told him had left him feeling shaken. Remembering that pig farmer who'd come at him with the axe, it wasn't hard to imagine the Cleavers slitting a dog's throat and terrorizing a young woman as she begged for mercy.

'It's all true,' said Suki. 'I swear it.'

149

When Suki left the bar, Connor drained his whisky and departed the hotel, flicking up his coat collar against the deluge. People hurried past him under umbrellas, taxis swooshed past, water streaming into gutters like rivers. He went back to the Porsche, surprised to find it in place and not towed. He shook himself like a dog and then drove over to Henley and Mum's house. He let himself in with his front door key and walked through to the kitchen, where Shauna was usually to be found.

She was there, sitting at the coffee bar. She looked up when she saw him.

Connor found himself staring at her like she was a stranger.

'What, were you expecting Aysha?' he asked.

Shauna said nothing.

Simmering with barely suppressed fury, Connor walked over to where she sat, took the Magnum out of his coat pocket and placed it on the bar in front of her.

'Were you expecting her to come back here and tell you she'd done it? That she'd blown Claire or Suki's brains out? Or both?'

Still, Shauna was silent. Her eyes were on the gun.

'Have you any *fucking idea* of what that would have done to Aysha? There were witnesses by the dozen. She'd have gone down for certain. Her life would have been totally *fucked*. She'd have spent years inside. *Years*. All to give you your bloody *revenge*.'

He was shouting. Shauna's eyes raised and she looked at him, unblinking.

'Don't talk to me like that,' she said.

'You're fucking *mental*,' Connor went on, uncaring.

'I want her gone,' said Shauna.

'Yeah, you wanted her gone a long time ago too, didn't you.' Connor rested his hands on the worktop and stared at her, this unknown person, his mother. 'I've been hearing about that. You know I have. About the Cleaver brothers and what they did to her. About the dog. All of it.'

Shauna's face grew still. 'I *told* you. I don't know what you're talking about,' she said.

'Yeah, you do. You wanted her gone and they helped you. Claire vanished, didn't she, on the night you and my dad got together. She ran for her life. But those bastards had already done the damage, and she was pregnant.'

Shauna's eyes were like daggers. 'Yes, she ran off. Nothing to do with me though. She broke up with Josh and just cleared out. That's all.' She got to her feet, stalked to one end of the kitchen, then turned and came back to the coffee bar.

He could see she was lying. It was true, what Suki had told him. All of it.

'Fuck it, you know what I think?' said Connor. 'I think that Dad should never have been with you at all. He should have been with Claire Milo, but you derailed his entire life, didn't you. If he'd been with Claire, if he'd been *happy*, then he wouldn't have fucked off to America to book fights, he would have stayed *here*.'

'You *what*?' roared Shauna. 'You little *shit*,' she said, and came across the kitchen, eyes mad with rage. She snatched up the Magnum and pointed it straight at his chest.

150

'Don't be bloody silly,' said Connor, staring down the large black barrel of the gun.

His mother was actually pointing the Magnum at him. She'd really lost it this time.

'Come on,' he said. 'Calm down and give me the gun, Mum. This is stupid.'

For a moment she glared at him and he thought, *Shit, she's going to do it. She's actually going to shoot me.*

Slowly Shauna's hand went down. She placed the gun back on the counter between them. Then she slumped down on the bar stool. 'I'm sorry, I'm sorry,' she said in a trembling voice. 'Look, I need some time alone, OK? Just go, will you. Fuck off, Connor,' she said. She sounded exhausted.

'Mum . . .'

'*Leave me alone*. Josh betrayed me and you know what? Now both of my kids have too. Just *go*.'

Connor went.

Shauna sat there afterwards, shaking with fear and anger as she watched the rain dribble down the kitchen windows, listened to it hitting the roof of the house. She wondered what was happening to her life, the life she had always been in such control of but which was now hurtling into chaos. She would never have hurt Connor. Not really. What had she been thinking, turning the gun on him? And oh Christ, what he'd said before, about Jeb coming after him with an axe. What the *fuck*?

Josh was gone.

Josh hadn't loved her.

A shriek of pain escaped from her lips as she thought it. First, last and always for her, it had been Josh. He had been the centre of her world. Oh, she had formed 'friendships' – not friendships at all really, but ways to advance herself in the circles she wanted to be moving in. Her old neighbour Chloe, who still lived at the house y the river, was a 'friend', she supposed. Actually, Shauna couldn't stand the snobby, alcoholic cow. But she was useful for down the tennis club and on the golf course and at the charitable events Shauna relished; Chloe had been Shauna's stepping-stone into that world.

But had Shauna really been accepted there? She didn't think so. She thought they still laughed at her behind her back. Well, fuck them. She laughed at them, too, with their 'mwah, mwah' kisses and their 'dahlings'; false as fuck, they were.

Ah, she didn't have much of a knack for friendship anyway. Never had, really. Her family, Josh and the kids – they were her world. Anything outside didn't count.

But Josh was dead.

And the kids? The one time she needed their help, begged for it, they'd disappointed her.

Feeling fidgety, Shauna slipped the Magnum into a drawer and wondered what to do. She was going mad here, alone in this house. She snatched up her car keys. She might go out for a drive, she decided. Fuck the rain. Her life was over, the way she saw it, but she was still breathing. She might pop over to Chloe's, pass some time, get out of here because the walls seemed to be closing in on her and things were coming to light that should have stayed buried forever. And it had all started when that bitch Claire had come back with that fucking daughter of hers.

That was all her life was coming down to, now: passing time, trying not to lose her grip on sanity. She felt shaky, like everything was falling apart.

Somehow, she would press on with her life. There were accounts that needed settling, and since no one else was going to help, she'd have to sort it all out herself. For a start, Claire Milo and her fucking offspring were going to have to go, she thought, taking the gun out of the drawer and tucking it into her handbag. And then there was Jeb Cleaver. He was going to have to pay for threatening Connor, trying to hurt him.

But in the meantime she was going to take Connor's advice and calm down, get control of herself. Let them all think it was business as usual. She'd arranged to meet Chloe to discuss the seating plan for the Heart Foundation dinner on Friday, so that's what she'd do: get on with things, be on the outside the smiling society hostess she was born to be – even though inside she felt as if she was cracking apart like a clay riverbed in the baking summer heat.

151

Shauna got into her car and was backing out of the gates when someone rapped hard on her window. She saw Jeb Cleaver standing there, that *bastard*. She pulled on the handbrake, ready for this fucker right now, and was about to let down the window and give him the hairdryer treatment when he yanked her door open, leaned in, unclipped her seat belt and dragged her out of the car.

'You arsehole!' she spat. 'Get the fuck *off* me, you shit.'

'Is that any way to speak to the bloke that's helped you so much?' said Jeb, shaking her like a dog would a rat. 'Don't try coming the posh bird with me, Shauna – I know you, remember? I know all your dirty secrets. Have you forgotten the time I helped you with that bitch neighbour of yours, held her under the water while she struggled? And all those other favours you wanted doing, people you wanted sorted.'

'Yeah? Well, I've been hearing some things about you. You son of a bitch, you came at my boy with a fucking axe in your hand.' Shauna glanced back at the car. The engine was still running. Her bag was there on the passenger seat. The gun was inside it. If she could only reach it . . . but she couldn't. He held her in a grip hard as iron. Jeb was dangerous, she was realizing that now; she'd had a tiger by the tail for so long, she'd stopped being aware of it.

'Oh, you didn't like that?' He was grinning at her now. 'Listen, you upset me. Hurt me *bad*. So this is me getting even, OK? You're a real keen mother, right? You drool over those kids so much it's sickening to see. And trust me, I *seen* it. You organize their love lives – telling me to sort out that hairdresser girl who got a bit too friendly with your boy Connor. You *told* me to see to it she didn't make you a grandmother – and I did. Now, you don't want to know me. Want to push me aside. Well, I got news for you, Shauna Flynn – I ain't going to let that happen.'

'You come near my kids again and I'll kill you,' hissed Shauna, right in his face.

'Yeah, fine words,' he laughed, and shoved her away from him. 'I'll see you around, Shauna. Love to the kiddies! Or maybe I'll see them first!'

And he turned away and was gone while she was still standing there shivering with shock on the pavement.

152

To her dismay, Shauna found she felt too unsteady to continue her journey after her confrontation with Jeb. Gingerly she inched the car back on to the drive, parked up, and switched off the engine. She grabbed her bag and tottered indoors, going into the kitchen and swigging back a glass of water at the sink. Then the doorbell rang.

Fuck!

She'd forgotten to close the gates when she'd driven back up and now Jeb had come for another go at her. Well by Christ she'd teach *that* bastard a lesson he'd never forget. Threaten her kids, would he? She yanked the Magnum out of her bag, weaved her way back into the hall and opened the front door.

It wasn't Jeb.

Claire Milo was standing there.

'Hello, Shauna,' said Claire.

Shauna stared at her like she was a ghost. Then she stepped backwards, holding the gun behind her back. Claire came past her into the hall, and Shauna shoved the door closed. She couldn't believe it. The gutless little wonder had come *here*.

'What the hell do you want?' said Shauna, following Claire into the kitchen.

Claire turned, and saw the gun in Shauna's hand. Her eyes widened, but she didn't plead or cry. Shauna wished that she would. She'd enjoy that.

'You know what?' Claire's eyes held Shauna's steadily. 'I've been frightened of you for a long, long time.'

'Well, you're right to be.' Shauna gave a mirthless, faltering grin. After getting shoved about by Jeb, it was good to feel in control again, on top of the situation. 'Shame you didn't do as you were told in the first place, and stay clear.'

'I couldn't do that,' said Claire. 'Not when I met up with Josh again. We loved each other.'

'Shut up,' said Shauna, raising the gun, the grin dropping from her face. 'Just shut your fucking yap or I'll finish you right now.'

'You know Josh was Fearless Flynn? Well, aren't all us Romanies meant to be that, really? Fearless? But I've lived in fear for too long. And now I'm sick of it. I've had enough. So I wanted to come here today, and tell you that I'm not afraid of you any more.'

'Why's that?' asked Shauna, holding the gun steady on Claire's heart. *Christ*, it would feel so good to pull the trigger, to see her go down for the last time. This *bitch* who'd stolen Josh off her.

'Easy to be brave with a gun in your hand,' said Claire.

'With or without the gun, I could sort you out. Easily,' said Shauna.

'Yeah, but you couldn't stop Josh loving me, could you?'

'You *bitch*,' said Shauna, the gun quivering in her hand.

'He was mine. Always,' said Claire. She spread her arms. 'So go on then. Get it over with. You want to kill me? Do it. I'll be with Josh then and we'll be happy. But, Shauna – you will still be alone.'

Shauna felt her finger itching on the trigger. *Do it*, she

thought. *Christ, just do it.* Her hand shook. She blinked. Nervous sweat was stinging her eyes.

'What's stopping you?' asked Claire.

Shauna's hand was shaking harder. The gun wavered.

'You're like all bullies, aren't you?' said Claire, staring at her old enemy. 'You feed on the fear of your victims, but at heart you're just a lousy coward.'

'*Shut up!*' yelled Shauna. The gun shook in her hand.

'So do it. Go on,' said Claire.

Somehow she couldn't hold the damned thing steady. '*Shit!*' Shauna said, explosively, and she slapped the gun down on the countertop and then clutched at the counter, her head spinning, feeling sick, feeling faint and weak.

Claire walked over to Shauna and stood there looking at her. Shauna raised her head and stared into Claire's calm, pitying blue eyes.

'Shauna?' said Claire, leaning her head down close to Shauna's own.

'What?' Her mouth was trembling; words were difficult to get out.

'Just this,' said Claire, and hauled her arm back and struck Shauna hard across the face.

Shauna reeled away, clutching at the countertop, a hand flying to her cheek. She stared at Claire and knew she'd lost. The bitch was right. Dead or alive, Claire had always held Josh's heart. So she'd won.

'Goodbye, Shauna,' said Claire, and she walked out of the kitchen, out of the house, and away.

153

Shauna didn't know how she drove over to Chloe's, but somehow she made it. She was shaking like a leaf in a high wind after her meeting with Claire. What was wrong with her? She should have *killed* that bitch while she had the chance. And she was flooded with fear for Connor and Aysha. *Jesus, what did I start the day I decided to mix with the Cleaver boys?* All those years, Jeb had been at her beck and call, but now she was aware that her hold over him had grown perilously thin. She had to think this over. Think what her next step should be. She had so much to deal with. *Too* much.

Chloe greeted her with the usual false show of affection. She was air-kissed on both cheeks, hugged, ushered inside. Chloe took her raincoat and hung it up.

'Dahling, how lovely to see you,' said Chloe, masking her surprise, thinking that Shauna looked like a drowned rat and one side of her face was vivid red, like she'd been slapped or something. The rain was torrential. Shauna must be demented, driving about in this weather.

'I thought we could talk over the seating plan for Friday night,' said Shauna, her movements jittery. She walked ahead of Chloe into the lovely lounge with its purple-and-gold colour scheme. Easy to see a redhead lived here.

'The seating plan? Yes of course,' said Chloe. 'But I

thought . . . with Josh going like he did, I'm sorry, I should have phoned you, but I thought you'd be so upset still . . .'

'I'm fine,' said Shauna, walking over to the big picture window and looking out over the expanse of striped green lawn and down to the river. When she and Josh had lived next door, their view had been practically identical to this one. Then she focused, frowning. There was something big and yellow moving down there. The loud hum of motors penetrated the double glazing.

'Oh, I see you've noticed,' said Chloe, coming to stand beside her. 'It's most inconvenient,' she tutted. 'So noisy. And the smell when the mud comes up! I tell you, I can't even go out in the garden, it's *unbearable*.'

'What . . . ?' Shauna was aware of her own heartbeat, very fast and painfully heavy in her chest. Her head was humming. She wondered if she was going to be vomit, or pass out. She watched the men, watched the machine. 'Oh Jesus,' she said.

'I suppose they had to do it eventually, because of the flooding,' said Chloe. 'Nearly left it too late, didn't they? It's been raining non-stop this past fortnight. Now at long last they're dredging the river.'

154

Connor went back to his flat. He couldn't eat, he felt too keyed-up. He phoned Benedict, told him what had happened in the park and told him to keep an eye on Aysha.

Fucking Mum.

His sister could have been banged up right now and destined for a life in Holloway if their mother's poison had done its work. He made tea, and then sat there and thought of Suki. Pale hair, long legs, eyes that could break a man's heart. All right, he'd followed her back to the hotel because . . . she fascinated him. Because she was stunning. And because . . . he wanted her. He wanted her in bed, just as soon as he could get her there. *If* he could get her there. Which seemed pretty damned unlikely, given the circumstances. But first, he had things to do.

He'd heard so many conflicting stories these last few days, it was hard to know what to believe. Time he went looking for answers.

He picked up his keys and went back out to the Porsche.

Connor drove past Winchester and carried on going until he reached the place. Avoiding the campsite where Josh had spent his childhood, he parked up in the lane and walked down through the fields until he reached the disused church. It was unlocked because there was nothing in there to steal. He stepped inside, hearing the echoing silence and feeling the steady chilling march of centuries all around him.

Slowly he walked up the aisle, looking left and right. Creepy in here, his footsteps echoing in the darkness. It had happened here, Claire's rape – that's what Suki had told him. He paused at the top of the aisle and looked down at the grave she had told him about, the one in front of the altar. The inscription read:

HERE LIES POLLY JAMES
FIANCÉE OF WILLIAM CODY
1745–1762

Died of the fever on the night before her wedding.
MAY SHE REST ETERNAL

Something Old
Something New
Something Borrowed
Something Blue

He stood there and stared at it for a long time, then he turned and walked back outside, closing the door behind him.

155

Aysha opened the door at Benedict's place to find Connor standing on the doorstep.

'Oh! It's you,' she said, her face falling. She turned without another word and led the way back into the lounge. Benedict looked up from the sofa. Then the phone started ringing.

'I'll get it,' he said.

'So what do you want?' said Aysha.

'Don't be like that, Aysh. I saved your bloody bacon. You ought to be grateful.'

'I should have done it.'

'For what? Mum was pushing your buttons, that's all. You can't alter history, Aysh. I know it's hard for you to hear, but if he'd lived, Dad was going to divorce Mum and marry Claire. Look – he was our dad and we both loved him. D'you really think he'd want harm coming to her? Or her daughter? Do you?'

She stared at him, arms folded. 'She told me he'd never loved me.'

'Well, I think he did. She was being a bitch, that's what she does best. She was manipulating you into doing something fucking stupid, and you fell for it. Just be glad you didn't do it and fuck yourself up for good.'

'I wanted to kill that—'

'I know. But you didn't. That's what counts. Come on, Aysh. Let's not fall out. I need your help.'

Benedict came back into the room, pulling on his jacket. 'Going out.' He kissed Aysha's cheek, flashed a grin at Connor. 'See you both later.'

When the door closed after Benedict, Connor looked at the window. In a little over an hour, it would be full dark.

'Put the kettle on, Aysh,' he said, settling down on the sofa. What they had to do was best done at night, under the cover of darkness. They had time to kill. And then, at last, he was going to find out once and for all what was lies, and what was truth.

156

'Shauna? Are you all right? You look . . .'

To Shauna, Chloe's voice seemed to be coming from a thousand miles away. Her eyes, her whole being, was centred on what she could see through the window. The roar of the machinery, the massive grab of the thing swinging up and down, dipping like a huge feeding animal, scooping up vast dripping weed-hung sections of mud from the bottom right of Chloe's garden. It was heading toward the house next door. The house where Shauna and Josh had lived. And the rain had stopped.

'They put a note through the door, told everyone up and down the road. But the stench! You would not believe it. We've complained, of course, to the council, but . . . Shauna? Where are you going?'

Shauna was hardly aware of moving, but she turned and walked to the end of the big lounge, then through the hallway and out into the kitchen. She didn't stop to get her coat. She unlocked the back door and set off across the terrace and down the steps.

'Shauna?' called Chloe, following her out. 'What's the matter?'

Shauna was panting, walking fast. Her stiletto heels caught on the rain-softened turf and she stumbled. She paused, kicked the heels off and then she carried on, bare-

544

foot, toward the monster machine and the men in the hi-viz jackets on the bank, who were watching as the driver manoeuvred the thing.

'No, no, no . . .' she muttered under her breath. This couldn't be happening!

She broke into a shambling trot and then into a run. She had to stop them.

'Shauna . . .'

Chloe's voice was growing fainter as she struggled to keep up with Shauna's pace. Shauna raced on, because if she got there in time she would stop them.

Stop them how?

She didn't know. She would think of something.

'Stop!' she started shouting.

The light was fading. It would be dark soon. Then they would *have* to stop.

The men had their backs to her and the machine was making its hellish noise; they didn't hear her.

'Stop for God's sake!' she yelled, aware that she was crying, that this was the final straw and now her life really was in bits.

'I said *stop!*' she screamed when she was within ten paces of them. She fell to her knees on the grass, the pungent smell of the churned-up river mud making her gag.

'Stop, for Christ's sake, stop it,' she moaned, sobbing.

Chloe hurried up to Shauna, bent over her.

'God, Shauna, are you all right?' she asked, but all Shauna could hear was the machine roaring like a lion, all she could see was the gang of workmen, the looks on their faces as they turned one by one to stare at her. But one of them was still watching the grab, and he stiffened as something caught his eye.

He put up a hand, waved. *Stop.*

The machine's roar died to a shuddering halt.

One of the men turned back to the river. Then another. And another.

Shauna's breath caught in her throat.

'What . . . ?' Chloe said, her hand on Shauna's shoulder. Now she looked ahead, too.

'What the *fuck*?' asked one of the men loudly.

Shauna looked. Hanging out of the side of the grab was a skeletal hand and arm. The bones were a pale luminous green-white from years submerged in the river.

'Christ!' said Chloe, putting a hand to her mouth. 'That's—'

'Holy *shit*! That's someone's arm, that is,' said one of the men.

They all stood there, frozen, fascinated. Disbelieving.

'Better call the police,' said one of the other men, his face white as milk. 'Tell them we've found a body.'

157

Night had fallen. The torch was weaving back and forth in Aysha Flynn's hand, which was shaking hard. Its cone of light, feeble in the total country blackness of the night, was wavering all over the place.

'Hold it *steady*, damn it,' snapped Connor.

Aysha put both hands on the torch. Teeth chattering with nerves, she tried to do as her brother said.

'This is wrong,' she told him. 'This is *crazy*.'

They were inside the tiny church near the gypsy camp, way out in the middle of nowhere. No one came here. It was near-derelict; no alarms, nothing. According to Connor, who'd looked it up, the church hadn't been in use since Gilbert White trotted past it on his famous white horse in the eighteenth century. It had never been big enough to seat more than twenty people, tops. It had no electricity, no heating or light. It was a place of deep peace and tranquillity.

Tonight, it was being desecrated.

We're going to be cursed for this, thought Aysha with a shudder.

Connor had brought a sledgehammer and a pickaxe along. Then he had led the way to the big gravestone at the top of the aisle, the one that lay right in front of the altar; last resting place of Polly James, 1745–1762, fiancée of

William Cody. The inscriptions had almost been worn away by footsteps over the years, but Aysha could still read them, just about.

May She Rest Eternal

Jesus! Spooky, or what?

Polly James had died the night before her wedding, it said. And then there was the old wedding rhyme:

Something Old
Something New
Something Borrowed
Something Blue

Connor tried to get the pickaxe under the edge to lift the stone. But it was huge and too bloody heavy for one man to budge. So now Connor flung the pickaxe aside and took up the sledgehammer again. He was taking aim . . .

Oh shit, thought Aysha.

. . . and the hammer swung fast, up and then down. It hit the ancient stone and bounced off.

'Fuck,' said Connor, peeling off his shirt and tossing it aside.

Despite the bitter chill, there was a sheen of sweat on his brow and an alarming intensity to his face when the torchlight caught it. Aysha watched him, thinking that this was crazy, that they couldn't be doing this, that he must be wrong.

Connor shot his sister a look. 'Steady,' he said, and swung again.

No luck.

'Connor, we shouldn't—' said Aysha.

'We have to,' he cut her off, and swung again, and again, and . . .

Suddenly it happened: the stone cracked. Connor hit it once more, and the crack widened into a fork and split. Connor downed the sledgehammer, grabbed the pickaxe again and levered one of the smaller sections away. It tipped up and then crashed to the side, echoing mournfully in the tomb-like silence of the church. Dust plumed up, and Aysha recoiled, coughing. Connor levered the pick under the remaining section, and heaved. That too gave up and fell aside.

'What the hell is *that?*' asked Aysha, her voice shaking as she focused the torch's beam on what was revealed.

Connor leaned forward. He'd hoped to find nothing but an ancient skeleton. It was Aysha who stretched down a hand. With a shiver of revulsion she brushed away dirt from the stuff Connor's blows had revealed.

'It's fur,' she said. 'Grey-blue fur. Oh *yuck.*'

'Something blue,' said Connor. 'Holy shit. That's Blue. That's Claire Milo's dog. They killed him and put him in here. You know what this means? It's true. It's all fucking true.'

'*What?*' Aysha looked ghostly pale in the torchlight.

'Fuck it,' said Connor.

He hadn't wanted to believe it, but here was the proof. The Cleavers really had killed the dog and raped Claire on his mother's say-so. Given her a child; given her Suki. He believed it all now.

158

There was very little left of Blue except fur, bones, teeth, and bits of catgut where he'd been stitched up time and again by Claire's dad after running through barbed wire after hares.

'Christ,' said Aysha, coughing and almost gagging as Connor started lifting bits of the dead dog out to see what lay beneath. The smell in here was ancient, dusty. It clawed at the back of her throat and made her breath catch.

Blue crumbled and fell apart as Connor moved him, rib bones detaching, leg bones coming loose, bits of insect-eaten fur detaching and drifting around like dust motes in the torchlight. Bit by bit, Connor laid the pieces of the dead dog beside the open tomb.

'Hiya, kids,' said a male voice behind them in the darkness.

Then something smacked Connor hard behind the ear and the torch fell. Blackness and light merged into a kaleidoscope and he pitched forward across the skeleton in the grave like a lover. He heard Aysha scream, and then there was nothing.

159

Connor was coming back to himself, inch by inch. His head hurt. He could hear someone crying. He opened his eyes and he was in a room. It was a dump of a room. Old beer cans all over the place, big dogs roaming around, threadbare sofas and enough dirt on the floor to plant an acre of spuds. The smell in here was ripe, fetid.

What happened?

For a long moment he couldn't even think straight. Then his eyes fell on Aysha, sitting hunched on a couch opposite, her face wet with tears. And he was sitting on another one. Christ, there were probably fleas in here, the dogs were scratching, wandering around, slobbering everywhere.

'Connor? Oh God, I thought they'd killed you!' Aysha burst out.

Connor tried to sit up straighter, tried to focus. His head was one screaming, writhing mass of pain. His shirt collar was damp; someone had hit him, and he was bleeding. One of the dogs, an ugly black-and-white bruiser, sniffed his leg and he feebly booted it away. He could hear voices, talking in another room.

Then a door opened and in came a squat, massive bear of a man, grey-bearded and mean-eyed. He had a small pursed mouth and a stare that could freeze hot water. His eyes fastened on Connor sitting there. Then on Aysha.

'So here's the kids,' he said. 'The girl I ain't seen before. But *you*, you're Fearless Flynn's boy,' he said. 'You're Connor. Looks like we meet again.'

It was Jeb Cleaver.

I'm a dead man, thought Connor.

160

Coming in behind Jeb was a smaller, older version from the same shallow end of the gene pool. Also bearded, wearing boots – and carrying Connor's own pickaxe.

Bill came over to Connor and looked down at him. 'Shauna Flynn's boy, right?' He grinned with blackened teeth at Aysha. 'And the girl too.' He reached down, grabbed Aysha's arm and hauled her to her feet. 'Her we'll save for later,' he said, leering at her.

'No! Christ, let go of me!' she screamed. 'Connor—'

'Shut up! We're going,' said the older Cleaver, and dragged her from the room. The dogs followed.

'Now I'm going to break you up,' said Jeb as the door closed after his dad and Aysha. Jeb gave Connor a broad smile. 'Piece by piece.'

Connor winced as he touched the sore spot behind his ear. It was still bleeding. He felt dizzy.

'That hurt? Don't worry. You won't be feelin' it for long,' said Jeb, coming closer.

Christ, what was happening here? 'I was in the church . . .' Connor started, dazed.

Jeb nodded. 'A little clue there on the stone: something *blue* – a nice touch, don't you think? Shauna liked that, she said the useless Milo cunt had always said she liked the

553

place, so why not bury her dog there? So we cut the mutt's throat and put it in there. Might have put the Milo girl to rest there too, but the mood was on us so we had some fun with her instead. All on your mum's say-so. Real dark horse, your mother.'

Connor took this in, staring at Jeb's brutish, uncaring face. 'It's true then. She was behind it all.'

'Shauna wanted the job done and we were willing.'

Christ, thought Connor.

Jeb let out a low whistle. 'Used to be the best fuck for miles around, that Shauna. And in return? She wanted Claire Milo gone so she could have Josh Flynn for keeps. But she's let me down, your mother, and I've been thinking of ways to get even. And what would hurt her most? Some shit happening to her baby boy and girl, I reckon.'

Connor felt like he wanted to puke.

'All I done for her,' said Jeb. 'Sorted things out, lots of things. *Including* that little hairdresser of yours she wanted rid of. Now she thinks she can blow me out like I was nothing? So let's see what she makes of this, yeah? Knees first,' said Jed, and surged forward, swinging the pickaxe high.

161

The kitchen was as disgusting as the lounge, but Aysha barely noted any of it as Bill Cleaver dragged her in there and slammed the door after them. He went to the back door, yanked it open, said: '*Get!*' and the dogs swarmed outside. He shut the door after them and then stood looking at her. Aysha shrank back.

'You piece of shit!' she said, her face wet with terrified tears.

Bill only grinned at that and crossed the room. 'See you in a second, girly,' he said, and went back out into the hall.

The minute he was gone, Aysha started yanking open drawers. Forks, spoons, knives but too small to be any use. She looked on the worktops. Threw open the cupboards, banging her shin on a toolbox. 'Fuck!' she yelped, and bent and rubbed her leg and then lifted the lid and looked inside. No good. Well, maybe. Then she saw something else, in the far corner of the worktop. She grabbed what she needed, gathered her courage, and surged out into the hallway.

Connor saw the pickaxe coming down and lurched to one side, out of the way. The axe buried itself in the sofa. Jeb swore, spat, then took another swing as Connor staggered, dizzy, trying to get to his feet and away.

'You'll just make it harder for yourself,' said Jeb, shaking his head. 'The punishment's due, boy, so take it. We'll send your ma a little something to remember you by, but the rest? We'll let our old porkers have you. Yeah, we'll feed you to the pigs. How about that?'

Connor was swaying, his legs unsteady. He saw the axe coming at him again and shoved aside a dirty, dusty old chair and went sprawling against the wall.

Thunk!

This time the wall got it, right beside Connor's head. Jeb yanked the thing back out. Plaster dust flew, and bits of shredded wallpaper. Connor tried to lever himself to his feet once again, but the room was spinning and he couldn't seem to get his legs to work.

'Stay *still*, cunt face,' said Jeb, and he was grinning, enjoying this as he drew the pickaxe back for the third time.

Can't move, thought Connor. *Can't do it.*

He watched the pick swinging back.

This is it then.

Back it went . . .

'Now take your punishment, boy,' he heard Jeb say as if from a great distance away.

Gonna die here tonight . . .

Then, at the top of the arc, the pickaxe stopped moving. Jeb froze there, his eyes wide. A thin trickle of blood came snaking down the side of his thick neck, staining the front of his filthy shirt a dull red. Slowly, he pitched forward and hit the wall beside Connor. Then Connor saw the meat chopper attached to the back of Jeb's neck, its blade buried deep, cutting his spine clean in half.

Connor looked up, trying to focus. He saw Aysha standing there, weaving back and forth. She looked like she was about to throw up. But she'd stopped Jeb Cleaver.

Then with a roar Bill came thundering into the room and threw himself at Aysha. She went down hard, the head of the Cleaver clan's hands locked around her throat.

162

Christ, the bastard's killing her, thought Connor.

His brain felt scrambled. Aysha's face was going purple. Bill was sitting on her chest in grief and fury, having seen that she'd killed his son, and was now throttling the life out of her.

Got to do something.

But he couldn't. All Connor could do was watch in horror as Bill killed his sister.

Must do something.

Couldn't, though. Couldn't get up. Soon, maybe, but by then it would be too late.

Shit.

Then he saw there was a hammer in Aysha's hand. She swung it up in a desperate move. It *clunked* against Bill's head and he swayed to one side. Blood was running down from his forehead, where the hammer had struck him.

Aysha felt the world reeling around her as the force of Bill's grip on her neck increased. Fighting for air and unable to get it, in panic she swung the hammer back again at the big man. It *smacked* into Bill Cleaver's temple this time, but he had a head like granite. He ducked sideways, wincing, but didn't release his grip.

Consciousness fading fast, Aysha gave it one last des-

558

perate shot. This time she aimed for his face. There was a *crunch* as his nose was broken wide open. Blood gushed down over his mouth. But he still didn't let go. She could hear choking noises coming from somewhere and realized that it was her making them. She swung again. The hammer hit him right between the eyes with an almighty dull *thunk*. Blood started pulsing down over his face in a steady stream, blurring his features.

Then in slow motion Bill toppled sideways and lay stretched out on the dirty old carpet. Aysha, free at last, took in a whooping breath and sat up, both hands on her throat.

'Holy *shit*! Oh Christ! That *bastard*,' she croaked.

Aysha crawled and then staggered to her feet and gave Bill another hard swipe around the head. Then again, and again. Finally, Connor was able to lurch to his feet and grab her arm.

'He's done for,' he gasped out.

Still eyeing Bill with loathing and fear, gasping, shaking, Aysha kept hold of the hammer and leaned hard into Connor, nearly upending the pair of them. They stood there swaying like drunks out on a Friday night.

'You OK?' Aysha choked out, coughing, clutching at her throat.

'I'll be fine,' said Connor, trying to raise a smile and failing. 'Just give me a mo.'

'D'you think he's dead?' asked Aysha, looking at Bill's blood-soaked form with a shudder. Shock setting in, she let the hammer fall to the floor.

'I should fucking hope so, after that,' he said.

163

The woman was acting weird.

Shauna could remember them saying that to the police when they arrived. The men, the ones who had been working, joking between themselves, clearing the river of weed, dredging the channel deeper so that boats could pass unimpeded and the river no longer was a flood risk in rainy periods on this stretch – they had told the police that she was behaving oddly.

Weird as nine pence, that one. Screaming and yelling and crawling about on the ground.

The dredger had unearthed a body. A skeleton, actually. First one, then – to the men's horror – another. And two rusted shotguns. All wrapped in a crumbling tarpaulin, weighted down. Shauna thought that this should never have happened; Ciaran and Rowan Cleaver should have lain there forever in their watery grave.

She was acting funny. Seemed very upset.

Wouldn't anyone be upset, seeing a sight like that? Of course they would.

'I'd better go home,' Shauna had said to Chloe when she had pulled herself together. But by then of course the harm was done. They had seen her acting weird, on her knees, saying no, no, no, it shouldn't happen, it shouldn't *be* this way.

'But won't the police want us as witnesses?' Chloe said.

Shauna ignored that. She drove home in a daze and sat in the half-dark in her kitchen as night closed in, wondering where the kids were, what they were up to. She made herself a strong cup of coffee and lit a cigarette and noticed that her hands were still trembling. She glanced down. Her tapestry-covered high-heeled shoes, her favourites, were caked in mud and grass clippings, ruined. She kicked them off, uncaring. Her feet were mud-covered too. No matter.

Ah, what the hell. The whole thing was over anyway. Josh was dead. The kids didn't even seem to like her and they wouldn't do a damned thing for her. And now the bodies had been discovered. How long would it be before the police pieced it together? She'd been acting weird, the men were right. They wouldn't forget that and neither would that gobby, snobby cow Chloe.

Chloe would tell them that the woman they were talking about was Shauna Flynn who'd once owned the property next door that backed on to the river where the bodies were found.

Should have taken them downstream somewhere, thought Shauna. But then – that night – she and Josh had been desperate, in a panic, thinking that it would be good enough, that no one would ever find them.

But they had.

Shit.

She put the big Magnum, the same one she had used to kill the Cleaver brothers, on the kitchen counter and looked at it. She'd been going to finish Claire Milo and her daughter, and then Jeb – but really, what was the point? She didn't seem to have any control over anything any more. Everything she did turned out a bloody disaster. And Josh was gone. Claire had been right, what she said:

Shauna had won the battle, for sure. But in the end, Claire had won the war.

Slowly, Shauna drained her coffee and stubbed out the remains of her cigarette. Looked around her beautiful, expensive and empty home. You had a good view of the driveway from where she was sitting. Saw everyone coming and going, right down to the gate on the road. She liked that.

She was tired now, tired to death. Yes, she could say that Josh had done it. She could get rid of the gun. She could say it was him, not her, who shot Ciaran and Rowan dead, but she was too exhausted to even speak the lie.

So fuck it.

Fuck it *all*.

She was still sitting there in the dark hours later when headlights lit the drive. A car had stopped at the gates. There were blue lights flashing. Now the intercom was buzzing, someone was speaking. Shauna stood up, went over to the intercom and pressed it, to let in the police.

Then she went back to the counter, picked up the Magnum, took careful aim, and shot herself in the head.

164

Connor and Aysha had cleared away the mess at the Cleaver place. Once they were done with it, that hell hole had probably never *been* so clean. They had hauled the bodies out on to one of the pickups, then they had buried Bill and Jeb way out in the woods, far away, working long into the night despite all their cuts and bruises to make sure the bastards would never be found. After that, they'd pushed the pickup into a flooded quarry and watched it sink out of sight.

The dogs?

Aysha hadn't liked to do it, but Connor had said someone would pick them up, so they had taken them halfway up country and then set them loose. They had no collars, nothing to identify them as Cleaver dogs, and that was good. The alternative would be to keep them locked inside the house to starve, or leave the doors open and risk the dogs tracking to Bill and Jeb's grave, unearthing their remains and eating what was left of the bastards. They made an anonymous phone call days later to the RSPCA concerning the maltreatment of pigs on the farm, and left it at that.

When they got back to Connor's flat in the early morning, they took turns to wash the blood away in the shower, and drank brandy to steady their shattered nerves. Connor settled Aysha in the spare room for the night, and fell into his bed, but his mind was full of nightmares, he couldn't rest. He got up early next morning, showered again – he still felt dirty from all that he'd done – and made coffee. It was then that the doorbell rang. He answered the intercom.

'Police, sir. Can we come up?' said a male voice.

Shit!

'Yeah. Come up.'

Aysha came out from the bedroom, her eyes full of guilt and fright, pulling on a robe one of Connor's girlfriends had left there. They stared at one another as there came the sound of heavy boots on the stairs outside. Had someone spotted them loading the bodies? Or dumping the truck?

'Oh Christ,' said Aysha, looking sick.

'Say nothing,' he told her, feeling pretty sick himself.

He opened the door and two youngish policemen came into the flat, removing their hats.

Jesus, here it comes . . .

'Mr Connor Flynn, is it?' asked one of them.

'Yeah, that's me.'

'And this is . . . ?' They looked at Aysha.

'My sister.'

The policeman who'd spoken first said: 'I'm sorry, sir, miss . . . we have some bad news.'

And then he told them the shocking news.

Their mother, Shauna Flynn, was dead.

165

Six months later . . .

Finally it was time for Dad's headstone to be installed. The mason said the ground was settled enough, and that they were doing it today. If Connor wanted to come tomorrow, see the finished article in place, then that would be fine.

Connor made two calls and then he drove down to the cemetery, walking along in the sunshine until he reached the area where the gypsy graves were situated.

There, he stopped and stood in front of Dad's big black granite headstone.

JOSH 'FEARLESS' FLYNN
KING OF THE GYPSIES
NEVER FORGOTTEN

was picked out in gold Gothic script. Carved beside his name was a pair of bare-knuckle fighters, arms raised defensively. Dad was dead and gone. Mum too. Hard to take in. But he had to. Shauna wasn't at rest in the Flynn plot, though: she was in with the Everctts.

Then Benedict and Aysha arrived. Aysha looked well now; she'd been shattered these past few months after hearing about Mum's suicide. It had hit her the hardest, but Connor thought, shocking though it was, it had worked out for the best. Had Shauna lived, she would have done a lot of time in prison for the murders of Ciaran and Rowan Cleaver, and that wouldn't have suited her at all. Mum had been a wicked woman. He knew that now, and accepted it. Poor Dad had been worth a hundred of her.

'I'm not mad at Dad any more for trying to find some happiness with someone else,' said Aysha as the three of them stood there staring at the headstone. It was magnificent; awesome.

Connor sent her a glance. 'No?'

'After what you told me about Mum and those fucking hillbillies? After all she did, and all she wanted them to do? No. I don't know how the hell Dad got hooked up with her, but I do know he was sorry he did.'

'Sod all we can do about any of it now,' said Connor. Aysha had been sickened when he'd filled her in on what Shauna had done to Claire, and she had softened toward Claire and her daughter as a result, outraged at their mistreatment. The Henley house was up for sale now; the proceeds would be split between Connor and Aysha, and he was looking forward to the day when it was off their hands for good. Neither of them wanted to keep it. First and last, it had been *Shauna's* house, not Josh's, and not theirs.

'He was a good man, wasn't he? Dad?' said Aysha.

'The best,' said Connor.

'Josh was a diamond,' said Benedict.

'What about the Milo woman? What about her daughter, Suki?' said Aysha.

'What about them?'

'I dunno.' Aysha shrugged and looked at his face. 'I just

thought there was something there. A spark of something. You and Suki. Is that crazy?'

Connor opened his mouth to deny it, and then found that he couldn't say the words.

'Connor, I wouldn't mind. You and her. OK?' said Aysha.

He thought back to the time he had found Suki here in the mud in the cemetery, crying her heart out. Hating her, then. Despising her. Feeling almost ready to wring her neck with his bare hands. But . . . yeah, Aysha was right. There *had* been something, for sure. A powerful erotic attraction which he thought – or *wished* – had cut both ways.

'OK,' he said, but he didn't even know where Suki was these days, *or* her mother. Back in the States, probably.

A month after Josh's headstone was erected, the Henley house got sold. Connor was there clearing stuff out when he saw someone had left a message on the phone. Shit, he ought to have cancelled the contract, but he'd forgotten. There'd been so much to think about over these last months, none of it pleasant.

The message was from Suki. He phoned her back, and told her all that had happened.

When Suki got off the phone to Connor – she was using Donna's office phone at Sylvester's – she went straight in to see Claire.

Suki sat down and looked at her mother. 'I've just got off the phone to Connor Flynn,' said Suki.

'Oh?' Claire put her pen down and eyed her daughter with a smile. 'You liked him, didn't you.'

Suki looked embarrassed. 'Was it obvious? I *really* liked him. Couldn't seem to get him out of my mind. So I called

Josh's home number, since I didn't know Connor's. Left a message. Heard nothing, and I thought, oh well, that's it then. But he's just phoned back. And . . . he gave me some news. Pretty shocking news, really.'

'Go on.'

'She's dead.'

'Who . . . ?'

'Shauna Flynn. She . . . she shot herself.'

Claire went very still. Then, to Suki's alarm, her mother's eyes filled with tears.

'Oh Christ!' said Claire, putting her hands to her face.

'It's over, Mom,' said Suki, going round the desk and hugging her hard. 'Don't cry. It's all over,' she repeated.

At last.

166

At Connor's request, Suki and Claire returned to England. Claire was reluctant, but finally she agreed to meet up with him at the place he suggested. When they got to the camp-site by taxi, he was waiting there in the black Porsche. The guard dogs were already out, baying. Trace Milo came down the steps of her parents' old van and called them off. Connor got out of his car and walked over to her. Claire and Suki got out of their taxi and joined Connor.

Claire looked uncertain as she came face to face with her sister after so many years. Trace stood and stared at her for a long, long time. Then Claire started to smile and so did Trace, and suddenly both sisters were crying and laughing. They ran forward and hugged each other.

'Fuck it, where the hell have you *been*?' Trace gasped out. She pushed Claire back a step and looked at her, smoothing her hands over her sister's face in wonderment. 'Jesus, you've got older!'

'Well, so have you,' said Claire with a laugh, sniffing back tears. 'Oh, Trace – it's so good to see you.'

Trace turned and hollered: 'Dad! Come out here!'

In the doorway of the van appeared an old man, bent over, a stick in his hand. His eyes were squinting against the daylight, and he was shabbily dressed. He stared down at Trace and at the woman with her, and blinked like he couldn't be sure of what he was seeing.

'Claire . . . ?' he said shakily.

Claire detached herself from Trace and slowly walked over to the van. She was crying hard now, finding it difficult to speak. 'It's me, Dad. It's Claire. I'm back,' she sobbed out.

'Is it really you?' Pally was hobbling down the steps.

Claire nodded, unable to say more. Her father came close. Then closer. Slowly, trembling, he spread his arms wide and Claire fell into them, crushing him against her. 'Oh Dad,' she cried. 'I didn't think I'd ever see you again.'

'Nor me.' Pally drew back and kissed her cheek. 'My little girl, my Claire.'

Connor and Suki stood side by side, watching all this. Suddenly Trace turned to them, glancing between the two of them. Her eyes fastened on Suki. Trace swiped at her eyes, swallowed hard and said: 'And who's this then?'

'This is Suki,' said Connor. 'Claire's daughter.'

'You wha—' Trace looked gobsmacked. She stared at Suki and then she ran up and enfolded her in her arms. 'Christ! I'm an auntie! I'm your Auntie Trace!'

'A *daughter*?' Pally had heard what they were saying. He pushed Claire gently away, his eyes on Suki. Then he looked back at Claire. 'You had a child. I have a grandchild.' He was shaking his head. 'I should have known, I should have been *told*. Ah Jesus, if only my poor Eva had lived to see this.'

'I'm sorry, Dad. I'm so sorry how it all turned out. But things will be better now. And I'll tell you everything,' said Claire. 'I'll explain. I promise.'

'Christ! What a turn-up,' said Trace, laughing and grinning for once in her miserable life. She went to Claire and hugged her again. Then she slipped an arm around her dad's shoulders, another around Claire's. 'I'll stick the kettle on,' she said. 'Come on, we've a lot to talk about.' She glanced back at Connor and Suki.

Connor opened his mouth to speak, but to his surprise Suki got in first.

'It's such a nice day,' she said with a smile. 'You three catch up for a while, OK? We'll take a walk, give you a little time.'

EPILOGUE

The sun beat down as Connor and Suki walked away from the camp and trod the path down past the line of shimmering poplar trees toward the church in the dell, walking between a field that was brown, empty of crops, striped like corduroy from fresh tilling, and another where the corn stubble scratched at their legs as they passed.

When they reached the church, Suki hesitated. 'This is where it all happened, isn't it?' she said, turning anxious eyes to Connor.

'Yeah. It is.'

Connor pushed open the door. Back at the beginning of the year he'd filled in the grave at the top of the aisle, reburying Blue the dog. He'd even said a quick prayer over the poor little blighter, he didn't know why; he wasn't particularly religious. Now, all that showed the grave had ever been touched at all was a split in the stones where he'd struck with the sledgehammer.

He walked in, up the aisle. Slowly, Suki followed, uncertain.

'This is weird,' she said, her voice echoing. 'I was *conceived* here. By violence.'

Connor looked at her. 'There's nothing here now. It's all gone.' Finishing the Cleavers and then his mother taking her own life had drawn a line under everything.

'Yeah.'

Suki gazed nervously around her at the big arch of the roof and the stained-glass windows, feeling she'd come full circle in her life, first finding her mother and now visiting this place where her life had begun. Then she looked at Connor; such a big handsome guy with his pale-brown hair and his light, leonine grey eyes. She couldn't deny she felt a deep attraction to him, had felt it almost from the moment they met in the solicitor's office. And *that* was weird, too, because this was like history repeating itself. This had been Josh and Claire's special place. And now, here were their children, standing here together.

'What?' he asked, watching her.

'It's just funny, isn't it. That we're here.'

'Hilarious,' he said, not understanding.

Suki turned on her heel and led the way outside again. Early autumn storms had raged for the past few weeks, but for now the sun was shining. She leaned back against the stones of the church and felt their warmth seep into her. Connor came outside and shut the door.

'So you're a gypsy,' she said.

'Romany,' said Connor. 'And so are you.'

'Tell me some gypsy words then. Mom never did.'

'My dad used to tell me them all the time. And my mum always chewed his arse over it.' Connor sighed and leaned back against the church wall beside her, trawling his memory for the words. '*Jotter*? That's a monkey. My dad used to call me that. *Gorgis* are house-dwellers. *Tan*'s a stopping place. *Jeal* is kin. *Yoggers* are guns. A *tan-tan buggo* is someone of mixed race. And the sun is Phoebe.'

Suki flashed him a smile. 'You ever eat a hedgehog baked in clay? I hear tell gypsies do that.'

'God, no. You know, I wasn't a boxer, but I always

wanted to be like my dad in his ways. I looked up to him. I wanted to be *kushto* and *tacho*, like him.'

'*Kushto* and *tacho*? What's that mean?'

'Good. And true.'

Suki was silent for a moment, thinking of Josh. When she spoke again, her voice was lower, more serious. 'Connor?'

'Hm?' He was very close to her, breathing in her scent, which smelled delicious, listening to her voice, which was as warm and smooth as maple syrup, and thinking that she was absolutely fucking fabulous. If she went back to New York again anytime soon, then he was going to keel over and die.

'You can kiss me, if you want,' she said.

Connor turned his shoulder to the wall so that he was facing her, staring into her eyes from inches away.

'If I *want*?' He smiled, and put his mouth on hers and kissed her long and slow. When he came up for air, he let out a quivering sigh, rested his brow against hers. 'I've wanted to do that for so long.'

'Then why the hell didn't you?' demanded Suki breathlessly, slipping her arms around his neck, her fingers smoothing through his hair.

'You seemed afraid of me. Maybe you had good reason.'

'I *was* afraid of you. You're very fierce. In a sexy sort of way.'

'And you're fucking beautiful,' said Connor, kissing her again, deeply, relishing the feel of her in his arms.

'Let's not talk about old stuff any more,' he said when he stopped kissing her. 'Let's just be happy we're here, like this. Why don't you stay for a while? Let me show you the sights?'

'OK,' said Suki with a smile.

Really, there was nowhere else she would rather be.

Right now, she *never* wanted to leave.

AUTHOR'S NOTE

I took a little artistic licence (OK – a lot) with the gypsy funeral of Eva Milo. Romanies often burn the wagon and possessions of the deceased, but I've yet to hear of any burning the actual *person* too. Still, who knows. And it's a great scene. All the time I was writing it, I could hear my mother saying, 'You just *had* to go too far, didn't you!' Guilty, Mum. As usual.

NAMELESS
JESSIE KEANE

**They took her children away, and she will
fight to the end to get them back . . .**

In 1941, mixed-race Ruby Darke is born into a family
that seems to hate her, but why?

While her two brothers dive into a life of gangland
violence, Ruby has to work in their family store. As
she blossoms into a beautiful young woman, she
crosses paths with aristocrat Cornelius Bray, a chance
meeting that will change her life forever. When she
finds herself pregnant, and then has twins, she is
forced to give her children away. At that point she
vows never to trust another man again.

As the years pass, Ruby never forgets her babies,
and as the family store turns into a retail empire, she
wants her children back. But secrets were whispered
and bargains made, and if Ruby wants to stay alive
she needs to forget the past, or the past will come
back and kill her.

Nameless is a gripping underworld
thriller by bestselling author Jessie Keane.

RUTHLESS
JESSIE KEANE

She thought she'd seen the back of
the Delaneys. How wrong could she be . . .

Annie Carter should have demanded to see their bodies lying on a slab in the morgue, but she really believed the Delaney twins were gone from her life for good.

Now, sinister things are happening around her and Annie is led to one terrifying conclusion: the Delaneys, her bitter enemies, didn't die all those years ago. They're back and they want her, and her family, dead.

This isn't the first time someone has made an attempt on her life, yet she's determined to make it the last. Nobody threatens Annie Carter and lives to tell the tale . . .

Ruthless is the fifth book in the
compelling Annie Carter series by
hit crime writer Jessie Keane.

LAWLESS
JESSIE KEANE

Only the lawless will survive . . .

It is 1975 and Ruby Darke is struggling to deal with the brutal murder of her lover, Michael Ward.

As her children, Daisy and Kit, battle their own demons, her retail empire starts to crumble.

Meanwhile, after the revenge killing of Tito Danieri, Kit is the lowest he's ever been. But soon doubt is thrown over whether Kit killed the right person, and now the Danieris are out for his blood and the blood of the entire Darke family.

As the bodies pile up, the chase is on – can the Darkes resolve their own family conflicts and find Michael Ward's true killer before the vengeful Danieris kill them? Or will they take the law into their own hands?

Lawless is the heart-racing sequel to *Nameless*, from bestselling author Jessie Keane.

DANGEROUS
JESSIE KEANE

Whatever the cost, she would pay it . . .

Fifteen-year-old Clara Dolan's world is blown apart following the death of her mother. Battling to keep what remains of her family together, Clara vows to protect her younger siblings, Bernadette and Henry, from danger, whatever the cost.

With the arrival of the swinging Sixties, Clara finds herself swept up in London's dark underworld where the glamour of Soho's dazzling nightclubs sits in stark contrast to the terrifying gangland violence that threatens the new life she has worked so hard to build.

Sinking further into an existence defined by murder and betrayal, Clara soon realizes that success often comes at a very high price . . .

STAY DEAD
JESSIE KEANE

When you bury your secrets, bury them deep

Annie Carter finally believes that life is good.

She and Max are back together and she has a new and uncomplicated life sunning herself in Barbados. It's what she's always dreamed of.

Then she gets the news that her old friend Dolly Farrell is dead, and suddenly she finds herself back in London and hunting down a murderer with only one thing on her mind: revenge.

But the hunter can so quickly become the hunted, and Annie has been keeping too many secrets. She's crossed and bettered a lot of people over the years, but this time the enemy is a lot closer to home and she may just have met her match . . .

Stay Dead is the heart-stopping sixth book in Jessie Keane's bestselling Annie Carter series.